To my Mother and Father

It would take another whole book to list the reasons

ACKNOWLEDGEMENTS

I would like to thank the very many people and organizations who have, in person or through their publications, given me invaluable assistance in my writing of *Atom Bomb Angel*: in particular, my wife, Georgina, for endless patience and encouragement, and Jesse, for not eating all the manuscript; Peter Bunyard, the Central Electricity Generating Board, Peter Taylor and the Political Ecology Research Group Ltd, the United Kingdom Atomic Energy Authority, the Union of Concerned Scientists, the Nuclear Installations Inspectorate, Dungeness Power Station, Ontario Hydro, Louis Kates, Atomic Energy of Canada Ltd, Hilary Woolley, Margot Kirk, Phillip Cochrane, the Namibia Information Office, Via Rail Canada, Laurie Drury, and many, many others.

ATOM BOMB ANGEL

PETER JAMES

PAN BOOKS

First published 1982 by W. H. Allen

This edition published in 2014 by Pan Books
an imprint of Pan Macmillan
20 New Wharf Road, London N1 9RR
Associated companies throughout the world
www.panmacmillan.com

ISBN 978-1-4472-5597-0

3 5 7 9 8 6 4 2

A CIP catalogue record for this book is available from the British Library.

Typeset by Ellipsis Digital Limited, Glasgow
Printed and bound by CPI Group (UK) Ltd, Croydon, CR0 4YY

Visit www.panmacmillan.com to read more about all our books
and to buy them. You will also find features, author interviews and
news of any author events, and you can sign up for e-newsletters
so that you're always first to hear about our new releases.

The ignorant man always adores what
he cannot understand.

CESARE LOMBROSO (1836–1909)

FOREWORD

Welcome to the second novel I ever had published, back in 1982. I was cutting my teeth on my craft then (although I guess I still am!) so please forgive any rough edges and, hopefully, enjoy *Atom Bomb Angel* for the period piece it now is.

Although it was the second novel I had published, *Atom Bomb Angel* was actually my fifth novel: there are four that I wrote in my late teens and early twenties that, fortunately, never got published – although the first got me an agent – and these manuscripts will remain for ever in a trunk in the attic.

Through an odd quirk of fate, Terry Pratchett gave me some research help on this novel – or rather didn't! You will notice if you read the Acknowledgements that one is to the Central Electricity Generating Board: atomic energy and nuclear power stations are key components of the plot of *Atom Bomb Angel* and in 1981, as part of my research, I made an appointment to visit the Press Officer of the Central Electricity Generating Board, a Mr Terry Pratchett – then a completely unknown fledgling writer himself. As I sat down and explained my story – and that I wanted to have access to a nuclear power station – he said to me, very pragmatically, 'Well, I cannot possibly give you any help. Look at it from my perspective: if I help you with this book and then when it's published it frightens people off nuclear power, then the whole industry could go into decline and I could find myself being made redundant.' And he was not joking! It was a very short meeting. He gave me a CEGB brochure (which I gather he had written) which argued in favour of nuclear power stations by pointing out that, in Victorian times, an average of one person per week died by drowning in a mill-pond, whereas there had been only one than death caused by the entire British nuclear power programme since the opening of Calder Hall in 1956 – the world's first nuclear power station!

Atom Bomb Angel is a book that had a profound impact on the way I was to research my novels from then on. I needed some short scenes in Namibia but I was short of money, so instead of going out there I gleaned all my information from books (this was before the Internet) and from talking to someone who had worked there. When *Atom Bomb Angel* was published, I was asked about my experiences in Namibia in one of my first newspaper interviews. With my face bright red, I fibbed and squirmed my way through the interview, mumbling about it being quite hot and a lot of sand, and surprisingly lush in places.

I vowed then and there that never again would I write about anywhere that I had not visited, nor anything that I had not in some way experienced – death excepted! I think that has helped the authenticity of my writing hugely, although it has also led to many moments of terror – perhaps the worst being when I was incarcerated in a coffin with the lid screwed down, for thirty minutes, during my research for my first Roy Grace novel, *Dead Simple*. And I am very deeply claustrophobic . . .

Through this novel, I also learned a lot about publicity. One of the most exciting days of my life had been the day, back in 1979, that I got a call from my literary agent telling me that WH Allen, then one of the leading publishing houses, had accepted my first novel – *Dead Letter Drop* – for publication and wanted to make a two-book deal. It was followed a year-and-a-half later by one of the most disappointing days of my life – publication day for *Dead Letter Drop*.

Early that morning, I got up and went into Brighton, rushing around looking in each bookshop window in turn, and could see no sign of my book in any of them. Worse, when I went inside and mumbled, 'Erm, do you have a novel called *Dead Letter Drop* by the author Peter James?' none of them had heard of it!

I then found out to my dismay that a mere 1,750 copies had been printed, of which about 1,600 had gone to libraries. WH Smith, God bless them – I will eternally be grateful to them – had been the only bookstore chain to buy it, with a whopping order of thirty copies. Or, to put it more positively, twenty per cent of the entire available print run after the libraries had bought their share! WH Smith had them all in their flagship store in London's Sloane Square, but nowhere else.

Feeling very downhearted, I picked up a copy of the *Bookseller* magazine and began browsing through it, looking enviously at the success stories of other authors and at the bestseller lists, showing each of the names listed selling many thousands of hardbacks of their titles. Then I came across an article on independent publicists, and it was a light-bulb moment for me. Yes! Publicity! That's exactly what I needed!

There was one firm – Pengelly-Mulliken – which got a bigger mention than all the others, so I made an appointment to go and meet with the two bosses, Carole Pengelly and Tony Mulliken. It was to be a fateful meeting. Today Tony Mulliken is one of my closest mates, and his firm – Midas PR – have been my brilliant publicists for many years. But it didn't start too well.

I explained that there was a lot of controversy in the UK about the siting of new nuclear power stations and, with a clever publicity campaign, we could stir up a lot of interest in the novel. Carole and Tony agreed enthusiastically. Then came the cruncher. How much would it cost, I asked.

'Well, a full nationwide tour, including Scotland, would be three thousand pounds,' Tony replied.

I then explained, rather embarrassed, that my entire

advance for the book was only two thousand pounds – not a big sum even back then. The two of them left the room, then returned a few minutes later. Tony said, 'If you could drive yourself – or better, have your wife drive you – then we could do it for *two* thousand!'

So, the following year, starting on publication day, I began the most intensive UK publicity tour I've ever done. The nuclear issue was a hot ticket not just in the UK but around the globe; every VW Beetle and Camper on the planet was stickered-up with the yellow smiling-sun symbol and the words 'Nuclear Power – *nein danke*!'

Tony Mulliken and his team had earned their money. I was on the road for three weeks, and in those days you did interviews in every town and city in England, Wales and Scotland, on both BBC radio and the local commercial station, as well as two or even three newspapers, plus television appearances. By the time we had finished I was exhausted, but excitedly and expectantly looking at the *Sunday Times* bestseller listings. But my name was nowhere to be seen. A few days later I found out why.

My publishers had yet again printed a meagre 1,750 copies. Yet again 1,600 of those had gone to the libraries. At least good old WH Smith had not let me down – they doubled their order to a whopping 60 copies! That left just 90 for the whole of the rest of the UK!

A salutary lesson learned, very early on: behind every successful author there is a publisher with faith in them. It was some years before I was to find that publisher . . .

There is a standing joke among authors that the rarest thing in the world is an unsigned copy of one of their books. But I guess in the case of those early copies of *Atom Bomb Angel* the joke is probably true. I hope you find it fun to read.

Peter James

1

There were five men in the rear section of the railway carriage. Two read, one watched the scenery, one slept, one picked his nose. The train was travelling across Canada, from Vancouver to Montreal. It was fourteen and a half hours out of Winnipeg, and would be arriving in Montreal in just over twenty-four hours' time. The intention was that by the time the train got to Montreal, one of the men in this section of the carriage would be dead. Me.

If any of the five had met before, they didn't show it, and, as is often the way with strangers flung together in railway carriages, none had as yet acknowledged even the existence of any of the others. Without wishing to draw the attention of the rest, two of the men were particularly anxious to make each other's acquaintance: myself and the man who had come to kill me.

I flicked, mechanically, through the pages of my book. It was by Lillian Beckwith, and was called *The Hills is Lonely*. I could have assured her it wasn't just the hills: the hectares of December prairie that drifted endlessly past the window were lonely too. Almost as lonely as being in this railway compartment.

The other man who was reading put down his *Time Life* and stood up, unsteadily for a moment as the train swayed, then he made his way to the aisle, standing on my foot in the process.

'I'm sorry,' he said.

'That's what it's there for,' I replied.

1

He didn't appear to know how to take it, so he left it. He stood indecisively in the doorway for a few moments, then slid the door shut behind him and disappeared into the next carriage. I caught the eye of the one picking his nose; he looked down, then shot me two furtive glances in rapid succession. On both glances he found I was still watching him; he looked down again and frowned, then tugged his finger out sharply, and began to study it with great intent, as if perhaps there was some problem with it that inserting it up his nose might have cured.

The one who was watching the scenery raised his fingers to his chin, and started to check the growth of stubble; after a few moments, apparently satisfied that his jaw and cheeks had not disappeared into an undergrowth of hair, he leaned back in his seat and closed his eyes tightly for a few moments, then opened them wide and began to stare at the ceiling.

The one who slept was moving most of his head up and down in a slow rhythmic motion. The part that remained static was his lower jaw; as the upper part of his head lifted, his mouth opened, and as it lowered, it shut again. The effect reminded me of a rather gormless fish – the tall, thin type that hang around in the weeds in tropical fish tanks, waiting either to eat or be eaten, and not particularly caring which.

At the last station was a poster. It depicted a group of people in their seventies, in track suits, running through a field. The caption beneath said: 'You're not getting older, you're getting better.'

Getting better. I wondered, at what? I was getting older, for sure, a damn sight too fast for my liking, but I certainly wasn't getting any better – at anything – and that was a pity. Because right now I needed to be one whole lot better at a great many things if I was going to stay in this strange, tough, twisted temptress of a game that fatalists call 'the luck of the draw', clergymen call 'the ways of the Lord', and biologists call 'life'.

Right now the key to life was contained in the briefcase that one of my four travelling companions had on the rack above his head. There were five briefcases on the racks. Two black Samsonites, two cheap leather ones of the type made in Hong Kong and sold through mail-order firms from glossy adverts in Sunday colour supplements, and one Gucci, the real thing, not a copy.

One of the Samsonites could be ruled out, since it was mine, which left me four cases to worry about. The content of one of these would tell me who it was that was here to kill me – and he didn't have to open it up to show me. In fact, I was pretty damn sure he had no intention of opening that briefcase until long after this train had reached Montreal.

It would be highly unlikely for any man to carry a briefcase with him on a long train journey, and not to open that case at any time during that journey. On an hour-long commuter ride, most men click their cases open at least once; on a forty-hour journey, the man who did not open his briefcase would start to stand out like a sore thumb to anyone interested enough to take the trouble to notice. And I was plenty interested enough.

I put down my book and picked up my *New York Sunday Times* magazine and turned to the mammoth crossword. I pulled my gold Cross ball-point from my pocket, looked down towards the crossword, and tapped the top of the pen thoughtfully in my mouth. Gripping the pen in my teeth I looked up after some moments, then lowered my eyes back down towards the crossword. Fourteen across: *Short Richard's offspring divides nation with friendly underground railroad?* Where the hell did I begin on that one? Normally I liked crosswords; in the long and boring hours of tailing someone, when it wasn't possible to read a book in case one missed something, at least the clues of a crossword gave me something to chew on. But right now, I had plenty to chew on without this particular puzzle. I had a puzzle that was far more complex, and if I didn't solve it fast, there was a pension-fund manager in England who was going to have one less pension to worry about. I squinted my eyes down towards the crossword, but it wasn't the clues that were printed on the paper that were going to help me – it was the rotating digits in the dial that was concealed in the barrel of my pen.

After a few minutes my right leg went to sleep for the fifteenth time. I tried to move it and it hurt like hell, but not moving it hurt even more. I needed to go for a walk – if I was even capable of standing up. Apart from a brief trip to the washroom earlier, I hadn't moved since boarding the train at Winnipeg last night. I had reclined my seat to go to sleep, and tilted it up again to eat the breakfast that appeared on a tray. I had a splitting headache, and my nose was running. The way I must have looked, I was worth gold nuggets to the advertising agency of any airline.

I memorized the exact positions of the briefcases, so that I could tell if any had been moved, and limped awkwardly down the aisle and through into the next carriage, a first-class sleeper. And then I saw her. She was in a compartment on her own, and she looked up for a brief moment as I passed. I caught her eye. She must have caught mine too, but she didn't show anything on her face. She had red hair and glasses. Last time she had blonde hair and no glasses, and she wore different make-up. It was a shade over two years. Long enough for someone to change, but not long

4

enough to forget. Had she forgotten, or was I just making a mistake? The man who had trodden on my foot was walking back down the corridor. Now was not the time to find out.

2

ATOM BOMB ANGEL

It had all begun for me with a telephone call on a wet September morning, less than four months before. The man had used the code of one of our operatives in Libya to get through to me, and he had sounded very frightened.

When the switchboard had first put him through he came across in an extremely irritating way, as people who can't speak one's language often do. At first, I thought it was just nervousness at speaking to a stranger in a strange language.

'Hello Mr Flynn, I am Ahmed.'

'Yes?'

'How are you?'

'I'm fine thanks, what do you want?'

'Pardon?'

'What do you want? What–can–I–do–for–you?'

'No – it is me. I am Ahmed.'

I decided that I was on the receiving end of a sales pitch from a Middle-Eastern life-assurance salesman on his first venture into England, and nearly hung up on him. It might have been a good thing for both our futures if I had, but I was obliged to listen, and so I did.

'I am call for Donald Frome. In bad trouble. Please you must come.'

'What sort of trouble?'

'Pardon?'

'What sort of trouble is Donald Frome in?'

'I cannot talk more, here, please. You come right away,

please. Men's wash place, Royal Lancaster Hotel, twelve o'clock. You must, please.' He hung up.

I looked at my watch: it was almost eleven thirty. I wondered whether it was a set-up, and decided it wasn't. The man had sounded genuine. One can fake a lot of emotions, but fear is probably the hardest, and my skull was still ringing with the fear in his voice.

I had the cab drop me off a couple of hundred yards up the Bayswater Road; the traffic was light and we were there a few minutes earlier than I had expected, and I didn't want to have to hang around either the hotel lobby or the lavatory.

I was feeling depressed, and the weather wasn't helping my mood. It had rained almost continuously throughout June, July and August, and the Indian summer the weathermen had promised us for September hadn't turned up, although there appeared to be more curry houses than ever before, so maybe that was what they meant. I walked through steady drizzle, with my hands in my jacket pockets, and I couldn't remember feeling so rotten. Everything right now was bloody rotten, and the days were getting short and the air was getting chilly, and there was a long, long winter ahead with nothing much to look forward to.

I was thirty-two years old, and in my eighth year as an agent for MI5. Eight summers ago had been a glorious summer, and I had spent most of it in Paris. That was where the MI5 talent spotters had stumbled across me, and decided I was a sufficiently unpleasant piece of work to fit nicely into their little company. Not that they'd bothered to ask me first: with a little co-operation from their chums in the Paris *Sûreté*, I was set up and flung into a Parisian slammer, with little hope of getting out until long past retirement age – unless I joined MI5.

To be completely accurate, it was a combination of

greed and laziness that had put me into this situation in the first place, but for MI5 to demand a lifetime's allegiance in return for their help, was, in my opinion, even more greedy. Mostly, I forgot about the background, and got on with my work, but there were occasions, like today, when I could think of a lot of other things I'd prefer to be doing, and I became morose.

I hate paperwork, and the assignment I was currently on was all paperwork. I had been attached to C4, the anti-terrorist division of MI5, with the task of preparing for my boss, MI5's Director General, Sir Charles Cunningham-Hope – better known as Fifeshire – what was to be virtually an encyclopaedia of terrorists in the United Kingdom. I think what he had in mind was one of those glossy coffee-table books, of the type that people like giving as presents to friends they know will never read them, called something like *Fifeshire's Compleat Terrorist*, and featuring every known terrorist in bright colour, with a few lines of text on their breeding habits.

He had, however, set about it in the very thorough manner that was typical of him, and, treading hard on the toes of MI6, as he liked to do, had embarked upon a massively ambitious programme to infiltrate all the key terrorist organizations of the world. Donald Frome had managed to penetrate the Marzoc camp – the Eton of Colonel Quadhafi's terrorist training schools – and had been sending back immensely valuable information for several months. It was not good news that he was in trouble, not for us or him, and I felt damn sorry for the poor bastard. I walked around to the front of the dismal grey slab of a hotel and marched in through a revolving door.

There was nothing inside to lift the gloom: a bank of shops selling cigarettes, confectionery, newspapers and

Braemar sweaters looked very empty, with sales staff standing to unenthusiastic attention, and a few hotel staff in their differing grades of uniform milled around with only the vaguest semblance of being active.

I went up some stairs, along a corridor past a battery of show-cases, and into the men's room. It was empty. I ran a tap to look busy, but almost immediately, the door opened, and an Arab, in a dirty white jellaba and brown sandals, hurried in. I put him at about thirty-five. He stared at me, several times in succession, with tiny frightened eyes. He was short and very thin, and spoke in quick bursts, without bothering to check my identity.

'Please – in there, in there – we must not be seen.' He flapped his hands towards the cubicles; at the same time he went over to the entrance door and jammed a silver coin underneath it – to make a scraping noise if anyone should come in. He ushered me into a cubicle and went into the adjacent one. I took down my trousers, so that if anyone did come in and looked underneath the door, they would see nothing unusual, and sat on the seat.

'Thank you for come, thank you,' said the Arab.

'That's all right, my friend.'

'I be quick.'

'Take your time.'

'Donald Frome in – very bad – I think now he dead.'

'What happened?'

'He is caught – somehow – I don't know how – someone find out. He give me message to bring you – he write down – I am too frightened – I read and then burn; he tell me it is very important I must give you message – it is difficult – I no speak much good the English.'

'You're doing fine.'

'I try to read – it not easy – I have not anyone to ask for

9

help. He say Operation Angel. Most important. Operation Angel. Many countries. Very bad. Nuclear power stations – they will blow up – many—'

'Who will?'

The silver coin screeched across the marble floor. There was a flat clacking of footsteps across the floor; it was the clacking of a pair of sandals. A whispered voice said, 'Ahmed?'

The Arab in the cubicle beside me said something in Arabic, which I didn't understand. I heard the splintering sound of a wooden door parting company with its hinges, followed by a scream of terror, which then turned to a scream of pain, a terrible scream. Suddenly, it stopped completely and was replaced by a weird gurgling sound. I struggled with one hand to pull up my trousers and with the other to yank my Beretta out of its shoulder holster, as I heard the fast patter of sandals retreating from the room.

I dashed out of my cubicle, struggling with my zip, and looked into Ahmed's cubicle. The door had been kicked off its hinges, and was suspended by its lock. Seated on the lavatory was just a volcano of blood. Ahmed's head had been almost completely severed, and hung at a strange angle to his neck, from which blood was erupting and running down his jellaba. His arms were outstretched and rigid. The only movement of his body was a macabre twitch in his left cheek.

I gagged twice and had to swallow hard to prevent myself from throwing up. I gaped in horror, and as I gaped, a fury grew inside me. I turned away. If any man had ever wanted to convince me that he had been telling the truth, he couldn't have done a better job than this.

The fury turned to a rage, a rage against all the terrorist bastards in London, in my town, in my world, for their ever-increasing gross outrages. I was going to get the bastards that had done this particular outrage, and I was going to teach them a lesson they would never forget. I hurtled out into the corridor. There was no one to be seen. I sprinted to the end of the corridor and dived down the stairs. As I hit the foyer, I looked in every direction, and saw a side door down one end swinging shut. I sprinted towards and through that door, just in time to see an Arab scramble into the back of a dirty grey Fiat, which drove off before he had time to close the door. I looked desperately around for a vehicle to commandeer. Almost on top of me was a taxi with its 'For Hire' sign illuminated. I scrambled into the back.

'Follow that grey Fiat.'

'You what?'

'Follow that Fiat!'

'What is this? The movies?'

'No – it's a ten quid tip if you do what I say.'

He did. The Fiat had slowed right down in a bottleneck at a roundabout and the cab got onto its tail.

'Stay right behind it, and don't lose it.'

'Orl try.'

For fifteen minutes the cabbie was a damn good trier. There were three Arabs in the car, and they were beginning to panic. They kept looking behind them, and every time they looked they saw the same view: the nose of the Austin taxi. We were heading towards Wembley, on a very erratic course, with the Fiat doing a fast U-turn at every red light it came to, and slowly making its way over towards the M40, where they knew they would be able to outrun us. Suddenly, one Arab in the back thrust his hand out of the window and fired two shots at us. One missed, the other punched a neat hole in the left side of the windscreen.

'Oh no, mate, this is where you get off,' said the driver,

slamming on the brakes. 'Ar'm not gettin' shot at for a bleedin' tenner. Ar'm not getting shot at for a bleeding monkey. Out!' He turned to face me and found himself staring down the wrong end of my Beretta.

'Either get this crate going or get out.'

He gave a weak grin, his face twitched, then broke into an exaggerated nervous grin. 'If it's all right with you, I'll get out – weak heart, got a pacemaker.' He jumped out the door. 'Tank's full. I'm not a coward, like, it's just I—'

I wasn't interested. I clambered into the driving seat, crashed the gear-lever forward and did the nearest thing to a wheelie that any London cab is ever going to do. The Arabs were stuck at the back of a queue at a red light, all peering around. There was an island in the middle of the road which prevented them from doing a U-turn. They backed up several feet and then drove onto the pavement, and Ghengis Khan in the back loosed off two more shots at me. There were too many other cars and people around for me to risk firing back. They stopped at the end of the pavement as a giant articulated lorry thundered across their bows, followed closely by another. I carried on with the accelerator pressed flat on the floor and hit them full in the back. I stopped dead, but on the pavement greasy with the drizzle, they cannoned forward, neatly into the gap between the front and the rear wheels of the second artic's heavily laden trailer. Above the roar of the lorry was a swift metallic crunch, a sound like a foot crushing a metal biscuit-tin, as the little Fiat was blotted, for a fraction of a second, from view by the huge wheels of the lorry, then the lorry was past and the Fiat reappeared, alone in the road, the boot and bonnet reasonably intact, but the entire passenger compartment no higher than ten centimetres off the road at its highest point.

I was aware of nothing for a moment but the staccato of the taxi's diesel engine. I realized I was holding the clutch down. I lifted my foot a fraction and, with a loud protest from somewhere up front, we began to move. I let the clutch right out and accelerated hard. We lurched forward. I was amazed. The bumper must have absorbed almost all the impact. There was a grating sound, but it wasn't loud. I looked around. People were clambering from their cars and running over towards the Fiat. The lorry had stopped and the driver was walking, puzzled and dazed around the side.

I decided the best place for me to be right now was anywhere but here. The police would get their report in due course and we would get ours, but there wasn't a great deal of love lost between the police and MI5, particularly when it came to corpses in wholesale quantities as it was always them that had to do the clearing up, and I didn't want to be stuck for the rest of the day with a bunch of sarcastic traffic boys from Ealing.

I accelerated off to the left, ignoring several shouts. Five hundred yards down the road a woman with suitcases hailed me. I ignored her and she waved furiously as I drove past. I wanted to make my report to Fifeshire and make it fast. I wanted to know what else anybody knew about Operation Angel, and if nobody knew anything about it, how we were going to find out more, and find out fast.

After a couple of miles, I started looking out for a phone booth. I wanted to make a call to the forensic boys to make sure they went through that car, and what bits of its occupants they could separate from it, with something considerably finer than a toothcomb. After about a quarter of a mile a booth came up on the left.

The vandals hadn't messed about with this one: all

they'd left were the Yellow Pages and a length of wire. It's funny, but I'd had a feeling that morning when I woke up that somehow it wasn't going to be my day.

3

'The basic principle of a nuclear power station is no different from any other form of electricity generating station. It is very important to remember this. Everyone gets blinded by science when they hear about nuclear power stations, but we are not all about fission cycles and fast neutrons and complicated formulas. All we do is to generate steam which is then forced past turbines that rotate and cause electricity to be generated – just as the wheel of a bicycle rubs against the dynamo, turning the knob at the top of the dynamo, which then generates the electricity that lights the lamps.

'Steam power is the key. Nothing has changed since James Watt invented the steam engine – it is exactly the same principle of operation. The only technological advance in a nuclear power station is the way we heat the water to get the steam – that's what we're all about. Ninety per cent of what you're going to find if you walk around this plant is the same as what you will find if you walk around any coal-fired or oil-fired or gas-fired power station anywhere in the world. The ten per cent that's different is the way we make the steam – that's what's important, that's what nuclear power is all about.'

The man paused for a moment, looking nervously through his spectacles, which were fast sliding down his nose. He wrung his hands together, sweat glistened on his brow, and his brown hair cut like a pudding basin clung greasily to his head as the sweat poured into it. He swayed on his feet, occasionally elevating himself onto tiptoe as he spoke, occasionally shoving his hands deep into the pockets of his tweed jacket, so deep at times I thought the jacket was going to come apart at the shoulders. He was used to parties of school children and university students. He wasn't used to a crowd like this lot; they could eat him for breakfast, and he knew it.

In an effort to swing ever-increasing public hostility to nuclear power stations into some measure of support for their construction programme, and to try and gain export orders, the British government had thrown open to the international press their latest star-studded masterpiece, Huntspill Head on the shore of North Somerset. It was the first pressurized-water reactor to be built in Britain and its one major drawback, as far as public relations went, was that it was based on the same system as the infamous Three Mile Island reactor which, in 1979, had come perilously close to wiping out a large chunk of Pennsylvania.

The future of the government's energy policy was in jeopardy, and a favourable outcome today would be a big boost for it. It was essential they got the right message across, and to get the right message across, it was essential they used the right man. Douglas Yeodall had been chosen for his school-teacher-from-next-door appearance and manner, his extensive knowledge on the subject of nuclear power, his honest face and, as much as anything else, for his thick Somerset accent. It had been decided that his accent, with its strongly rural flavour – an accent that reminded one of crude jokes about lecherous farmers – would put people at ease. The journalists present were of a different opinion. Half of them couldn't understand a single word; the other half, which could, with some difficulty, make out the general gist of what he was saying, had decided that the British government had deliberately laid on the village idiot.

It wasn't just the journalists who thought Douglas Yeodall was a lousy choice; so did Douglas Yeodall. He stared out across the sea of seven hundred faces, at one thousand, four hundred eyeballs, across the battery of cameras and microphones and shorthand note pads, and a silence as thick as a mushroom cloud of fall-out dust, and soldiered on.

'I'm sure there are many of you who understand the principles of nuclear physics,' he paused for a murmur of assent, but none was forthcoming, 'I'm sure there are many of you here today who know a great deal more about this subject than I do – I just work here!' He paused for a titter of laughter; there was none. His audience ate ordinary statesmen and prime ministers for lunch, and presidents and kings for dinner; they weren't going to start laughing at the wisecracks of a two-bit lecturer from the backwoods of Somerset. Any more gags and Douglas Yeodall wasn't even going to make the peanut bowl at cocktail hour. He appeared to realize this, and straightened up his body, and aimed the tip of his nose at the back of the hall. His eyes were now staring straight into the floodlights. They dazzled him, but he didn't mind. At least he wasn't staring into the eyeballs of those stony-faced bastards any more.

'If I bang my two fists together . . .' He did so, close up to the microphones, and winced; he'd done it too hard and it hurt. He shook his hands, and the audience burst into a roar of laughter. Yeodall looked puzzled for a moment, then smiled to himself; he had a feeling he'd scored a point.

'If I bang my fists together – it hurts!' He continued. 'It also makes them warmer, because the friction of the two hands banging together has made heat. If my hands were to disintegrate on collision, even more heat would be generated. It is the way in which heat is generated that makes nuclear power stations different from all other types of power station. I'm going to put this as much into layman terms as I can, but if I lose you – or you lose me – it is explained in the booklet you have been given.

'Everything in life is made up of atoms – that, I think, everybody now knows – but atoms also are made up of something. They are made up of particles called protons and neutrons; to give you an idea of the size of these particles, one thousand billion neutrons placed side by side in a single line would just about stretch the width of a pin-head.' He waited for a gasp of amazement. There wasn't one.

'Now, uranium, which is a metal mined from the earth, is made up of three different atoms; one of these is called U 235, and in U 235 the neutron particles are very active and a few are constantly flying out.' A diagram illustrating what he said was projected onto a large screen behind him. 'If one of these particles, which fly out at about twenty-five thousand miles per second, hits another U 235 atom, that atom will split into two, and sometimes three, separate atoms. It is that collision and that splitting of the atom that generates heat, just the way the banging of my fists does.' He banged his fists again, more gently this time.

'At the same time as splitting into two or three, more neutron particles fly out; if these particles can also be made to hit atoms, then we have what is known as a chain reaction.

'Now the way we make this work for us is, in outline, very simple. Uranium is processed and refined and then put into metal tubes, which are called fuel rods. Several hundred rods are then inserted into what we call the core – you can think of it as being like the barrel of a revolver, the rods being the bullets. The rods are insulated from each other by what are called control rods, through which neutron particles cannot pass. As the control rods start to be withdrawn, the neutron particles start flying out and splitting the atoms in the other rods, and the fuel rods start to get very, very hot. The control rods are not withdrawn completely, but adjusted to maintain the temperature required.

'The entire core is immersed in water; the water is kept under very high pressure to prevent it from boiling so that it will act as a coolant for the core – like a car's radiator system. After the water leaves the core, heated to a temperature many times higher than boiling point, it is then converted into steam, which is then pushed through the turbines.

'If anything goes wrong, the control rods are dropped straight back into the core and the reaction stops. The core, which you'll see when we make our tour, is suspended above the ground, in its tank, with the control rods directly above it. The reason it is suspended above the ground is for ease of access to all parts of it. Almost all maintenance is done by remote control from outside the containment – that's the name of the building in which the core is housed.'

Yeodall paused for some moments. He'd got through the toughest bit for his audience, but the easiest bit for him; he bit his lip, took a deep breath, and ploughed on.

'Unfortunately, this process of nuclear fission produces a lot of by-products which are known collectively by a name which has a sinister connotation these days: radioactivity. Certainly, radioactivity has a lot of nasty things in it that have got to be controlled and kept well away from human beings, except in areas of medicine, which I'll come on to later. You've got neutron particles, which aren't going to do you a whole lot of good coming through you at twenty-five thousand miles a second; there's Cobalt 60 and Iodine 131, Krypton 85, Strontium 90, Plutonium 239, with alpha rays, beta rays, gamma rays – none of which are going to do you any good. Alpha rays are damaging if breathed in, gamma rays and beta rays do damage if they hit human tissue.

'A lot of them have a short life-span – we measure their life-spans in what we call half-life. That means the length of time it takes for a radioactive substance to lose half its strength. Some have a very short half-life – a matter of seconds only – but others, such as Krypton, have long half-lives – Krypton's is nine and a half years, Strontium 90 is twenty-eight years, and Plutonium 239 is twenty-four thousand three hundred years – so we have to take a great many precautions to make sure mankind is shielded from this radioactivity, and is going to remain shielded for ever.

'The first stage is the reactor core itself. The containment wall around that is two-metre-thick reinforced concrete; it is dome-shaped for maximum structural strength, and it will withstand very great stress. In tests on this type of dome, a simulation of a fully laden jumbo jet crashing into it at six hundred miles an hour was done – and the aircraft lost the fight. It didn't even make a noticeable dent.

'But even in the event of the containment dome being fractured, we have a fall-back here at Huntspill Head. The containment is connected to a second building, with the same internal capacity, which is kept permanently as a vacuum. If there were any crack in the core containment, a series of valves between the two buildings would automatically open, and all the steam would be sucked straight through.' His eyes were running from the glare of the lights, his throat was parched, and he badly wanted to scratch his balls.

'Apart from all the security which all of you have witnessed on coming to this station, there is a great deal more hidden security here as well. The entire station is monitored by no less than three completely separate computers. If at any stage the three do not tally, they are all programmed to automatically start shut-down procedures until the reason for the difference is known and corrected.'

Yeodall talked at great length on the subject of safety, and in particular the safety of the population of Huntspill, the local town. He talked as if Huntspill were the hub of the universe, and should the rest of the world fall apart, the fact that Huntspill would not be eradicated by its power plant – from which, incidentally, it received no power – would make it all better again.

'When we talk about dangers to the public of radiation, we define the individual member of public as a "fence-post man" – that is to say, an individual who spends all the years of his life, twenty-four hours a day, seven days a week, on the station boundary, eating fish reared in the station effluent and drinking the effluent water. This person would in one year be subject to about the same amount of radiation as someone who lives on the fortieth floor of a high-rise building, or who once flies in an aeroplane from London to New York. In more technical terms, he will receive a dose of radiation that is less than one per cent of what is considered to be a safe annual dosage.'

Yeodall beamed out at his audience. They still weren't impressed. Many of them had flown a good deal further than from London to New York to get here, and they weren't happy to hear they had received any dosages of radiation at all, however slight. If he'd gained a point earlier, he'd just lost it now. He launched a volley of statistics about the cost-effectiveness of nuclear-generated electricity. His audience had been blinded by statistics before; they all knew that any competent statistician could make his figures prove anything he wanted them to prove. They were getting bored; they were getting fed up with sitting on the hard plastic seats, watching large and dreary slides appear behind Douglas

Yeodall's head, and trying to translate the language as this well-meaning fellow droned on. They wanted to get to the meat, to the bit where they could ask questions, where they could do some ripping apart; and then bugger off and have lunch.

'One hundred and fifty million diagnostic procedures a year are conducted with radioactive isotopes produced in power stations such as this,' he said. He was into the benefits of medicine now, and the audience began to take more notice; they were interested in survival, as everyone is interested in survival.

'Cobalt-radiation treatment units have extended the useful lives of people throughout the world by an estimated eleven million years; over the next twenty years, this could jump to over fifty million years. Without nuclear power stations providing cobalt as a waste by-product most of this cobalt treatment would not be possible, as the cost of producing cobalt would be out of reach of even the richest hospitals.'

Seven hundred journalists scribbled onto their note pads. Yeodall had scored his second point.

'Radiation is also playing an important new role in sterilization. Peaches on the food shelves of South African supermarkets are being given small doses of gamma rays. These kill the bacteria and increase the shelf-life of the peaches by ten times. The World Health Organization estimates that thirty per cent of all the food in the world is not eaten because it has gone off before it ever reaches a table. The life of milk can be prolonged by doses of radiation; salmonella in chickens can be killed off without affecting the flavour; and these rays leave no toxic residue whatsoever.'

The thought of eating gamma-ray blasted chickens, and of South Africans not having to hurry over their purchase of peaches did not leave any visible marks of excitement on the faces of the seven hundred.

Yeodall announced that the lecture was over, and that question time had now begun. As an insurance policy against the length of his grilling, he informed his audience that the commencement of lunch awaited the conclusion of the questions.

From the battery of hands that shot into the air, lunch looked in distinct danger of becoming supper. A woman with a strong Australian accent spoke. 'Sir, what in your opinion is the worst kind of an accident that could happen in a nuclear power station?'

'There is very little room for accidents in the operation here; as I told you, we have three automatic shut-down systems, all independent of one another. We've fed every kind of accident possible, and every kind of sabotage possible, into the simulators, and we are totally confident in the safety systems here. If we weren't, we wouldn't work here; I'm sure I wouldn't. We have over one thousand people working here, and I don't think any of them would be here if they were worried. In dangerous jobs, people get paid danger money. Nobody gets paid danger money here. Does that answer your question?'

'No, sir, it doesn't; my concern is not whether an accident could happen – it is what sort of accident could happen. What is the worst sort of accident that could happen?'

'The worst accident that could happen here is if one of the steam pipes were to fracture; but in the event of that happening, the valves to the vacuum building would open and the steam would be sucked straight in there.'

The science editor of *The Times* stood up. 'You say that an accident could not happen, and yet in 1979 there was a very serious accident in a power station at Three Mile Island in the United States, with the same type of reactor as this. Why could this not happen again, over here?'

'The result of a number of malfunctions and human errors at Three Mile Island was that a large bubble of hydrogen gas built up inside the containment and they had no way of getting rid of it – they had no vacuum chamber into which they could syphon it. We have such a chamber, so even if we had a similar set of initial problems as Three Mile Island, which is unlikely, there would be no danger.'

A tall black reporter stood up. 'What would be the result of a terrorist organization either blowing up this power station, or getting their hands on the uranium that is used here and using it themselves to make nuclear bombs?'

'To answer the first part of your question: there are an enormous number of buildings that make up this complex. It would take a mammoth amount of explosive just to blow up the containment, let alone the entire complex. In any event, the terrorists wouldn't be achieving much: if they wanted to knock out the supply of electricity, it would be much more sensible merely to blow up the power cables.

'To answer the second part: the uranium that is used here would not be of much use to terrorists in the making of nuclear explosives. The level of enrichment is very low, so if they did succeed in stealing some, it would have to go through an enrichment process – for which they would need access to an enrichment plant. There are very few of these in the world, and they are very strictly controlled. But in any case, if terrorists wanted to get their hands on uranium, they wouldn't bother trying to steal it from here – the place is much too well guarded – it would be far easier to steal it while it was in transit.'

An English reporter stood up and spoke with a high-pitched, snide North Country accent. 'What I would like to know is what would happen if, just supposing, somehow, radioactive steam did escape out of the containment – you know, let's say the valves to the vacuum building jammed and the steam got out into the air. What would happen?'

Douglas Yeodall looked twitchy. 'Well – er – well, if that happened, you'd surely get a lot of nasty stuff in the air – precisely what would happen would depend upon which way the wind was blowing. If the wind was blowing northwesterly at the time, well, that stuff is going to head straight towards Huntspill, and there would be a major emergency. We'd either have to evacuate the town – there is an evacuation plan which the townspeople know about – or if it wasn't too serious, we'd make them all stay indoors and keep their windows shut. But this couldn't happen.'

The English reporter spoke again. 'What if the wind were blowing in a different direction?'

'Well, then the people of Huntspill would be fine, there'd be no real problem then.'

The Englishman wasn't going to let that one go quite so easily. 'The people of Huntspill might be all right – but what about other places downwind? What about Bristol? Bath? Reading? Basingstoke? Oxford? And what about London?'

'Well – the steam should have dispersed into the atmosphere by the time it reached any of those cities; but depending on the strength of the wind, people close to the station could be in some danger, that's true.'

Yeodall looked anxiously about the sea of faces, searching for a fresh hand so he could move away from this Englishman, but he could only see the Englishman's hand. 'The steam might disperse into the atmosphere, but there is no reason why the radioactive particles should stay in the steam. They would drop out of it, into the wind, and eventually down to earth. It could take hours before they all come down to ground. There was a volcanic eruption in Washington in 1980 that showered ash onto countries up to five thousand miles away. And you have just told us that some of these particles will live for decades and some for tens of thousands of years, so wherever this stuff lands will be contaminated for a very long time.'

'We think that there would be such small radioactive particles ending up inside human beings that they would do absolutely no harm at all.'

'You might think that, Mr Yeodall, but do you know that for sure? Or are you going to wait until it happens and use the whole world as your guinea pig?'

'No, it is not our intention to use the world as our testing ground. Radiation is only harmful in large and prolonged quantities. There is a great deal of radiation in natural life – from the sun, from the burning of fires, from minerals. It is a naturally occurring phenomenon, and humans ingest it daily. You, walking down a street, will ingest in one day more radiation than a worker in this station is permitted to receive, working indoors, in that same period. The worst possible disaster in a nuclear power station would put the most insignificant amount of radiation into the atmosphere.'

Ron Tenney, the station's general manager, poured a hefty measure of Scotch over the ice cubes, and handed me the glass. He turned down the volume control on the video monitor and grinned at me. He was a jovial man in his early forties, with the same sort of rugged good looks as the successful businessmen-hero characters that are portrayed in television soap operas – dark hair, slightly rugged features, and skin pockmarked from childhood acne – and he spoke with a smooth confident voice that was given an added warmth by the faintest drawl of an Irish brogue.

'Well, he's holding up – I think he'll stay the course! Jesus! I wouldn't want to be out there with that pack of dogs. He's doing a fine job. I hate the press. Bad news sells newspapers; that's all those bastards are out there for, selling their newspapers. The more they can twist Doug's words into prophesies of doom, the more copies they'll sell. Bad news is the only thing that sells newspapers – when do you remember reading a newspaper article in support of nuclear power stations?' He didn't wait for my reply. 'Never, that's when you last read one. Never!' He pulled hard on his drink.

It was two weeks since my meeting with Ahmed in the men's room at the Royal Lancaster, and I was now ten days into my new job: hatchet man for the Secretary of State for Energy. With a faked background of ten years' training with the consultancy arm of Peat, Marwick and Mitchell, I had been given an office and *carte blanche* at the United Kingdom Atomic Energy Authority to go anywhere, anytime, and look at anything, in order to produce a report on productivity and cost-efficiency within the British nuclear energy industry. The industry was so vast, and spread out, both geographically and in terms of different companies and organizations, that it was an impossible task for one person. The person responsible for putting me in this job knew that too; it was the Director General of MI5, Fifeshire. He didn't care a damn about their cost-efficiency: he just cared about keeping them intact.

This was the third power station I had visited in a week, and I would be visiting the remaining thirteen within the next few weeks.

'What's your view on the safety of these things?' I asked Tenney.

'They're fine – but they're not infallible. Nothing is. It's possible for things to go wrong. It would be possible for terrorists to sabotage this place – not easy, but possible. God knows what damage would be done if anything did happen.'

'So why are you here?'

'I'm here because I don't believe it will happen; the odds are small enough to make it an acceptable risk. Any place has hazards, and any job has hazards. I don't feel I'm any more at risk working here than doing anything else – just as long as no bunch of crazed loonies anywhere out beyond that perimeter fencing is plotting to blow us up!'

'Do you believe what Doug Yeodall was saying about an escape of steam?'

He paused for some moments. 'No. That's crap. Well, I say that's crap, but I don't know for sure. No one does. But what we generally think would happen is that that steam would stay together in a concentrated mass, and spread out a few hundred yards in every mile on either side, so it gets wider and wider. There would be so much radioactivity in it, it would be a killer at a hundred miles long and thirty wide. It wouldn't disperse for weeks, not unless there was a hurricane. But we're not going to tell the press that! No way! Why worry them? It's never going to happen.' He grinned, and chinked the ice cubes in his glass.

4

The canopied stern of *Chanson II* moved little in the calm St Tropez dusk. Two stout hemp ropes held her secure to the bollards on the quay, and a battery of smart navy and white fenders protected her port and starboard sides. Her teak decks shone with polish, her white paintwork glistened, and the gold lettering of her name and the word *Panama* underneath were immaculate.

She was a rich man's boat, in a parade of rich men's boats. One of a dozen and a half genuine gin palaces that sat swanking in silence down the most public part of the quay, opposite the cafés and the restaurants where thousands of holiday-makers from campsites and pensions mingled with the few wealthy villa owners to sip their *cafés au lait* and pernods and pick at giant ice-creams in glass bowls, and ogle in awe at the passing crumpet, and the stunning white bums of the boats of the super-rich.

Chanson II was one hundred and forty foot, and had fourteen private berths, all with *en suite* bath or shower, plus generous quarters for a crew of sixteen. One of the berths was a sizeable state room with a bedroom off it, that had a circular bed, with mirrored walls and ceiling. The private bathroom had a double bath and a Jacuzzi. In one corner of the state room was a twenty-six-inch Bang and Olufsen colour television set, and next to it was a matching B & O stereo. Down one wall, under a large expanse of glass that was more a picture window than a porthole, was an exquisite, genuine George the Third writing desk, with two telephones on it.

The telephones, the desk, the hi-fi, the television, the bathroom, the bedroom and the boat belonged to a handsome 46-year-old German named Deke Sleder. Sleder was a familiar name to the readers of gossip columns and glossy magazines as one of the world's international playboys. A doyen of the jet set, five times married – once to an heiress, twice to film starlets, once to a rock singer and the last time to a black fashion-model – he was one of the world's most publicized ageing trendies.

But living glamorously was not the only thing he was good at. He was also well known to the readers of *Fortune* magazine, *Business Week*, the *Financial Times*, the *Wall Street Journal* and many other financial publications, as a businessman to be reckoned with. Having inherited from his father a fortune in excess of four hundred million Deutschmark in interests ranging from textiles to oil, from high explosives to wheat farming and to the manufacture of ball bearings for railway carriage wheels, and having turned these not entirely humble origins into a combine turning over more than five hundred million pounds annually, Deke Sleder could not be reasonably described as either lacking in grey matter or being short of a bob or two.

A taxi drew up at the barrier at the end of the quay, and a short, plump American in a loud, checked jacket, tangerine Polyester trousers, white shoes with tassels, and a thin silver chain inside his open-neck shirt, clambered out. He was struggling simultaneously with the French language, a large Gladstone bag and the French currency. Judging from the expression of thunder on the taxi driver's face, he had won his struggle with the French currency.

The American picked up his bag and strutted jauntily up

the quay, reading off the names of the boats as he went along, until he reached the *Chanson II*. As he started to walk up the gangway, he didn't notice a man at a café on the quay lower his copy of *France-Soir* and study him carefully through the 200mm lens of his Nikon before pressing the shutter button.

The American was excited. Invitations to spend long weekends on yachts in the South of France did not come often to Adamsville, Ohio, and he sure as hell was going to make the most of this one, even though he fully expected to spend most of the time discussing important business. That was what he had assured his wife, and he had assured her that in good faith, because it was what his host-to-be had told him. He was, all the same, a trifle curious as to what deal was so important it was worthwhile his host-to-be's flying him all the way out here – and first class at that.

The American's appalling dress sense and poorly kept body masked an intelligent, if limited, brain. He was at the peak of his career and would go no higher than where he was, although there were more rungs available for the climbing. He worked for the American Fossilized Corporation, a massive combine which specialized in the manufacture of aviation and rocket fuels, as plant manager of their Adamsville, Ohio, operation. It was public knowledge that American Fossilized was under scrutiny for a take-over bid from Gebruder Sleder GMBH (US) Inc., and it was public knowledge that the boss of Gebruder Sleder was one Deke Sleder. It was not, however, public knowledge that the principle business these days of American Fossilized, and in particular of its Adamsville plant, was the manufacture of uranium-filled fuel rods for nuclear power stations.

As the American stepped onto the deck, two burly men in double-breasted navy blazers, white trousers, peaked caps and white plimsolls, materialized from the stern cabin.

'Can we help you?' said one, guessing the man's mother tongue first go. He spoke with a heavy German accent.

'My name is Slan – er – Harry Slan. Mr Sleder is – er – expecting me.'

'Good afternoon, Mr Slan,' the henchman smiled. 'Herr Sleder is expecting you.' He stretched out his hand and took Slan's bag. 'Please, you follow me. Herr Sleder is sure you would like to take a rest after your journey, and he will welcome you aboard himself at drinks before dinner in two hours' time at eight o'clock.' The man led the way off down into the boat. Harry Slan could not see the wink that was exchanged between the man who remained behind and the man on the quay who was so short-sighted, he needed a 200mm lens in order to read his *France-Soir*.

They went down two flights of polished wooden stairs and then along a carpeted corridor. They went past a door marked *Tirpitz*, another marked *Graf Spee*, and stopped outside one marked *Bismark*. The man turned to Slan. 'This is your cabin. On behalf of Herr Sleder, I wish you a very comfortable stay.' With that he put down the bag and walked off.

Harry Slan picked the bag up and entered the cabin. Halfway in, he stopped in his tracks. Standing in the room, facing him, was a tall dark-haired girl, with a strong, beautifully proportioned body that almost rippled with energy. She put her hands on her hips and smiled at him. Her breasts were large and firm, and lifted up and down slightly as she breathed. The only stitch of clothing on her entire body was a minute bikini bottom, either side of the front of which sprouted thick black tufts of hair.

Harry Slan gulped and started to back out of the room. 'Sorry – I'm sorry – er – wrong room.'

'You must be Harry?' she said, with a soft German accent.

'Er – yes – er – sorry.'

'Welcome to your cabin, Harry. I am your cabin hostess. Let me fix you a drink and unpack your bag for you. What would you like – a nice cold beer, or an American cocktail?' She marched over to the door, took Slan's bag in one hand and Slan in the other, and pushed the door shut behind them with her foot.

5

Horace Whalley was a pragmatic-looking man, in his early fifties. He had a thick-set face at the front of a conical head, with a large nose that dipped slightly downwards, and grey hair that was cropped short, and he looked as though he carried the burdens of the world on his shoulders. He was about five foot seven, wore unassuming worsted suits, drab wool ties, and had a generally meek air. He stooped slightly, and never took large footsteps. Unknown to him, there was a tiny electronic microphone concealed in every room of his house, inside his car, inside his office, and inside his Rotary Club tie-pin, which normally he always wore but had recently mislaid.

He munched his bran and prunes breakfast, unaware that the sounds of his eating were being heard, with perfect fidelity, by six men in three motor cars, parked in the vicinity of his house, in the tree-lined Surbiton avenue, in such a manner that they could follow him unobtrusively, regardless of which direction he decided to take on leaving his house.

It was the seventeenth morning of their vigil, and they had heard him, as usual, take his wife a cup of tea in bed, murmur. 'Goodbye, dear, I'll see you later,' go downstairs, pick up his briefcase and umbrella from beside the door, go out and into the garage. A few moments later, the tail of a powder blue Vauxhall Cavalier would start pouring out choked exhaust smoke, the reversing lights would shine on, and the car would start to move backwards down the short concrete driveway. None of the six men needed to look at their wristwatches: they knew it was 6.15 a.m. precisely.

There were twelve men in the team altogether, six were always on while the other six rested. All twelve of them had come to the conclusion several days ago that following Horace Whalley was a waste of time. His routine each day was exactly the same: from the time he left the office at four forty-five in the afternoon to the time he returned to it at seven in the morning, any one of them could have told me, with his eyes shut and his ears blocked, exactly where Whalley was and what he was doing. But they were professional enough to understand that this was the point. Whalley's normal routine was completely taped; any deviation from it would stand out like a sore thumb – and it was a deviation that we all waited for.

The three cars that followed him in the morning, changing places every few miles, were different makes and colours from the ones that followed him in the evening, and none of the cars was ever used more than once in the same week. At six twenty as usual the three cars that followed him in towards central London heard him turn on Radio 4, keeping the volume control low as he listened to the end of the Farming Report, and then turning the volume up to listen to the news headlines. The men thought perhaps he'd turned it up louder than usual on this particular morning, but they couldn't be sure.

The first item on the Monday morning headlines was the shooting of four soldiers in Belfast. The second item was a sharp fall in the cost of living. The third item was the disappearance of the chairman of the United Kingdom Atomic Energy Authority, Sir Isaac Quoit. He had last been seen, the announcer informed listeners, on Saturday afternoon, walking his pointer across Ashdown Forest, near his Sussex home. The dog had returned home alone, but nothing had been seen or heard of Sir Isaac. The breakfast programme newscaster gave the information to the nation, or at least to that portion of the nation that were up at this hour, tuned into Radio 4 and actually listening to their sets, with a degree of gravity in his voice that was ideally suited to the occasion, and had been selected from a file of fifty different tones of gravity for fifty different types of serious announcements stored in the memory banks of his brain after a quarter of a century doing this job. The police, he stated, were treating the matter as 'foul play', and left his audience to decide for themselves whether this implied that the police were intending, shortly, to arrest the dog.

By the time the blue Cavalier's radio reception had faded into nothing but a crackle as the car descended the ramp to the car park underneath the United Kingdom Atomic Energy Authority's Charles II Street headquarters, Horace Whalley and the six men who were following him had listened to the newscaster report the same story, in the same tone, five more times. They had also listened twice to Sir Isaac Quoit's wife relating precisely what Sir Isaac was wearing when he set off, what he had said to her, which was pretty much what anybody who was setting off to walk the dog for forty-five minutes might say to his wife, and debating whether the fact that he had had a second helping of pudding might indicate he had been stoking up for a long journey. They had also listened to her relate how the dog had come home with someone else's frozen leg of mutton in its mouth, which didn't indicate anything at all, except that either the dog was underfed or it was a kleptomaniac.

'Daphne's coming in.'

I switched off the tiny radio receiver built into my propelling pencil. Daphne was the code name for Horace

Whalley. I looked at my watch and knew I needn't have bothered. It was exactly 7.00 a.m. I yawned, and cursed Whalley. Having to be at work at 7.00 a.m. was not my idea of fun, and after seventeen days I still had not got used to it. I decided I probably wouldn't ever get used to it. My circadian cycle, as the twenty-four-hour clock in one's body is called, is not geared to be in harmony with the gentle glow of dawn; it prefers to commence its daily cycle several hours after the sun has first appeared over the far horizon, and it likes to be jolted into action by a succession of cups of thick, black coffee delivered by a warm, naked girl. Much to the chagrin of myself and my much abused innards, my current coffee-mate wasn't into 6.15 a.m. deliveries.

I took out my first Marlboro of the day and then stuck it back in the pack. I wasn't giving up – I like smoking – but I had promised myself I was going to cut down drastically, and that definitely meant not lighting up at 7.00 a.m., for openers. If my metabolism was in ruins and my lungs in tatters, it was Whalley who was to blame. My hatred of his working hours, and the knowledge that the sooner I either gave him up as a bad job or nailed him doing something, the sooner I might have some chance of returning to a normal existence – or at any rate, to as near to a normal existence as my job would ever allow – spurred me to a degree of application to this task that appeared dangerously like enthusiasm.

The office at the Authority, which the Energy Secretary had commandeered for his hot-shot analyst, was small, and tucked away in a quiet corner of the building, with a window that looked down onto Charles II Street, and it had two features uncommon to the other offices in the building: firstly, with the door shut, it was completely sound-proof; secondly, concealed in the back of the desk was a twenty-one-inch television monitor, linked, via closed-circuit to three television cameras and as many microphones elaborately concealed in the office of Horace Whalley two floors above.

From seven in the morning to a quarter to five in the afternoon, I watched and listened to Horace Whalley at work. From ten until five past ten he slurped at a cup of hot coffee that was brought to him, and from one until a quarter past he munched his way through an egg and cress wholemeal bread sandwich, followed by a spam and chutney wholemeal bread sandwich, followed by two chocolate digestive biscuits and a small carton of milk, all supplied by his wife. From a quarter past three until twenty past three he slurped at a cup of hot tea. His daily adventures into the world of gastronomy were unlikely to land him a job as an inspector for the *Michelin Guide*.

Apart from the brief interludes to nourish the inner man, Whalley was a prolific worker. His official title was controller of system safeguards, and his job was to ensure that the safety systems and procedures at the sixteen nuclear power stations in Great Britain were properly maintained and adhered to, within the confines of their budgets. Much of his work was to check up on the work done by the Nuclear Installations Inspectorate and the National Radiological Protection Board, and to analyze their recommendations.

Whilst most of Whalley's work was done from his office, he was entitled to, and did frequently, make random checks on the stations, and in order to be able to carry out these checks effectively he was allowed access, without having to seek any permission whatsoever, to every square inch of every power station in Britain.

For the past seventeen days he hadn't made any such

checks; in fact he had done nothing of any interest at all. From the camera that was concealed above his desk, I could read any of his documents that I wanted to; I hadn't yet noticed anything that was my taste in literature. It was the third week of October, over six weeks since my rudely curtailed meeting with Ahmed in the lavatory, and in that short time, I had added a new subject to that list of subjects upon which I could talk, if required, at great length, without actually knowing very much at all: this new subject was, not surprisingly, nuclear power. From my visits to each of the stations in Britain, and my seventeen days in the Atomic Energy Authority, I had acquired, whilst certainly not sufficient knowledge to build a nuclear power station, more than was adequate to blow one up. But if this was what was in the mind of my friend Whalley, in seventeen days he hadn't yet showed his hand. Not at any rate until this particular day when, at 1.00 p.m., instead of taking out his sandwiches, he got up from his desk, put on his coat, picked up his briefcase and left the office.

I pulled out my propelling pencil, pushed the tip in and spoke into the clip. 'She's coming out.' I pushed the button a second time, which switched it onto the receiving cycle and walked over to the window. A couple of minutes passed and there was no sign of Whalley. I figured he must have gone down into the car park, and if he had I wouldn't see him come out from here, since the car park entrance was at the back of the building. I held the pointed end of the pencil up to my ear. It contained a tiny directional speaker, through which, if pointed at my ear, I could hear perfectly clearly, although someone standing right beside me would not hear a thing.

Another minute passed, then a voice came out of the pencil.

'This is Sheila. We've got her.'

It was our practice to code name both the person being tailed, and the cars tailing, with girls' names. The names of the three cars today were Sheila, Mavis and Ethel. My name for today was Carol.

'Stay with her, Sheila,' I said, 'I'm coming out too.'

I left the building by the front entrance, turned left and walked up to a grey Cortina that was parked on a jammed meter. It was one of five different cars that were parked on this meter on a daily rotation; I had keys to all five. I started the engine, then pushed into my ear a device that looked like a miniature hearing aid, but was a radio receiver tuned in to the frequency of the three surveillance cars. I could have tuned in to Whalley as well, had I wanted, but I didn't think he would have a great deal to say to himself whilst driving along on his own. I clicked the top of my propelling pencil and spoke into it. 'This is Carol. Where's the party?'

'At the fairground. Looks like we're going on the helter skelter.'

The fairground was code for Hyde Park Corner and the helter skelter was Park Lane. It was highly unlikely that Whalley was eavesdropping on us, but in surveillance we avoid taking risks. Although we changed our frequency daily, and sometimes more often than that, there was always the danger he could stumble across it accidentally, and if he heard places mentioned where he was actually driving at the time, it wouldn't take him long to put two and two together. So, like the police, we had an elaborate language for tailing, complete with its own vocabulary and key-place nicknames.

I caught up with Ethel, the back-marker of the cars, going around Swiss Cottage; Ethel was a brown Morris Ital. I overtook Ethel and sat behind Mavis, a mustard Chrysler

Horizon. That's one thing about the security services – they always buy British cars. Anyone worried about being tailed by MI5 can relax if he sees foreign cars behind him.

We headed onto the M1, and the traffic was thin. About half a mile ahead, I could see Sheila, a navy Ford Escort. Somewhere in front of him was Whalley.

After about ten minutes, Ethel moved into the fast lane and passed me, then Mavis and Sheila, to give Horace Whalley a change of view in his mirrors. In spite of the seventy miles per hour permitted limit, we maintained a steady fifty-five. Whalley was no speed merchant, but it helped us in tailing him on the exposed motorway, for it meant that plenty of cars passed, reducing further the very slim chance that Whalley might notice us.

After a while, to break the monotony, I pulled into the fast lane and accelerated past Mavis, and then past Ethel, and saw Whalley's Cavalier for the first time on this journey. I passed Sheila and drew level, after first making sure there were no turn-offs for a good way ahead, and passed him. As I went past, I looked at him out of the corner of my eye; he was driving like a frightened rabbit, hunched up over the wheel, and concentrating far too much on the business of keeping his car going forward and in a straight line to take notice of anything at all going on around him.

I carried on pulling away from him until he was nothing but a speck in my rear-view mirror, and then saw a sign for services in one mile, followed by another sign indicating junction fourteen in five miles. I pulled off into the service area, but Whalley carried on down the motorway; I waited some moments, then pulled out and sat some way behind Mavis. None of the cars spoke to each other; there was no need.

We passed Birmingham and turned off onto the A5. We

passed Telford and Shrewsbury and hacked through into Wales. I was glad I had a full tank, as Whalley showed no signs of stopping either for fuel or food. The light was fading fast and I put my sidelights on, and then, after another twenty minutes, my headlights. The road became little more than an Alpine pass, twisting through the Welsh hills, and tiny villages containing ten craft shops per head of their population. It was seven o'clock and for the past two hours our average speed had been no more than thirty miles per hour. For another hour it remained the same, and Ethel made a stop for fuel.

When Ethel had caught us up, Mavis stopped for fuel, and Sheila sat behind Whalley. Just after half past eight, the left indicator of the Cavalier started flashing, and the car pulled off the road onto the crowded forecourt of a pub. Sheila's driver, evidently numbed with the monotony of the tail, nearly rammed him up the back, his car snaking about the road with a howl of rubber; he then hooted angrily, flashed his lights and accelerated sharply forwards, which was textbook procedure for a near-accident when tailing. Whalley would never see that car again.

I pulled up a hundred yards past the pub and spoke into the microphone. 'She's gone in the German cruiser.' German cruiser was rhyming slang for boozer. Cockney was alive and well and living in British Intelligence.

Ethel went past me, and didn't stop, but I knew a short way up the road he would turn round, come back and find a discreet place to wait and watch the pub's entrance. Mavis would be waiting a hundred yards or so back from the pub, also with a clear view of any vehicle or person leaving it.

I got out of the car and sprinted back towards the pub. As I came in sight, I stopped running and began to walk normally. A dark-coloured Capri – bottle green, I thought, but couldn't be sure in the poor lighting – pulled out of the parking lot, with one man at the wheel and no one else in the car.

'Pick up a fare, Mavis.' I spoke into my breast pocket, whilst memorizing the Capri's number at the same time. I had instructed the Chrysler to follow the Capri. There was probably no connection between the Capri and Whalley's stop, but having come all this way, I wasn't in any mood to take chances.

I could see Whalley's Cavalier, empty. Whalley must have gone into the pub. I looked through the window into the lounge bar; it was a large L-shaped room, with chintzy, rose-coloured lighting, a long bar with a drab buffet selection at one end, and a battery of slot machines, including an ageing Space Invaders.

It was a dreary-looking pub, large, granite-walled, with about as much character as a multi-storey car park. Whalley was standing by the buffet, with a pint of beer in his hand, ordering some food. I thought about it for a moment. The pub was fairly full. Horace Whalley wasn't a man of particularly striking presence. From the time Whalley had pulled off the road into that parking lot, to the time I had driven a hundred yards, stopped, got out of my car and sprinted back up to the pub, a maximum of ninety seconds could have passed. It would have taken Whalley at least twenty seconds to park his car, and another twenty seconds to get to the pub, assuming he was moving like lightning – unlikely after a seven and a half hour drive without a break. If he'd marched straight to the bar, and been served immediately, and had given the exact money, he would have beaten the world record for time taken to get a pint of beer in one's hand from entering a pub door. There was a throng of people at the bar trying to get served, and the staff behind the bar were slow old biddies. No way.

The woman behind the buffet buttered two slices of white bread, plonked a couple of pieces of white turkey meat onto one slice, closed the second slice on top of it, placed the sandwich on a plate, added a sprig of parsley that looked like it had been cultured in the Gobi Desert, and passed it over the glass counter to Whalley. He produced his wallet and handed her a bank note. All the while, he kept the elbow of his left arm pressed tightly to his chest, as though there were something in his coat he didn't want to let drop.

Dismal though that sandwich looked, I could have paid a very handsome sum for it right now; I was starving. I tried to remember if I'd eaten anything yet today: one Twix bar at about half six this morning on my way in to the Atomic Energy Authority. That was all. I was hungry right now – damned hungry – but something told me I had a long night ahead and that there wasn't going to be much food in that night for me.

Whalley took his sandwich and his beer and sat down in a corner on his own. Someone had bought that beer for Whalley, but Whalley had been late, and that someone couldn't stay to drink with him. Only one person had left the pub since I'd arrived. I decided I had been right to have the Capri tailed. What I needed to know was whether Whalley was collecting, or delivering, or both. From the way he continued to hold his arm tight to his chest, he had certainly done a spot of collecting.

I left the window and ran back out to the road. Diagonally across from the pub, backed deep into a gap in the bushes, was the Morris Ital, Ethel. I walked over and spoke to the driver, then went to my car, opened the boot, and removed the items I needed. Then I ran back down to the pub and looked in through the window. Whalley had finished his sandwich, and was draining the last of his beer.

I went to the car park, opened the Cavalier's door with the duplicate key I had had made a couple of weeks back, and wedged myself down onto the floor behind the front seats, carefully stretching the black blanket I had brought over me. I positioned a gas mask close to my face, and removed the safety cap on the tiny cylinder that I gripped in my hand.

Some moments later, I heard footsteps approaching the car, the sound of a key in the lock, the sharp click of the black lock-pin popping up, and the sharp creak of the driver's door opening – it was in desperate need of oil on its hinges. Even under the black blanket, the glow from the interior light seemed as bright as a floodlit cup-replay football pitch. I felt the seat-back sag as Whalley lowered his body with all the gentleness of an elephant bouncing onto a trampoline.

The door slammed shut, and the interior light, mercifully, went out. Whalley belched, then let out a loud fart.

I heard the click of a seat belt, and then the sound of the engine starting, followed by the sound of an unsuccessful attempt at marrying a motionless gear cog with a rotating gear cog without the assistance of a clutch. There was another belch. Whalley to me sounded dangerously drunk on his one pint of bitter. He finally got the sequence right, and I felt the car begin to move forward. We slowed, and then accelerated out, onto what I presumed was the main road. Several hundred yards behind, and without front lights, I knew the Morris would be starting to follow.

I secured the gas mask over my nose and mouth, and then turned the valve. Whalley would have had to have been listening very closely indeed to have heard the tiny hiss, and right now the organs that conveyed sound waves to his brain were flooded with the sound of one Welsh and seven French radio stations in rapid succession, as he struggled to find the elusive one that played music that was not accompanied by undulating wailings and distant Germans holding earnest conversations.

I closed the valve and allowed time for Whalley to inhale the sleeping gas into his lungs. I waited some moments, then opened the valve again for a five-second burst. A sudden blast of cold air, accompanied by the noise of rushing wind, told me Whalley must have wound down his window. No one does that on a cold night unless they are getting tired.

I was a little concerned about the gas. It was the first time I had used this particular type, fresh off the production line of the Playroom – the dirty tricks department of British Intelligence. Messrs Trout and Trumbull, its inventors, claimed it was the first non-inflammable sleeping gas in the world; not having used it before, I had no real idea of its strength.

I waited the minute and a half it took him to decide he had had enough fresh air and wind up the window, which he did, then opened the valve again, this time for eight seconds. Again he opened the window. I hoped to hell he would do the sensible thing and pull over and stop, and not fall asleep at the wheel with an articulated lorry coming the other way.

The window went up again, and I released another five-second burst. This time, the car slowed noticeably. Suddenly he braked very hard, the car swerved, and I felt a bumpy surface under the wheels. We carried on for some yards, then stopped, and Whalley switched off the engine. He yawned loudly, and I released another burst as he yawned. There was the click of a lever in front of me, and the driver's seat tilted back a few degrees. Whalley was sound asleep before he had even leaned back into it.

Everything was quiet for a few moments. There were some clicking sounds from the engine as the coolant dribbled through the pipes, the roar of a lorry in the distance, then the heavy rhythmic breathing of Whalley. It was pitch dark, we were either in a lay-by or on the grass verge. I put the valve right under Whalley's nose and opened it for four seconds. According to my instructions, he would wake up in a couple of hours, feeling very thirsty and slightly queasy – neither sensation being particularly out of the ordinary for someone who is attempting to shake off fatigue by sleeping in his motor car.

A lorry thundered past and the Cavalier shook. I switched on the car's interior light, and right away saw a small Jiffybag on the front passenger seat. Fortunately, it had not been sealed, and I removed its only content: a thick plastic container. I pulled out my torch and shone it on the container. Nothing was written on the outside, but I knew what it would contain. I had frequently seen such containers before. I opened it, and I was right: it was a video-cassette.

I searched Whalley thoroughly, but there was nothing else of interest on him. The most common subject matter recorded on unmarked video-cassettes in plain brown wrappers is hard-core pornography. But if it was hard-core pornography my friend Whalley was after, there were easier places for him to obtain it within a few minutes' walk of his office. He didn't have to drive half-way across England and Wales. No. I had a distinct feeling that naked girls with thongs and spurs were not going to start performing on any video-screen this particular tape was played into. My feeling told me that the vigil of the past seventeen days had paid its first dividend.

I put the tap back in the bag. and placed it onto the seat, then I picked up my various bits of equipment, left the Cavalier and walked a couple of hundred yards back up the road to where Mavis was stopped. I opened the front passenger door, and spoke to the two men inside.

'Can you drive back to the pub and pick up my car? I'll stay here, but I don't think he's going anywhere for quite a while.'

'Why don't you come with us?'

'I'll wait – just in case he's got any friends that come looking for him.'

'One of us will stay if you want.'

'No, it's okay, I'll do it.' Until I'd found out where he was taking that tape, I wasn't going to let either Whalley or the tape out of my sight for one second. I slammed shut the Morris door. Chris Allen, the driver, started up, and put the car into gear, and the car moved forward. I ran after it and tapped on the window. He stopped and wound down the window.

'While you're at the pub,' I said, 'you might get me a turkey sandwich – and ask for a double portion of parsley, preferably green, if they've got any.'

'Yes, boss,' he grinned.

Either the pub was further back than I had thought, or there was a problem finding green parsley, or the pub served a particularly good pint of beer, for it took the crew of Mavis one hell of a lot longer to return with my car and sandwich than I had expected, and standing on a freezing-cold Welsh roadside watching a car with a slumbering man in it wasn't my idea of fun. They say that food tastes better when you are hungry, and if that is true, I wondered what the hell the sandwich would have tasted like if I hadn't been hungry. The bread had the texture of mildewed asbestos and the meat tasted as if it had been marinated in creosote. Somewhere between the pub and me the double portion of parsley had gone on the missing list. If I'd had any sense, I should have thrown away the sandwich and eaten the paper napkin it came in – it would have probably been a lot tastier and a damned sight more nourishing.

I must have been over-generous with the gas, because it was nearly three hours before Whalley started up his engine and drove on. Two cars followed him through the night as he headed back towards London. I sat, yawning dangerously, behind the wheel of one of them. At a quarter to seven, Whalley stopped a short distance from the BBC Television Centre in Shepherd's Bush. He went in, with the Jiffybag, and came out, thirty seconds later, without it.

I waited until he had driven off, with Mavis following him, then went into the Television Centre myself and up to the twenty-four-hour reception desk.

6

Harry Slan stared through the hairs on his plump belly at the thick black bush of the strong German girl, and at her taut stomach, the muscles of which rippled as the stomach contracted and expanded, and then he stared up at her huge breasts that swung down to his face and then up to the heavens, as she rode up and down his diminutive but rigid organ. She held his wrists in a pincer grip against the mattress, and gritted her teeth in a maniacal smile. Although it was only the last week of September, behind her clenched-shut eyes she was working out her Christmas shopping list for her boyfriend, her three sisters, her brother and her two ex-husbands.

Harry Slan thrust for all he was worth, pushing his tiny circumcized stump deep inside that black patch; he was excited, very excited, for he knew he was driving her wild with ecstasy. He pulled down, then thrust deeper still inside her. She groaned with delight; he sweated with pleasure.

She had just decided that Griselda, her youngest sister, a keen cook, would like a nice casserole dish; yes, she remembered Griselda's embarrassment at having to serve up a veal stew in a tin saucepan when she had last been to dinner. Unthinkingly, she contracted her pelvis tightly and gave it two sharp gyrations. Before Slan could do anything about it, he found he was coming for the second time since he had arrived on the boat. Uttering a noise not unlike that of a man losing his foot-hold on the roof of a house, he fell back into the soft bedding.

Eva snapped out of her shopping list just in time to notice and add some finishing touches. As he sank back, she caressed his brow. 'Wonderful,' she whispered into his ear, 'I came so many times, so many times.'

Slan beamed with delight. Not once in all the forty-eight years of his life, could he remember having come twice in one hour. Then he remembered where he was, and leaned his head over to look at his watch. 'Shit,' he said, 'I'll have to start getting ready for dinner.'

Eva stayed on top of him. 'Don't worry darling, Deke is not a punctual man. Relax, we have plenty of time.'

Slan looked up into her eyes. He was completely and utterly exhausted, but he was determined to make the most of every minute. Tonight, he was going to set a record that was going to make every man back at the American Fossil-ized Corporation's Adamsville, Ohio, plant goddam eat his fucking heart out.

Unbeknown to Slan, eleven men in eleven cabins similar to his own, on the *Chanson II* at this very moment, were receiving a not dissimilar treatment. The only thing that singled him out, at this particular moment, was that his host, Deke Sleder, was watching his every action on the twenty-six-inch Bang and Olufsen colour television screen in his private state room, while the video-recorder rolled steadily on.

During the long weekend that was just beginning, each of the eleven men in turn would be recorded – and not for posterity – on the same Betamax that rolled away now, each performing acts much the same, some more imaginative, some more lazy, as those in which Harry Slan currently wallowed; each with a beautiful girl, stark naked, or clad in anything they fancied, from a morris-dancing costume to a lifebelt. Like Harry Slan, each of these eleven men was reasonably happily married. Each too worked, in some capacity, at senior management level, in their country's nuclear energy industry. One of the men came from England, two from France, two from Spain, five came from the USA and one from Canada.

In the cabin next to Harry Slan was a man who had never been very successful with women. He had taken out a few before he had met the one who was to become his wife, but he had never got anywhere near seducing them, much as, timid though he was, he would have liked to. Marriage provided a sex life that he supposed was adequate, not that his wife was ever the whore in the bedroom he had read that good wives were supposed to be. There was something in particular which had begun as mild curiosity, but had been slowly turning into an obsession as the years went by: his wife was fair-haired; he wanted to know what it would be like to make love to a dark-haired woman. For the past twenty-one years, every remotely attractive woman who smiled at him, unwittingly sent him reeling into an erotic fantasy. One day, he had been promising himself, he would take off to Shepherd Market, and buy himself an hour or two with one, but he knew, that when it came to it, he would not have the courage.

But now, finally, his fantasy had come true; he was lying naked on a bed, on top of an equally naked raven-haired woman. She was more beautiful than anyone he had ever dared to hope he might conquer. And here she was, naked in bed with him, on a paradise boat in a paradise port on a balmy late-summer's evening, a million miles away from his home, from his wife, from, he thought happily, any possible chance of being found out. Like Harry Slan, he too had wondered why he had been invited; but right now, he didn't give a damn. He opened his eyes to look at her, to reassure himself that she was real, that his dream had come true; that he was finally – after all the years of dreaming – making love to a dark-haired woman. His name was Horace Whalley. Whalley wasn't under any suspicion the night I made a routine search of his office, and the search was no more and no less thorough than the search I made that week of half the other offices of the staff of the Atomic Energy Authority. But the letter of invitation from Deke Sleder to spend a long weekend on his boat, earned Whalley his position between the glass slides under the Maximilian Flynn microscope. Deke Sleder might have been on *Cosmopolitan*'s 'ten sexiest men in the world' list; he was on quite a different list in the files of British Intelligence.

7

The small brass plate to the right of the front door of the building had engraved on it the words *Portico Investments Ltd*. Nothing else gave the casual passer-by any clue as to the activities that went on behind the white-painted, five-storey Regency façade of 46 Carlton House Terrace.

There was nothing to hint to the casual passer-by that number forty-six did not in fact stop at basement level, but continued down into the ground for another five storeys, and continued along, down the Mall, occupying five more houses.

Inside the entrance hall of number forty-six was an attractive brunette in her mid-thirties. What singled her out from the thousands of receptionists in London that looked not unlike her was a cabinet on her sitting-room wall at home which contained some forty-five cups and medals; most were from Bisley, but one had pride of place: it was an Olympic Silver for Rapid Pistol Fire. By making the most local of movements with the hand she used for pushing her intercom buttons, she could, within one and a half seconds of anyone coming through that front door, have produced a hefty Colt revolver and started firing it.

To her left was a glass display booth featuring an array of extremely large uncut gemstones, including a diamond, sapphire, emerald and ruby. A montage of colour photographs behind the stones depicted a drill-bit grinding into the earth, with the caption *Amarillo, 1935*, a pair of tongs holding up a ruby ring, with the caption *Nairobi, 1955*, and an aerial photograph of an area of hilly desert.

The display was for the benefit of visitors, not that this building had many strangers visit it, nor did it encourage them. The regular inhabitants of the building knew that the gemstones were nothing but bits of glass, and the photographs were prints from a handful of negatives found in the vaults of the Science Museum.

The entire complex onto which the front door of number forty-six opened housed a daytime staff of seven hundred and fifty people, the majority of whom entered and left via a battery of innocent-looking doorways dotted around the Mall, Trafalgar Square and Cockspur Street, or by one of the three entrances to the car park which sprawled below the complex.

On the fifth floor, through a secretary's anteroom, and through a massive, heavily beaded double door, was the man who presided over this domain. He was a powerfully built man with a bullet-shaped head rising from a bull-neck; a nose that was long, but did not protrude much, and was broken in a couple of places like a prize fighter's; his hair was a mixture of dark greys, with occasional black strands, and there were elegant silver streaks either side of his temples. He wore a Turnbull and Asser lawn-cotton shirt, pin-striped down the chest, but with plain white collar and cuffs, a very up-to-date Lanvin tie, and the entire package elegantly wrapped in five hundred pounds' worth of Dormeuil navy-blue chalk-striped cloth and Hawes and Curtis expertise. He wasn't a particularly tall man, being no more than five foot nine, but he had the sort of presence that would make the most belligerently drunk of rugger-buggers move over to make room for him at crowded pub bars.

A close look at the wrinkles around his eyes would

indicate he was in his late sixties, but in spite of that age, he looked capable of vaulting the giant desk, which he dwarfed with his presence, in one leap – that was, unless you knew that, tucked somewhere under the back of that massive expanse of mahogany, was a thin but strong walking stick. It wasn't age that had brought on the necessity of this stick, but a hail of bullets from a would-be assassin's sub-machine gun just over a year ago.

Closeted behind the front door of 46 Carlton House Terrace, behind the brass plate with *Portico Investments Ltd* engraved on it, was an organization that could trace its roots back to the days of Queen Elizabeth I and the Spanish Armada. It was a secret organization, so secret, in fact, that it did not officially exist, in spite of the fact that it spent its way, annually, through some one hundred and forty million pounds' worth of British taxpayers' money. Outside the organization itself, there were only two people, at any one time, who had the faintest clue what it was up to: the Home Secretary and the Prime Minister, and what they knew could be written with a fairly thick felt-tipped marker on the back of a postage stamp.

The organization sprawled across three other complexes of its own in London, largely as a result of Fifeshire's expansion plans, as well as sharing a massive complex beneath the Hyde Park underground car park with the Army, the police Special Branch, the Secret Intelligence Service – MI6 – and no doubt, half the leading Russian moles in England. The organization was MI5, and the man who sat on the fifth floor of Portico Investments, Sir Charles Cunningham-Hope OBE, better known by his code name, Fifeshire, was its Director General.

Fifeshire rarely saw most of his operatives from year in to year out, but I was privileged – if any of the hundred, different, rotten assignments I have had could be called a privilege – to work directly for him. He was my control. We had got on extremely well at my first ever interview with him – whether he had taken pity on a waif in distress, or had spotted a gullible mark who could be manipulated, or had any of a thousand other reasons, I could not tell, so I consoled myself by believing that Fifeshire was intelligent enough to recognize a fine man when he saw one.

Fifeshire's ace agent had, however, little desire to be the most admired man in the graveyard, and for that reason I kept more than a wary eye open whenever I went to see him. I walked in to the familiar room, and he stood up behind his desk, and stretched out his massive hand. It was the kind of hand that leaves delicate ladies who shake it with speechless smiles on their faces, while their cheeks flush bright red, and they transfer their weight from one foot to the other for several moments, until the numbness in their hand subsides and the full strength of the agony hits them; then they let out a short, sharp, but elegant and restrained, 'Owww'.

I was prepared for his clamp, and braced my hand against it; he held my hand for a few seconds, shaking it hard, and just at the moment at which the knuckles were about to crumble to dust, he mercifully let go and waved me to sit down. Beside his desk was a twenty-six-inch television monitor, wired to a video-cassette player. They had been put there on my instructions.

'How are you, Flynn?' he asked.

'A bit better than last week,' I replied. It was last week that I had reported that I was bored stiff watching Whalley do nothing. I wasn't bored any more.

Fifeshire looked wryly at the monitor. 'How kind of you to be concerned I might miss *Coronation Street*.'

'I know you like to be kept informed,' I said.

'Well I wish more people did,' he said. He threw a copy of the morning's *Times* across the desk top. 'Did you read the paper this morning?'

'No, I was busy watching a television programme called *Horace Whalley Goes to the Office.*'

Fifeshire grinned for a brief moment. 'Look at the front page.'

The headline read: *Prince and Princess of Wales start Belfast Tour.*

'Did you know they were going on a Belfast tour?' he asked.

'No.'

'Well, nor did I. Forty million pounds is the budget I have this year to spend on spying on Northern Ireland terrorism, and there isn't anyone that knows more about the subject than I do, yet they go and send the Prince and Princess over there without even asking our opinion. Anyhow,' he said, abruptly changing the subject, 'that's not your problem. Let's hear what you have to say.'

'On Monday Whalley left his office and drove to a pub ten miles this side of Porthmadog in Wales. Moments after he arrived, a Ford Capri drove out. I had the Capri tailed, and whether or not the Capri knew he was being tailed, I don't know, but he shook our men off after about fifteen minutes. From the description of the way he did it, my guess is he's a professional, but didn't know whether he was being followed and just went through a standard routine – a security procedure. What is interesting is that he had false plates on his car – he certainly wasn't taking any chances. The plates bore the registration number of a Datsun that was written off in a smash four years ago. Now there might not be any connection between him and Whalley, but I watched Whalley most of the time he was in the pub and he didn't communicate with anybody, yet when he came out he had a package on him, which contained the videotape he delivered to the BBC, a copy of which is ready to roll on your machine.'

Fifeshire nodded. 'As you don't have any information about this man in the Capri and, by the sound of it, little chance of finding out any more unless he shows himself again, it's not of much help is it?'

'No,' I said.

'Would you recognize him if you saw him again?'

'No, I might recognize the car. I'm having all possible leads followed up – anyone that might have sold the fake plates, all the usual.'

The intercom buzzed and Fifeshire pushed a button on the machine on his desk. The voice of his secretary, the Honourable Violet-Elizabeth Trepp, came out. 'Mr Wardle and Captain Coleman are here to see you, Sir Charles.'

'Send them in please, Miss Trepp.'

To call the Honourable V.-E. Trepp a battleaxe would be to do a cruel injustice to battleaxes. She was to gorgons what a neutron bomb is to a pea-shooter. The whole of MI5, Fifeshire included, were terrified of her. If one didn't know the personnel department better, one might have thought she was a joke perpetrated by them; but personnel didn't have a sense of humour.

Her efficiency, or at least her view of what efficiency should be, drove everyone to the depths of despair. She was not merely protective towards Fifeshire, she protected him like a nuclear-blast shelter. To get a telephone call put through to Fifeshire required a university degree in diplomacy, an enormous amount of patience, and plenty of time to spare. 'Who is calling?' she would say, followed by, 'Is he expecting you?', followed by 'I'll see if he wishes to speak to you.' No one escaped this treatment – not even those who called every day; nor those who called several times every day; not the low-grade bosses, nor the middle-grade bosses, nor the top bosses; not even the Home Secretary, nor the Prime Minister. All got exactly the same treatment. She had been mentally strangled a thousand times, and several hundred of those times by me alone.

By an act of secrecy worthy of the entire organization, Fifeshire had had installed a direct line of which she was unaware, so that he could once again receive urgent calls in time to take some action.

The double doors opened and two men came in; one, a short man, balding, with greying strands of hair, aged about fifty-five, in a green worsted suit that was too small for him and a cream shirt that was too big; the other was in his late thirties, with jet black hair, about six foot tall, wearing a brown double-breasted blazer with plain gold buttons and dark-grey flannel trousers.

'Sir Charles,' I said, introducing them, 'this is Ken Wardle and Dick Coleman from the Playroom.' The Playroom was the nickname given to the gadgetry department of the Combined Central Information base underneath Hyde Park. Some of the most up-to-date equipment in the world was down there, constantly being improved and adapted and applied to all forms of Intelligence work by a team of some of the finest underpaid technicians in the country. Wardle and Coleman were two of these.

'How do you do,' said Fifeshire. 'How very nice of you to come. I'm looking forward to seeing the show!'

Wardle and Coleman smiled politely, and caught my eye. Without moving an eyelid, the three of us winked at each other. We were together in the big boss man's room, like privileged schoolboys; we had to be on our best behaviour and as time was even more precious to Fifeshire than to most people, we hoped he wasn't going to feel we'd wasted his time.

'Shall we start?' I said.

Fifeshire nodded. Wardle switched on the monitor, and Coleman pushed the play button on the video-cassette machine.

The picture that came on the screen was a steady pan across Moscow's Red Square. Into the camera, wearing a Burberry mackintosh over a suit, walked Sir Isaac Quoit. He strode straight up towards the camera, until he was in full close-up, and then stopped.

'Hallo,' he said. 'I am Sir Isaac Quoit and I am the chairman of the United Kingdom Atomic Energy Authority. For those of you who have not heard of this organization, it is the body responsible for the development and organization of the nuclear energy industry in the United Kingdom.

'The reason I am here in Russia is that I do not feel safe in England, nor virtually anywhere in the free world. You may wonder if I have gone mad. The answer is no, I have not gone mad; but I am tired of lying to you, the British public, of feeding you an endless farrago of twisted statistics, of statements from corrupt scientists who have been paid to make statements that they do not themselves believe; I am fed up with doing nothing but heading and running a massive propaganda machine that has been set in motion by the government to cover up its complete inability to understand the implications and dangers of nuclear power, to cover up the fact that it has ruinously overestimated the demand for electricity for both the immediate and the long term, and has, even more ruinously, underestimated the cost of generating this electricity.

'I am tired, in a nutshell, of lying to you that nuclear

power is safe and cheap. It is not. It is immensely dangerous; not only has it been responsible, almost totally, for the ever-increasing incidence of death from cancer in the last twenty years, but it can, and almost certainly will, one day wipe out our entire country. And during the next five years, the cost of nuclear-generated electricity will become as much as eight times higher than the cost of conventionally generated electricity.

'These lies are put upon you to protect the face of the government, and to protect the jobs of the many thousands involved in the nuclear energy industry. On the question of jobs, I can say that many thousands more jobs would be created as a result of generating electricity by conventional methods, and exploring new methods, than are currently available in the nuclear energy industry.

'Why, you might ask, is this massive and lethal deceit maintained? Look back to the origins of the nuclear industry in this country, and an answer may begin to emerge.

'Our first reactor, Calder Hall, became operational – went critical, as they say – in 1956. In front of the press of the whole world, the Queen switched the power from Calder Hall into the national grid, and the nuclear age was born. But the amount of power Calder Hall put into the grid was miniscule. That was not the reason why Calder Hall was built; it was built to produce plutonium for nuclear weapons. The electricity was a by-product.

'The answer becomes clearer still if you look behind the scenes at the British government's commitments to NATO; that same answer emerges again if you look behind the scenes at the British government's commitments to the US – and we do have a major, very secret, defence treaty with the US. With regard to both these commitments, the major part of our contribution is not in ships, or in tanks, or in guns, or aircraft, or personnel; it is in plutonium. Our contribution is to supply NATO and the US with plutonium for nuclear weapons. The easiest way to manufacture plutonium is through nuclear power stations. Plutonium, at close to the ideal level of enrichment for nuclear weapons, is a waste product of nuclear power stations. The major percentage of the defence budget of the British government is concealed in your electricity bills.'

Sir Isaac continued for a further twenty minutes' worth of impassioned and highly plausible-sounding speech. His theme seemed to drift at times, and he didn't always explain clearly what he meant, but he got the basics of his message through loud and clear: the British public were being conned by a government that was too clever by half, and the result of this conning was a spreading network of nuclear power stations on an island far too small to cope with them. Britain, he said, was on the edge of a dark and deep nuclear abyss. She was about to ride, like her countrymen a century and a half before in the Charge of the Light Brigade, into a valley of death and despair from which she could never return. She was too small a land to have so many nuclear power stations, not to mention the fuel-reprocessing plants and the waste plants. One major accident in any of a couple of dozen of nuclear establishments could distribute, across every inch of the land, a cocktail of radioactive horrors so thick and so strong, that nobody would be able to inhabit Britain for generations to come.

Fifeshire watched the speech in stunned silence. At the end, Coleman pushed the pause button, and the picture froze. The chairman of the United Kingdom Atomic Energy Authority stood silhouetted against Lenin's Mausoleum, looking much as I had seen him in the flesh, on a couple of occasions, in the corridors of the Charles II Street building.

He was, I remembered, much more jovial-looking than the strained and tired man he appeared to be here. He was a good six foot tall and very bulky, with a deeply sagging treble chin. The top of his head was completely bald, but tufts of unkempt curly hair sprouted either side of his head and stuck out over his ears. His raincoat was unbuttoned and he wore a Prince of Wales check suit underneath, with all three buttons on his jacket awkwardly done up. He looked like a cross between an eccentric scientist, a giant teddy bear and a Dickensian publican. He was fifty-nine years of age, but had married late in life and had four children all still at school, the youngest being only seven. Although his expression was serious, his eyes had a strange warmth in them.

Fifeshire shook his head slowly, then looked at me. 'He's lost his trolley. He's had a brainstorm, flipped his lid – must have done. I know him well. Dammit, I had a drink with him two weeks ago, he's as straight as they come, dedicated to his work – absolutely dedicated. There's something very strange about all this – very strange.'

'Take a look at Sir Isaac's wrist-watch, sir.'

I nodded at Coleman who pushed the pause button again, and the tape started rolling. Quoit remained on the screen, but now there was a zoom shot in to his right wrist, until the wrist filled the screen. We could see the time clearly on his Rolex wrist-watch: it was seven ten. The second hand was moving steadily around, so the watch wasn't broken.

'Seven ten,' I said, 'yet Red Square is in broad daylight and humming with people. At this time of the year, Moscow is in darkness at both seven in the morning and seven in the evening.'

'Moscow is three hours ahead of us,' said Fifeshire, 'It's probably ten thirty in the morning, Quoit has forgotten to adjust his watch – it's still on English time.'

'Possibly, sir. I think you might change your mind about that.'

The picture changed to a close-up of Quoit's feet and the cobbled ground right beside them, then a series of close-ups of the feet of other people in the Square.

'I asked Ken Wardle and Dick Coleman to take a close look at this videotape and see if they could come up with anything interesting, and I think you'll agree with me, shortly, that they have. The time on Sir Isaac's watch is one thing, and it doesn't prove anything at all, but the next thing certainly does. Ken perhaps you'd be good enough to explain?'

'Certainly, Max,' said Wardle. 'What you're looking at right now is a close-up of Sir Isaac's feet and the feet of other people in the Square through a magnification of the videotape; what you cannot see with the naked eye, even on this magnification, are the shadows on the ground. If it had been a bright sunny day, you could have seen those shadows reasonably clearly, but it was obviously an overcast day, the lighting is flat, and the only shadow that there is, is beyond the range of normal television contrast. You are now going to see this same section of tape put through what we call an image booster – and what I mean by that, in layman's terms, is that we have put it under a microscope.'

The image on the screen changed from feet on the ground to a mass of large and small, dark and less dark shapes. Always, there were two large dark shapes with two smaller, less dark shapes attached.

'What you are now seeing are the feet of people in the Square, and the ground beside their feet, greatly magnified. The dark shapes are the feet themselves, the lighter shapes are the shadows on the ground. Now, there is one pair of feet – these here, that do not have a lighter shape attached – that do not have a shadow. This is most extraordinary. Everyone in Red Square is casting a shadow, except for one person; those feet belong to Sir Isaac.'

'Are you implying what I think you are implying?' said Fifeshire.

'The only possible explanation,' said Wardle, 'is that Sir Isaac was not in Red Square whilst this was being filmed. He was either in a studio with a clever front-projection system, or else was filmed against a neutral background and then superimposed onto a tape of Red Square.'

'The next thing is even more interesting,' I said before Fifeshire could comment, and I nodded at Wardle.

The picture rolled on. The shadows went and two graphs appeared, one above the other. They looked like annual sales comparison charts of some company, the top one showing a good year, the lower one a horrendous year. Coleman again froze the image, and Wardle spoke.

'As you are no doubt aware, Sir Charles, we have the ability now, from recordings of people's voices, to make what we call voice-prints. These are as individual as finger-prints: no two people have the same voice-prints. On the screen you are looking at, the top graph is a voice-print made from a recording of a speech Sir Isaac made three months ago at Oxford University. The bottom graph is a voice-print made from part of the speech we have just heard. Without any doubt at all, these voice-prints were from different people.' Wardle pulled out a pack of Du Maurier cigarettes and offered them around; I took one and lit it. Fifeshire removed a large Havana from the silver box on his desk, and began a surgical operation on it. After some moments, he spoke.

'So who is the person we have just been watching?'

'Sir Isaac Quoit,' said Wardle. 'But he wasn't in Red Square and it wasn't his voice that you heard. You are familiar, I am sure, with the term dubbing when applied to a motion picture – when the film is made in one language, but a different language is recorded onto the sound-track, in as close synchronization with the lip movements of the characters talking as is possible?'

'Yes. I prefer subtitles, but go on.'

'In video, there are techniques available now that are far more sophisticated than the method of dubbing used for celluloid. An electronic dubbing job has been done that would be quite impossible to detect with the naked eye – the only possible way of detection is through the voice-print technique.'

'The thing that baffles me,' said Coleman, 'is that it seems very naive of the Russians to believe no one would run the checks that we have done.'

'You must remember,' said Fifeshire, 'that although the Russians are bang up-to-date – and, indeed, even ahead of us in some areas, particularly medicine, and some space technology – there are many technological areas where they are way behind the West. Just look at their motor cars, their cameras, their navigational equipment! It's more than likely that in this particular field, they are simply not aware of these detection capabilities you have demonstrated.'

Coleman nodded.

'I must say,' continued Fifeshire, 'this certainly sheds a new light on Quoit's disappearance, wouldn't you agree, Flynn?'

'I think one would be a trifle unwise to ignore it completely.' I grinned. 'I think the Director General of the BBC would be more than a little miffed as well. He has kindly given us the best half hour of video he's likely to have all week, and I'm sure he would be most upset if he felt it wasn't fully appreciated.'

'How very kind of him to put his country before his viewer ratings,' said Fifeshire cuttingly. 'It was only because I threatened to have banned completely the six-part series on British Intelligence they've just finished making that he agreed to hand the tape over to you at all. I wouldn't lose a great deal of sleep over his feelings; we've got enough to lose sleep over as it is. We have on the surface a straightforward defection. Quoit goes on television and delivers his justification for his defection – something he feels strongly enough about to give up everything, family, dog, friends, the lot, and plump for Russia, a country where, so far as we know, he has never set foot before. An unusual action to take, but it has been done by others before.

'However, look beneath the surface, and we find three interesting facts. Firstly, Quoit has not adjusted his watch to local time – unusual, for someone as meticulous as Quoit. Secondly, while the impression given is that Quoit is in Red Square, he is in fact not there at all. Thirdly, it is not the voice of Quoit we hear, but of someone else.' Fifeshire looked at me, then at Coleman, then Wardle. 'Does the cassette tell us anything?'

'No, sir,' said Wardle. 'It's a Philips which could have been bought almost anywhere in the world.'

'What about the lines – doesn't Russian television operate on a different lines system from our own?'

'Yes,' said Wardle, 'it does. But they could have taped it on their own system and then converted it to our 625 lines system and the fact that it had been taped on their system wouldn't show up.'

'So apart from some footage of Red Square, is there anything in this videotape that proves beyond doubt that Quoit was not actually in Russia when it was made?'

Wardle and Coleman looked at each other. Wardle

spoke. 'Nothing at all, Sir Charles. Sir Isaac could have been taped anywhere. The footage of Red Square could have come from any stock footage library. The superimposing and the dubbing could have been done by a competent tape-editor with the right facilities – which are not hard to come by – anywhere in the world.'

Fifeshire nodded. 'Well, gentlemen,' he addressed Wardle and Coleman, 'you have given us plenty to chew on. I am sure you are both extremely busy, so I won't keep you any longer. You have been most helpful. Do you have any more questions, Flynn?'

'No, Sir Charles.'

Fifeshire stood up. It was a technique he must have perfected years ago, because he had it to a fine art and it always worked. I knew, because he had used it on me a hundred times. It was his way of getting rid of people quickly, with the minimum loss of time wasted on common courtesies, and yet with extraordinary grace and politeness. He would stand up, looking as though he had to dash somewhere in a hurry. This had the effect of making anyone in his presence want to help him by getting out of his way quickly. They would leap to their feet, grab briefcases or any other articles they had brought, give him a hasty handshake and sprint for the door. Fifeshire would stand rooted to the spot, looking like an athlete awaiting the starting gun for the marathon, until the door had closed, whereupon he would relax and sink back into his chair, with a slightly smug grin on his face. It was by means of this technique that Wardle and Coleman were despatched from the room.

Fifeshire put his cigar in his mouth and lit it. He drew on it slowly and deliberately. 'So,' he said slowly, 'it is quite possible that Quoit is in England. But wherever he is, is he a free man or is he a captive?'

'Captive. Must be. If he was doing this of his own free will, there wouldn't be any need for his voice to be faked.'

Fifeshire nodded. 'I agree with you. And what's more, he's in this country.'

The last time I had come here, Fifeshire had chewed my head off. He wasn't a man who had bad moods often, but when he did, the last place on earth to be was in his office. I had made that mistake two days after the unfortunate Ahmed had shuffled off his mortal coil in the men's lavatory in the Royal Lancaster. In Fifeshire's words, severed heads rolling about four-star-hotel lavatory floors were in extreme cases, perhaps, just about tolerable. Severed heads rolling about lavatory floors, playing dodgems with stolen taxis, and a car-load of flat Arabs under the wheels of an articulated lorry, was, in the none too superfluous wordage of Fifeshire's oratorial flow, 'Not bloody tolerable'.

'No, sir,' I'd agreed.

'I've got Scotland Yard down my throat. I've got Special Branch down my throat. I've got the Home Secretary down my throat. I've got the Foreign Office down my throat. I've got MI6 down my throat. I've got the Minister of Defence down my throat, and now I've got the bloody Libyans down my throat as well. It's bloody lucky I had my tonsils out, or I'd be choking to death. The Prime Minister wants a special report, the press are crawling in every orifice in the wall. Did you have to kill them all? Did you really have to shunt them under that lorry?'

'I was just trying to stop them.'

'Well, you succeeded, Flynn, didn't you? You certainly stopped them. The Cultural Attaché to the Libyan Embassy, his private secretary, the Deputy Minister for Arts, and Libya's leading expert on icons.'

'They shouldn't go around cutting people's heads off and shooting at people.'

'There were no knives and no guns found in the wreckage of that car.'

'Then, with no disrespect, sir, they must have eaten them.'

Fifeshire had been very upset by the news Ahmed had given about Donald Frome. Reports had stopped coming through, which indicated Frome was in trouble. He was one of Fifeshire's key moles, and had successfully infiltrated the international terrorist circuit and gained a position of considerable trust. If he was blown or dead, it would take years to replace him, and if what Ahmed had said was true, by now he was almost certainly both. Further, the news Ahmed had relayed, about the threat to nuclear power stations, did nothing to alter his mood. It fitted in with a lot of feedback Fifeshire had been getting lately from some of his other sources.

It was this not entirely amicable meeting with Fifeshire which had led to my study of the British nuclear energy industry, its power stations and its organizations; which in turn had led to the twenty-four-hour surveillance of Whalley; which led to the tape frozen on the screen to the right of Fifeshire's desk. Nothing suspicious whatsoever had checked out about the four Arabs who had been crushed to death in their car, and it was on my persuasion alone that Fifeshire had, with not a little reluctance, sanctioned the whole study. I was going to have a lot to answer for if I didn't come up with the goods. Today, however, was the first bright day. I could tell by the expression on Fifeshire's face that, although we hadn't yet found the pot of gold, we had at least stumbled across what might turn out to be a rainbow.

'What makes you so sure Sir Isaac is still in Britain, sir? He might not be in Russia, but he could be anywhere.'

'All the passport staff at Britain's seaports and airports who have been on duty since Quoit disappeared have been interviewed. Flight lists of all airlines have been checked; the flight crews of almost all aircraft on which anyone remotely fitting his description has travelled, and, likewise, all ferry staff, have been interviewed. No one has seen him. And yet he is an unusual-looking man, a distinctive man, a man whom, once seen, is never forgotten, and yet no one saw him. That in itself is no proof at all – thousands of flights and boats leave this country every hour – but I have an Intelligence report from Moscow that seems to tie in with this.

'Someone is going to be smuggled out of England next Monday, on the 10.00 a.m. Aeroflot flight to Moscow. Our contact does not know who this person is, but believes he is either a scientist or has detailed knowledge of certain scientific advances in this country.'

'Our friend could fit that bill,' I said.

'Very neatly indeed.' Fifeshire relit his cigar, which was burning down one side only.

'If we're on the right track with our thinking, Sir Isaac has been kidnapped by the Russians. The Russians have taken him to a secret television studio somewhere in England and got him to speak. Maybe he didn't realize it was a studio, and maybe he didn't realize he was being videotaped. Afterwards, they dub over, in perfect lip-sync, someone who sounds very like him making a strong defection and anti-nuclear speech. Then they bang him against a back-drop of Red Square and send the tape off to the BBC. All perfectly possible, except it doesn't make any sense. It sounds more like a prank pulled by the anti-nuclear people – the Ecologists – some group like that.'

'Possible,' said Fifeshire, 'but I would have thought most unlikely.'

I nodded, and lit a cigarette.

The Honourable Violet-Elizabeth Trepp produced coffee. It was the colour of tea made with a five-year-old tea bag, and tasted like paraffin. Fifeshire waited until she had left, then poured his into an ornate pot containing a rubber plant. 'She doesn't understand why none of my plants ever live more than a few weeks,' he said, then continued.

'If it is the Russians, and I'm certain it is, I cannot think why they want Quoit. Information about our nuclear energy programme is freely available, and the Russians themselves are more advanced in many areas of nuclear energy technology than we are. This scaremongering speech is most peculiar. What do the Russians hope to gain by kicking up dirt about nuclear power stations? All right, they get the anti-nuclear protestors out, and get public feeling going against everything nuclear, and disarmament will no doubt rear its head and become a major issue. The government may back down a few steps on its current nuclear policies, perhaps make a token cut in some area which doesn't matter, and agree to look into the situation regarding US missile bases. But the Russians have got easier ways to whip up public feeling than this. They've got dozens of members of CND on their payroll, doing a good noisy job. Maybe they feel they're not doing a good enough job – but I don't think that's what's behind this.'

'You think it's a cover for something?'

'It must be – Operation Angel, whatever that is. Horace Whalley, Operation Angel, Libya, Deke Sleder, the Russians – what a pretty package. We need to open it up, Flynn, and I think we need to open it up quick. There's an international game going on, and they've forgotten to send us a copy of the rules; we'll have to figure them out for ourselves.'

'I don't understand about Whalley and this cassette –

why on earth did he have to drive all the way to Wales to pick up the tape and take it to London? It seems very odd to me.'

'Could be a number of reasons: to see if he is being tailed; or, more likely, to help break him in – start him off doing fairly simple jobs, get him used to operating. It was a simple job, but a bit demanding, physically, and clandestine enough to give him a small taste of excitement. They could have been checking to see whether he would obey instructions – standard practice with a new recruit. It also gets him implicated – makes it harder for him to back out at a later stage if he suddenly decides he wants out. And besides, you don't know for sure that he wasn't delivering anything. What did he do after he dropped the tape off?'

'Nothing. After I dropped the tape in to you on Tuesday morning, I went in and took his office apart, but I couldn't find anything. I had a damn good look through it – I had the whole day. He drove straight home after going to the BBC, and telephoned the office to say he wouldn't be coming in because he felt under the weather. I'm not surprised; I was bloody knackered too – and at least he'd had three hours' kip. He stayed home the whole day – slept, did a bit of gardening, watched some television.'

'Didn't his wife wonder where he had been?'

'No. It's normal in his job – he does midnight swoop operations on various power stations quite regularly. Yesterday, he went into work and didn't speak to a soul all day – no phone calls, nothing.'

'Proper little Jekyll and Hyde,' said Fifeshire.

'Aren't the Russians going to think it odd if the BBC don't put this tape out – or don't mention it at least? Surely they would expect that in the search for Quoit, news of this tape would spread across every paper and every television screen in the country?'

'I think the BBC should put it out, put the whole thing out. They can explain the delay by saying they wanted to check whether or not it was a hoax, and now they are satisfied that it is genuine. After all, we don't want our Russian chums to think we know something do we?'

'Not if we're to have any chance of finding Quoit before they get him on that plane.'

'Finding Quoit isn't exactly going to be easy.'

'If he's going on a plane, and a schedule flight at that, then he'll have to go to Heathrow Airport – they can hardly get the plane to swoop low over wherever they're holding him and hoist him up on the end of a rope.'

'And where do you suppose he's going to be at Heathrow?' said Fifeshire, dryly. 'In the first-class lounge carrying a big placard which says, "I'm defecting to Russia"?'

I ignored his remark. 'The baggage hold.'

'The Russians don't let anyone near their baggage or their holds. We wouldn't have a hope of getting a look-in there.'

'Couldn't we pick him up before they get him to the baggage hold?'

'You'd have to stop and search every single vehicle coming into Heathrow, both to the passenger and the cargo terminals; there'd be a traffic jam fifty miles long – and still no guarantee of finding him. He could be packed away in a container at the back of a goods truck – you couldn't possibly search every container going into Heathrow.'

'Maybe we could find him before they move him to the airport. He's probably in a Russian safe-house – there must be a list of Russian safe-houses?'

'There's a terraced house in north-west Leeds. There's a twenty-seven-bedroom mansion outside Sevenoaks; there's an eleven-bedroom manor house near Cirencester. There's a forty-four-bedroomed castle near Angmering in Sussex which is used as a country club. There's a nine-bedroomed house with an estate of 18,500 acres, including two villages and forty-eight outbuildings, thirty miles from Aberdeen in Scotland. There are seven houses of varying sizes dotted across London. Those are twelve of the safe-houses that we know about; and we are certain, that sprinkled around the British Isles, there are at least another twenty-five more. It's Thursday morning, and Quoit's plane leaves at 10.00 a.m. next Monday – which gives us somewhat less than four days. You'd have to get an awful lot of search warrants, knock on an awful lot of front doors, and look inside a great many cupboards.'

I got Fifeshire's point.

There was a long pause, while Fifeshire drew on his cigar a few times in slow succession.

'If we can get our hands on Quoit,' I said, 'then we might find out what the Russians are up to; if we let him go, we might have to wait for their next move. What about Whalley's yachting holiday with Sleder – have you found out anything more about Sleder?'

'Yes,' said Fifeshire grimly, 'rather a lot.'

8

The full Aeroflot Illushyn 62 accelerated down the runway, its four Kuznetsov turbo-fan engines greedily gobbling kerosene, and converting the precious liquid into something that was even more precious at this particular moment, as far as the pilot was concerned: the 92,600 pounds of thrust that would accelerate the Illushyn to the one hundred and forty miles per hour needed in order to lift off from the runway and avoid ploughing through the snow-covered perimeter and into the office buildings that lay a few hundred yards beyond.

Captain Yuri Gromkyan preferred, on balance, to fly in the summer; but when the aircraft was jam-packed, like today, to its maximum take-off weight, the denser air of winter was safer for take-off. He knew that on this November day, with the outside temperature hovering around the zero mark at four o'clock in the afternoon, the Illushyn needed four hundred yards less length of runway to take off than in the heat of summer.

He saw his co-pilot, Viktor Kieviz, out of the corner of his eye, scanning the engine and flight instruments, ready to call out the airspeed readings, leaving him free to concentrate on the ribbon of Moscow's Sheremetieva Airport tarmac rapidly shortening in front of him.

'One hundred twenty . . . one hundred thirty . . . one hundred thirty-five,' read Kieviz.

In three seconds they would be past the point of no return for this runway, past the point beyond which, no matter what happened, he had to lift off. because he could never stop the aircraft in time to avoid going through that perimeter fencing, across the highway, and into the office complex.

'One four O.'

Gromkyan pulled back the control column, the nose came up instantly and the tarmac began to drop away. When he had first learned to fly, on single-engined planes, he learned to push the control column forward a little immediately after lifting off, to let the flow of air build up under the wings, before starting the climb up to cruising altitude; but in this massive aircraft, it was the thrust of the jet engines rather than the airflow which propelled it upwards into the sky. He just kept the nose pointed at a seventeen-degree angle upwards, the throttles wide open, and instructed Kieviz to retract the undercarriage. Kieviz pushed the lever to the up position, and then flicked the switch that would extinguish the No Smoking sign in the 169 seat cabin behind the locked door at the rear of the cockpit.

There was, they both knew, a VIP in that cabin: Nicholai Ztachinov, deputy head of the KGB. He was coming out on this Sunday afternoon flight to Heathrow, London, and would be returning to Moscow in the morning. Ztachinov was a chain-smoker, and it had been made very clear to Gromkyan that Ztachinov did not like to be kept waiting for his smokes.

At two thousand feet, as they came up into the first wisps of cloud, Gromkyan engaged the automatic flight-control system, which was already programmed to fly to London. Almost immediately, the aircraft adopted a banking attitude, in a long slow sweep around, upwards and to the left, and then began to level out.

'What do you fancy doing in London tonight, Viktor?' asked Gromkyan.

'A McDonald's hamburger followed by a negress with big bazonkas.'

'Count me in,' said Yolef Stiz, the flight engineer who sat behind them.

'And me too,' grinned Gromkyan.

'I'll go along with that,' said Vasilik, the radio operator. Korshov, the navigator nodded his assent also.

'Botnick at the Embassy's promised to arrange it all. He can get negresses for forty roubles.'

'Forty roubles!' said Stiz. 'I don't want one with gold teeth – just an ordinary one will do.'

'Yes, well, you don't want an ugly one do you?' said Gromkyan. 'Remember the story you told us when you were on the New York run?'

Stiz remembered. The negress he had picked up who was so cheap – so stunningly beautiful and yet so cheap. He'd clambered into bed and discovered she was possessed not of breasts and vagina, but of a pair of testicles and eight inches of penis.

Gromkyan scanned the instruments carefully, checking each one in turn. At seventeen thousand feet they broke through the cloud into the rich orange sky. The winter sun, a weak red ball, hung only a short distance above them. In one hour it would be almost dark. In sixty-five minutes they would be south of Riga, and in a further hour and a quarter they would be over Heligoland. There they would turn a few degrees to the left, cross the North Sea and fly over Clacton VOR and into London. It would be five in the afternoon local time when they arrived, and they should be in their Embassy quarters by six thirty. Gromkyan wondered whether Botnick was laying on the party in the Embassy, or whether they would be going out. He hoped they would be going out; he liked the atmosphere of London at night, even on a Sunday.

Behind the crew in the cockpit was a bullet-proof door which could only be opened from inside the cockpit – an anti-hijacking measure. On the other side of that door, one hundred and fifty passengers, including the deputy chief of the KGB, several Russian diplomats – including one KGB and two GRU agents – two English diplomats, a group of Russian buyers of agricultural machinery, twelve Englishmen in the overcoat-manufacturing industry, a Welsh university lecturer and his wife returning from their honeymoon, and a motley group of tourists and businessmen, together with the standard Aeroflot plain-clothed armed guard, were beginning to relax. They had survived take-off; they now had to survive only the service and the landing.

I stood outside the boundary of Heathrow, near a maintenance-area entrance. It was the kind of afternoon that makes organizers of garden fêtes hang themselves from marquee guy-ropes. It was filthy wet, and a continuous, thick spray of rain drove down, which was whipped into every pore on my face by a wind that blew solidly and strongly, without pausing to gust. It was exactly the sort of afternoon I had been praying for. It was five o'clock and nearly dark, and I knew nobody would want to know anything except getting his body inside a dry hot room and getting a cup of wet hot tea inside his body.

The guard in the hut at the entrance to the airside didn't give a monkey's about me, and unless he was about to qualify for the world speed-reading championships, he couldn't have absorbed much of my pass – not that it would have mattered if he had, for it was a pretty authentic document. Nor did Hawkeye appear to think the orange boiler suit that I wore, and the blue metal tool box that I carried, to be out of order. He might have perhaps wondered why I was on foot and not in a vehicle, but he knew that the Russians were a strange lot, and if being communists meant they had to walk outside on a day like this, then that was their problem.

Fifteen miles to the east, an Aeroflot Illushyn 62 had just been given clearance by the Heathrow tower to land after a Quantas jumbo. Because of the high winds. Captain Gromkyan switched the controls to manual and began his landing descent, his eyes and Kieviz's eyes glued to the instrument panels. Sinking slowly from the sky, the Illushyn moved onto the correct course for Heathrow's runway 28 Left, and headed towards the airport at its approach speed of two hundred and ten knots.

I walked towards the maintenance hangars. Pan Am's massive maintenance complex was over to the left, and beyond that was Air India's.

The air filled with the howl of the Quantas jumbo coming in overhead, its flaps fully extended and hanging down, its undercarriage poised like talons, a bright light urgently winking, the air below shaking from the noise and the wake; it glided smoothly down and out of sight beyond the sheds, like some gigantic condor.

I reached the shadows of the British Airways hangars, and stayed there, walking around until I could get a clear view of the massive concrete parking area, and the particular section of it that interested me – Delta 32. An Air India Boeing 707 taxied across the apron. A fuel tanker drove off behind its tail into the murky dark. Another roar built up overhead, and with landing lights full on and belly lights winking furiously, full flaps down, and the rudder no doubt angled several degrees to the right into the vicious cross-wind an Illushyn 62 sank down out of the wet sky, through the wake turbulence of the jumbo before it, and onto the wet tarmac of the lighted runway.

Captain Gromkyan allowed the plane to cruise down the runway for some moments, then, satisfied that all wheels were down and the course was true, and assuming there were no obstructions ahead that should make him slam open the throttles and abort the landing – because he couldn't see anything other than the lights which stretched out towards the horizon and converged some distance before it – he reached out his right arm, and pulled the throttle levers into full reverse thrust.

The four turbo-fan jet engines bellowed against the rain and the wind, their roar echoing across the acres of wet tarmac, grass and concrete, bouncing off the walls of the hangars, and then dying down as the aircraft slowed to taxiing speed. I stood, in the dark, with the rain concentrated above my head, by a poor gutter, into a raging stream that tore down the back of the neck of my boiler suit.

Outside the small French town of Carentan; on the *route nationale* 13, about fifty kilometres from Cherbourg, is a Routier restaurant much loved by French lorry drivers. One driver, Jean-Pierre Edier, had been looking forward to having dinner there all the way up from Montélimar, which he had left that morning. He had in fact already driven through Carentan on his way up to Cherbourg to deliver his load of nougat, bound for Quebec. Now he was shot of his load, he could relax, eat his dinner and have a good long sleep in the bunk bed at the back of the Volvo's luxurious cab – since it was a Sunday, he could only deliver, he couldn't collect. In the morning, he would pick up a load of cane sugar which he would deliver to Montélimar.

As Edier reached the doorway of the restaurant, he belched. A massive bowl of oysters, winkles, whelks, shrimps and crab, followed by white fish in cognac, followed by a hefty tournedos marinated in red wine, followed by a greedy chunk of camembert, followed by apple-and-meringue pie, washed down by a litre of *vin ordinaire* and a half-pint of cognac *très* rough, was getting near the limit the much-abused belly inside his sprawling frame could cope with. He shoved two francs inside a Space Invaders machine and lost all three of his men without firing a shot. He shoved two francs into a pinball machine and lost all five balls in rapid succession. He wisely decided it was time to call it a day.

As he negotiated his bulk through the flimsy doorway, the chilly night air blasted his face. He blinked twice, and stared across the road at where he was certain he had parked his company's thirty-two tons of lorry and trailer; he blinked again, because what he was now staring at was an empty space, and none of the spaces nearby that were occupied by other vehicles was occupied by the vehicle that his gaze sought.

'*Merde!*' said Jean-Pierre Edier, wondering if calling the police in his inebriated state would be the smartest thing. '*Merde!*' he repeated.

Captain Gromkyan obeyed the parking instructions at Heathrow Tower, and brought the Illushyn to a standstill at Delta 32. He closed the fuel cocks in front of him and slightly to the right, and the whine of the four engines slowly faded away. The electric gangway transporter was already heading out across the concrete towards them, and four men raced out of the gloom to place chocks under the wheels of the aircraft. A fuelling tender started its engine, and the sewage removal tender and the baggage trucks started forward.

I left my hiding place and, clutching my tool box, joined in the general throng of activity. A bunch of men and women in boiler suits identical to mine clutching boxes, brushes, pails, cloths and black bags, stood waiting quietly, heads bowed against the driving rain. Two passenger coaches pulled up at the foot of the gangway.

First down the gangway came Ztachinov, which gave me a shock; I had no idea he was on the plane. I recognized him from photographs. He had one of those faces one never forgets, and can never mistake – an ugly face, a face that bore a thousand grudges: a long thin nose; high cheek-bones; short hair with a hint of a quiff at the front; cold eyes, one of them was glass – a legacy from a car accident – and it was a common joke that it was easy to tell which was the glass eye – it was the warmer-looking of the two.

After the last of the passengers had disembarked, the group of cleaners raced to get up to the top of the gangway and out of the cold and wet, and I placed myself in their midst. Nobody even stood at the entrance to look at the identity card each man and woman held out.

The interior of the plane was a drab green colour, and the atmosphere was more that of a troop transporter than a passenger liner. I marched straight down to the back and stopped at the last row of seats before the lavatories. From the top of my tool box, I took a screwdriver and pliers, and began to dismantle a reading light above one seat.

A cleaning lady walked past me, without paying me any attention at all and went into the first lavatory on the left. In the space of about thirty seconds, she had wiped the basin, checked the towels and tissues and the soap, mopped some urine off the floor, and moved on to the next lavatory. I continued to fiddle with the light. Less than a minute and a half later, her job with the three lavatories was done, and she walked off back down the aisle.

I screwed the cover back onto the light and slipped into the first lavatory on the left. I shut the door behind me, but didn't lock it, and put my tool box on the floor. I took out a large adjustable spanner, wound it open until it fitted over one of the four bolts that secured the steel lavatory to the floor, and wound it tight onto the bolt.

The bolt wouldn't budge at first, and a small amount of thread came away, but then it slackened and began to turn easily. I worked through the other three, lifting them out in turn and putting them carefully to one side; then I lifted up the entire lavatory, to reveal a black hole, about eighteen inches in diameter, which stank worse than the breath of a London Underground commuter. I put the seat down in the tiny space beside me. There was a sucking and gurgling, which told me the sewage tender had begun pumping the tank out.

At least the aircraft boffin at Combined Central Information knew his stuff. His tiny office was crammed full of model aeroplanes, and he looked more like an errant schoolboy than the three-times decorated Squadron Leader and fighter-pilot ace he had been in the Second World War. Reginald Braithwaite was known to the whole of British Intelligence as Biggles, and those that ever had dealings with him discovered one thing: there was nothing he didn't know about aircraft. He had assured me that the Illushyn had a manhole directly underneath this lavatory seat, for inspection purposes, and he had been right; he'd also told me I would need a gas mask, an aqualung, and a wet-suit, and on that he was also right.

I already had the wet-suit on underneath the boiler suit, which I peeled off, and I removed the rest of the kit from the bottom two layers of the tool box; the kit included a stubby weapon with a bulbous magazine that looked not unlike an early Sten gun, and another weapon that resembled a Very pistol, and clipped them both onto the belt of my wet-suit. Then I took a bolt cutter, and snapped off the ends of the four bolts, so that they would lie in their holes without protruding, and look, to anyone that did not try to turn them, as if they were holding the bowl to the floor.

I waited until the tender had finished pumping, and then I put on the gas mask, pulled up the hood of my wet-suit, pulled on a pair of rubber gloves, packed up the overalls and the bolt-cutter into the tool box, and squeezed down into the hole.

My feet dangled into space, and for a moment I wondered if Biggles had got his measurements wrong and it was more than four feet to the bottom; but then my feet squelched into several inches of a slimy substance that I preferred not to think too hard about, and I touched the floor. I reached up my hands, and pulled the tool box down, placing it on the floor beside my feet, then reached up again, took hold of the lavatory bowl, and manoeuvred it back into its correct position. I took four bolts from the tool box, pushed them up through the four holes into the base of the lavatory, and hand-turned them until they were sufficiently tight to prevent the lavatory from moving. There was a small hole in the centre of the lavatory, through which I could see up into the tiny room; the light was on, but that would go off soon, when the maintenance men switched off the generator.

I stood bent double in this hell-hole, where I was to spend the next sixteen hours, listening to the sound of my breathing through the gas mask, idly hoping that some giant man-eating alligator hadn't decided to make this place his home. It was cold, very cold, and I was already getting cramp from being arched. I didn't want to sit down in that horrible mire, but I had a tough day ahead, and if I didn't get some sleep tonight, I wasn't going to be any good for anything.

As I gingerly began to lower myself down, I decided that, compared to this place, the Black Hole of Calcutta would be like a honeymoon suite at the Savoy.

9

Totes is a small town that lies midway between Dieppe and Rouen, and is really more a large village. Like many sleepy French places, it straddles two main roads. At one end of Totes is an outstandingly beautiful manor house, with red brick walls and white shutters, set some way back from the road. Half a mile up a cart track behind it, is a cluster of barns, silos, cowsheds, chickens, dogs and pigs, the central point of which is an ancient, grey stone farmhouse.

The proprietor, Gaston Leuf, was a wizened old farmer, with a shrivelled body and a wrinkled face. Except when he was sleeping, he had never been seen without a blue beret on his head and the stump of a yellow Gauloise sticking out of his mouth. If you ever wanted a photograph of a classic French farmer, you'd travel a long way to find a better specimen than Gaston Leuf.

It was a glorious early November morning, and the whole of Normandy was shrouded in a three-foot-high mist that the sun was slowly dispersing. The whole land looked like a fairy-tale setting, and there was a feeling of serene peace.

Leuf had been looking forward to today, for today he was going to show off; today for the first time in his life, he would be driving to market in a new tractor. It was a gleaming orange and dark grey Renault TX 145-14 Turbo, with sixteen forward and sixteen reverse gears, all with synchromesh, a maximum forward speed of thirty kilometres per hour, and an air-conditioned all-weather cab.

Today, everyone would be jealous, as he thundered, not rattled, but positively thundered, into market, at the helm of the turbo-charged Renault, towing his covered cattle wagon behind him. He hurried into the kitchen, where his wife, Yvonne, was brewing the coffee.

'*Bonjour, ma cherie!*' He kissed her on the cheek. '*Voom, voom!*' he said, like the excited schoolboy he had once been, sixty years ago. The land he had sold to the council would be paying for a lot of things, but none would he enjoy more than his tractor.

Before sitting down to his breakfast of coffee and bread rolls, he hurried out to the large barn to look once again at his new machine. He pulled open the doors and marched in, beaming. Then he stopped in his tracks and the beam froze on his face. The tractor had gone. The trailer had gone too, but for several moments he did not notice that. He did not notice, either, that both his ladders were gone. He stood, staring in blank amazement. Who, in all the sleepy decades that Totes had passed through, had ever heard of one drop of milk, or one egg, or one chicken, let alone one whole great, spanking brand-new synchromesh-geared Renault tractor being stolen? Leuf spat on the ground. '*Vache!*' he said, and spat again. '*Qui?*' he said, '*mais qui?*'

If you happen to be a person who enjoys a good night's kip, the sewage tank of an Illushyn 62 aircraft is probably not the place for you; it sure as hell wasn't for me. I looked at my watch. It was five to seven. It was about the three hundredth time that I had looked at my watch since half past six the previous evening. Outside it would be light; people would be waking up, getting their morning papers, having hot showers and warm toast and splashing on sweet-smelling colognes and aftershaves and talcs.

Shortly after nine o'clock, I began to hear signs of activity: the electric whine of baggage-loader trucks, the rattle of a catering truck, then the thumping of footsteps, and the whole aircraft shaking – passengers were boarding.

At five past ten precisely, I heard the first engine fire up. The hissing whine started low at first, then built to a higher and higher pitch, and then the next engine started, and repeated the process, and then the next, until all four were whining fiercely, and then they died down to a quieter deeper pitch. A few moments later, I was sent skidding across the floor of the tank and crashed into the back wall; the plane couldn't have been moving more than a few miles per hour, but the floor was so slippery that it only needed the slightest motion to send me hurtling out of control like a clown on an ice rink. I got back underneath the lavatory and gripped onto the grab handles.

The plane was now taxiing at a good speed. I wondered which way the wind was blowing – that would decide the direction in which we took off. I wondered, if the plane crashed, whether anyone would ever find me in here. I checked all my equipment, and tried for the hundredth time to push my gas mask against my nose and get rid of the damn itch that had been there for at least ten of the last fourteen hours. I desperately wanted to blow my nose, but there was nothing, nothing whatsoever, however bad, that was going to induce me to remove that gas mask.

The aircraft stopped; I knew we were probably standing in a queue of aircraft all waiting for take-off clearance from the control tower, and we remained motionless for several minutes.

Then the engines built up to a crescendo once more, and the aircraft began to move forward. My arms, holding onto the handles above me, stretched to their full length as the rest of my body was yanked by the acceleration back towards the rear of the tank. The wheels bumped, bumped, bumped, then the bumping suddenly stopped, and I swayed madly, like a gorilla on a trapeze, smashed my back up against the roof of the tank, and swung wildly down, cracking my knees on the floor.

The aircraft's climb took an eternity, and my arms were aching like hell, but I was going to hang on; I was not going to go skidding across that damn floor any more. Finally the Illushyn began to level out, and the pressure came off my arms, and soon we were on an even keel. The four engines were all at the rear and the noise and the vibration down here was deafening me and shaking me to pieces at the same time. The steel chamber caused the noise to echo, and it seemed to be getting louder and louder. And then it began to happen: someone came into the lavatory.

I looked up, and watched trousers being pulled down, and then underpants, and then a pair of large pink cheeks descended towards me, with a hairy pair of balls and a long thin penis at the front. The whole lot dangled down inside the seat, blocking out almost all the tiny amount of light. I imagined the expression on the face of the owner of this apparatus. He had probably been holding his legs together since boarding the flight, and at the first opportunity, he had dashed in here, and was now seated with a gleam of blissful expectancy on his face. Had he known what lurked beneath him, I had a feeling the expression might have been somewhat different.

As I wondered, I took careful aim with my pistol: it was a Capchur gun, the type that zoo-keepers use for firing drugged darts into unapproachable animals. It works on compressed air, and the tiny pin-like darts dissolve in the skin they penetrate. With a 'plunk' that made a roar and an echo down here that sounded like a twenty-one-gun salute, a tiny dart filled with a large dose of Scoline embedded itself into the right cheek of the man's buttocks. Even as he exclaimed in surprise, and began to stand up to find out why he had felt this sudden pin-prick pain, the drug had started to travel through his blood stream, turning him, fraction of second by fraction of second from being wide awake into being dog-tired; so dog-tired that by the time he got to his feet, he could not remember why it was that he had stood up, and by the time he had sat down again, he was fast asleep.

I unscrewed the four bolts, removed them, and then, using all my weight, and all the leverage I could get from the slippery floor, I pushed the bowl sideways, being careful not to send it and its occupant tumbling over with a crash that would bring a stewardess running in. He was a heavy customer, and it took a full minute of pushing to clear a gap for me to climb through. I had had to wait for someone to come into the lavatory in order that the door be locked – it was the only way I could emerge safely from my hiding place. The man whose luck it had been to come in first was a well-built man in his late forties; from his close-cropped hair and his poor quality clothes, I guessed he was almost certainly a Russian, but I wasn't interested enough to start trying to make sure.

I rinsed my rubber-gloved hands, and dried them carefully, then peeled the gloves off – I didn't want slippery fingers right now. I pushed earplugs into my ears, and turned them until they were a snug fit, then I removed the two stun grenades that were clipped to my belt. With only a two-second fuse on each, I didn't want to go dropping them under my feet. At the same time, I didn't want to expose myself in the aisle of the aircraft for longer than was necessary. The armed guards on Aeroflot flights are instructed to shoot on sight anyone behaving suspiciously. Appearing from the lavatory in a wet-suit and gas mask, with a minor arsenal of weapons hanging from clips around my body, it was not unlikely I would have qualified under the category of 'suspicious behaviour'.

I unlocked the door, pulled it back, placed a grenade in each hand, and stepped out. I pulled out the pin of the first one with my mouth, lobbed the grenade as far down the aisle as I could, pulled the second pin out with my hand, and lobbed that grenade down towards the middle of the aisle, retreated into the lavatory and pulled the door hard shut.

There were two muffled booms in rapid succession, and I now had exactly ten seconds. The stun grenade is a device that was originally dreamed up by the SAS and developed for them. Known as flash-bangs, they had been modified by the Playroom boffins so as not to be a fire risk. They produce a combined flash and explosion that completely deafens, and their effect in a closed environment is to paralyze totally, for a minimum of ten seconds, anyone in their vicinity. They will not cause any actual bodily damage, other than to eardrums, and therefore would not, in theory, damage the structure of the aircraft. For the next ten seconds, everyone in the passenger compartment of the aircraft, including the KGB vigilante, would be paralyzed. The flight crew in the cockpit would be unaffected. They would have heard the two bangs, muffled somewhat, and they would doubtless be wondering what on earth had happened.

By the time four of the ten seconds had elapsed, I had sprinted the length of the aisle, negotiated two rigid stewardesses in the process, and was pressing the intercom button to the cockpit: in what the lingo expert at Combined Central Intelligence had informed me was a perfect

Muscovite accent, I yelled the rough Russian equivalent of 'Don't sit there, you dumb motherfuckers. Come back and help us!'

It had the desired effect. As the eighth second elapsed, the door opened, and an inquisitive engineer poked his head out into what he expected would be the normal, pressurized air of the cabin, but was in fact a cloud of the same sleeping gas Horace Whalley had enjoyed, squirting hard out of the nozzle of the device that was now clamped under my right arm and looked not unlike an early-model Sten gun, but which was in fact a very recent model gas-gun. By the time the ninth second had elapsed, he was fast asleep, and after the tenth second had passed, so were his chums – the pilot, co-pilot, navigator and radio operator. I turned the nozzle down towards the aisle of the aircraft and squeezed the trigger much harder. Within seconds, the entire cabin was filled with the gas.

I pulled the flight crew out into the aisle, then went back into the cockpit and pulled the door firmly shut behind me. I looked at my watch: one minute and twenty seconds had elapsed. From the dose I had given, it would be some minutes yet before the people back in the cabin would begin to come round, although I couldn't be sure. I hoped for their sakes it wouldn't be much more.

It was five minutes to eleven. The sky was clear blue without a cloud to be seen, and Margate was twenty-three thousand feet below our port wing, as the plane continued its course on auto-pilot.

Didier Garner looked at his watch and grimaced. It was five to ten, Paris time; one hour and twenty minutes of his ten-hour working day had so far elapsed without his lighting up a single Winston. Normally he would be lighting his fourth about now, but today he was finished with smoking; he had quit, and he was going to stay quit. The last hour and twenty minutes had been hell, but he had got through them, and he would get through the rest of the day – somehow. He looked out of his window into Place Vendôme, out across the square towards the Ritz. It was a bright sunny November morning, and everything looked good for the director of Heli-Transport France. It was about time. For six weeks the company's three Aérospatiale Puma helicopters, the backbone of his fleet, had been grounded by the authorities after a piece of engine cowling had sheared off one and plummeted through the roof of a parked car. The problem had been traced to a mechanic carrying out faulty maintenance work, but the grounding had cost the company a fortune. From today, the grounding had been lifted, and there was a full schedule for the helicopters for several weeks ahead, which would quickly resolve the company's financial crisis.

The white telephone on his desk buzzed and he picked up the receiver to take a call from his chief engineer at their operational base in Senlis. Within sixty seconds of picking up the receiver, he had reached inside his desk, taken out a Winston cigarette, placed it between his lips, and was now holding the flame of his gold Dupont lighter to the end. During the night, someone had stolen all three Pumas.

I sat in the pilot's seat of the Illushyn, and ran my eyes systematically over the controls. Up until three days ago, the largest aircraft I had ever flown was a twin-engined Piper Aztec, and now I was at the helm of an aircraft that was a Russian copy of a VC 10.

For the past three days, I had done nothing but take off, circuit and land a VC 10 at the British Airways training school; take off, circuit, land, until I was sick to the back teeth of doing it; take off, circuit, land until I could do it, do it all, without asking one single question. Right now, I was glad of those last three days, damned glad.

I checked the altimeter, the airspeed, and the rest of the instruments, took the control column in my left hand, and with my right hand, reached out and switched off the automatic pilot. A voice behind me suddenly bellowed through the intercom in Russian. I didn't speak a great deal of Russian, but I knew enough to understand what the voice was saying. It was saying 'Who the hell are you?'

I replied, in the best Russian I could muster. 'Your plane is in the hands of the Israeli Freedom Front. Remain calm and nothing will happen to you; attempt to come through this door, and everyone on this aircraft will die.' I knew there was no way they could get through the door. It had been designed to keep out the most determined of hijackers. The Stechkin pistol that the security guard doubtlessly carried, would in no way be capable of penetrating either the door or its bolts. I switched off the intercom, leaving them to stew.

Ten miles out over the North Sea, I looked carefully at the radar screen, and scanned the clear sky with my eyes. Then I started a long banking turn to the right and the English Channel. I was going to have to keep a sharp eye out. I had no flight plan filed for the course I was flying, and, moreover, I was heading up the Channel and straight across one of the world's busiest air corridors.

Down below, and a long way to the left, I could make out Calais. Calais passed by and then Boulogne began to appear. Dover passed by on my right, and then Beachy Head came into view. Scanning every inch of the sky with my eyes, I descended to eighteen thousand feet, and then banked sharply to the left and headed straight for the French coast.

I didn't bother to switch the radio on; I knew that a torrent of abuse would pour out from the French air-traffic control boys. I descended to ten thousand feet.

After a few minutes, I could see Dieppe dead ahead and very clear. I cut the airspeed to two hundred and fifty knots, and started a sharper descent. We crossed Dieppe at seven thousand feet, and the Illushyn was beginning to respond very sluggishly to my movements of the control column. It was twenty-one minutes past eleven.

Two gendarmes were operating a speed trap on the N27 Dieppe to Rouen road. They sat on their Motoguzzi 1,000cc motor bikes, one of them beaming a vascar detector down the empty road behind them. It was a long, straight and very wide stretch of dual carriageway, and it was busy only in the summer months.

Behind the gendarmes was a large cornfield, across which a tractor chugged, pulling a large covered trailer. It was a smart new Renault tractor, but neither of the gendarmes paid any attention to it. Their eyes were on a silver sports car, a kilometre up the road, and coming their way at what looked considerably faster than the one hundred and forty kilometres per hour that were permitted. The gendarme holding the vascar detector aimed the device carefully and squeezed the trigger. The needle raced past the one hundred and forty mark, and carried on, past the two hundred mark, hit the stop at two hundred and twenty and snapped off.

The driver of the Aston Martin DBS Vantage held the slim steering wheel tightly in his hands. The Super-Snooper radar detector on his dash screeched loudly as he rocketed past the articulated lorry at one hundred and forty-five miles an hour, and he then saw the two gendarmes up ahead, by the roadside.

His reaction was to drop from fifth gear into fourth, and flatten the accelerator pedal. In spite of the speed at which he was already travelling, the massive brake-horsepower of the engine thrust the small of his back deeper into the rich leather of his seat-back, and the speedometer climbed up to one hundred and sixty-five miles an hour. He allowed himself a fraction of a second to look in the mirror and see that the police were setting off after him, and then they ceased to become even specks in the distance. He shifted into fifth gear, and the car surged forward. The speedometer swept past the one hundred and seventy mark, one hundred and seventy-five, flickered up past one hundred and eighty, and then finally hovered around the one hundred and eighty-five mark. He passed an orange 2CV Citroen and nearly blew it off the road with his slipstream. The driver was enjoying himself, and his enjoyment of the fine car and the thrill of the speed was all the more satisfying because he was actually being paid to do this.

A mile and a half behind him, the two Motoguzzis accelerated down the road, their sirens bleating. Half a mile behind them, the articulated lorry, with the Montélimar licence plates, suddenly acted very strangely, slewing across the road, and then reversing, so that it blocked the road completely.

My airspeed was now one hundred and forty knots. The stall-warning buzzer shrieked almost continuously. There was hardly any response to my movements of the control column. Down below, the road stretched out. Then the articulated lorry came into view, exactly in the right place. We passed barely fifty feet over its roof; I had full flap, the undercarriage down and locked, and beneath that bulbous nose in front of me, the road was rushing up to meet us. We sank down, down; I fought with the column to keep the nose up, and with the rudder to keep the aircraft straight. It must be now, I thought, it must be now! I pushed the four throttle levers forward, and as the surge of acceleration came, I felt the centre wheels touch, ever so gently, and I was about to congratulate myself. I pulled the throttle levers back to cut the thrust, but to my surprise, the aircraft at that moment lifted several feet back up into the air, and then thumped back down with a jarring I could feel through every bone in my body. We lifted up again and crashed down again, then up again, then down again, and this time, to my relief, we stayed down, racing along the road. Then finally, the nose came down and the nose-wheel touched. I waited for a moment for it to settle, then I wrenched the throttle levers right back into full reverse thrust, and stood on the brakes for all I was worth.

The speedometer sank: one hundred and twenty, one hundred, eighty, seventy, sixty, and finally down to ten knots. I turned the aircraft sharply to the right, off the road and into the cornfield, and halted about one hundred yards from the tractor, which was already pounding its way over to us.

I switched on the intercom. 'There are detonators aboard this aircraft which will destroy it in exactly four minutes; you must open all exits, including the emergency exits, and you are to leave by the escape chutes, and get as far away from the aircraft as you can. Anyone who tries to interfere will be shot. Long live Israel! Freedom to the Jews in the Soviet Union!'

The tailgate of the articulated lorry lowered, and an Aérospatiale Puma helicopter appeared from inside.

Another two followed it. All three had emblazoned on the sides the name: Heli-Transport France.

The tractor and trailer stopped at the rear of the aircraft. Among the contents of the trailer was a corpse with a new set of dentures. That corpse, which had been acquired through the services of the Department of Anatomy at the Elephant and Castle, had probably been given the best dental treatment to which any corpse had ever been treated. If the soldier who had died of a heart attack had known that the body he had donated to medical science would so serve his country, he would, for sure, have died a proud man.

The new dentures with which the corpse had been kitted were for the purpose of identification. They had been made, correct to the last detail, from the dental records of Sir Isaac Quoit. I sure as hell hoped Quoit was aboard this aircraft after the lengths to which we had been.

I could see passengers scurrying from the aircraft across the cornfield. Among them I recognized tough KGB deputy chief Ztachinov, evidently not as tough as he had thought. He was going to have some red-faced explaining to do when he got home, if he wanted to hang on to his job.

There were three taps on the door in rapid succession, followed by two slow ones, and then three more quick ones. I opened it up. Two men, wearing the blue denim peasant clothes of the French farming fraternity, but distinguishable from ordinary French farmers by the balaclavas that concealed their faces and the Sterling sub-machine-guns in their hands, stood outside.

'Ready to go, sir. We've got Sir Isaac.'

'Where was he?'

'In the hold, surrounded by two thousand chickens.'

Two minutes later, the three Pumas lifted up into the sky. I looked down at the stubble of the cornfield, at the great silver bird with the red-star markings and the hammer and sickle on its tailplane, and the crowd of people standing, looking like bewildered ants, a few hundred yards off from the Illushyn. Suddenly the plane produced two orange bursts, followed by two thick puffs of black smoke, then a massive flame ripped down its entire length like a knife-blade, before turning into a blazing ball of fire that enveloped the plane completely. I looked across at the man who sat in the seat opposite me: a large, portly man, with nine days' stubble on his chin, crumpled clothes on his body, and confusion in his eyes.

'Don't worry, Sir Isaac,' I said cheerfully, 'you'll be back home within a few hours.'

Quoit smiled feebly. He would smile even more feebly when the news was broken to him that he was officially dead, and was going to have to stay dead for a considerable time to come.

One Puma peeled off and headed down towards the centre of France. The second peeled off and headed east towards Germany. We headed north, out towards the Channel. A long way west, down the Channel, beyond the control of the French coastguards, a Special Boat Service high-powered launch awaited us. Heli-Transport France would eventually get back two of its Pumas. One would be found abandoned in Germany, the other abandoned in central France. The third wouldn't be found until the day the English Channel was drained.

The French coast slipped away beneath us. I looked at my watch: it was eight minutes to twelve, British time. At the switchboard of the *France-Soir* newspaper, one telephone line in particular would be engaged: the caller was telling the news editor about the successful hijack and the destruction of the Illushyn by the Israeli Freedom Front, a new faction whose aim was to rain blows upon the Soviet Union until every last Jew in Russia had either been released or was granted full rights as a citizen. Their first blow had just been dealt.

As the world read its papers, and heard its news, during the next twenty-four hours, I wondered how many people would ever guess that the Israeli Freedom Front's name had been dreamed up on the fifth floor of MI5's Carlton House Terrace headquarters, and that the group in question were not an assortment of fanatical Jews, but fourteen professional soldiers from a regiment of the British Army called the SAS, and one, not entirely unhappy, very hungry, and exceedingly smelly spy.

10

It was 10 November, and the temperature in Adamsville, Ohio, was minus two degrees Celsius. The underfloor heating ducts pumped out warm air for all they were worth, their strenuous effort masked by the quiet and gentle hush of blowing air, which was the only sound that could be heard in Harry Slan's office.

Harry Slan sat down at his desk. It was two minutes to nine, and he was frozen stiff. He stared through the window, the lower half of which was misted up, at the glow of the weak sun on the snow-covered ground, and at a gritting truck that moved slowly down the road outside, its blue lights flashing brightly.

There was a large pile of mail on his desk, which he looked forward to opening. He enjoyed opening mail, especially when he couldn't tell from the outside what the contents were, or who this or that letter was from. There was always a chance it could be from some anonymous benefactor enclosing a cheque for vast riches – unlikely, as he knew, but possible.

Third down in the pile was a postcard from a workmate on holiday in Hawaii. The picture showed a glorious stretch of white beach, with a scattering of yachts anchored a short way out to sea. A grin came across his face as he cast his mind back to *Chanson II*. Nearly two months had passed since that glorious, incredible, utterly decadent, utterly filthy, most wonderful long weekend of his life. He had toyed with the idea of writing to Eva, but fear of being discovered by his wife, Myrtle, had so far prevented him. On many occasions during the past six weeks he had sat back, his eyes open, but the shutters at the back of them drawn, his mind four thousand miles away, inside a body that lay on soft cushions on a hard teak deck, under the glow of a hot Mediterranean sun, out of sight of the rest of the boat, while his stunning German beauty gently nibbled away at a very hard object she had just removed from his bathing trunks.

He was snapped out of his reveries by the sound of his office door opening, and Matt Krosnick, the chief engineer of the Adamsville plant of American Fossilized Corporation, came in. It was Thursday morning, inspection morning, when the two of them would walk through the entire plant.

'Morning, Matt,' said Slan. He started to get up from his desk, and then stopped, and felt himself blush a little, and tried not to blush, which made things worse. He couldn't stand up, not in front of anyone, not right now: he had a gigantic erection.

'Morning, Harry,' Krosnick looked at him oddly. 'Oh – you haven't finished your mail. Want me to come back in ten minutes?'

'No,' said Slan, desperately wanting him to go away and come back in ten minutes. 'No, don't worry.'

Slan stood up from his desk in an almost doubled-up position. He buttoned up his jacket and sank his hands deep inside his trouser pockets, and began to walk around to the front of his desk, whilst keeping his body turned away from Krosnick. Krosnick wondered if he was suffering from a slipped disc.

American Fossilized's Adamsville plant employed nine hundred and thirty men. In fifteen years of operation, working with lethally radioactive uranium hexa-fluoride gas, producing the fuel elements that would eventually spend a year or so inside the core of one of many nuclear reactors, followed by six months to a year at the bottom of a cooling tank, followed by several centuries encased in massive radiation-proof casks and entombed at the bottom of oceans, or deep underground, not a single man had been killed, injured, or even suffered the slightest overdose of radiation; and this was due to Slan's vigilance. He was proud of the safety record, and he had reason to be.

After the morning's inspection, Slan and Krosnick lunched in the canteen, then Slan returned to his office, sat down, and continued with his morning's post. Halfway through the pile, was a large white envelope addressed to him, and marked 'Private and Confidential'. The postmark was New York. He wondered who could have sent it, but didn't come up with any ideas. Taking his paper knife, he slit the envelope open along the top. He pulled out first a type-written note. It read simply: '*Sorry to send these to you at work, but not sure of your home address. Thought you'd enjoy a little souvenir!*' He then pulled out four photographs. They were colour photographs, taken with a camera with a very expensive lens, and taken by a photographer who, without any doubt, judging from the clarity of the picture, the excellent composition, depth of field, and colour fidelity, knew his trade.

The first depicted Harry Slan and a very attractive dark-haired girl, lying on a bed side by side, naked, and apparently joined together at the naval. The second depicted Slan, again completely naked, bent double in the middle of a room, whilst the same dark-haired girl, wearing nothing but yellow wellingtons, administered the lash of a rope across his backside. Slan winced at the memory, not of the whipping, but of how he had had to avoid letting his wife see his backside for three weeks afterwards. The third showed Slan and this same girl sitting side by side in a large swing chair on what appeared to be the deck of a yacht; behind them was an expanse of flat blue sea, and a long way back towards the horizon was the unmistakable outline of the French port of St Tropez. Closer inspection of the photograph revealed that Harry Slan's bathing trunks were hanging around his ankles, and the girl, who was topless, was holding his very erect penis firmly between her forefinger and her thumb. The fourth photograph showed them making love in a cabin, doggy-style.

Slan had turned very white, and his hands were shaking. For two months, he had been convinced that the reason Deke Sleder had invited him for that weekend was because Sleder was going to buy American Fossilized, and he wanted to meet his future works manager. He had thought it odd that there should have been so many people from the nuclear energy industry on that yacht together, but, with Eva there, he really hadn't been too interested in wasting time conversing with other men. Since he had returned home, he had begun taking the *Wall Street Journal*. He scoured its pages, and whenever he saw mention of one of Sleder's companies, or of Sleder himself, he positively beamed with smugness at knowing this great man personally.

He wasn't beaming any more. 'Sorry to send these to you at work, but not sure of your home address' – was whoever sent this crazy? 'Thought you'd enjoy a little souvenir!' Had Deke Sleder, if it was he who had sent this, gone stark raving mad? His wife, Myrtle, opened all the mail that came to their house, regardless of whether it was marked *Private*, *Confidential*, or *Danger, do not open – contains nuclear bomb.* Ever since a colleague, for a joke, had bought him a subscription to a monthly pornographic magazine which arrived in a plain brown wrapper. Myrtle had taken command of the mail. She was a violently jealous woman, convinced that every woman in Adamsville was after her husband's body, and she had informed him, more times than he could count, and in great detail, of the very many unpleasant things she would do to him if she ever found out he had been unfaithful to her.

He stuffed the photographs into the central drawer of his desk, then pulled them out, marched them over to a filing cabinet and stuffed them into a file marked *Personal*. Then he took them out of that file and stuffed them into a file marked *Overseas enquiries – dormant*. Then he took them out of that file, had one more careful look, then tore each into a hundred pieces, and burned the pieces in his ashtray.

He studied the note for some clue, but none was forthcoming. He tore the note into shreds and dropped the pieces into his waste paper basket.

He wondered if it was a joke. If it was, then it was a damned strange joke, and he couldn't think who could have perpetrated it. He hadn't become friendly enough with any of the other people on the boat that weekend for any of them to have pulled a prank. If it wasn't a joke, then what was the purpose? There was no demand for money, not even a hint of a demand. Whatever the purpose was, Harry Slan didn't like it; he didn't like it one bit.

11

Anyone who wanted to be a fly on the wall of the conference room on the fifth floor of 46 Carlton House Terrace would have needed fog-lights to see through the canopy of smoke that encircled the massive oval-shaped mahogany table, and completely concealed the fine stuccoed ceiling.

All four walls were heavily panelled, with several layers of sound-proofing materials, and an outer layer of oak. To reduce the possibility of any eavesdropping to an absolute minimum, the room had no windows.

Against the far end wall, looking imperiously down on the room, hung a portrait of the Queen; above it were the crossed flags of the Union Jack and the flag of St George. This end-piece was designed to impress visitors to this room, and it seldom failed to do so. It was a reminder to all who sat at this mahogany table that they were there to serve their Queen and country. In the business of spying, it was all too easy to lose one's focus on reality and on one's goal – if one was ever lucky enough to be given a clear one.

In the chair at the head of the table – his customary position – sat Fifeshire. Occupying another five of the eighteen available chairs, were Peter Nettlefold, Commander of C4; Sir William Atling, Director General of MI6; Kieran Ross, the Home Secretary; Sir Isaac Quoit; and myself. Everyone watched Fifeshire.

'Littlejohn,' he said, 'had killed one hundred and forty thousand people by the day World War Two was over. Eighty-five thousand of those were either killed instantly or died within a few hours of the bomb exploding, the rest over the following months. Many thousands more who were in Hiroshima and in Nagasaki at the time the bomb was dropped there have died prematurely young, and there has been a high rate of deformed children born not only to women pregnant then, but women pregnant many years after. It is estimated that over a quarter of a million human lives were either lost or seriously and irreparably damaged as a result of the bomb on Hiroshima.

'How many of those that died in Hiroshima died from the actual blast?' asked Kieran Ross, the Home Secretary.

'It's difficult to be precise about figures,' replied Fifeshire, 'but the general view on those eighty-five thousand who died more or less immediately is that about twenty per cent died from the blast itself, the rest from a massive dose of radiation.' He sucked a generous helping of not particularly radioactive Havana smoke into his mouth, and blew it out. 'The principal effect of radiation is the destruction of the body's tissues: the limbs malfunction, the digestive system packs up, hair falls out, vomiting starts, the brain malfunctions and delirium sets in. None of it is very pleasant, and what is even less pleasant is that, once someone has been exposed to that kind of radiation, there is very little that anyone can do to help. As far as radiation goes, medicine is still in the dark ages.

'The secondary effects are slower-acting, but no less hideous. These effects are caused by the debris in a cloud of radioactivity, the fall-out left in the air. Strontium 90, for example, which attacks the bone tissues, causing bone cancer, it has a half-life of twenty-eight years. Iodine 131, which escaped from Windscale in 1957, attacks the thyroids. That has a half-life of only eight days; that means that after a mere twenty-seven days it would stop killing people.

There's Radium 226, which attacks the bones and has a half-life of one thousand six hundred and twenty years. There's Plutonium 239 which attacks the sex organs, causing birth defects, mutations and miscarriages for several generations after exposure. Plutonium 239 spontaneously ignites on contact with the air and becomes Plutonium dioxide. Plutonium dioxide has a habit of clinging to dust particles; if just one particle – just one particle – is breathed into someone's lungs, that tiny grain of plutonium will attach itself to a cell, lie dormant for fifteen years, and then after almost exactly fifteen years, it will cause that cell to start multiplying: the multiplying of that cell is called, in layman's language, lung cancer. And the half-life of plutonium is a mere twenty-four thousand years.'

The group in the room listened in silence. Fifeshire drew on his cigar again, and continued.

'Naturally, in most cases the strength of the dosage affects the seriousness of primary and secondary radiation exposure. A small degree of exposure might increase one's risk of contracting cancer by one in a thousand – not much, you might say, since cancer already kills off prematurely one in four people on the face of the earth. And yet, as I have just mentioned, it is not always true that small doses are less harmful: just one particle of plutonium dioxide is all that's required. You wouldn't know if you breathed that particle in. You cannot see, smell or feel radiation, except with a Geiger counter. It is the potential of radiation as a killer that I find gravely disturbing, and the quantities of radioactivity inside nuclear reactors are positively alarming. The bomb that killed one hundred and forty thousand people within thirty days at Hiroshima, was a fifteen-kiloton bomb, a very small bomb indeed by today's standards. Inside the containment building of the average nuclear reactor in service in the world today is seven hundred times the amount of radioactivity released onto Hiroshima by Littlejohn.'

Fifeshire looked at a sheet of notepaper. 'That, by calculations that have been prepared for me, is enough to kill eighty-four million people – or, if you like, the entire population of the British Isles, Canada and Australia, with ten million to spare – and this from the contents of just one reactor. There are, in the British Isles, at the present time, sixteen operating nuclear power stations, with a total of forty-two reactors – and I am excluding other nuclear establishments, such as fuel-reprocessing plants like Windscale. There are thirteen reactors in Canada, two hundred and four reactors in the United States. You will probably remember the fire at Windscale in 1957, which caused the release of a cloud of radio-isotopes into the atmosphere. As a result of this, a million gallons of milk from cows within a two-hundred square-mile radius had to be thrown away – and this was a very minor incident indeed. The locals report a greatly increased incidence of cancer in the region, but this has not been substantiated, as no records were kept.

'During the past week, I have myself spoken to a number of eminent scientists in the nuclear energy industry, including Sir Isaac. Some are anti nuclear and some pro. I put to each the same question: What would be the immediate, the short-term and the long-term effects of a nuclear reactor being blown up? I asked them to concentrate on the three systems in use in this country: the magnox, the advanced gas-cooled reactors, and the pressurized-water reactors. We have only two of the latter at the present time – at Sizewell and at Huntspill Head – but it is the most commonly used system in the United States and France, and more will be built in this country.

'Each of the ten men I spoke to prefaced their replies by

saying that, basically, they had no real idea what would happen, and gave me educated guesses. I find that incredible. No real idea! There are few other man-made potential disasters the results of which could not be reasonably accurately predicted. The scientists said that the blowing up of a nuclear reactor would result in an uncontained disaster of a magnitude that would depend on force and type of explosion – whether it was caused by internal malfunction, or by a conventional bomb, or a nuclear device – and on the strength and direction of the wind, and the general weather conditions at the time.

'If a crowded jumbo crashes into a town, everyone on board is likely to be killed, as is everyone within two hundred yards of the crash, but it would go no further than that. Similarly, a car careering off a road might kill the people on board, and anyone in its path, but the effects would go no further. Nor would a terrorist's bomb in a street kill more than those people within the immediate vicinity. But with nuclear reactors, the situation would be quite different.

'A massive range of permutations were fed into a computer at the Atomic Energy Research Commission, and this is what the machine came up with.' Fifeshire paused for a moment, and relit his cigar. Then he picked up a computer print-out and read aloud. '"Worst conceivable accident: likely to be achieved only by sabotage with a nuclear explosive device. Assuming wind speed of fifteen miles per hour, there would be a cloud of radiation fifteen miles long and forty-five miles wide within one hour. In three hours it would be forty-five miles long and nine miles wide and would be lethal to anyone in this area. Further it would be almost certainly fatal for anyone to enter this area for at least four weeks, and this area would be permanently uninhabitable for at least one hundred years. In twenty-four hours the cloud would be three hundred and sixty miles long and eighty miles wide, and fifty per cent of the people in its path would die within ten years, if they were not evacuated for a very minimum period of at least one year. There would be long-term restrictions on agriculture, and dairy farming would be prohibited for ever in this area. The cloud would continue to expand and still be sufficiently dangerous to warrant, for a period of one to six months, the evacuation of the population in its path within a radius of between one thousand and two thousand miles."'

Fifeshire put down the print-outs. 'If we just take the first twenty-four hours: in this area, everyone would have to be evacuated for one year. The total size of this area is just under thirty thousand square miles. It may be of help to know, if you are trying to work out exactly what kind of area we are talking about, that the entire land mass of England, Scotland and Wales combined comes to only 89,038 square miles.' He paused for a few moments. 'These figures are not based purely on calculated estimates; they are also based on hard factual evidence. Data from previous instances of leakage of radiation, and from atomic blasts, was fed into the computer, including details of the nuclear-waste explosion that occurred at Kyshtym in the Urals in the winter of 1957. That was a small explosion, but it totally devastated an area of five hundred square miles.

'Thousands of people died then, and thousands are still dying from the effects of the fall-out today. Ten years after the explosion, women who had lived nearby were still being advised to abort if they became pregnant, and today, over a quarter of a century later, massive signs on the north-south highway which runs through the entire region warn drivers to drive at maximum speed for thirty miles, to keep windows closed, and not to stop for any reason.

'Also fed into the computer was data derived from the analysis of ash movements from volcanic eruptions during the past three decades. There are many recorded instances of volcanic ash pouring down thousands of miles away from the volcanoes,

'This print-out is, I believe, a soundly researched document. It might, perhaps, be exaggerating the dangers; but, equally, it might be underestimating them. I know that Sir Isaac, in more than broad outline, agrees with it.'

Quoit nodded his head. He looked a good deal more *compos mentis* than he had a week ago after being freed from a portable chicken coop on the Illushyn.

'In the event of the worst happening to a single reactor, a major portion of the United Kingdom would have to be evacuated, and evacuated within hours. This would be impossible. Air-raid shelters might be some solution, but air-raid shelter filter-systems cannot filter out all the very fine particles of fall-out that would come from a power station. Their filters would be effective against fall-out from nuclear bombs, but not as effective against nuclear reactor fall-out. The basic difference is that nuclear reactor fall-out is much finer. It actually dissolves into the air itself, making it very hard – in fact, impossible – for filtration systems to keep it out. Wherever air, however finely filtered, gets in, so will nuclear reactor fall-out. Only those places with their own internal air supplies would be completely protected. The second problem is that after a bomb attack the fall-out level would subside to the point where people could come back out into the open within a few weeks. But with reactor fall-out, this period would be very much longer. Within twenty-four hours downwind, they would have to stay in their shelters for a year. And in any event, we are only talking about a tiny minority who would have any shelter protection at all. For the majority, we would have an insurmountable problem in that nothing could be grown on massive areas of British soil for years. We know it is impossible to evacuate the population, but it may well be equally impossible to feed the people if they stay – and survive.

'And this would be the result of blowing up one, just one, of the forty-two reactors in the sixteen nuclear power stations on this island.' He tapped the ash off his cigar.

'I have read out to you the worst that could happen. With conventional explosives, or with an explosion caused by malfunction due to sabotage, the radiation hazards would be considerably reduced. But we should think in terms of the worst, and if something less bad happens, we can regard it as a bonus. There are plenty of people who say it is not possible to blow up a reactor and cause a serious radiation leakage; so far as I am concerned, they are the direct descendants of those people who knew the Titanic could never sink.

'It is my opinion, from the evidence that has been presented to me, that somewhere out beyond these walls people are plotting against one or more of our nuclear power stations – and not only against our power stations, but those of other countries as well. There are three nuclear power stations on the north coast of France. If any of these were blown up when there was a southerly wind, great tracts of this country would be in grave danger.

'We cannot take the kidnapping of Sir Isaac by the Russians too seriously. We must examine all the possible motives, and take every possible step to safeguard ourselves.'

Everyone in the room nodded in assent. I looked at Quoit, and the strain showed in his face. From the time the van with the two men in it had pulled up beside him while he was walking his dog, to the time a man in a balaclava had stuck his head into the chicken coop in the hold of the Illushyn and said, 'All right, Sir Isaac, you're safe now!', he had lived in a drugged half-world, with little conception of time, and none at all of place. Since arriving back in England, he had been under almost continuous hypnosis, as the MI5 interrogation team had attempted, as kindly and gently as they could – two things which didn't come naturally to them – to prise from out of the deeper recesses of his mind descriptions of his captors, of where he was taken and held, of the making of the videotape, of the food he had eaten, of the taste of the water he had drunk, the crockery, the cutlery, right down to the name Thomas Crapper & Sons inscribed on the porcelain at the bottom of the lavatory bowl. He had produced very little that was of help; the only detail of his entire ordeal that he was able to recall clearly and accurately was the clucking noise of the chickens.

'Do you have any idea, Sir Charles, what the Soviets' motives might have been in kidnapping Sir Isaac?' asked the Home Secretary.

'There are a number of possibilities. The first is that the Russians simply want to stir up unrest, as they do from time to time. They often do this to distract Western attention from something that is going on inside the Soviet Union – a trial of dissidents, or a purge of some minority sect, something like that. But I don't think it is so in this case.'

'The television programme that the BBC put out has certainly stirred up unrest – the Energy Secretary has made my life merry hell for letting that go out.'

Fifeshire grinned. 'You mean he actually had to answer questions about nuclear energy? I should think it did him some good. It's about time, after two years in office, that he actually read a book on the subject.' Fifeshire turned his eyes away from the Home Secretary, summarily dismissing him from his attention, and stared for a brief moment at the rest of us, one by one. 'The second possibility is that the Russians are becoming concerned about the world supplies of uranium. We know that the Soviet Union has very large uranium reserves in the ground, but we are also beginning to learn, from intelligence sources, that because of its geographical locations, and its relatively low grade, much of it cannot be mined economically.

'The Soviet Union has at the present time forty-seven operating nuclear reactors; in five years' time, this figure will have trebled. They're going to have to get their uranium from somewhere. Perhaps they feel that by stirring up anti-nuclear-energy fever in the West, they will effectively cause a reduction in the nuclear construction programme, leaving more uranium available for them.

'But really, we're just guessing at the moment what the Russians are up to, and trying to make sense of the new facts we have. The first information we had on this whole business that was in anyway tangible was from the Arab named Ahmed that Flynn met in the lavatory of the Royal Lancaster. But before he could really tell us much of value, the unfortunate man was killed – not by Flynn, I should add, which does make a welcome change.'

There was a titter of laughter from everyone except the Home Secretary, who just glared at me. I wasn't convinced I liked the image of me, as the Security Services' hangman, that Fifeshire was cultivating.

'The information this Arab gave Mr Flynn,' Fifeshire continued, 'was, firstly, that one of our operatives in Libya, who had penetrated a terrorist training camp, had been blown – and from the sound of it, probably captured and killed. Secondly, he mentioned the words "Operation

Angel". He said it was to do with nuclear power stations, that many countries were involved. He wasn't terribly specific, was he, Flynn?'

'No, sir. He said that many power stations would be blown up, presumably in many countries – but that was all he managed to get out.'

'Couldn't you have prevented him from being killed?' asked Ross.

'If I'd been sharing the same lavatory cubicle with him, I might have done,' I said. I saw Fifeshire conceal a grin, and Ross glared at me.

'The man who killed this Arab,' continued Fifeshire, 'fled in a car with three others. Due to a spot of carelessness on Flynn's part, all four of them met an untimely death under the wheels of an articulated lorry.'

There was another titter from all except Kieran Ross. I had the distinct feeling I had not made a big hit with the Home Secretary.

'All four men were from Libya. The Libyans are claiming that they were high-grade politicians and diplomats, but on looking into these claims, our sources suggest that they were nothing but a bunch of hit-men.'

I caught Fifeshire's eye, and he winked at me. Sometimes, I decided, he wasn't so bad.

'As a result of this, we decided to take a very close look at the British nuclear energy industry – power stations and all other related areas. A short while after this incident, the controller of system safeguards at the United Kingdom Atomic Energy Authority, a man called Horace Whalley, was invited to spend a short holiday on a yacht in the South of France by none other than Deke Sleder, the German industrialist. Sleder is a man on whom we have always kept an eye. His business practices are nothing if not sharp, and his allegiances have from time to time been a trifle dubious. In the last two years, Sleder has made big strides into the nuclear energy business – not in this country, yet, I might add. Sleder was joined, on this jolly boating trip, by a total of a dozen men from five countries: from the United States, Canada, France and Spain, and the United Kingdom was represented by Mr Whalley. Judging by the bevvy of girls on board, it wasn't just a working holiday.

'Now, at this point, it could be that Sleder merely wanted to get inside information on the nuclear energy business in these countries; the men came from different fields – some were working for governments, some for private industry.

'The next thing that happened was that Sir Isaac disappeared. There was no immediate connection at all – until Mr Flynn, following Whalley, saw him pick up a videotape from a contact in Wales and deliver this tape to the BBC. That was the videotape that went out on the air last Monday.

'The final thing, of course, was the discovery and rescue of Sir Isaac from the Aeroflot plane.'

'Do you think, Sir Charles,' asked Peter Nettlefold, the Commander of C4, 'that the Russians are planning some form of worldwide sabotage of nuclear power stations?'

'We received a report yesterday from Sir William's department,' Fifeshire was referring to MI6, an organization for which he normally had little regard, 'perhaps you'd like to relate it, Bill.'

Sir William Atling had a dark sunken face, and his eyes were a long way back in their sockets, shrouded by enormous, squirrel-like eyebrows. He was fairly tall, but very thin, and wore a sombre dark suit and dark tie that would not have made him look out of place in the clerical department of a firm of undertakers.

'This "Operation Angel" was mentioned in a report I

received from Moscow in July, and it has been mentioned several times since. I do not know what it is – no one has been able to find out, and my people are trying very, very hard. In Moscow there is a complete veil of secrecy drawn over it. The only thing I can tell you for sure is that something is going on that is greatly exciting the Politburo. What it is, I do not at the moment know. It could well be this Operation Angel.

'As you probably know, the Politburo is mainly a bunch of old men, and it is not often that old men get excited. I know from experience that if the Politburo is excited, gentlemen, then we should be worried – very, very worried.'

There was a long silence. Nettlefold broke it. 'What are your views on the Libyan connection, Bill?'

'Well – Libya is a major international terrorist base. Its neighbour, Chad, has massive uranium reserves, and the Libyans have been moving in on Chad for a long time – but that's not necessarily relevant here. Maybe the Russians are going to get the Libyans to blow up all these power stations for them. Perhaps it's not the Russians' baby at all – it could be someone else's plot and they're just footing the bill, or someone could be fronting for them – there are a lot of possibilities.'

'Could it be an IRA plot?' asked Ross.

'There's no evidence at the moment to suppose it is,' said Fifeshire, 'and the IRA would be concerned only with Britain.'

'What about the other Intelligence services?' said Ross, flapping a pair of bony white hands like an excited schoolboy.

If you met him in the street, and didn't know he was the Home Secretary, you would think he was a complete twerp. He was gangly, very thin, and boyish-looking, with a conical head thinly layered with neat, mousey hair. He had a penchant for bright flowery ties which did not go with the grey chalk-striped suits he wore, and he walked with a distinctive bounce on flat, white, rubber-soled lace-ups. His voice and gestures had become, by the month, increasingly camp, ever since he had taken the opportunity of his appointment as Home Secretary to announce to the world that he had decided to 'come out'. His problem was that, having come out, he didn't have any idea where he was. He was an embarrassment to the entire government, yet the Prime Minister dared not sack him, for fear of upsetting the not inconsiderable gay electorate.

'Which other countries have you informed?' he asked.

'None, and at the moment I don't intend to.' Fifeshire said emphatically. He didn't like Ross at all, and referred to him, when he was out of earshot, as 'the pogo-stick'. 'If I tell any of those organizations, or the Canadians, I might as well send a copy of anything I say directly to the Russians. Besides, we do not know for sure that any of these countries are involved. I don't want to go raking up a hornet's nest that could blow our only chance of finding out what's going on before it's too late. If I feel we need their help, or if I find out something that they must be told, then at the appropriate moment they will be told. Until then, we must play this whole affair close to our vests and find out what we can ourselves.' Fifeshire looked at the Director General of MI6, and Atling nodded pensively. It was rare that the two men ever communicated with each other, such was their mistrust for each other's organization. MI5, under Fifeshire, and without the knowledge of any politicians of any party, had over the past fifteen years built up a formidable overseas espionage division – something quite outside the original sphere of responsibility for the internal security of Britain.

Fifeshire maintained that internal security could not be effective without deep inside-knowledge of what was happening elsewhere in the world, and he did not trust MI6's information. Similarly, Sir William Atling and his predecessors had always felt that an overseas intelligence network could not be run without an effective home intelligence network, and he did not want to be in the hands of MI5. So the two men ran their organizations independently, both doing similar work, spying often on the same people, Fifeshire with a slight edge in the United Kingdom, and Atling with the edge overseas. It was Fifeshire who had made the overture to Atling, because he felt that that edge, however small, might right now be needed.

'Secrecy,' Fifeshire continued, 'is to be our major weapon. The Russians do not know we have Sir Isaac back. A corpse will have been found in the plane in the exact part of the hold where Sir Isaac was concealed. The Russians will have told the French that it is the body of one of the hijackers – a Jewish dissident—'

'Won't the French want proof of identity?' interrupted Ross.

'No, I doubt it very much. This whole incident is immensely embarrassing to them, particularly at a time when *détente* for them has never been better, and their trade with Russia is booming. I should think the French are relieved as hell there's only one corpse, and they've probably already got it off their hands and sent it to Russia. In case the Russians try and check up on its identity, and manage to steal Sir Isaac's dental records, we've had it equipped with an exact copy of Sir Isaac's set of teeth – it was fairly easy, as Sir Isaac has no teeth at all, only dentures.'

Quoit blushed. At least it brought some colour to his face.

'Wouldn't it have been easier to alter Sir Isaac's dental records?' asked Ross.

'Of course it would have been,' snapped Fifeshire. He didn't like people questioning his methods – particularly people he didn't like. 'But for all we know, the Russians might have made a copy before the kidnap took place; we didn't want to take the risk. Now are there any questions on what I have said so far?' Fifeshire looked around the group.

'Yes,' said Ross. 'How are the Russians going to explain Quoit's death to us?'

'The Russians don't know that we have Sir Isaac back; they will believe we assume Quoit to be in Russia, and that, having said his piece, he probably doesn't need to make any more public appearances. In a few months' time, I expect they will notify us that he has been killed in some sort of acci-dent – probably a car crash – and that will be the end of it.'

'Thank you. Now, my next question,' said Ross, assum-ing command of question time, 'is what precisely are the steps you are taking, and how much time do you think we have?'

'I don't know how long we have. I'm assuming it's only a matter of weeks. With regard to the steps we are taking: Flynn has a twenty-four-hour surveillance on Whalley. We are hoping Whalley will soon meet again with his contact – the man from whom he collected the videotape. The contact gave Flynn's men the slip last time, but next time they will hang onto him with glue. Unfortunately, we know nothing about him except that he drives a dark-coloured Ford Capri with false licence plates. The owners of every dark-coloured Ford Capri in Britain are being checked on, but it's a massive task. Frankly, we'll be lucky if anything comes from that. Whalley is by far our best bet; he'll lead us somewhere, I'm certain.

'We're also taking a close look at Sleder, and we hope that Sir William's team in Moscow is going to come up with something. Other than that, Mr Ross, we'll just have to sit on our pert little bottoms, and wait.'

12

It was probably because I was deep in thought after the meeting that I didn't think hard enough about the message waiting for me on my desk. It was short and clear, and read: *A man telephoned. He said he was a friend of Ahmed. He will wait for you at the farthest table at the back of the downstairs floor of Richoux in Knightsbridge until three o'clock.*

I grilled the girl who had taken the message, but she could give me very little help. The voice was foreign, unsteady, and the caller obviously had a limited vocabulary. I could have had the voice played back, as all incoming telephone calls are automatically taped, but there wasn't enough time to go winding backwards and forwards through the tape, and since I didn't know anyone who didn't speak English fluently, hearing the voice probably wouldn't have helped me. I put my jacket and coat on and went out through the front entrance of number forty-six into Carlton House Terrace.

It was a bitterly cold day, sleeting slightly. I did up my coat buttons, put my hands in my pockets, and started to walk down towards Pall Mall to find a taxi. I was surprised to hear the familiar diesel rattle after only a few moments, and turned around, to see a taxi with its 'For Hire' light on, coming down right behind me. I flagged it down and climbed in. 'Harrods,' I said, Richoux being right across the road from the department store, which would give me a chance to see if there was anyone hanging around watching Richoux who shouldn't have been.

'Pardon?' he said in a thick accent. He was young – couldn't have been much more than twenty-two – with a Middle-Eastern complexion, and a large gold-coloured watch.

'Harrods,' I repeated.

'Harrods, Knightsbridge?' he asked.

'Correct.' During the best part of thirty-two years living in London, I had never come across more than one Harrods. This man obviously knew better. The watch was a genuine Rolex. I wondered at which branch of Harrods he'd bought it. The cab was smart – almost brand new; maybe it came from Harrods too. I leaned forward to the partition window. 'Nice new cab,' I said.

'Yes,' he laughed nervously, 'yes, this is my cab.'

An advert on the back panel told me I needed a new postal franking machine. The driver crashed the gears badly going from third to fourth as he negotiated St James's Street. I have always had a love-hate relationship with London's taxi drivers. When I am driving myself, I think the entire bunch of them are miserable bastards who reckon they own every inch of the road, who never let anyone out, and who carve anyone up given the slightest chance, even if they have to go out of their way to do it. When I am a passenger in a cab, I think they're bloody marvellous, terrific people, ace drivers, and I can more than fully understand their contempt for the average drivelling moron creeping his saloon around the centre of London's roads at five miles per hour, and letting the whole world and his dog go before him at every opportunity.

But right now, my confidence in the London cabbie was taking a severe battering. For the privilege of having to stump up the best part of a week's wages for every tenth of a mile that I travelled, I felt I was entitled to expect someone who was at least able to drive, who could, at the minimum, string a few sentences of the English language together, and who didn't think there was a Harrods on every street corner.

As we rounded the corner into Piccadilly, we stopped at a red light. At least Mustapha wasn't colour blind. He opened his door and hopped out. 'You wait please, one moment – I buy *Standard*.' He darted off towards a news kiosk.

I wasn't sure afterwards whether it was his Rolex watch, or his lack of knowledge of London, or his lack of driving skill, or my sheer disbelief that with his limited grasp of the English language he could have any use for a newspaper, or the fact that for a quarter to three on a Monday afternoon he had just appeared too damn quickly, but something made me lean forward and look into his cab. There was a hand grenade on the seat and there was no pin in the grenade.

The explosion happened as I was somewhere between the door and the pavement. It picked me up, and blasted me clean over the railings into St James's Park, and blasted most of my trousers away. It turned the cab into a ball of fire, and sprinkled smaller balls of fire around the foyer of the Ritz, and other parts of the immediate vicinity.

I lay for a moment on the cold grass, my ears completely numb, my face stinging, my legs hurting like mad, as I gulped in air; and as I gulped in air, I got mad, and as I got mad, I gulped in more air still, and as I gulped in more air still, I got even madder, and I reached for the inside of my jacket, only to discover I no longer had either a coat or a jacket, but I did still have my holster with a Beretta inside it. I pulled out the Beretta, and snapped off the safety catch. I checked the selector was on single fire. I was going to get that Arab; I was going to get that sodding bastard. I climbed over the rails, gingerly, for everything hurt. There was complete silence. The whole of Piccadilly had come to a halt. I pinched my nostrils with my fingers and blew hard until my ears popped; but still there was silence – silence except for the ticking of car engines. Somewhere in the distance I heard the blast of a horn. The cab burned fiercely, crackling viciously. The paintwork of a Ford Granada parked on a meter next to it was blistering and bubbling. The newspaper vendor was wide-eyed and blinking.

I stared up and down for the Arab. He was nowhere in sight. I looked at doorways, inside cars, up and down the street, but I didn't move. I waited. I looked for that one movement, somewhere – but there was none. A pretty girl in a Metro was staring at me; her face was frozen in a mixture of horror, pity and puzzlement. I couldn't blame her; standing there dressed in nothing but black calf-length boots, blue Marks and Sparks Y-fronts, half a gingham-check blue and white shirt, and a hefty great 9mm Beretta 93R, I couldn't have looked the world's prettiest sight.

I tried to conceal the gun, by sticking it inside my shirt, and I became conscious of the fact that I wasn't going to be able to stand here much longer without attracting a crowd of several thousand. A front-page news story and my mug plastered over every newspaper would not greatly enhance my career prospects. I needed to move away from here, fast. I began walking; somehow, I just didn't fancy a taxi.

13

Happy fucking birthday. The note was written on my hall mirror in lipstick, in big scrawling letters. Her car was gone and so was she, and I could hardly blame her for going. I had promised, faithfully, that I would be home by seven; it was now eleven hours later. Being a spy isn't a good career for steady relationships; it's even worse for rocky relationships, and ours would have been described, in nautical terms, as a 'force 10 gale on the nose'.

The first time I met her, she was in my bed. She had a shock of hair that was bright green on one side and bright orange on the other. I didn't know whether to make love to her or to dust my furniture with her; either way, I decided it would be courteous to wake her up first.

'Screw off,' were her first words to me. She rolled over and her feet came out the end of the bed. I didn't need a tape measure to figure out she was tall, very tall – quite a bit taller than me; I ruled out dusting the furniture.

I shook her again gently. 'Wakey, wakey,' I said, 'you've broken into my house and now you're sleeping in my bed.'

'How very observant you are,' she replied sleepily. 'Anyhow, what kept you?'

'What kept me? Who the hell are you?'

'Light me a cigarette, sit down and I'll tell you.' She had an Australian accent. It's normally an accent I don't care for, but she made it sound good. I lit a cigarette, handed it to her and sat down in the chair at the end of the bed.

'If you're that scared of me, why don't you go stand in the street and I'll shout to you through the window?'

It was one o'clock in the morning, I was feeling more than a little drunk, and my brain was taking a little time to figure out all this.

She sat up a little. 'You can sit nearer,' she said, 'I won't bite.'

'None of you?'

'I don't like jokes about my height – I'm sensitive about it.'

I went and sat down beside her. 'I'm sorry,' I said, 'I didn't know you were sensitive about your height. All I can see is your head and your feet – how do I know how much is in between?'

I looked at her face carefully. It was a sulky face, about twenty-four years old, with pouting lips and a small chin on top of a very long neck; she had rich blue eyes, with fair eyebrows, and a beautifully clear skin with the trace of a tan. She smiled, and the face sprang to life. Apart from a little mascara and a couple of dashes of rouge, she wore no make-up at all, and didn't need to. Her hair really didn't do her justice at all. She had the kind of face men shoot each other over.

'Who are you?' I said.

For a reply, I got a long deep kiss – in about forty different places. It was four o'clock in the morning before I was able to talk again.

She had seen me arrive at the party, and had decided, for whatever mysterious reason that sometimes triggers the jackpot switch in a woman's brain, that I was to be the lucky man. She had gone to my coat, taken my keys, made a wax impression of them, then put them back. Noticing that the car keys had a Jaguar tag, she had gone outside, walked up the street to the first Jaguar she had come to. It was an old one, a 1953 XK120 convertible, and as far as she was concerned it fitted me. To be sure, she had felt the radiator. It was hot, so she knew it had recently been driven, and figured it was definitely mine.

She had then telephoned what she described as 'a chum' at Scotland Yard, given him the Jaguar licence number, and asked for the name and address of the owner. Then she went to a late-opening locksmith in the Earls Court Road and had a duplicate of my keys made, then went straight to my Holland Park mews house. Somehow, the talent scouts for British Intelligence had missed her. She wasn't a spy. She had a trendy up-market gym-cum-solarium for trimming the fat and tanning the face of anyone willing to stump up eighteen pounds an hour to lie in a make-believe tropical island, listening to taped sounds of Pacific breakers, and tropical monkeys fucking.

'How did you know I was coming back alone?' I asked.

'There were only two spare girls at the party, and neither of them was your type. I decided that if you hadn't come with a girl, then you wouldn't be going home with one.'

'I didn't see you at the party.'

'I was there – all six foot three of me.'

'I can't have been looking high enough.'

I felt something cool and firm grip an important part of my reproductive apparatus. 'Careful what you say, Max Flynn. I don't want any gags about the mountain going to Muhammad because Muhammad wouldn't go to the mountain.'

'You're one hell of a gorgeous mountain,' I said.

She released her grip, and set to work on my body again, and we didn't talk for another hour. When we did, it was she who opened the dialogue; she did it by prodding me very hard in the stomach and bringing me out of my not entirely unpleasant coma.

'Max Flynn,' she said, 'what do you do?'

'What? You don't already know?'

'No. I can tell you're not an interior decorator.'

'Is that a compliment or an insult?'

She stuck a Rothmans in my mouth, then held the flame of a platinum-cased Zippo to the end of it. Then she took the cigarette, lit her own with it, and put it back. 'It's an insult!' she said.

'Thanks a lot. It's my home you're talking about, and I don't think it's the role of a housebreaker to criticize the victim's taste.'

'I love your taste,' she said. 'Thousands wouldn't, but I do. It's sort of post nuclear holocaust.'

'The cleaning lady's away sick.'

'Has she been away long?'

'About eighteen months.'

'You haven't answered my question. What do you do?'

'I'm a spy. I work for MI5.'

She giggled. 'Spies are short and fat and old, and wear grubby mackintoshes. I don't believe you. What do you really do?'

'I work for a venture capital company.'

'Your own firm?'

'Afraid not. If it was, I'd have a mansion in Belgravia, with a pet interior decorator in a cage, and an unpickable butler on the door.'

'Wouldn't even I be able to pick him?'

'No, not even you, Sherlock. Not unless you asked him very, very nicely.'

'I think I would,' she said. 'Very, very nicely. What does your venture capital firm put venture capital into?'

'Almost anything that's risky but has a chance of a fat profit: a mini-computer firm; a company with a revolutionary method of making maps; a chain of do-it-yourself shops; a cargo airline; a shipping firm; an oil-exploration company; a chain of medical clinics specializing in sports injuries; a firm that manufactures mini tractors; a geological exploration company; a nickel-mining company in Australia; and a whole load of other things.'

'My father owns a mine,' she said.

'Does he? What do they mine? Front-door keys?'

She ignored the taunt. 'No, plutonium, I think it is.'

'You don't mine plutonium; it isn't a raw material.'

'Oh, well, it's the raw material – whatever you call it.'

'Uranium?'

'Yes, that sounds right. I'm not really sure though, he does so many different things. It's in Namibia, I think.'

'Where the hell's that?'

'South West Africa, ignoramus.'

'All right, Einstein, don't get smart with me.'

She took the cigarette out of my mouth and placed it in the ashtray. Her hand started moving menacingly down my body.

Suddenly, something ice-cold hit my stomach, and for a moment I tensed right up. It was a trap. She had stabbed me. Then the coldness spread further over my stomach. I pulled back the sheet. In her hand was a blue-and-white tube out of which she was squirting a clear-coloured liquid.

'What's the matter?' she asked, moving further down my anatomy.

Talking became difficult. 'I wondered what it was,' I was able to gasp.

'KY Jelly,' she said, 'like it?'

I liked it a lot. After a few minutes I didn't know whether I was going to come or die. I lived.

When I came around, she was dozing. Bright daylight was shoving its way through the curtains. She opened her eyes. 'You haven't told me your name,' I said.

'You never asked.'

'I'm asking you now.'

'You've got to guess.'

I thought hard for some moments, and memories of a short while ago came flooding back. 'I've got it,' I said.

'What is it?'

'Gelignite.'

That had been four months ago. Since then she had all but moved into the house, and the normal far too few hours of sleep I usually snatched had been reduced by a good seventy-five per cent. She couldn't understand why the job I did required me to arrive home late some nights, extremely late other nights, and quite frequently not at all.

After a while the explanations began to wear a bit thin. It was a problem that wasn't new to me; after all, there is a limit to the amount of times any intelligent girl will accept the excuse that one's car has broken down, her feminine logic will cut across the problem with one clear solution: 'Why don't you scrap that old banger and get yourself a sensible car?'

To have my Jaguar XK120 referred to as an 'old banger' was hardly music to my ears, but for four months I'd been heaping the blame, quite unfairly, on the car's shoulders, so Gelignite's comment, in the circumstances, was perhaps not entirely unreasonable. At least, from her point of view.

It was clear from the message on the mirror that last night, my birthday, had seen the end of her patience. She had said she was going to cook me a special birthday dinner, and I had promised to be back by seven. After Whalley had left the Atomic Energy Authority as usual at five o'clock, I had gone over to Carlton House Terrace to check through a list of owners of dark-coloured Ford Capris with police or Intelligence files on them for whatever reason.

At twenty-five to seven, I got up from my desk. I had timed it so that if I left now, I should be home on the dot of seven. The phone rang. I was tempted not to answer it, but like a lot of people I know, I just can't leave a telephone ringing.

'Hallo?' I said.

'Daphne's not going home. She's heading down the M40.'

'Shit.' Why did Whalley have to pick tonight? Stupid miserable bastard! If he didn't one day swing from the gallows for what he was doing to my country, he was damned well going to swing from his testicles for what he was doing to my sex life. 'All three of you there?'

'Yes, sir. Don't worry.'

With the team of surveillance monkeys I had under me, I knew I had every reason to worry. They were all so good at losing things they could have made a fortune on the stage making members of audiences disappear – the only problem being that they would have been incapable of bringing them back. Since my press-ganging into MI5, I had never had people working under me and I didn't like it. I understood now why most agents prefer to operate on their own; at least that way, if there are any screw-ups, you know who's made them and what they are. But as I didn't have wings on my back and jet-packs attached to my ankles, and there wasn't always a handy telephone kiosk around to charge into, I had to use the services of others to be in three places at once for me. But if it looked as if anything interesting was going to happen, I wanted to be right there in the front line. I especially wanted to be there the next time Whalley met up with his chum in the dark Capri.

'I'm on my way. Daphne going as fast as usual?'

'Yes.'

'Call me if she deviates. I'll catch you up at the Porn Shop.' Deviation meant turning off the motorway. Porn Shop was code for Oxford – derived from the Oxford colour of blue. Cambridge, with its lighter blue, was coded Cinema, implying soft porn. I hung up, and bashed my elbow on the edge of the desk. It was still sore as hell from where I had landed on it after being blown out of the taxi a week before.

I picked up the phone again, and dialled my home number. It rang on without being answered. After fifteen rings I hung up. I decided Gelignite couldn't have got in yet. I buzzed down to one of the three night-operators who would have just come on duty. 'Could you please ring my home in half an hour's time and tell the lady that answers that I had to fly to Shannon to look at a weaving plant, and the plane's got engine trouble, and I won't be back until very late – and give her my apologies.'

'Yes, Mr Flynn.'

I took the lift down into the underground car park, and walked over to my Jaguar. Her midnight-blue paintwork still managed to gleam under a heavy layer of London grime, and her wire wheels needed an energetic Sunday afternoon with a tin of spirit, a toothbrush and a duster, but they were going to have to wait a good while yet for that. Gelignite and the XK had no need to be jealous of each other: they both received an equal amount of neglect.

I climbed into the driver's seat, pulled the door shut by the red leather tongue, pushed in the ignition key, and turned it. There was a deep clunk sound, followed by a rapid ticking sound, and the gauges in front of me began to quiver with life. I pulled out the choke and waited for the fuel pump to finish its ticking. I pressed the starter button. There was a woosh from the air intakes followed by a boom from the twin exhaust pipes as she fired first time. She sat, vibrating with energy, engine thumping on full choke, sounding a little lumpy, as she usually did until she warmed up.

I removed some dust from the boss of the four-spoked steering wheel, a thick conical boss that would have made a hole in my chest the size of a cannon ball had I been flung against it in an accident, but then this gorgeous brute had been built in the days before padded dashes and collapsible steering columns, and progressive body crumple. She had a solid steel chassis, and the theory was that if anything got in her path once she was under steam, she would shunt it clean out of the way, or cut it in half like a battleship slicing through a smuggler's yawl. I let the choke in a little, pushed the clutch pedal down hard, pushed the short thin gear lever into first, let off the handbrake, and we moved forward. I stayed in first gear as we went up the steep ramp. The guard just inside the metal gate pushed the button that sent it clattering upwards, and nodded me a goodnight; I waved a finger back at him in reply.

The Jag is not the best car in which to try and follow someone discreetly, but it was dark, and I didn't feel like driving one of the department's dreary machines tonight. I felt, it being my birthday, I had a right to some compensation for missing what had promised to be, as Gelignite had put it, an 'interesting' celebration. Since she had an extremely fertile mind regarding pastimes not unrelated to the reproductive processes, I had a feeling that I was going to be missing out on something that ought not to be missed out on.

I wrenched my thoughts away from Gelignite and onto more mundane matters, such as remaining alive, at least for long enough to complete my exploration of her mental and physical erotic treasure-chest. One week ago an Arab had tried to murder me. He had failed, but he had escaped, and it was possible he might try again. The taxi had been stolen the day before and had false plates. There was more than a little evidence to suggest that he was not just a lone crackpot with a grudge against people who travelled in taxis. But there was no evidence yet to suggest exactly who he was. He was probably a Libyan hit man, flown over for the one job, chosen because there were no records on him in England. I didn't know either, what his purpose in trying to kill me had been. Possibly it was to silence me in case I had picked up any information from Ahmed in the Royal Lancaster lavatory, but if that was the case, they had left it a long time. Possibly, it was to avenge the deaths of the four Libyans. The third possibility was that it may have been to get me off Whalley's back. That was the possibility I most feared, for it would have meant Whalley knew he was being followed, and would therefore do nothing except waste our time. But I didn't think whoever it was could be so naive as to think that if they got rid of me everyone would leave Whalley alone.

Possibly it was someone settling an old score. In this game, we never know when we are making enemies, nor, often, who our enemies are.

There were too many possibilities and not enough clues. I would have to wait until whoever it was tried again, and endeavour not to break his neck before he talked.

The three exit ramps from the car park were rotated in irregular sequence, to make life harder for anyone trying to keep tabs on the movements of the staff of 46 Carlton House

Terrace. The one in use tonight took me out into Cockspur Street, opposite Canada House. Whether they didn't know there were any other ramps, or whether they knew which one was in use tonight, or whether they had all three covered, I did not find out, but I spotted them before the registration number of my car had even sunk into their brain cells – not that they could have learned a lot from it; the day after Gelignite had succeeded in cracking my private fortress, I had had the name and address of the owner of the Jaguar changed on the police files, and on the Swansea central vehicle registration files, to one Angus McTavish, who resided on a remote atoll thirty miles north-west off the coast of John o'Groats, Scotland's most northern tip. McTavish did not exist, but the island did. Anyone else who had the bright idea of trying to track me down through my car licence number was in for one hell of a long journey, with little to show for their efforts, other than, perhaps, some snapshots of an uninhabitable rock covered in bird-shit.

The dark blue Marina crept up through the busy traffic in the Mall, and stuck two cars back from me; it stayed with me up St James's, and down left into Piccadilly. There were still scorch marks on the tarmac from the previous week. The Marina forked left behind me into Hyde Park Corner, but still I couldn't be one hundred per cent sure. I still couldn't be completely sure as I went around and took the Park Lane turn-off, and held my speed to thirty, although the legal limit was forty. The Marina stayed back, letting other cars pass. There were two men in the Marina. Caucasians.

I turned sharply left, down the ramp to the filling station; they didn't follow. If I was right and they were tailing me, they had just shown that I wasn't dealing with complete amateurs. I stuck five pounds worth of petrol in the tank, which topped it to the brim, and drove out again. The Marina was circling Marble Arch.

I drove around Marble Arch and headed back down Park Lane, sticking to the inside lane. The Marina came down, three cars back, also in the inside lane. No one but an idiot, or someone wanting to turn left, drives down the inside lane of this part of Park Lane. We crossed the Brook Street lights, then on down, past the Dorchester lights, still in the left lane, the Marina two cars back now. The traffic was thick ahead and to the right of me; then there was a gap. I cursed the side-screens of the Jag, wishing that at this moment I had glass windows with clearer vision. I looked out; there was a truck coming down fast. I slammed the gear-lever into first, flattened the accelerator, hung the tail out all over the road, rev counter thrashing into the red, blast of horn from the truck, ferocious hoot from a taxi as I rocketed clean across his bows – Christ, a bicycle – missed the back wheel by an inch. MGB going slowly down the outside lane, but I won't get in front. Hurry, MGB, for chrissake – oh shit, XJ6 belting down second lane – move your ass MGB. The gap opened and I got out of the path of the XJ6, and behind the ass of the MGB, down the tiny slip road in the central divider which was the last exit before Hyde Park Corner, and away from the jam that the Marina now had no chance of missing.

As I started to drive back up Park Lane, I could see the Marina, still in the inside lane on the far side of the carriage-way. Both driver and passenger were looking my way, and while I was too far away to see and memorize their features, I could, even from this distance, make out the expression on their faces: they looked very pissed off.

I pulled a receiver from my pocket and put it in my ear. Then I took my propelling pencil out, and spoke into the clip. 'This is Ursula' – Ursula was my code name for the day

– 'I want urgent tail on navy Marina registration AEX 659Y. Currently in southbound jam at Park Lane-Hyde Park junction. And gen too.'

'Roger Ursula. Reply Halo.'

The words 'Reply Halo' told me on which of the channels the reply would be coming. When we were in contact with Central London Control, or with any other central control point – there were several in key cities across Britain – to minimize the risk of one's conversation being monitored, each radio transmission would be made on a different frequency. If I wanted to speak to CLC again, it would next be on the frequency for which Halo was the code. I set the dial on the pencil to this frequency and switched the transmitter off to conserve the battery; it would be some minutes before the reply came.

At Marble Arch, I turned left down the Bayswater Road, and then threaded my way around the back of Paddington Station. One hundred years ago, this had been the smart side of the Park to live. Then the station had been built, and the smart set fled over to South Kensington to escape the smut and the soot. Now the trains were electric or diesel and there was no smut and no soot, but few of the smart set had moved back. Terrace upon terrace of handsome white buildings sat decaying, with paint flaking off; the ones that weren't hotels were jam-packed with as many apartments any landlord, with access to a cheap carpenter and even cheaper plumber, could cram in.

My ear plug bleeped; I pressed the button on my pencil. 'Ursula,' I said.

'It's a Hertz rental. Taken out this morning by one Michael Allen Keating, of 67 Harewood Drive, Leeds. He paid cash in advance for three days' rental, and left cash deposit for the car. It was taken from the Russell Square branch and was to be returned there. It has been found abandoned north side of Piccadilly. Will check further on Keating. Over.'

'Thanks. I'm going around the block. I'll call you later.'

'Going around the block' was code for leaving London.

'Roger Ursula, reply Fairy.'

It was some way down the M40 motorway before the traffic lightened and I could see a clear stretch of road ahead of me. When the gap finally came, I dropped down into third, and pushed the accelerator hard down. The car surged from fifty up to ninety, the engine missing a couple of times as the oil was blown off the plugs, and then on up to ninety-five, where I changed back into fourth. Still the car surged forward, the pit of my stomach trying to force its way into the soft leather seat-back behind me. The needle whipped past one hundred and ten, one hundred and twenty, one hundred and twenty-five, and I eased off there, before the rev counter went into the red, and held her at one hundred and twenty. Although she would soon be entering her fourth decade, she felt as if she was hardly run in, and clung to her line on the road like a limpet.

In the event of being stopped by the police, I had a small plastic card in my wallet. It was issued by the Home Office and it had on one side my photograph and a Home Office seal, and on the reverse the words: *This person is on special duties. Please give him any help he may require. By authority of the Home Secretary.* But I didn't need to use the card tonight. Whatever any of Britain's answers to Starsky and Hutch might have been up to, they weren't waiting for speedsters down this particular stretch of highway. After a few minutes, I eased down to one hundred.

I mulled things over as I drove. I wondered whether the Marina had been tailing me to see where I was going, or was tailing me to see if I would stop anywhere long enough for them to get some vital part of the top half of my anatomy into the cross-hairs of a telescopic sight. I wasn't enjoying this assignment, but there wasn't a lot I could do about that. Before I could move off it, I had to see it through; and to see it through I had to survive, and right now, that didn't seem like the easiest of things to do.

I was out of my depth, but so, it seemed, was everyone else – from Fifeshire downwards – out of our depths and in the dark, playing a game of chance that would pay us no prizes if we won, but could cost dearly if we lost. At least they were the kind of options we were used to.

I was so wrapped up in thought that I went straight past the brown Triumph Dolomite, Sarah, the rear of the three tail cars, the grey Chevette, Alison, and the beige Allegro, Debbie. I was about to go straight past Whalley's Cavalier when the alarm bells started clanging in my head. I braked hard, and dropped back behind the Allegro. We were on the A44, between Worcester and Leominster, having left the motorway a long way back. There were no street lights and no houses; it was pitch dark. The traffic was heavy.

Suddenly, the Allegro's brake lights came on, and I nearly slammed into the back of the car. A car a short distance ahead of him was turning right. It was Whalley's Cavalier, and he was turning into a small lane.

The Allegro went straight on. I snapped off my lights and turned into the lane to follow. Whalley was driving very slowly now, obviously looking for something. I saw what appeared to be a cart-track on the left, and swung into it. There was a splintering crash. I cursed; without my lights on, I hadn't noticed the closed gate. I switched off the engine, leapt out of the car, not worrying about the gate for the moment, ran around to the boot, grabbed a briefcase from it, then sprinted off up the road after Whalley's car.

I was in luck; around the next corner, I saw him put his brake lights on, and then I saw him shine a torch out of his right-hand window. He held it steady for a moment, then switched it off, turned right, and drove straight in between the bushes. I ran up to where he had gone in. There was a gap which led through to a huge field. Sitting at the edge of the field, glinting slightly in the moonlight, was a dark-coloured Ford Capri. I pressed down the tip of my pencil. 'Daphne's stopped for a picnic. She'll need some ice.' My code words told the team to keep both ends of this lane covered.

Whalley drove up towards the Capri. I snapped open my case, and drew out my image-intensifier binoculars, and looked firstly at the Capri's registration. It was different from the last time, but I had little doubt it was the same car. I looked up through the windscreen. The driver wore a large pair of sun-glasses and a cap pulled down over his forehead. His mouth was covered by a thick moustache. Whether by accident or design, he had made it quite impossible to identify any of his facial features.

I took a set of headphones from my case and put them on. There was a wire running from them to a device with a telescopic sight, that was long and pointed, like a gun with no stock or breech. I stared through the image-intensifier sight and picked up Whalley. I pushed the switch on the side of the device, and was nearly deafened by the grating of a handbrake being pulled on. I turned the volume control down.

Whalley, methodical as always, removed his ignition key, then left his car, walked over to the Capri, and got into the front passenger seat of the Capri.

I aimed the cross-hairs of the sight onto the front wind-screen of the Capri, midway between their heads. The device was the very latest in eavesdropping from Messrs Trout and Trumbull of the Playroom, British Intelligence's answer to Alexander Graham Bell, Oppenheimer, the Atari Corporation, and Heath Robinson, all rolled into one. Their inventiveness knew no bounds. Among this month's collection of essential items for the Spy-Who-Has-Everything were a rubber plant containing a concealed gun that could be aimed with deadly accuracy and fired, by remote control, from a distance of up to five miles; an apple that was a hand grenade – the removal of the stalk primed it; and an aerosol that, if sprayed onto the trunk of a tree, coated it in a substance that turned it into a highly effective radio aerial. Trout and Trumbull were heavily into Mother Earth this month; all the past few years' publicity on ecology had obviously suddenly got through to them.

The most extraordinary thing about these two pasty-faced boffins, who looked more like elderly sales assistants in a dignified men's outfitters of a nearly bygone age, was that everything they produced could be relied upon to work. Of the hundreds of weird devices they came up with, few were ever offered by them for service; but, with very rare exceptions indeed, one had the greatest of confidence that, if they did offer something, it would work.

The device I held in my hands now wasn't actually their invention. In fact, they invented very little. Their brilliance lay in their ability to find and adapt inventions of others to the needs of the British field operative of the 1980s. This particular device was a laser microphone which could pick up a conversation with the most perfect clarity and fidelity of tone from a range of up to five miles. It did this by picking up the vibrations that the words made on any solid object nearby, and translating the vibrations back into speech. Glass was ideal for this, and no piece of glass could have been more ideal than the Triplex toughened-zone windscreen behind which they now sat.

'You're late. Jesus, you had me worried.'

'I'm sorry – the traffic was bad getting out of London.'

'The traffic's always bad in London. You got stuck in it last time – why couldn't you have left earlier?'

I recognized the man's voice. I had heard it before. I racked my brains to think where, but I couldn't remember; but I had definitely heard that voice.

'I couldn't. It would have looked suspicious.'

'You were hours late last time. I've driven a hundred miles to make your journey shorter for you this time, and you're still late.'

'I'm sorry; I'm not good at this sort of thing.'

'Maybe I should send some of these to your wife – would it help your punctuality?'

There was the sound of stiff paper; they both looked down at something the contact held.

'You told me the negatives had been destroyed.'

'Did I? I must have lied.'

'I'll be on time in the future.'

'I'm glad to hear it, but I'm hoping there won't be too many more times.'

'Good. I don't think my nerves can take it much longer.'

'You're sure you weren't followed here?'

'Of course not. I've told you, the Authority has no security worth speaking of.'

'We're worried there's been a leak. I was going to tell you last time, but I didn't want to frighten you. The Libyans caught a British agent operating in the training camp where we had our briefing sessions. Under torture, he admitted that he had bribed a Libyan friend to go to London and tell his control. The Libyan was tracked down and silenced, but not until after he arrived in London. We know who he contacted, but we don't know how much he managed to tell. We know it can't have been a great deal, because the specific details hadn't been decided then, and I advised we should let the matter drop. But now there's been a real fuck-up. Wojara didn't agree. He wanted to have the person the Libyan contacted silenced as well – someone at MI5. They had a go at him and screwed up. You probably read in the paper last week about the bomb in a taxi?'

Whalley nodded.

'Well, if that MI5 man's got half a brain, it can't take him too long to put two and two together and figure out a connection. I knew there was going to be trouble dealing with niggers. You're going to have to keep your ears to the ground and a careful eye out.'

'Yes,' said Whalley unhappily. In the gloom, his face looked as cheerful as the inside of an empty curry house.

'It could open up a whole can of worms, this screw-up, and this operation has to succeed, Mr Whalley, it has to succeed; and you're the man that's going to make it succeed, aren't you?'

Whalley nodded silently.

'And you know what will happen if this operation fails for any reason, any reason at all, or even if it has to be aborted, you know what your wife is going to get through the post, don't you?'

'Yes.'

'I'm glad we still understand each other. Now, we have a date: 4 January – provided the wind is right: westerly. If not, it's the first day after that that it is right.'

'I can gear for a specific day – but I don't know how I can delay after that day.'

'That's your problem.'

'I also don't know if I can be ready by then.'

'You'll have to be.'

'Can you give me to the middle of next week to confirm it?'

'You can have until next Tuesday.'

'All right,' Whalley sighed, 'how shall I let you know?'

'You'll send a postcard to Oxford University with a picture of Westminster Abbey on it. Now, write this down: you'll send it to Ben Tsenong – I'll spell that for you: B-E-N T-S-E-N-O-N-G – Balliol College, Oxford; and you'll write the message: "You're right, London is beautiful. See you again soon. Marsha." Got it?'

'Yes.'

'I'll contact you again soon. Goodbye.'

'Goodbye.' Whalley got out of the car and walked back to his Cavalier. The man in the Capri did nothing until Whalley had driven back out through the gap. When he had gone, the man started the Capri; but instead of following Whalley's tracks out through the gap, he turned the Capri in a large arc and, accelerating smartly, headed out across towards the far side of the field. I followed him with my binoculars. He went through an open gate and into a wood which dipped down into a valley. There was no point in my trying to sprint after him – he was driving much too fast. The cunning bastard! I don't think he knew we were here, but he certainly wasn't taking any chances. I spoke into the pencil. 'Contact in Capri SFG 77R. Coming out backstage; send out a soft alert.'

A soft alert is an instruction to all police patrols to look out for the Capri, and to stop it for any traffic offence, however minor, that they can. The intention was, that by stopping the Capri and notifying our surveillance team where it was stopped, it would give them time to get back onto its tail. But there weren't that many police around in this part of the world, and if the man was a professional, of which there seemed little doubt, then he was likely to stick to the quiet back-roads. It was also likely that by the time he emerged from the other side of those woods, the Capri would have yet another registration number.

I tried hard to remember where I had heard that voice before. It was recently, I knew that. Maybe I was mistaken, but I didn't think so.

It was half past eleven, and I had a good three and a half hour's drive back to London; for the moment, I had forgotten all about my birthday, and Gelignite's treat, because right now there was one thought, and one thought only, racing around inside my skull: for the first time since I had begun this assignment, I felt I was in with a sporting chance of hitting the jackpot.

I rewound the tape a little, pressed the play button, and listened for long enough to be satisfied that the conversation had been safely recorded. So Whalley was being blackmailed. Interesting. Very interesting. The whole dialogue had been most interesting.

The gate was an elaborate, if ancient, job, made from timber and barbed wire, and I had done a damn good job of wrapping the barbed wire through the spokes of the Jaguar's wire wheels and around the hub wing-nuts. No amount of tugging would do any good; I was faced with the choice of either driving back to London with the gate attached to my wheels, or jacking up the car, removing the wheels, and disentangling the wire in the freezing-cold, pitch dark. Unhappily, the latter was the more realistic of the two alternatives.

I was not, therefore, in the most cheerful of frames of mind when, at a few minutes to six in the morning, I finally drove into the mews, to see that Gelignite's black Golf GTI was not parked, as it normally was, eight feet away from my front door and blocking the entire mews; in fact, it was not in the mews at all.

I stared again at the note on the hall mirror. *Happy fucking birthday.* That just about summed it up. I picked up the telephone, and dialled the night operator at Portico.

'Didn't you call my home and give the message I asked you to?'

'We did.'

'Well – what did she say?'

'Do you really want to know, Mr Flynn?' She was hesitant.

'Yes, I do.'

'Well – she said, "Bullshit".'

I dialled Gelignite's flat. The phone rang, once, twice, three times, four times, then 'Hello'. It was the voice of someone arousing from a deep sleep.

'It's me.'

There was a long pause. 'Thanks for a great evening.' Yawn. 'What time is it?'

'Five past six.'

'Was she a good fuck?'

'What do you mean?'

'Next time you get your secretary to call up your girlfriend and tell her you're going to be late because you're strapped to a totem pole and surrounded by savages brandishing tomahawks deep in the Amazon bush, let me give you some advice: make sure your girlfriend hasn't seen you driving down Park Lane fifteen minutes earlier, and, what's more, driving like a loony to get out of her line of vision because you think she hasn't spotted you, because I did spot you, you shit!' She hung up.

I stood staring into the receiver, and decided that people were right about birthdays: they do get less fun as you get older.

14

Harry Slan entered the plush reception area of Gebruder Sleder GMBH (US) Inc., on the sixty-fourth floor of 101 Dag Hammarskjöld Plaza, an imposing skyscraper in the United Nations complex between Second and Third Avenues in Manhattan. His glum mood of the past three weeks had finally been lifted somewhere around his third glass of Dom Perignon 66 consumed aboard Deke Sleder's personal LearJet, approximately half-way between Adamsville, Ohio, and La Guardia Airport, New York.

Two weeks after the photographs had landed on his desk, a call had come from Sleder's office, not from Sleder himself but from his personal assistant, saying that Mr Sleder would very much like to see Mr Slan. Mr Slan replied that he would very much like to see Mr Sleder. The assistant sounded perfectly charming – she always did, whoever she spoke to; that was the way Sleder liked his company to sound.

So the plane was laid on, as was a vehicle to collect Slan from his home and transport him to Columbus Airport, as was a limousine at La Guardia to transport him to Sleder's Manhattan headquarters. If it wasn't for his silly carelessness in sending souvenir photographs, thought Slan, through his pleasant haze of vintage champagne – if it was him who had sent the photographs – one could get to like Deke Sleder and his way of life one hell of a lot.

He walked slightly unsteadily towards the receptionist. From across the room, she looked to him like a knockout. As he got close up to her, he realized she was a knockout, and he felt a surge of animal lust for her which surprised even him. She wore a loose black dress that hung, as if suspended by air, half-way down her otherwise totally exposed and very firm breasts. As she leaned forward to stub out a cigarette in the ashtray, and greet him with a rich, wanton smile, he too leaned forward, and could see her nipples as her breasts lifted back from the dress; he could see her firm white stomach below her breasts, and, he wasn't quite sure, but he thought he could see beyond that.

'Good morning,' she said.

'I – er – I – er – I'm Harry Slan. I have an appointment – eleven o'clock, with Mr Sleder.' He realized she was watching him look down the front of her dress; what surprised him was that she smiled.

'Yes, Mr Slan. Mr Sleder is expecting you. I'll tell him you're here.'

Slan opened his mouth to say thank you, but nothing came out. Her perfume had just hit him, and it drove him mad with desire; he was in love with her. He had to get back to Adamsville by this evening; it was his wife Myrtle's birthday, and they were having a party. The Jonklins and the Ormsbys were coming round, and he had promised Myrtle faithfully that he would not be late back. 'Would you care to join me for dinner tonight?' he asked.

She smiled at him, a long smile that was full of desire. He started to compose his letter to Myrtle. The letter told her he was sorry, but life was too short and he felt he had not seen enough of it. Maybe he'd come back some day, and maybe he wouldn't; he hoped she'd understand. They'd had a lot of good times together, she wasn't to take it personally. There wasn't anyone else. It was just – well – he wanted to be alone for a while, have time to think things over, think what it was he really wanted to do with his life, or at least the rest of his life until Myrtle tracked him down.

'I'm sorry, I already have a date.' The smile, for a moment, went from her face. Slan's stomach hit the floor, and stayed there for several long seconds.

All Gebruder Sleder's receptionists, and several other members of his office staff, at offices all around the world, were paid salaries way above the going rate for the posts. The reason for this was that the girls' duties included sleeping with whoever they were instructed to, and when they were instructed to. But no one had instructed Barbara Lindell to sleep with this fat, sweating, half-cut stump of a man who stood leering at her from the other side of her ITT switchboard, and she counted her blessings. She smiled sweetly at Slan, pressed the intercom button to Deke Sleder's private secretary and spoke into the telephone receiver. 'Mr Harry Slan is here.' She listened for a moment, smiled, and replaced the receiver. 'Go right up, Mr Slan, take the internal elevator over there to the seventy-third floor, and you'll be met.'

'Thank you.' Slan paused, but he hadn't ever been much good at chatting up women, and although his ego had been boosted by his four days with Eva, at the age of forty-five he was discovering that his patter was even slower in coming now than when he was twenty. He grinned a rather unsure grin, and fled for the elevator. As the doors shut, he kicked himself. He should have tried harder; then he thought about Myrtle, and decided it was best that she had said no.

The doors opened again, and he stepped out into a large anteroom. Two burly security guards stood up from their chairs. 'Good morning, Mr Slan,' they said courteously. 'Routine security – I'm afraid we'll have to do a quick body-search, if you don't mind.'

Slan did mind, but his brain was weakened by the mixture of expensive alcohol and the girl nine floors below, and he put his hands in the air and grinned.

When they were satisfied that the fat man was not carrying any apparatus that could either blow holes in their boss, or cut bits off him, they allowed him to pass into the next room, in which sat the most sexy girl in the world. She wore a charcoal-grey, knitted dress, that appeared to have been made at a time when there was a severe, international wool-shortage. What Slan saw was the almost naked body of a girl, decorated with the odd grey strand of wool; the only item of clothing that actually covered any of her body was the Woolmark label.

Slan was swept in a trance through polished-wood double doors into Sleder's office. Now, he thought, he was beginning to understand why men fought and cheated and stole and killed to get to the top; because if this was what awaited them, then to hell with the wrath of God. There was nothing any devil could come up with in the hereafter that could possibly make one regret having lived a life like this.

The office was enormous, with a staggering view through the blinds – which took the glare but not the warmth from the streaming November sun – down towards the Empire State Building, the Chrysler Building, and a panorama of other high-rise buildings. Up here was an intimate little village in the sky. One looked out at other high-rises as equals, instead of up at them as towering dominating monsters. It was a view that could make any man happy to come to work. The office was the size of a football pitch, and Sleder's desk the size of a tennis court. Sleder sat behind it, in total command of it, wearing a white sports jumper and a cream open-necked shirt. The desk was almost bare, with just an intercom, dictating machine and, surprisingly thought Slan, just one telephone.

Sleder extended a hand, and Slan marched over. As he got near, Sleder stood up. Slan didn't even attempt to reach across the desk, but walked round the side and shook the outstretched hand.

'It's very good to see you again,' said Sleder in an accent that made even the toughest of the Anglo-Saxon female breed go weak at the knees. 'I trust you had a good journey?'

'Terrific!' said Slan. 'I'd travel Sleder any time!'

They both laughed, then Slan stiffened. He didn't know why Sleder wanted to see him, but he knew why he wanted to see Sleder. He'd drunk too much and he had let his guard drop; he'd better pull himself together now – fast.

'Will you have a glass of coffee, or would you prefer something stronger?'

'Coffee will be fine, thank you.'

Sleder pushed a cigar box at him. 'Havana?'

Slan shook his head.

Sleder pushed an onyx cigarette box. 'Cigarette?'

'I gave up.'

'Did you? So did I. I don't find it easy, though, do you?'

'It takes a while. Five years now, I haven't touched one.'

'That's good. Did you smoke many?'

'Two packs a day.'

'It's good you gave it up; that's too many, much too many.'

Slan was beginning to wonder whether Sleder had summoned him all the way here merely for a discussion about giving up smoking.

'I agree,' he said. He wanted to say, 'Who the hell was responsible for sending me those photographs?' Instead he said, 'How many did you smoke?'

'About one pack. But that was too many also.' Sleder smiled – a big, warm smile.

The girl with the outfit that could have bankrupted the International Wool Secretariat delivered coffee and reduced Slan to a jellied mass. When she had departed and his senses began to return to him, he decided he was going to recommend to American Fossilized that they trade in their coffee-vending machine for one like her. He wondered whether Sleder regarded her merely as an ornament, or whether his interests in her extended to extra-curricular activities.

'Did you enjoy your trip with us on *Chanson II*?' asked Sleder.

The girl came in again and placed a dispenser of saccharin tablets on the coffee tray. Slan longingly watched her firm buttocks and taut thighs rub past each other as she walked out of the room with a careless stride.

'I had one hell of a time. A real ball! Any time you're short of a crew member, let me know!' Slan laughed, but this time Sleder didn't laugh; he merely smiled politely.

'You looked as if you were enjoying yourself. I thought the photographs were great fun – you got them all right?'

Slan snapped out of his fantasies. 'I got them all right. Why the hell did you send them?'

'Why?' Sleder looked hurt. For a moment, Slan felt guilty that he had offended him. 'I thought everyone who goes on holiday likes to have their . . . holiday snaps – a little souvenir, memento, something to look back at when you are old and grey and you can't get your pecker up any more.' Sleder grinned.

Slan grinned too, but it was a nervous grin. Something in Sleder's tone of voice wasn't quite right. 'But let us hope there are – how is the expression – many more summers before the swan dies!'

Slan looked curiously at him.

'It's an expression I took from a book by an English writer – Huxley – about a rich man, a very rich man who does not want to grow old, he wants to find the key to eternal life. The book is called *After Many a Summer Dies the Swan*.'

Slan looked blank. He only understood three things in life: eating, sex and the manufacture of fuels. Literature had always been beyond him; he never even read the words in girlie magazines.

'You are probably wondering why I asked you to come and see me?'

Slan nodded.

'Well, it is because I consider you a friend – a personal friend, a good personal friend, a friend with whom I share my summer holiday – that I'm asking you this, if the answer is no, then just tell me, and we won't say any more. I need a favour – a very small favour.'

Slan now had a feeling that his reaction when the photographs landed on his desk had been the right one, a feeling that he had bolstered when Sleder's personal assistant had telephoned, and a feeling that was being further bolstered now. He had a feeling that today was pay-day and it was he who was going to be writing out the cheques. 'What – er – what sort of favour?'

'A very small one, Harry. Well, one that is small to you, but will mean much to me.'

Slan stared Sleder in the eye.

'My company is having problems at the moment, big problems. The whole world economy – it is not good. I have a large company – turnover last year is eleven hundred million dollars – and it is a private company – I own it all. But now there are big problems: we manufacture textiles – fabrics for curtains, for dresses, for seat covers – but the world textile trade is in severe recession. We are producing oil and exploring for more, but the exploration is costing more than the profits we are making from the production. We are producing explosives, but there is a world surplus, and there are many legal restrictions, and many countries are cutting back on their spending on defence. We are farming, but the profits in food at the moment are slim. We produce component parts for railway trains, but the railways are in decline.

'You see, this business was founded by my grandfather, and was rooted in the areas that were growth areas in his lifetime; they were still growth areas in my father's lifetime; but now, for me, times are changed. I must find new areas. And we have moved into one new area where there is real potential for growth: the manufacture of nuclear fuels.'

Slan nodded. 'You want me to give you information?'

'No. I don't need information; that I have – all I want. What I need are customers; I need orders! I need orders for AtomSled! This is the name of my new company: AtomSled. Punchy, eh? It has balls, don't you think?'

Slan nodded. If Sleder thought it had balls, then it had balls.

'Gebruder Sleder has a good reputation throughout the world. Everyone knows that Gebruder Sleder delivers on time, and it delivers what has been ordered! Because of our reputation for reliability, we have been granted licences to produce nuclear fuel for power stations in eleven countries, including the United States; but we cannot seem to break through and get the big meaty orders that we need.'

'I thought you were going to buy American Fossilized. It was widely rumoured – still is. We've got plenty of orders; if you buy the company, you'll get them all!'

'Ha! I would love to, but I cannot afford it. Your turnover

is five thousand million dollars, with a profit last year of seven hundred million. I do not have the kind of money that would buy a company of that size. I know there has been speculation in the financial press, and I have not discouraged such rumours – they are good for prestige – but the press do not know the size of my business, nor the money I have. My company is spread across the world; there are holding companies in Liechtenstein, Switzerland, Panama, and other, very private places. The press can only guess at the size of my business and the extent of my personal wealth, and, as is usually the case when the press don't know something, they err on the large side. Big sums of money, big deals – that sells newspapers.'

The wind had suddenly gone from Slan's sails. He had been assuming all along that Sleder was going to buy the company, which was why Sleder was interested in him, probably saw in him the company's future president, and now this was not the case, not the case at all. 'What – er – what are you wanting me to do?'

'Harry, I want you to buy our fuel rods and our fuel assemblies.'

'You're joking. How can I do that? We don't buy either rods or complete assemblies from other companies. We make them ourselves. That's our business.'

'I know this. You are the exclusive manufacturer of fuel for fifteen power stations in the United States, and for two in Canada. In addition, you supply many other power stations with some of their requirements. American Fossilized manufactures twenty-three per cent of all the nuclear fuel used on the North American continent. If you were to stop manufacturing overnight, that would leave a very big gap in the market . . .'

Slan's mouth dropped open.

'. . . and we would have the stocks ready to fill in right away.'

'What do you mean?' Slan's face had turned a deep shade of ivory.

'Harry, I want you to sabotage your plant.'

'You're mad.'

Sleder grinned. 'No, I am not mad. It's simple. You fix for an accident to happen in the plant – you know there are plenty of ways an accident can happen, you are the expert in these things, not I. You make it a good accident, and cause a radiation leak, contaminating your plant. Obviously, the plant has to be shut down right away. It cannot continue with production until the contamination has been cleared up, and this will be a long process. Your company has two options: either you tell the United States Nuclear Regulatory Commission what has happened, in which case they will close you down – for a minimum of many months, until they have investigated and until you have cleaned up – and your customers will have to look for other suppliers. Naturally, they will come to us. Or, you keep quiet, you do not tell the NRC anything has happened. Keep the whole thing under wraps, quietly get on and clear up, and quietly buy the fuel from us to supply to your customers.'

'And then you blow the gaff when it suits you?'

Sleder smiled. 'Maybe, maybe not. It would depend on how trade goes.'

Slan shook his head. 'There's no way,' he said, 'no way under the sun. I like my company, and I like my job, and I'm not going to do that. No way. It's totally immoral; a lot of people could get hurt, maybe killed – and they're my friends. You picked the wrong guy; count me out.'

'No,' said Sleder, 'I will not count you out.'

A little colour had returned to Harry Slan's face; it now drained out again. 'What do you mean?'

'If you do not agree, I shall arrange for a considerably more comprehensive set of holiday photographs than I sent to you to be mailed to your wife. They are at the present moment sitting in a sealed envelope, addressed to Mrs Myrtle Slan, at the address I have written on this piece of paper – your correct home address, I believe? They will be sent in the noon post unless I ring down to stop them.'

Slan glared at him, then looked down at his watch. It was five to twelve. 'You said when I arrived that if I didn't want to help you, then I didn't have to.'

Sleder leaned even further forward; his blue eyes turned to a menacing shade of grey, but his lips broke into a warm, cheerful smile. 'I lied.'

Slan didn't speak for well over a minute. He was searching desperately for some alternative, and he knew his search was a waste of time, because there was no alternative. Sleder had him hook, line and sinker, and Sleder knew it. It was over the third glass of vintage Remy Martin, that Slan had quietly confided to his host, after a magnificent dinner on *Chanson II*, that he had never before been unfaithful to his wife – not because he didn't lust after other women, but because of his terror of her. It all came flooding back now, and it was too late to start cursing. He shrugged his shoulders. 'I'll do it.'

Sleder's smile turned to a big grin. 'Thank you, Harry, that's what friends are for.'

'Don't give me any more of that "friends" crap.'

Sleder sounded hurt again. 'It's not crap, Harry. I can't afford to do without this business. American Fossilized Corporation can. No one's going to suffer. So the shares might dip a little, if the news gets out, but this plant of yours in Adamsville, it is only a part of the whole business; it would not affect it too dramatically. And besides, the news isn't going to get out. So it will cost your company a little more to buy the fuel than to make it, but I will be fair with my prices; I am going to give your company good prices.'

'What about the danger to my men?'

'That, I'm afraid, is your problem. I am sure you can find a time when no one is around – I don't know when: the middle of the night, or a Saturday – you will have to choose.'

'And when do you want me to do this?'

'Very soon. Before the end of November.'

'That gives me less than three weeks.'

'So how long does it take you to throw a few switches and undo a couple of bolts?'

'I think you are as aware as I am that it will not be as simple as that. There are elaborate safety systems at all stages. I'm going to have to give it very careful thought.'

'Don't look so gloomy, Harry. Cheer up, I am full of confidence in you! By the way,' he lied, 'Eva sends her love. She said, if you ever get to Germany, give her a call.' Sleder was a maestro.

'Really?' said Slan.

'Yes. I think she's pretty hooked on you – it's too bad you have a wife when there are so many nice girls around in the world.'

'You have some pretty good-looking ones in here.'

'Yeah, not bad, eh? New York is an okay place for the not bad-looking girls.' Sleder grinned.

'You're right. That receptionist you've got – she's really something.'

'Yeah, she's quite something.' Sleder waved his hand in an expansive gesture. 'Why don't you ask her out tonight –

have a bit of fun in New York before you go back to your wife?'

'I can't – it's her birthday today.'

'So? She'll have another one next year.'

'But I—'

Sleder silenced him with a wave of his hand, and pressed the intercom. 'Barbara, darling, what are you doing this evening?'

'Well, I – er, I – do have a date, Mr Sleder.'

'An important one?'

'Well, I guess not.'

'Perhaps you could cancel it? My good friend Mr Slan is stopping over in New York tonight and he doesn't know his way around the city too well. It would be a good idea for him to have a pretty girl to keep him out of trouble, don't you think?'

She didn't think it was a good idea at all, in fact she thought it was a rotten idea; but her contract stated that unless she'd given two weeks' prior notice of any date, she could be requested to cancel it.

'Why don't you book a table for two,' continued Sleder, 'somewhere nice and romantic. I would join you, but I have a meeting that I'm afraid is going to continue until very late.'

'Yes, Mr Sleder.'

The meeting that was going to continue very late came in and asked if anyone would like more coffee, then removed the dirty cups and herself from Slan's transfixed gaze.

'Er – I really do have to get back to Adamsville tonight. My wife – she'll—'

'There is no schedule airline that can get you back today. The earliest is tomorrow morning. If my aeroplane were to break down, the earliest you could be back home would be midday tomorrow.'

'But your jet hasn't broken down,' said Slan.

Sleder grinned. 'If I tell you I've just heard that it has, does that clear your conscience?'

'You've already shown me what a high regard you have for the truth.'

'Well, it has broken down. So, to make up for everything, there's a limousine and driver at your disposal to take you around New York, anywhere you'd like to go. My secretary will give you some expenses money, and a bit over to buy your wife a nice little something. Come back about half five and collect Barbara. And you don't have to worry about a hotel – we have a hospitality apartment here that I am sure you will find more than adequate. You'll get a good night's sleep – if you want it – but who needs sleep when you're in New York, eh Harry?'

'Sure, who the hell does!' grinned Slan, beginning to feel a bit better.

'I'll call you in three weeks, and you can tell me whether you are going to start buying the fuel direct, or whether I should start contacting your customers. Have a nice day!'

The grin fell from Slan's face, but before he had time to ask any more questions, Sleder had shaken his hand, steered him through the double doors into the anteroom, where the girl in the Woolmark label had placed an envelope containing one thousand dollars in cash into his hand, and steered him into the outer room; the security guards had guided him into the elevator, which deposited him at the sixty-fourth floor reception area.

He walked up to the receptionist. 'Call for you at five thirty, Barbara?'

'Can hardly wait, Harry,' she beamed warmly, lying through her glistening teeth and Peach-Blossom Glow Max Factor lipstick.

Slan took the lift down to the ground floor. He was looking forward to tonight; he hadn't much to look forward to beyond that.

15

After Gelignite hung up on me, I despatched the least incompetent of my fresh-faced minions to go and watch Whalley for me, and then crashed out for a couple of hours. I woke up at eight feeling considerably worse than when I had lain down, made myself three cups of thick black coffee in a row, then drove in to Portico. I drove past the entrance of all three ramps to see if anyone was keeping watch, and it didn't seem that anyone was.

I first made a couple of calls. The navy Marina of the night before hadn't yielded any clues, and the address on the licence the driver had given Hertz was false. The contact with the Capri had got away without being spotted. It was a good start.

I switched on the tape recorder and played the tape of Whalley and his contact several times. After an hour and a half, I was satisfied I had picked up all that was of interest: the name Wojara, which at the moment meant nothing; and the name Ben Tsenong, which also meant nothing; the contact's voice, which I had heard before, meant something, although right now, I didn't know what. He had driven one hundred miles; that was interesting, but there are one hell of a lot of places within a one-hundred-mile radius of Worcester. The contact had said 'niggers'; that was very interesting. Up until now, we had only encountered Arabs; Arabs weren't blacks. Whalley talked about gearing for a specific day, what did he mean by that? 4 January or the first day after that on which there is a westerly wind. Wind;

Fifeshire had talked about wind – wind spread radiation. Westerlies were the prevailing winds over the British Isles. 4 January; I tried to figure out the significance of that date; it was a Monday. New Year's Day was on the Friday. I went down to the library, one floor below, and looked up religious holidays; there were none on 4 January. There was no event scheduled for 4 January in any publication at all. I turned my attention to the wind, and pulled out the massive *Times* atlas of the world, and furrowed through until I came to the world wind-flow charts. The January chart showed the westerly winds sweeping across the Atlantic, across Spain, France and the British Isles, and then on, up towards the Arctic. In the months following January, the charts showed the same wind direction across the Atlantic, but after crossing Northern Europe, instead of curving up towards the Arctic, the winds curved down and across Russia. I thought about it for some moments; if nuclear power stations in England were going to be blown up and Fifeshire was right with his figures that fall-out could be damaging two thousand miles downwind, if the Russians wanted to be sure of not being swept by winds that had crossed England, then the safest month for them would be January.

It could well be that there was a completely different and much better explanation for the significance of 4 January, but I had to start trying to put the pieces somewhere. I went back up to my tiny office – cubicle would be a more accurate definition. The Security Services' answer to defence-budget cuts was to reduce the amount of space its staff occupied. If they cut the size of my office much further, it was going to require a shoe-horn to get me in and out. Part of the idea was, of course, to discourage us from spending too much time indoors on our backsides; it was very effective.

I telephoned the bursar's office at Balliol College, Oxford.

The woman who answered was polite and helpful. I told her I was from *The Times*, preparing an article for the next *Educational Supplement*, on overseas students at Britain's universities, and asked her what she could tell me about Ben Tsenong. She confirmed that a Ben Tsenong was registered. He was studying nuclear physics, in his third year; he came from Namibia, and was on a United Nations scholarship. She suggested that if I wanted more information, I should write to him.

Not having any great conviction that becoming a pen pal with Tsenong would provide me with the sort of information I was after, I decided to go and pay his room a visit. Two hours later, I was in my Jag, negotiating the double hazard of driving rain and a thick wadge of cyclists pedalling with their eyes shut against it. Oxford didn't look its best in the November rain; it wasn't the sort of day for whipping out the Instamatic and snapping the sights. The windscreen had decided it was going to fog up and stay fogged up, and no amount of persuasion from either the de-mister or a duster could make it change its mind.

There was a parking bay in the centre of the street past the Sheldonian Theatre, and I pulled in there. I shoved three coins in the parking ticket dispenser and lost them all. I banged the machine with my fist, then walked across to Balliol and into the porter's lodge. A list of students was pinned up on the wall; Tsenong's name and room number was on it, and I was relieved that he was staying in college, and I didn't have to go traipsing around Oxford looking for his lodgings.

On the wall behind the porter's desk was a plaque which read: *Ezra Hancock d. 1911 A better friend no man had.* I hoped the same applied to his replacement. 'Can you tell me where 11/7 is, please?'

PETER JAMES

Ezra Hancock's replacement turned out to be a chip off the old block. I got the directions to Tsenong's room, and I got the names of all his immediate neighbours. Other than knowing he was black, the porter couldn't give me much information about Tsenong. I thanked him and went out. I stopped in the shelter of the arch outside the lodge door, checked to make sure no one was looking, then pulled a cap from my pocket and pulled it over my head; I also put on a large pair of dark glasses, pulled my coat collar right up, then took a scarf from my pocket and wrapped it around my neck several times. It would have taken someone with X-ray eyes to know it was me inside that lot.

I walked through the arch, round the edge of the oval lawn of the Front Quad, with its grass that would make the surface of the snooker table look like a derelict golf course, through the Old Balliol gates and across the Garden Quad. I went in the entrance to staircase eleven, and climbed the steps. Number seven was on the second floor. I knocked on the door. A rather strained voice said, 'Come in,' and I cursed. I had hoped no one would be in. I pushed the door open, and saw a thin black youth seated at a desk by the window. His face could have been good-looking but for a pallor of tiredness and a scowl that made thick lines across it. He looked over his shoulder at me and I saw hatred in his eyes. It wasn't hatred of me in particular. The hatred in those eyes had been there a long time before I knocked on the door.

'James Gilbert?' I said.

'No – the floor below.'

'The floor below? That's where I was – they said he was on this floor.'

'Well, he isn't; he's right below me.'

'Ah – you must be Mr Kershaw?'

170

'No. My name is Tsenong. Kershaw is further down the corridor.'

'I thought that porter was a bit dim. Sorry to have bothered you.'

Tsenong turned back to his studies without replying. I closed the door. Right. Now I knew what he looked like. The next step was to wait until he went out. I walked back across the Quad and into the shelter of the archway. The porter had told me there were only two exits from Tsenong's room – either the door or the fire escape. Both would bring him out into the Quad, and from the shelter of the arch I had a clear view. I removed my cap, glasses and scarf, and turned my coat inside out; it was reversible, and now showed black on the outside instead of white. If Tsenong walked right past me, he would have no reason to recognize me. I had a feeling I was in for a long wait, because he had looked settled into his books. I looked idly out at the teeming rain, and thought about the events of the day.

After leaving Portico, by a different exit from the one I had used the previous night, I spotted a shiny green Ford Escort slide out into the traffic. There was only a driver in the car; no one else. I turned down to the Mall, around Buckingham Palace and up towards Hyde Park Corner. The Escort sat well back. More for amusement than anything else, I turned from Hyde Park Corner into St George's Street and drove into Belgrave Square, where I suddenly pulled over sharply to the left to a florist stand. The Escort was caught completely on the hop. I left him to circle several times around Belgrave Square, while I made a slow and ponderous attempt to decide which bunch to buy for my sick aunt in Maidenhead, before telling the not very amused vendor that I had just remembered she was allergic to flowers, and then drove off.

I decided I would take the Escort for a drive down Walton

Street. Walton Street is a smart, narrow street, lined with restaurants, art galleries, and precious little shops staffed by horsey ladies who talk to each other as if they are shouting from distant lavatory seats.

The doyen of the Walton Street restaurants is Walton's, which once had the dubious distinction of being blown up by the IRA. In front of this restaurant, the road hooks sharply to the right and comes to a traffic light. It is rare to find an occasion, day or night, when there isn't a bottleneck in Walton Street and today, fortunately, was no exception. I ground to a halt in the jam, about fifty yards back from Walton's, with the Escort four cars behind me. I pulled the handbrake on, then, ducking my head, I slid across and climbed out the passenger door.

Crouched right down, and ignoring the curious gaze of the driver in the van behind me, I crept down the side of the van, and down the side of the two cars behind it. As I reached the Escort, out of the driver's line of vision, with one hand I unholstered my Beretta from an inside pocket – clicking off the safety catch in the process – and with the other hand I opened the Escort's door.

'Good morning,' I said, climbing in.

He looked at me, at the gun, and at me again. It was either the gun or me that he didn't like the look of, but I couldn't immediately tell which. He was a youngster, no more than twenty, in a cheap brown suit, nylon shirt with broad stripes, and a vulgar blue tie with red blobs and yellow zig-zags. He had a thin layer of hair on his upper lip, where he thought he was growing a moustache, and a comb and a short ruler sticking out of his breast pocket. His eyes were open wide, and getting wider; his initial expression of dislike was fast turning to one of fear.

'You've got five seconds to tell me who you're working for

before I shoot your balls off,' I said. 'One . . . two . . .' A car in front started hooting – the traffic in front of the Jaguar had started to move. 'Three . . .'

'I don't know what you mean.' He spoke with an Irish accent.

'Unless you tell me, I am going to pull the trigger in two seconds' time – and I don't really care whether you tell me or not,' I said.

He got the message.

'Four . . .'

'Cleary.'

'Clever boy!'

Another car and the van joined in the hooting.

'Patrick Cleary,' he said.

'And who is Uncle Patrick and how do you come to be working for him?'

He looked at the gun again. It was a particularly large and menacing-looking weapon. The wrong end of a Beretta 93R is not the most comforting sight in the world, and it's not meant to be. It's meant to scare, as much as blast, the living daylights out of people.

'I don't know who he is. I was offered the job by a bloke I met in a pub.'

It seemed to me that the underworld led a pretty cushy life. Its inhabitants appeared to spend all their daytimes – when they weren't on holiday on the Costa Brava – collecting things that had fallen off the backs of trucks, and all their evenings getting offered large sums of money for doing simple jobs for strangers they met in any pub they entered. 'Bullshit. Who is he?'

'I don't know.'

'What was the name of the pub?'

'Ring of Bells, Highgate.'

'Who is he?'

The car behind started hooting as well.

'I don't know, I told you.'

'Who was the bloke you met in the pub?'

'Mick.'

'Describe him.'

'Short guy, ginger hair.'

'Smile, please!'

'You what?'

'I'm taking your photo.' I pointed my watch at him, and pushed a small button above the winder. There was a sharp click and a tiny whirr. A cacophony of hooting began both in front of us and behind us, simultaneously. 'Mick who?'

'I don't know. He didn't say.'

'What did he ask you to do?'

'Said I had to follow you; see where you went.'

'And then what?'

'That's all.'

'How were you going to tell him?'

'He said he would contact me.'

'What's your name?'

'John – McEliney.'

'Where are you from, John?'

'London.'

'Can I see your driving licence?'

He pulled it out; it had his name on it and an address in Kilburn, North London. I photographed it and handed it back. The hooting was getting even worse.

'How long have you been following me, John?'

'This is the first time – just now.'

'How many days have you waited?'

'I just started today. He said you didn't show for long periods sometimes.'

'Who did?'

'Mick.'

'Mick who?'

'I told you, I don't know.'

I pulled out my notebook, and from the back I tugged a plastic strip; a sheet of plastic came out. 'Put your hands on that,' I said. He did so. 'Now push hard.' He was shaking like a leaf. I took his fingerprints. 'Now your thumb . . . good boy.'

I put the plastic back in the notebook and put it in my pocket.

'Was there anything else you wanted to see me about, John?'

He looked at me oddly, then shook his head.

'Good, then I'll be off.' I took hold of his ignition keys, switched off the ignition, then removed them, pocketing them as I left the car.

The van driver in front had gone puce. He leaned his head out of the window and recited a very inadequate list of sexual organs and what can be done with them. He finished just as I shut my car door. 'If that's all you know,' I said, 'you can't have a very interesting sex life.'

He could certainly run fast. Luckily the light was green, and I accelerated through it, leaving him to shake his fist impotently. I forgot him, and concentrated on McEliney.

I reckoned that McEliney had been telling the truth. He spoke with an Irish accent; Kilburn was an Irish colony in London. It was becoming pretty clear it wasn't only Arabs and Russians and blacks that were involved in this little bit of no good; it was also the IRA. After the failure of the Arab to kill me, they had probably been instructed to watch me and see if they could figure out anything from my movements. The first time I had spotted them had been last night, in the blue Marina, and then again this morning. I wondered if they had been following me last week, and decided they hadn't. I would have noticed them. No, the reason they hadn't followed me last week was almost certainly because they hadn't been able to find me. They had probably presumed I would be in my office at Portico, and had been keeping watch on that. They wouldn't have had any reason to know I was at the Atomic Energy Authority; if they had known, they would have been tailing me from there. That was a big relief. If they had tumbled me at the AEA, I would have been blown; the whole damn thing would have been blown. Last night was the first time I had been in to Carlton House Terrace since my somewhat bumpy taxi-ride. It was also the first time a tail had picked me up. It made sense, and I felt a bit better; they had no idea what we were up to.

Tsenong came through the doorway sooner than I had expected. He wore a yellow plastic anorak, and carried a barrel-shaped red and white nylon hold-all, which he was probably using as a satchel. He ran across the exposed Quad, and went out through the Back Gate into Magdalen Street, and disappeared from view. I would have liked to follow him to see where he was going and get some idea how long that would give me, but I was worried that I would waste valuable time if I did so, so I went straight up to his room.

It had an old-fashioned lock which was dead easy to pick. I locked it again from the inside and jammed the lock with a piece of metal so that if he did come back suddenly, he wouldn't be able to get in.

The room was a standard Oxford undergraduate room. It was very small, which indicated that Tsenong did not have much private means. There was an old green filing cabinet, a shelf full of books, a large battered armchair, a wooden chair at a small modern desk, a coffee table, an elderly wardrobe, a lumpy bed and a single-bar electric heater. The window overlooked Magdalen Street, and didn't do much of a job of keeping out the traffic noise.

What made this room different from the rooms of most undergraduates was a complete lack of personal touches. There were no photographs, pictures, decorative objects, nothing, except piles upon piles of books on the subjects of nuclear physics and nuclear energy.

I began with his desk. In the first drawer was an assortment of bills, an invitation to an Oxford Union debate on nuclear power, and a packet of Fisherman's throat lozenges. In the second drawer, on their own, were two telegrams. Both bore the same date: 10 August. One was from Otjosundu, Namibia; it said simply: *Dadda pass away yesterday morning. Stop. He is more peaceful now. Stop. Love you son. Stop. Mama.* The second was from Marzuc, Libya; it said: *All has been agreed. Stop. Will be in touch. Stop. Lukas.*

Most of the other drawers were filled with technical notes and papers. I scanned sheets at random, but there didn't seem to be much of interest. It looked mostly like university work, but I couldn't be sure as most of it was highly technical and way above my head. I photographed the sheets I pulled out, for the boffins at CCI to decide whether there was anything Tsenong was working on that he had no business to be working on.

I took each book off the shelf in turn, held it by the cover and shook it. Nothing fell out of any of them. I felt underneath the furniture, and went systematically through the entire list of possible hiding places: under the mattress, loose floorboards, cracks in the wall, everywhere – and nothing further turned up. Then I tried the most obvious place in the room: the filing cabinet. Inside the first drawer was a map of the world, with every nuclear power station clearly marked. I had no doubt that the map was an item he required for his studies, but I wondered for what particular reason someone had shaded in red pencil the whole of Britain, France, Spain, Canada and the United States of America. In addition, there was a flow of arrows around the world, and the flow struck me as looking not a bit unlike the flow of the January wind that I had studied earlier that morning. After the arrows passed through the shaded countries, they assumed the colour of the shading for some considerable distance. I photographed the map and replaced it. I went through the rest of the files, took a number of photographs, but did not come across anything else that struck me as being of particular interest.

I unlocked the door, listening carefully for any footsteps. This was always the moment I hated the most. I took a deep breath and marched out. The corridor was empty.

I got myself out of the building, out of the Quadrangle, out of the parking bay and out of Oxford. So far it had been a fruitful, if a trifle long, day – two hours' sleep was not my body's idea of a good night's kip; it wasn't my brain's idea either. The rain battered down, the wipers continued their mournful clumping, the de-mister fought with the damp for domination of the windscreen. It was three in the afternoon and growing very dark. I was pleased with my progress.

There was the sound of a horn blaring. It continued blaring, getting louder. I opened my eyes. 'Christ!' I swung the steering wheel hard to the left, and thirty-five tons of articulated Mercedes lorry thundered over the fourteen and a half feet of tarmac I had vacated about one thousandth of a second earlier. Shaking from the shock, and cursing myself for allowing myself to be so stupid as to fall asleep at the wheel, I slowed right down, pulled into a lay-by, slouched down in my seat, and slept for an hour and a quarter.

*

The rain had stopped by the time I drove into the mews. It was nearly eight o'clock. I turned the corner, swinging out wide in order to position myself for the garage, and missed a large dark shape in the middle of the mews by a good quarter of an inch. I didn't need to take a second look at the dark shape to know it was Gelignite's Golf. All of a sudden, I felt one whole lot better. Behind the thick curtains, I could see lights were on in the house. I put the Jag in the garage and opened the front door.

There was a smell of cooking. I went into the kitchen. Gelignite didn't look up. 'You're a shit, Max Flynn, you know that? You're a shit.'

'So I've heard,' I said wearily.

'What do you mean, you've heard?'

'If you think you're the first person on earth to discover that I am a shit, then you're badly mistaken. You're about seventy-five girls too late.'

Le Creuset were not particularly concerned with aerodynamics when they designed their casserole dish range. If they had been, the massive one Gelignite flung at me would have probably killed me. Fortunately, its full payload of couscous did not improve its airborne stability, and it crashed into the wall a good arm's length from my right ear. We both stood glaring at each other. A full minute passed before Gelignite broke the silence. 'Christ,' she said. 'You look awful.'

'I feel it.'

'Shall I fix you a drink?'

I nodded. 'I didn't think I'd be seeing you again.'

'You're lucky,' she said. 'I had to get my toothbrush.' Somewhere beneath her crazy hair, I thought I detected the merest trace of a smile.

16

After Harry Slan left Deke Sleder's office, the German Industrialist sat in silence for a long time thinking. He was not a happy man at that moment, and he did not like doing what he had just done. However, he liked being rich and he liked being powerful, and he was intelligent enough to understand that a family's empire does not always survive and prosper through three generations by putting ethics at the top of its list of priorities.

The man who had come to see him at his headquarters in Hamburg only a few months before hadn't exactly had ethics at the top of his list of priorities either. He had introduced himself to Sleder's personal assistant as one Walther Hauptmertz, stating that he had a business proposition that he wished to put to Herr Sleder in person; no one else in the organization would do. Intrigued, Sleder had granted him an appointment.

Hauptmertz was a stocky man, with a twinkle in his eye, and a face that was full of fun. He strode into Sleder's office in a fashionable herring-bone suit, that flattered his figure, but did not have the preciseness of fit, nor of detail, that a personally tailored suit would have done. The back of the jacket rose up a little too high behind his neck; one of Hauptmertz's shoulders was a fraction higher than the other, but the jacket did not compensate for this; there were buttons on the cuffs, but no buttonholes, not even fake ones; the jacket had a striped pattern, but the stripes did not match up at the shoulder seams, nor at the pockets. It was clearly an off-the-peg suit, and, judging from the good cloth from which it was made, had been bought from an expensive boutique. His narrow Cardin tie, and even narrower Etienne Aigner executive briefcase were further confirmation that he probably wasn't on the poverty line. He struck Sleder as looking like a cross between an international arms dealer and a marketing manager for a French cosmetics house.

They shook hands and sat down. The size of this office made Sleder's New York office look like a cupboard in comparison, but Hauptmertz did not show any sign of being impressed. He placed his briefcase on Sleder's desk, popped it open, but didn't remove anything, and leaned forward.

'Herr Sleder,' he said with a big smile, taking what appeared to be a gold Dunhill lighter from his pocket. 'Have you ever before seen one of these?' He held it up for inspection.

'I think so – it's a cigarette lighter, is it not?' Sleder wondered if the man was weak in the head.

'No. It looks like a cigarette lighter, Herr Sleder.' The man pulled hard and it snapped into two halves, and for a full second there was a high-pitched shrieking sound, which then subsided slightly. He laid the two halves on the desk top, and moved them around. As they moved, the shrieking got alternatively louder and then quieter. Hauptmertz finally moved them into a position that stopped the shrieking altogether. 'This is actually the very latest in anti-bugging equipment. No microphone, of any type, however close or powerful, can pick up one intelligible word with this device in operation. Both halves are transmitters and receivers; they are transmitting now on a new frequency – a frequency that you and I cannot hear. This frequency disintegrates electric sound waves, but does not affect ordinary human speech and hearing.' He smiled.

'Very clever,' said Sleder, 'provided, of course, it works. It could be most interesting . . . most interesting. And you are looking to sell this invention, are you?'

'Oh no, Herr Sleder, I just wanted to tell you about it in case you had decided to record our conversation – to let you know that it would be a waste of time.'

Sleder eyed him strangely.

'You see, Herr Sleder, what I am about to tell you is confidential. It would be in the interests of neither of us for this conversation to get beyond the walls of this room. That is my reason for putting this device on your desk.' The twinkle, for a moment, went from his eyes, like the sun on a rich blue sea suddenly going behind a cloud, leaving dark grey water and sinister white horses; then it bounced back again, and he smiled once more.

'I see,' said Sleder, not seeing very much at all. 'So what is your secret, my friend, that is so great I am the only person on earth who may share it with you?'

Hauptmertz stared him straight in the eye. 'I am going to destroy your business and personally bankrupt you,' he said.

Sleder put his hand out, flipped open the lid of his cigarette box, without offering the box to Hauptmertz, lit the cigarette with a table lighter on his desk, inhaled deeply, then blew the smoke out and leaned forward. 'And for your next trick after that?'

'I am not a magician, Herr Sleder, and I am not playing tricks.'

Sleder held the cigarette out in front of him, but did not draw any more smoke from it. 'That's a pity; I have a goddaughter, and I am sure she would have liked a white rabbit for her birthday.'

Hauptmertz didn't smile. Sleder wondered whether to push the button that would bring the two guards charging in with their guns, or whether to hear this man out a bit further. The man made his decision for him.

'Gebruder Sleder,' said Hauptmertz, 'owns, among its major assets, 842,000 acres of wheat ranch-land in Manitoba, Canada, Oregon in the United States, and Queensland, Australia. The revenues from this make up nine per cent of your company's total revenues.

'You own SledTex of Lecco, Italy, which is now among the world's five largest producers of sportswear textiles, making fabrics for everything from ski anoraks to footballers' shorts to scuba-divers' wet-suits to asbestos suits for motor racing drivers; SledTinta of Como, Italy, one of the world's largest textile printing plants; Sleder-Ykeng-Lee of Hong Kong, which is one of Hong Kong's largest manufacturers of jeans, and which now has a twenty-year contract to build factories and manufacture jeans inside the People's Republic of China. Your textile interests account for twelve per cent of your company's total revenues.

'Your interests in oil are spread fairly widely. You own a small field in the North Sea, but the drilling so far has been inconclusive, although you have hyped up the reports, and three major companies are interested in purchasing it at the present time. You have minor oil interests in Saskatchewan, Kenya and the North Sea, but your major oil holdings are in El Salvador, where you have made seven important strikes, and invested, if I may be permitted to say so, more than is wise, perhaps, for such an unstable country.'

Sleder continued to stare at Hauptmertz. He hadn't

moved an inch, and the ash was half an inch long on the end of his cigarette.

'Revenues from your oil fields in El Salvador account for twenty-three per cent of your company's total revenues.'

Sleder knocked the ash off the end of his cigarette, but did not lift the cigarette up to his mouth. So far everything Hauptmertz had said was completely accurate; and the only people in the world who knew the precise figures of the Gebruder Sleder empire were Sleder and his accountants. Someone had been giving Hauptmertz a lot of help with his homework.

Hauptmertz continued. 'You are producing high explosives under a licence from the Federal German Government which specifies that these explosives are for industrial purposes, such as mining, only. In fact, only ten per cent of the explosives you manufacture are sold for industrial purposes. Under the banner of your company, and behind the façade of your industrial explosives business, you have a sizeable munitions empire manufacturing, and going to great lengths to sell, hand grenades, shells, mortars, land-mines – and you don't discriminate over your clientele, do you? Terrorists are among your best customers. It is all done under a perfectly innocent-looking front, and the authorities are kept very happy by the substantial annual payments, both in cash and in beautiful girls, that you make to them. This munitions empire accounts for twenty-six per cent of your revenues.'

Sleder stubbed out his cigarette. He was starting to feel uncomfortable, and he wasn't used to feeling uncomfortable.

'Gebruder Sleder,' said Hauptmertz, 'manufactures wheels, ball bearings, brake parts and axles for railway loco-motives and carriages; you supply Germany, France, Italy,

Switzerland, Britain, Spain, Canada and the United States with these parts. This side of your business accounts for twenty-eight per cent of your company's total revenues.

'The remaining two per cent comes from a new development. Your company AtomSled has been set up with a massive capital investment – all provided by yourself – to cash in on the world boom in nuclear energy. AtomSled has been set up to manufacture the fuel rods and bundles for nuclear power stations. The amount of plant you have constructed, if worked at capacity, would contribute twenty-five per cent of your company's total revenues; all it contributes at the present time is two per cent. You have so far been unable to obtain sufficient contracts. Your factory workers are on short time, yet even so you are building up a massive stock-pile of fuel, which you cannot be sure you are going to be able to sell. The financial drain caused by this is serious, but at the moment not desperate.' Hauptmertz and Sleder stared for some moments at each other.

'Thank you,' said Sleder, 'for giving me such an elaborate account of my business; I would be curious to know your sources.'

'Yes,' said Hauptmertz, 'I have no doubt you would.'

'I would also like to know who you are, for whom you are working and why you are telling me all this?'

'My name is Carpov, Dimitri Carpov. I work for a small company in the Soviet Union which you may have heard of: it is called the *Komitet Gosudarstvennoi Bezopasnasti* – you probably know it better by its initials: the KGB.'

'And my name is James Bond,' said Sleder. 'I work for MI6.'

Carpov shook his head. The twinkle had gone again from his eyes. 'You are joking; I am not.'

'Please continue,' said Sleder.

'Your wheat and textile interests: they account in total for twenty-one per cent of your revenues, which is not a lot, so we shall not for the moment concern ourselves with them. But your oil – which alone accounts for twenty-three per cent – that is interesting. The backbone of your oil interests is in El Salvador, and we have some very good connections there. We can arrange very quickly for your plant to be destroyed, and we can make it impossible for you to put up new plant in its place.

'Your munitions interests, which account for twenty-six per cent of your revenues: I don't think I need to convince you any further that I know a great deal about your business; I know exactly who you are paying off, and how much you are paying; we could expose you in any of a dozen different ways, and wipe out your munitions business within a matter of months.

'Your railway components which contribute twenty-eight per cent of your total revenues: we have massive plant in the Soviet Union making the same types of components; we could go to all your customers and offer to supply them the same articles at a price you could never match. We could wipe out your components business within a year.'

Sleder drummed his fingers on top of his cigarette box. 'And what good will this do you?'

'I'm coming to that now. We have in mind to offer you a deal: you do a small favour for us, and in return we won't destroy you.'

Sleder took out another cigarette, and rolled it around between his fingers.

'We just want you to start supplying fuel rods and bundles to a number of nuclear power stations in the United States, Canada, Spain, France and Britain; that is all.' He sat back.

Sleder put the cigarette down on the desk. 'I don't know if I have missed something that you said, but that is precisely what I am trying to do at the moment. There are several other countries I would like to sell to as well.'

Carpov nodded. 'You didn't miss anything. We are not concerned about countries other than these – what you do there is your own affair – but with these five, we are prepared to give you plenty of assistance.'

'And what do you want out of this? Do you want to supply the uranium?'

'You'll find out what we want, when we are ready to tell you.'

Sleder's brain was churning over. The only possible reason he could think of was that the Russians needed an outlet for surplus uranium; but two years ago his company had approached the Russians to see whether they would be prepared to supply uranium and at what price, just as they had approached all the other uranium-producing countries with the same questions. The Soviet reply had been that they had no surplus uranium to sell. So why, Sleder wondered, had they changed their minds – or had they?

He didn't like Carpov, didn't like him one bit, but there was something in what the man said that made Sleder think. His own approach to the nuclear energy industry had been lethargic so far; it was time he pulled his finger out, and this was just the prompting he needed.

'I cannot see any advantage in not co-operating,' said Sleder.

'I think that sums it up very well,' said the Russian.

The box of *crème de menthe* Turkish Delight slid across the spotless grey desk top, sprinkling bits of icing sugar as it went. Arthur must have had a birthday recently, I decided; he normally carried his Turkish Delight in a paper bag. I took one and pushed the box back.

'They're good,' he said, taking one out of the box and lifting it up towards the cave-like orifice that had suddenly appeared between his thick moustache and even thicker beard. The beard was very uneven, as though every now and then, when the mood took him, he would have a go at trimming it with a pair of scissors, but got bored half-way through. With the jagged, uneven tufts, and the patches of white from the sugar that had fallen off the lump of Turkish Delight, his beard had taken on the appearance of a gorse bush struck by lightning.

Arthur Jephcott was in complete contrast to his office. He wore a thick, dark-green Harris Tweed suit, that, whilst looking as though it had been handed down to him by his father, had actually been made, at very great expense, by an elderly tailor who continued to labour under the 1930s view that suits that looked new were vulgar. Also, as he'd told the cheerful Arthur at the final fitting, he'd made plenty of allowance for Arthur to 'expand'. The man had not lied; in square footage, the outfit was more like a marquee than a suit. Arthur could have doubled in size and still had room for a few friends in there. Under the jacket, he wore a yellow-and-brown checked Viyella shirt, the collar of which had almost entirely frayed away, and appeared to be held together by his bright orange tie.

I thought it odd that his wife could have let him go out like this, but then, I hadn't met her, and maybe she was even stranger. He looked every inch an academic, with alert brown eyes, a tangle of curly hair on his head, and small, soft-looking hands of the type that appear to have spent their days caressing expensive leather-bound pages of print in quiet oak-panelled rooms. In fact his hands spent their days caressing the keys of a computer terminal, and the room was not oak-panelled, but lined with lead and concrete.

Arthur Jephcott was Director of Combined Central Information, an outfit shared by all the organizations that comprised the British Intelligence network. CCI was housed in a massive atom-bomb-proof office complex several hundred feet underneath the Hyde Park underground car park. Jephcott was responsible for an army of 5,000 people in this windowless subterranean town, and for one of the largest computers ever built; it was in fact four massive computers connected together, and the machine was known by the name of Wotan.

Arthur's office was a sterile white, with nothing at all in it except a grey metal desk. Behind his desk, was the keyboard of a terminal into Wotan, and on one side of the desk was a large visual display unit looking much like a television screen. Arthur had no pens, pencils or paper in his office; he never used them. Everything that he wanted to write down, he tapped straight into Wotan.

He finished chewing his piece of Turkish Delight. *Crème de menthe* Turkish Delight was Arthur's one vice in life; he was completely addicted to it. He never smoked, and never drank, but throughout his waking hours he would steadily munch his way through ten to twelve pounds of the stuff a week. Apart from a very sticky handshake, it didn't appear to do him any great harm.

Arthur Jephcott was a librarian, an archivist, a sorter and storer and retriever of facts; he would take facts, pull them apart, then put them back together, five different ways, ten different ways, one hundred different ways, without his face being lined with worries, because he never had to decide which was the right way. He merely presented the options for others to decide; presented the pros and the cons, loading first one end of the scale with weights, and then the other, but leaving someone else, always, to decide whether the end that finally sank down was, in this murky world of espionage that was forever grey, to be marked either *Black* or *White*.

Every piece of information that was gleaned by the Security Service, the Secret Intelligence Service, the Special Branch, GCHQ – Britain's round-the-world radio monitoring network – the Armed Forces and the police was passed, through Arthur, into Wotan.

'How's your very lovely lady?' he asked.

'Giving me a complex – she's too damned tall; she's also not terribly impressed with me at the moment. We came rather close to splitting up a couple of weeks ago.'

'What happened?'

'I got tripped up – the night Whalley went off to his meeting with Mr X. She was preparing me some special birthday surprise; I'd promised to be home early that night, and I had to stay with Whalley. I sent her a message saying I was stuck in Ireland with a broken-down aeroplane, and she'd seen me driving down Park Lane half an hour before. She's still convinced I spent the night with another bird.'

'Is there not a golden rule, Max? If you tell a lie, make

sure it is not only plausible, but that you can substantiate it within the context of your movements and actions? It's one thing to make a mistake like that with a girlfriend, but you could make a similar mistake in an operation which could jeopardize your life.'

'You haven't met Gelignite,' I said, 'it damned nearly did!'

He grinned.

I remembered coming straight to see Arthur the morning after Gelignite had broken into my house, and he ran her through Wotan backwards, forwards and inside out, cross-referencing three generations back, and every living relative we could find. She was clean Roedean, finishing school in Montreux, Lucy Clayton secretarial, and a personal bank account that would have made Croesius sit on the ground and beat the floor with his fists in a jealous rage. Great-great-grandpa had been transported to Botany Bay for rape – a trait that had evidently not entirely left the family's genes. Out there, he had founded the family empire in sheep farming. Great grandpa had expanded it into property and mining, and on his death it was divided between his two sons. One son lost his half on the baccarat tables of Monte Carlo; the other son trebled the size of his, and handed it down to his son. His son produced Gelignite.

'Don't mess this one about,' said Arthur, then, 'Marry her.'

'I'm not the marrying kind.'

'With a face like that, and a father rich enough to give her five million quid for her twenty-first birthday and not feel it missing out of the petty cash tin, what more do you want? With a pedigree like hers, if she were a dog, she'd clean up at Crufts.'

That summed up Arthur's romantic vision of life: he

looks at a super bird, and immediately conjures up visions of dogs winning prizes. I grinned at him. In spite of being surrounded by the most up-to-date technology in the world, and spending all his working hours in this weird, stark complex, without daylight and without natural fresh air, in the cold white light of neon strip bulbs, amid the constant distant hum of the air-conditioning units and the sound of tapping on keyboards of word processors and computers and push-button telephone dials, he retained a simple, almost rural outlook on life. His stout leather brogues and his car seats thick with the hair of his wife's hounds gave away his private life best: he was a man who relaxed away from work by walking across moors, not by wining and dining dusky mistresses.

'So what's new in British Intelligence?' I asked him. Arthur loved to gossip, not that he ever gave away state secrets, but he did pass on little snippets of personal information about my superiors.

'One little goodie for you,' said Arthur. 'The Home Secretary – you probably read that he's in hospital for a few days for medical tests?'

I nodded.

'Well, he's actually there because he is suffering from – er – damage to the rear quarters; he and some boyfriend got a bit carried away together.' Arthur grinned. It was an unusually fruity tale for him. 'I think he's a bloody liability that man; so does everyone. But that's the only one I have for you today. Since you moved on to grander places, I have been suffering from a serious lack of information!'

Arthur was referring to my previous assignment, a massive study of the staff of MI5. With a few breaks for 'quickie' jobs every few months, the assignment had taken me the best part of five years. During this time, Arthur and I traded a great many tales. It was a curious relationship we had developed, based on scandal that we could not pass on beyond the walls of the room, told through mouthfuls of Turkish Delight.

'That assignment was a damned sight simpler,' I said. 'I don't like this one at all. There's something about it – I don't know quite how to describe it – I just don't feel that, whatever I'm doing, I'm really making any progress. Just when I think I'm getting somewhere, whatever I'm onto dries up. It's almost like chipping away at a glacier with a hammer: take a bit off here, a bit off there, but it's not making any difference, not stopping the damn thing from advancing. Operation Angel, whatever it is, is big, damned big; it is scheduled to take place on 4 January, and it is now 14 December. Three weeks, and right now, where are we? Bloody nowhere.

'I reckoned I had it all figured out after I stopped McEliney in his car. Put the Ring of Bells pub under a microscope and wait for ginger-haired Mick to turn up; follow him, bug him, and between him and Whalley, we'd get to the pot of gold. I've drunk in that damn pub every night for the last three weeks, chatting up the thick-arsed locals until I'm blue in the face, waiting for Mick to come – then arriving home with Guinness all over my breath and trying to persuade Gelignite I've been working hard – Then I get a phone call last night: the police have found him on an abandoned building site with a bullet in his head; the bullet is from the same gun that shot McEliney dead two days before. Someone's doing a damned good job of tidying up their back yard.'

Arthur nodded. 'It's a familiar pattern – seen it many times before – eliminating unwanted witnesses before the stunt is pulled.'

'I think we're going to need one hell of a lot of luck in the next three weeks,' I said.

'Do you?' said Arthur, somewhat surprised. 'I didn't know you were a person who believed in leaving things to luck. It's certainly not the reputation you have. You're known by most people in Intelligence as the Digger, because that's exactly what you've always done; you've kept on digging until you've found something. That's the only way in our game; Fifeshire's Law of Intelligence: facts, facts, facts! We'd all be useless without them – Wotan would be fifteen million quid's worth of scrap ironmongery without facts. And facts aren't acquired by luck – at least, in my view, not often. People can say they got a lucky break, but I always disagree. People say a golfer is lucky if he gets a hole in one. I don't agree with that at all. Heck, that's what the chap's trying to do. When he drives off he aims at that pin – even if he can't see it, he's still aiming for it – and every time he stands on a tee throughout his life, he aims for that pin. If he goes to his grave without ever getting that hole in one, in my view he has been unlucky. If he has succeeded in getting a hole in one, I wouldn't say he had been lucky; I'd say he had been successful – he had done what he tried to do.'

'Well, I'm going to need an awful lot of golf balls, Arthur,' I said.

He grinned.

'Anyway, what have you come up with?'

'We'll go through it,' he said. He looked at his watch. 'We'll have to be quick – I have to leave here in exactly half an hour. Now that the Home Secretary has discovered, after eighteen months in office, that he has an Intelligence organization under him, he wants to know all about it – ruptured anus or no ruptured anus.'

'And what will you tell him?'

'What Fifeshire thinks he needs to know.'

'Which is?' I asked.

'Not a lot,' he said abruptly, and then grinned.

'Did you have any luck with the voice-prints?'

Arthur shook his head. 'It would be a damned sight easier if you could remember where you had heard that voice. What about hypnosis?'

'Tried it. Negative.'

'You don't think it's your imagination?'

'No. I am certain I heard it before.'

'Well, we've fed dark Capris into Wotan, and now we have fed in that voice. Your people are out interviewing everyone in the nuclear energy industry and they're sending the tapes to us. We are converting them into prints, and feeding them into Wotan in the hope he can match one print up with the conversation you recorded between Whalley and his contact. There are over two hundred thousand people who work in the nuclear energy industry – I have their files – it will take you until well past 4 January to inter-view them all – you'll be lucky if you get your man that way.'

'I thought you didn't believe in luck?'

He grinned. 'Let's just say I sometimes believe in miracles!'

'What about McEliney's fingerprints?'

'Nothing more than what I told you last week: his record was clean, but his father has a long record of IRA involve-ments; he was arrested in connection with the Hilton bombing back in the mid seventies, but there wasn't enough evidence to convict him.'

'But it does make it pretty clear there's an IRA involve-ment?'

'Oh, certainly. The voice you cannot place – the speech boffins have analyzed that, and they say the man was almost certainly born and brought up in Ireland, and has spent at least twenty years in this country since then. His accent may have faded naturally – but he might have deliberately worked at losing it.'

'Can't you single out everyone with an Irish background?'

'We have already done so, and we keep a special watch on them as their voice-prints come in. But if he's hiding his Irish background, he's almost certainly changed his name and his identity, and without knowing who the person is, it's a near-on-impossible job to find one person out of two hundred thousand who has changed his identity. Of course, it could possibly be this person Patrick Cleary that McEliney spoke of. There is nothing to prove it, though, and even if we could prove it, I don't think it would be of great help to us.'

'Why not?'

'Because I think that's a false name too. We've checked on every P. Cleary in all the phone books in the British Isles, and all the ex-directory listings – every possible way the name could be spelt. We've singled out all the Patricks, and checked on them, and we haven't been able to find any positive IRA links. All of them have been telephoned, and their voice-prints have been compared with your tape; negative. That leaves us with three possibilities: either he isn't on the phone, or he's using a pseudonym, or he doesn't exist.'

'Which do you think is the most likely?'

Arthur beamed smugly. 'You know I don't normally like to give opinions?'

'I had noticed.'

'Well, this time it's different. It's Wotan's doing, of course – you see, he has come up with something most interesting. As you probably know, as part of the Sharing of Intelligence

Treaty between the SIS and the CIA, they, and a few other of the world's intelligence networks, watch all the key international airports of the world, particularly those of countries endangered by terrorism and those of countries that support terrorism. All passenger lists, incoming and outgoing, are fed into Wotan, and to the CIA central computer system in Washington, and the computers are able to build up patterns of movement and link names to dates and events.'

'Yes.'

'Well, among the names you gave me were Ben Tsenong, Wajara and Lukas. Ben Tsenong is a student at Oxford, studying atomic energy; he is from Namibia, and on a United Nations scholarship. There are no records about him in Namibia – which is not unusual: records in South West Africa are appalling. However, Wajara could well be Felix Wajara. He's a key figure in the People's Liberation Army of Namibia and one of the most powerful blacks in the country – if they ever have free elections, he would stand a good chance of becoming prime minister. The name Lukas was harder, because that is a Christian name and not uncommon out there. However, on 10 August Felix Wajara arrived at Tripoli Airport in Libya with one Lukas Ogomo. Lukas Ogomo is a senior member of SWAPO – South West Africa People's Organization. On a separate flight, on the same day, the chairman of SWAPO, Hadino Dusab, also arrived in Tripoli. And now, what is most interesting of all, on 9 August, guess who else flew to Tripoli?'

'Stun me,' I said.

'Patrick Cleary.'

He stunned me.

'On 10 August Lukas Ogomo sends a telegram to Ben Tsenong in Oxford saying, "All has been agreed." The telegram was sent from Marzoc, which happens to be where

Quadhafi's top guerrilla-warfare training establishment is based.

'Tsenong gets a telegram from his mother on the same day telling him his father has died. Wotan has been able to discover that someone called Tsenong was buried in Otjitambi around that date, so the cable appears to be genuine – probably just coincidence that the two were sent on the same day. But not coincidence in my opinion that Cleary, Ogomo, Wajara and Dusab were in Libya that day – what do you think?'

'No, no way. But why Libya?'

'Quadhafi gives a considerable amount of assistance to terrorist organizations purely on ideological grounds. He also gives assistance for other reasons, and Namibia has something that Quadhafi can't get enough of at the moment.'

'Uranium?'

'That's right.'

'So that gives Libya's motive, but what about Namibia? What do the Namibians want with nuclear power stations in Britain?'

'Might not be just Britain,' said Arthur. 'On those same two days Jose Reythal, a key ETA man, Gunther Keller-Blaus, who runs Baader-Meinhof from a French hideout, Joel Ballard, an ex-CIA officer who is now a professional mercenary-terrorist, Mossif Kalib, who I am sure you have heard of – a key PLO man, and one of the most dangerous terrorists in the world – and a Russian, Leonid Posgnyet, a senior KGB officer – this entire bunch of charming individuals all arrived in Tripoli. Of course, terrorists are coming and going the whole time through Tripoli Airport, but this lot are a team of heavyweights, and it would be as well to bear in mind that their arrival might not be coincidence.

'The Namibians are trying hard right now to shake off South African control of their country. United Nations ordered the South Africans to give the Namibians full independence twenty years ago, and they still have not done so. There are plenty of Namibian political prisoners languishing in South African jails, and the country is under complete South African domination. Namibia is rich in a number of minerals, including diamonds, platinum and uranium, and it also has the only safe anchorage along fifteen hundred miles of coast: Walvis Bay, an important strategic port to the South Africans. It's not surprising they don't want to let go. The United Nations have made Britain, Canada, the United States, France and Germany what they term the "contact states" – that is to say, the United Nations have made those countries responsible for putting the pressure on South Africa to free Namibia; but other than token actions every now and then, the contact states aren't doing anything at all, because it's not in their interest. They want to keep communism out of Africa wherever they can, and they know that as soon as Namibia gets her independence, she may well go to the left.

'The map you photographed in Tsenong's room is very interesting – four of the five countries are contact states: Britain, Canada, the United States and France. The only exception is Spain.

'The Namibians are bound to feel that by really piling the pressure on South Africa, they might eventually get somewhere, and they might have come to the conclusion that a major outrage in one, perhaps in more than one, of the contact states might be the best way of furthering their aims. Nuclear power stations would of course be highly relevant targets, since one of Namibia's principal exports is uranium.'

'Hence Ben Tsenong's presence over here under the cover of studying nuclear energy: as an innocent student, he probably has easy access to nuclear power stations.'

'Undoubtedly,' said Arthur.

I thought hard for some moments. 'If we are right about Tsenong, then he's a major find, and he could lead us straight to the lion's den. But if he gets the slightest bit of wind up, you can be sure he'll just lead us up blind alleys. He's evidently working with a substantial team of accomplices and we don't know who they are beyond Horace Whalley and a man called Cleary who doesn't appear to exist. They could be anyone in the nuclear energy industry, at any level. If we start asking questions about where Tsenong has visited, word undoubtedly will get back to him. For the time being, we can trust no one in the nuclear energy industry. We can't tap Tsenong's phone, because he hasn't got one. We'll bug his room with a micro-video camera, and put a twenty-four-hour surveillance on him, but they will have to keep their distance – which won't make their task easy. We cannot risk his blowing us.'

Arthur nodded in agreement. 'Someone ought to go to Africa and have a chat with a Namibian or two.'

'I have a source through which I might be able to get some introductions out there,' I said.

'Oh really?' He smiled. 'Not unconnected with a certain lady friend?'

'Possibly not,' I grinned.

'Well, why not?' said Arthur. 'At least you'll get some warm weather.'

18

Arthur wasn't wrong about the warm weather; I could feel it through the walls of the Trident as we taxied along the runway at Windhoek, the capital of Namibia. With the country sandwiched between two deserts and straddling the Tropic of Capricorn, it wasn't surprising that it was hot.

Namibia, or South West Africa, is approximately the size of England and France combined, and has a population of between 900,000 and 1,500,000 depending on whom you talk to. It is bounded, on the north, east and south by Angola, Zambia, Botswana and South Africa, and on the west by eight hundred miles of shipwrecks, shifting sands and buried diamonds.

Like a great many other countries in the world, it had got along quite happily since time began without the assistance of the white man. When white men finally got there, in the late nineteenth century, they consisted not of wise people bearing gifts of frankincense and myrrh but of Trek-Boers who were tired, hot and extremely smelly. In 1885, by the Treaty of Berlin, Germany annexed South West Africa, and treated it to its first Governor, one Heinrich Göring. During the next twenty-five years, Göring proceeded to butcher seventy-five per cent of the black population, and produced a son, Hermann, who inherited his talent for genocide, and was given plenty of opportunity to exercise this talent a few decades later in the guise of Air Minister to Hitler.

In 1915, South Africa took over control of the country from Germany, and at the end of the First World War, South

West Africa was formally declared a protectorate of South Africa, a state of affairs that a substantial percentage of the population has been attempting to change ever since.

I mulled over the lengthy briefing I had been given on the country by Roger Brandywine, the Foreign Office resident expert on South West African affairs, as I stepped out to the top of the gangway steps. In the blinding sunlight it was hard to see anything for a few moments, and I trod on the heel of a large man in front of me, who wore long khaki-coloured trousers, a loose shirt with an orange goldfish pattern, and a straw pork pie hat on top of a very large head with a fat white face; he swivelled round, and in a strong German accent laced with an even stronger stench of garlic, spat out, 'Votch your step, you fucking man,' then proceeded to miss his own and fell headlong the entire length of the gangway. I didn't see any great banners saying *Welcome to Namibia*. Reckoned I didn't need to.

It was unlikely that anyone was keeping watch on Windheok Airport, waiting for me to turn up, and even more unlikely still that, if they had been, they would have recognized me when I did. I handed a German passport to the white immigration officer and he studied it closely for some moments. The photograph he looked at showed a man with a Zapato moustache, thick tortoiseshell glasses and hair lacquered down and brushed straight back. When he looked up at me, he saw exactly the same man. The name on the passport was Josef Shwartzenegger, and under the heading for occupation it said: Geologist. He closed the passport, handed it back to me and nodded. Geologists were a dime a dozen through this airport.

I took a cab the thirty-eight kilometres up into the centre of Windhoek, and checked into the Kalahari Sands Hotel in Kaiser Strasse. I put my bags in my room, and went out of the hotel into the street in search of a public call box. There was a possibility that the hotel's phones were bugged by the South African secret police, BOSS, and as I was going to have to use my real name to the person I was going to call, in spite of having checked into the country and into the hotel under the name of Shwartzenegger, I didn't want to arouse anyone's suspicions.

When the telephone rang at the Westondam Corporation's Dambe Mine, about fifty miles north-west of Windhoek, it was answered immediately. The Dambe Mine was one of Westondam's many worldwide interests. The chairman and chief executive of Westondam was one Sir Donald Loewe-Congleton, better known to readers of *Private Eye* as King Kongaroo, and better known to me as father of Gelignite.

The girl on the switchboard put me through to the foreman-manager right away.

'Smed here,' said a curt, thick South African accent.

'Pieter Smed?'

'Yes?'

'My name is Flynn – I'm a friend of Sir Donald—'

'Welcome to South West Africa – you have a good journey?' His tone had changed from the curt, defensive, to the welcoming.

'Thank you.'

'Sir Donald telexed that you would be coming.'

'Grand. When could we meet?'

'I am at your disposal. I could come into town – or I could send a car for you to bring you out here to see the mine?'

'I'd like to see the mine.'

'I am sure you want to rest this afternoon after your

journey. I'll send a car for you at nine o'clock tomorrow – it's only half an hour's drive out here.'

'Fine.'

'Where are you staying?'

'The Kalahari Sands. Describe the car and I'll be waiting outside.'

'It'll be a white Peugeot 505.'

'I look forward to meeting you tomorrow morning.'

'Me too, Mr Flynn. Goodbye.'

The car arrived ten minutes early, and luckily I was already outside waiting; it could have been embarrassing if they had paged me. The car was driven by a black in a white, open shirt and white shorts, and either he wasn't much of a conversationalist or he didn't like white people, or, most probably, both. He also appeared to be under the impression that the maximum speed in each gear was the speed one had to reach before charging up, and I wondered, as the engine howled flat out – the worst thing for it in this searing heat – how many gearboxes and engines he got through in a year. As we left the main road and started to climb what was little more than a pot-holed mountain cart-track, with the speedometer gyrating between seventy and ninety, I wondered also how many cars and passengers he got through in a year.

The scenery that jerked up and down outside the Peugeot's windows was dramatic; it was rocky terrain, with low hills, steep cliffs, massive boulders, and little shrubbery. We passed three wrecked cars in as many kilometres. I wondered why he didn't take the hint, and decided it was because they were all his.

He swept right across the road, taking a racing driver's line into a blind corner, and I gritted my teeth so tightly I thought my gums were going to collapse. 'Do you get much traffic on these roads?' I shouted, in the hope that getting him to talk might slow him down.

'No, you don't,' was the reply he shouted, and the next moment he was fighting for dear life with the steering wheel, brakes and gear-lever, as he struggled to fit the car into a gap between the rock side of the road and an articulated fuel-tanker that was also playing boy-racer through the corner in the oncoming direction. There was a bang, followed by the sound of rock ripping open metal as the near-side of the car rubbed itself against a piece of protruding cliff-face, but the driver didn't even bother to slow down.

It was to my great relief that we finally rounded a corner and could see a large valley a short way to the right, with buildings and machinery. 'Dambe Mine,' said the driver, sweeping off the road and stopping what remained of the Peugeot at a perimeter gate. Two men in white uniforms, with white blancoed webbing, and machine-guns hanging from their shoulders, looked in through the car windows and then waved us on. Just beyond the guards was a huge notice-board, at the top of which was the round, three-bladed, black-and-yellow, international radiation warning symbol, and underneath the words in red: *Danger. Radioactive materials mined here. No unauthorized persons permitted. Protective clothing must be worn at all times in controlled areas.* The message was repeated underneath in Afrikaans and in German.

We drove over to a large prefabricated but permanent-looking two-storey building, and the driver leaned back to me. 'You go through there.' He pointed to a doorway.

I got out, very relieved to be standing once again on terra firma, and looked around for a moment. We were in a huge bowl that appeared to have been hewn out of the rock. Apart from the fact there was no music and no jolly lights, the place had the atmosphere of a fairground. It was a massive complex of pipes, cranes, wires, overhead conveyors, pylons, vehicles and buildings, and the noise was deafening. I went in through the doorway, and gave my name. A few minutes later a blond-haired man with a thin, wrinkled face and clear blue eyes strode in. He was very tall, standing a good six inches above me, and he stretched out a hand the size of a boxing glove. I took a good look at my own hand, in case it was the last time I ever saw it, and offered it up like a sacrificial lamb. As he crushed it, I attempted to crush his back, but there was nothing to grip on at all; it was like trying to crush a block of polished granite.

'Nice to meet you, Mr Flynn. You had a good drive out here?'

'I got here in one piece – but I'm not quite sure how.'

'Niggers can't fucking drive,' he said. 'Lost three people this year on that road, but the management won't accept what I tell them. Come on up to my office. We'll get white drivers one day – but only when they make them pay nigger drivers the same.' He grinned. 'You got many niggers in England?'

'One or two,' I said, following him up the stairs to a small office with a large fan.

'You're lucky; they're all over the fucking place out here.' He pointed me into a chair, and sat down himself.

'I guess it was their land once.'

'And America belonged to the Indians. So what are they going to do – kick everyone out of New York, paint the Empire State Building up like a fucking totem pole, and fill the place with Indians? Everyone wants to go back, no one wants to go fucking forwards. Let the whites bust their guts to develop this country, get it all going well, then give it back to the fucking niggers. Smoke?'

'Thanks.'

He handed me a Chesterfield, shoved one in his mouth and produced a flame from somewhere within his hand. 'So your company is interested in buying some mining rights out here?'

'Well, this is a very exploratory visit.'

'Take my advice and go someplace else. Going to be a lot of problems here soon, lots of fucking problems.'

If there were many more like him around, I wasn't surprised. Although, judging from what was reported in the press from time to time about the strong-arm business tactics of Sir Donald Loewe-Congleton's empire, this particular example was probably one of the more kind-hearted employees.

'What problems do you get at the moment?'

'All sorts of problems, Rates of Pay in the mines; conditions in the mines; land ownership. There's a lot of change in the wind, and it's not blowing any good for the white man.'

'What exactly do you mean by conditions in the mines?'

'Health and safety; hours of work; length of years a man is permitted to work; monitoring it all, checking it all – we got ten miles of files out the back, it's a pain in the ass and it costs a lot of money.'

'Do you get many health problems?'

Smed looked at me slightly curiously. 'Sure you do. We don't get so much now they're wearing the masks and we're monitoring the air-dust levels – but then we don't get so much work done, either. We even have a full-time doctor now.'

'What kind of health problems do you get?'

'The normal ones for uranium miners – respiratory, mainly.'

'Lung cancer?'

'Pretty high rate in the past; it should come down now.'

'Have SWAPO put much pressure on you?'

'Not directly, but indirectly they have, through the bloody South African government – they're scared of the rest of the world. They've got the West telling them to pull out of here; the Russians are right behind SWAPO – they're treading very carefully. So now we have to look after our niggers and keep them fat and well.' Smed spat on the floor. 'I'm paid to run this mine at a profit for Westondam – if I don't, I'm out on my ass, and I got four kids at school. Every day that I work here, I'm meant to lead them to the bathroom and wipe their asses; but I don't. Because I'm not putting my neck on the block for any fucking niggers.'

I nodded, and stubbed out my cigarette. 'Did you ever have anyone by the name of Tsenong working for you?'

'Tsenong? Down on the face?'

'I don't know; he died in August.'

'Daniel Tsenong?'

I nodded.

'I remember the name all right. His son caused us one hell of a lot of problems. Came sniffing round here – we had to throw him out. Said we'd been covering up his father's medical records – he put the chief medical officer from Windhoek onto us.'

'What was his son's name?'

'Ben.'

'Can you tell me a bit more about his father?'

'I'll get his file – I still have it.' Smed went to a filing cabinet and pulled out a drawer, then rummaged through several files. He pulled one out and opened it up. 'Not much,

I'm afraid. He joined us thirty-three years ago: started at twelve; lived with his family in a shanty village about twenty miles west of here. Lot of our workers come from there and a few other villages in the same region; we bus them in each day. Got a wife, and two sons. Left us in May – or rather, we got rid of him. He couldn't get through a day's work; he had lung cancer.'

'Contracted as a result of working in the mine?'

'Probably.'

'What about his son, Ben – have you got any more information on him?'

'May I ask what your interest in him is?'

'He's just applied to us for a job.'

'To you?'

'My company advertised for an expert on South West Africa to advise us on mineral prospects. He was one of the applicants for the job,' I said.

'His son?'

'He's in his third year at Oxford University, studying atomic energy.'

'That's right. I knew he was at university in England. You want to be careful – smart niggers are dangerous niggers.'

I nodded. 'That's one of the reasons for my visit. We are thinking of hiring him – he's a bright youngster – but we suspect he might have other motives.'

Smed raised an eyebrow. He went back over to the filing cabinet, and pulled out a file that was an inch and a half thick. 'I suggest you take a read through this, Mr Flynn: it's a psychologist's report. I've got a couple of jobs I must go and do, which will take me about half an hour. We have to watch our backs the whole time in this country; we watch anyone we think is dangerous, or could one day become dangerous, very closely. We employ a team of psychologists, and their job is to alert us to any warning signs they see. Would you like some tea or coffee – or a drink?'

'Coffee, please.'

'I'll have it sent up. Have a good read.' Smed went out and I opened the file; it was not a cheerful read.

Ben Tsenong had been lucky enough to win one of only three science scholarships a year awarded to the whole of Namibia. After two years away at college, he had returned home for the summer holidays before commencing his third year. He had found his father very ill and his mother demented with worry. He then discovered Westondam's doctor had lied to his father about his illness; he'd told him he had bronchitis. Not having sufficient money to go to a doctor on his own account, Ben's father had accepted the Westondam doctor's diagnosis. Ben paid for a specialist, and found out the truth. If there had been a chance of curing his father when the disease was first discovered, there certainly wasn't now.

Ben Tsenong was eaten up with hatred – hatred against Westondam Mining Corporation, against the South African government, against Germany for beginning it all with their colonization. But the strongest hatred he had was for the country that he now knew best of all: England.

He hated England firstly for the way it took over where Germany left off. England could have done something to improve life for the Namibians, but instead did nothing. He hated England because he believed that it was England that was responsible for everything bad about South Africa and the way it ruled. He hated the fat cats of England who licked the cream its colonialism had raked off the world. He hated the fat people of England in their Jaguar cars most of all, but he hated them almost as much in their Fords or their

Vauxhalls or in their Minis, or their imported Renaults or BMWs or Mercedes, or any of their cars.

Ben Tsenong was a scientist, and he understood science. He did not understand the world, and most of what he knew of the world, he hated. He hated all the countries that used nuclear energy; he hated the people in those countries for the lights they left on, for their mindless television programmes, for their Space Invader machines, for their ice-crushing machines, for their neon lights and moving staircases and sunray lamps, for their electric toothbrushes, and toy train sets, for everything that was useless and mean-ingless and guzzled the energy that had made nuclear power at all necessary; and made it necessary for his father to spend his life down in that mine, breathing in those par-ticles of dust that had radon atoms clinging to them, which had gone down into his lungs, and sat there, and set to work, beaming out destruction, killing good cells and making bad cells, until the bad cells began to multiply on their own, without any assistance, and dreadfully, painfully, started to kill the life that was his father, and destroy forever the will to live that was his mother.

Namibia had no nuclear power stations. The uranium that was mined here went mostly to Europe and North America. His father had never switched on a light that was fuelled by the uranium he had dug from the ground.

Smed came back in. 'How's it going?'

'I can see what you mean,' I said.

Smed offered me another cigarette; I declined. He lit one for himself.

'Does the name Lukas Ogomo ring a bell?'

Smed's eyes opened wide, and he nodded. 'A very bad bell.'

'Why?'

'If he had his way, he would close down all uranium mines in the country, and if independence comes, he may well get his way. He's totally committed to it, and although generally speaking he's only a small noise in SWAPO, on uranium he is their leading spokesman. He's friendly with Tsenong's son too – but I don't know how they know each other.'

'Where is he based?'

'Windhoek. Operates from SWAPO's headquarters there. You thinking of employing him too?'

'No, but I'd like to have a chat with him.'

'I don't think you'll get very far.'

'How about if I went to see Felix Wajara?'

Smed grinned broadly. 'He eats white men for breakfast. You wouldn't get an audience; you'd be wasting your time. If you want to talk to anyone, Ogomo is your best bet – it's a slim bet, but at least he would be approachable. But be careful what you say.'

'I'll try.'

Smed looked at his watch. 'Do you want to see around the mine before lunch? Or shall we just have a large drink here?'

'Let's just have a large drink here,' I said.

'Quite right,' agreed Smed. 'Anything that's above ground you can see from here anyway. Below ground, there's nothing but niggers, darkness and dust.'

I thought I might be in luck having a different driver take me back to Windhoek, but I wasn't. He was a different driver, but there was no difference in the way he drove.

Shortly after we hit the main road, we passed a pull-in bar called the Beerstop, and I made a mental note of it.

We made it to Windhoek without being wiped out, and I thanked the driver out aloud, and God under my breath, and got out. It was three o'clock, and I had some business to do. I went first to hire a car; a slightly dented, but fairly recent model Datsun was all Avis had, and it suited me fine. I next went to a shop-fitters, and bought a male shop-window dummy, which I put in the boot of the car. From there I went to a hardware store, and bought a ball of twine, a packet of absorbent cloths and some long nails. Then I went to a chemist and bought a pack of disposable hypo-dermic syringes and some Elastoplast. Then I went to the public library, and asked to see some articles on Ogomo; never having seen him before, I wanted to look at some photographs of him so I would know what he looked like.

He was short, and quite fat, with goldfish eyes, a dimple in each cheek, and an inane smile. My first impression of the photographs were that they had been taken while he was stoned out of his mind. It was the same for everyone who saw him for the first time – everyone, that is, who didn't know that the dimple on the left cheek had been caused by a 2mm soft-nose bullet entering his mouth, and the dimple on the right cheek by the same 2mm soft-nose bullet leaving his mouth, courtesy the anonymous sniper, for whom no one had claimed responsibility, who had failed to test his new image-intensifier telescopic sight before firing, a test which would have revealed to him that, at a range of two hundred and fifty yards, the rifle was firing four inches too low.

The bullet had severed an important muscle in each cheek, the result of which being that Ogomo was left with a permanent grin on his face.

At a quarter to five I went to a call box and dialled the number of the SWAPO headquarters in Windhoek. A girl answered.

'May I speak to Lukas Ogomo – it is very urgent.'

'Hold a minute, please.'

I breathed a sigh of relief – at least she hadn't said he was out, or, worse still, abroad. Another woman's voice came on the phone.

'Who are you please?'

If they had gained one thing from one hundred years of white domination, it was the white man's art of vetting unwanted telephone callers. 'A friend of Ben Tsenong – from England.'

A surprisingly high-pitched man's voice came through the receiver. 'Ogomo speaking. Who are you, please?'

'A friend of Ben Tsenong – from England.'

'What do you want?' He sounded tense.

'I have a message from Ben. I must speak to you in private. I'm in danger, and it's very urgent.'

'Do you want to come here?'

'No good.'

'You tell me where?'

'Have you a car?'

'Of course.'

'Take the Okandja Road, and take the turning for Otjiwarongo. Go on for about three miles and you pass a bar on the right-hand side of the road – it's called the Beerstop. About four hundred yards further on, there's a turning to the right marked with a small post which says Otjosundu. You take that turning. Immediately on the left is a piece of flat land. You'll see a yellow Datsun parked there. I'll be in that car waiting for you. Leave your car and join me. If anyone comes with you I shall know something is wrong and will drive straight off.'

'I understand,' said Ogomo in a voice that sounded as if he didn't understand at all. However, he repeated correctly the directions I had given him.

'Half past nine this evening.'

'Half past nine,' he said.

I hung up and went back to the hotel, leaving everything locked in the boot of the car except for the syringes, which I took up to my room. I opened my briefcase, and removed a small black box containing two phials labelled with the names of chemicals used for rock-testing analysis. From each one I filled a syringe, then I emptied the remainder of the chemicals down the sink, and rinsed the phials out carefully. I put the syringes into a plastic bag, together with one of the cloths I had bought, sealed the bag carefully, and put it into my jacket pocket. Outside, dusk was beginning to fall. I wanted to get to the site before it was completely dark in case there was anything I hadn't noticed as I had jolted past on two occasions earlier that day.

The drive took about forty minutes. The place was even better than I had at first thought. The bar, with two battered cars and the remains of a bicycle outside, could not accurately be described as the hub of the universe, and there was no other building anywhere in view. I pulled the Datsun a good way off the road, switched off the lights, and settled down to wait until night had fallen completely. It was a calm, muggy evening; there was a new moon and the sky was quite dark, which pleased me – I didn't have any desire to be floodlit.

After about ten minutes, the quiet was broken by the clattering of bicycles, and I saw the silhouettes of a bunch of people pedalling past. They cycled off into the dark and then there was silence again.

When it was as dark as it was going to get, I unscrewed the cover of the interior light in the car, and removed the bulb. Next, I took the dummy out of the boot, assembled it, and placed it in the driving seat. I removed the bag of syringes from my pocket, wrapped one in the cloth, and put it back in my pocket. I laid the other, and the Elastoplast, on the front passenger seat of the car. I hoped no policeman would come along on a routine patrol and decide to do a check up on the car. I didn't know what he'd make of a junkie dummy.

I walked back down to the main road, where I could see clearly in all three directions. There were no lights on in the Beerstop, and the cars and bicycle were gone. A pick-up truck with several men crammed in the cab drove down the road, and I stepped back into the bushes to avoid being caught in the beam of its lights. It pulled into the forecourt of the Beerstop, and I heard the sound of cursing; they had evidently been expecting the bar to be open. They drove off down the road. I walked over to the bar. The door was padlocked, and there were large shutters pulled down to the ground. I walked all around the outside, safety catch off my gun, but there was no one there. I went back to my watch post.

I was glad to have my Beretta with me, and it is thanks to Trout and Trumbull that I am able to take it wherever I go. They constructed a shoulder holster for it, which, if assembled in a certain way, gives the whole thing the appearance of being a pistol-grip super-8 movie-camera. It never fails to fool airline security guards.

At nine twenty-five, I saw the bright glow of headlamps stab the sky some way in the distance. They disappeared, then stabbed the sky again, this time closer, and I began to hear the sound of a car. Two minutes later, a Toyota estate car slowed down and turned right onto the Otjosundu road. It drove slowly for some yards, and then turned left off the road. As quietly as I could, and keeping to the shadow of the bushes, I sprinted across towards where my car was parked. The Toyota placed itself so that its headlamp beams were full on the Datsun, and the dummy silhouetted perfectly; even to me it looked as though there were a real person sitting in the car. The driver got out of the Toyota and walked across to the Datsun. I took the rag from my pocket, and emptied the contents of the syringe into it. Holding the rag in my left hand, I ran up behind him, silent on my rubber shoes, passing the Toyota closely and glancing in to make sure no one was concealed in there.

I waited until he had put his hand on the handle of the Datsun's passenger door, then I clamped the chloroform-soaked rag over his nose. The shock of it must have made him take a deeper breath than usual, for he went limp right away. I had no trouble in recognizing him from the pictures of him I had seen in the library: it was Lukas Ogomo.

I removed his jacket, rolled up his right shirt sleeve, laid him out on the back seat of the Datsun, and tied his arms and legs firmly together. Then I picked up the syringe and waited for him to come round. The content of the syringe was a pale-yellow, liquid barbiturate, Pentothal. When Ogomo came round, I would inject into him just enough to put him into a happy, relaxed state of near-euphoria – the final point of consciousness before sleep – in which he should completely lose all his inhibitions.

It took about fifteen minutes before he began to stir, and then he started to come awake quite quickly. I stuck the needle into his arm, and pushed in a fairly generous helping of the mixture. His eyes rolled. I lashed the syringe to his arm with the Elastoplast.

'Hallo, Lukas,' I said.

'Man, hi!'

'Good, eh, Lukas?'

'That's good; feels real good.'

'You relax and enjoy yourself, Lukas.'

'Sure, sure. Where am I? Where am I? I can't move – what is all this? Hey? Hey?' He was starting to panic. I pushed the plunger in further and he relaxed immediately. 'Who the hell cares,' he said cheerfully, 'this is a nice place!'

I gave another gentle push on the plunger.

'What the fuck's going on, man?'

'Don't worry, relax, lie back, have a nice time.'

'I'm having a nice time.'

'Tell me some things, Lukas.'

'What would you like to know, man?'

'Tell me about Angel?'

'Angel's top secret, man, I can't talk about that.' He laughed. 'No way; that's my little secret – well, not just mine, everyone's, but – hey – I have to get back now. What's up? I can't move my hands—'

I pushed the plunger again.

'Aren't you meant to be telling me things?' he said.

'No, Lukas, you're telling me, you're giving me messages for Ben, for Ben Tsenong, and for Patrick, Patrick Cleary.'

'This feels good.'

'They're screwing you, Lukas.'

'Whatd'yer mean?'

'You'll find out.'

'How can they? Why would they?'

'You know better than I do. Ben isn't happy. He thinks you're ignoring him.' I pushed the plunger in a short way.

'Tsenong's just a boy. He's small fry. He's just a kid, just a kid. Cleary's the smart one in England. I like Cleary, he's nice.'

'Kind to you, is he?' I pushed on the plunger.

'Oh yes, I mean, we're not great buddies, you know, or anything like that, no, but – er – he's nice.'

'Who is your great buddy?'

'Felix is. He's always been good to me. Felix is my good friend.'

I pushed the plunger in further.

'I could stay like this for ever; feels so good, so good.'

'Felix who?'

'Wajara. And Hadino – Dusab: he's good to me too.'

'Is he in Angel?'

'Sure he is. Felix and Hadino and a lovely bunch of men.'

'Who are they?'

'Not all lovely; guy I can't stand – German – hate all Germans – they killed my grandparents, German bastards. I'll kill them all, fucking Germans. I can't move my feet.'

He was getting panicky. I injected more Pentothal and he relaxed.

'Who's the German?'

'Can't move my feet.'

I gave a long push of the plunger. 'Who's the German?'

'Killer, Keller, Keller-Bluff, no, Keller-Blaus, Gunther Keller-Blaus; he's in charge of France.'

'France? Why not Germany?'

'Not allowed to touch Germany.'

'Who isn't?'

'Angel.'

'Why not?'

'Konyenko said so. Said Spain instead. Much help from ETA.'

'Who's Konyenko?'

'Russian. Don't want the winds blowing over Russia. Don't want to radiate Russia. Radiate, radio, radio, rashio, russiate,' he rambled on.

'Radiate with what?'

'Fall-out from the nuclear power stations we're going to fucking blow apart, man.'

'Who is?'

'That would be telling.'

'Go on, tell.'

'All right – long as you promise not to tell anyone else.'

'I promise.'

'I believe you. You're a nice man. For a white man, you're pretty nice.'

I pushed in a drop more. 'Who is going to blow up the power stations?'

'Mossif Kaleb.'

'He's from the PLO?'

'Yeah, nice man. Doesn't talk a lot. But he acts! He and Ballard are going to sort out the US of fucking A. Wow! They're going to sort out Canada too. Wow! They've got connections in Quebec. Big connections. Big fucking bang. Wow!'

'Who else?'

'I can't remember. Oh yeah, the fat man Rey – er – Jose Reythal. Spanish man. Spaniard man? Spanner man? Spandard man? Something like that!'

'Who else?'

'Don't know. Posgnyet, but he's only in charge, he doesn't count, only a fucking Russian.' He laughed. 'They're nice to us, the Russians.'

'I'm glad, Lukas. Tell me about Angel? What is Angel?'

'Didn't I tell you, man?'

'No, you forgot.'

'Angel – Anti Nuclear Generated Electricity. Simple, eh?'

'Very simple, Lukas. Did you think that up yourself?'

'No. The Russians did.'

'Tell me more about the Russians.'

'Yes, they're nice. Lovely Russians; blonde ladies and

vodka. They pay bills – big bills, small bills – and screw blonde ladies.' He giggled.

'Which power stations are you going to blow up?'

'All over. I can't move my hands.'

I pushed the plunger again. There wasn't much left in the syringe.

'Which countries?'

'United States, Canada, France, Spain, England. All going to be big fucking bangs. All the contact states, man. Except Germany, Spain instead of Germany.'

'Why Spain instead of Germany?'

'Winds. Russians don't want radiation blowing over East Germany and into Russia. ETA in Spain keen to take action against nuclear energy – everyone decided it would be pity not to include them.'

'Which power stations in each country?'

'Whichever they decide on, man.'

'Which ones?'

'I don't know.'

'You're being screwed by everyone.'

'No, I'm not, they love me. I am big man.'

'There's a plot to kill you. I'm the only one who can save you, Lukas. I want to save you, Lukas, I want to save you very much.'

'Thank you. Please save me.'

'If you want me to save you, you'd better tell me everything, and tell it fast. Now, which power stations?'

'I don't know, I tell you, all over, some here, some there, some fucking everywhere!' He began to giggle again.

'Which power stations, Lukas?'

'Wherever the wind is good.'

'Why are you doing all this?'

'Whole goddam world's going to stop raping our land,

going to stop digging their greedy fists into that uranium, man. That's no-good stuff. We want to leave it in the land, man, and cover it up again – almost as much, man, as we want our freedom. Yeah! To be free! We are going to make the world take notice of us, man. After next month, nobody's going to ignore Namibia, man. No fucking way!' He laughed.

'Why are the Russians helping you?'

'Different Russians got different reasons,' he giggled. 'Konyenko – he's our contact here – he help us because we fix him up with blonde girls.'

'And Posgnyet?'

'He control Operation Angel. From Moscow. I don't remember why he help us.'

'Try and remember.' I squeezed in more of the drug. There was now only a tiny drop left.

'Russia helps us, because it is good for Russia, maybe. I don't know. Things not good for those countries are good for Russia. Who knows? Who knows with Russians at all?' He giggled. 'First they make things good and easy for us – then maybe later they make them hard. We must be on guard, eh? They think we are simple. But we are not. We will outsmart them.'

'Of course you will,' I said.

'Of course we will,' he agreed.

'Now why don't you tell me which power stations?'

'They only know in each country. Security, man. If we don't know, we can't tell. Good, man, eh? Smart!' He grinned.

I squeezed in the last of the drug.

'I like you,' he said.

'What else would you like to tell me?'

'Anything. I like talking to you. I want to go on talking to you for ever.'

'Who went to Libya last August?'

'Everyone, man, that was the big meeting. Yes, that was the big one!'

'Who was everyone?'

'Everyone I told you.' His eyelids closed.

'You, Hadino Dusab, Felix Wajara, Gunther Keller-Blaus, Jose Reythal, Mossif Kalib, Patrick Cleary, Joel Ballard and Ben Tsenong?'

'Not Tsenong, man, he had to go back to England.'

Ogomo was not lying.

'Tell me about Patrick Cleary, Lukas.'

'Irish. I don't know more. Met him only once. Nice man. Kind.'

He was showing signs of coming round. I placed the chloroformed cloth over his nose; he went unconscious at once. I removed the Elastoplast and pulled out the syringe. Then I untied him, rolled down his shirt sleeve, put his jacket on, and carried him over and put him behind the wheel of his own car. Then I took one of the large nails I had bought that afternoon, and pushed it up hard in the gap in the tread of his front off-side tyre. I didn't want it to burst the tyre then and there, but equally, I didn't want it to fall out.

I went to my car, and drove a short way further up the road, turned around, switched off the engine and the lights, and waited. After half an hour, I heard the sound of an engine starting, and then lights came on and what I presumed to be Ogomo's Toyota headed off back in the direction of Windhoek. I threw the syringes and the cloth out of the window into a thick clump of bushes. Ogomo, I figured, would have a pretty thick head at the moment, and be wondering just what on earth had been happening. He would have a pretty good idea and wouldn't be feeling too happy about it all. He wouldn't be able to remember much about what he had said, but he would remember enough to know that he had probably said a damned sight too much. He needn't have worried, however, about whatever anyone was going to say to him.

I looked at my watch. Four minutes had passed; that should be about right. I started up, but did not switch on the lights. My eyes were well accustomed to the dark now. I drove about a quarter of a mile, and came up over the brow of a hill. There, some way in front, were the tail-lights of a car that was certainly Ogomo's. I drove down into another dip, and put my headlights on. When I came to the next brow, the Toyota was only a few hundred yards ahead. It was at the side of the road and leaning slightly to the right.

I could see a figure kneeling by the front off-side wheel, winding up what looked like a jack. One hundred yards and there was no mistaking it was Ogomo. I kept my speed steady. He turned to look at me for a moment, then turned back to his jack. Then he turned to look at me again, and must have wondered why I wasn't giving him a wider berth, in fact, why I wasn't giving him any berth at all. By the time he realized that I was coming straight at him at sixty miles an hour and tried to do something about it, he had left it too late. The near-side section of the Datsun's bumper hit him straight in the chest, and the headlight hit him full in the face; the car shook, there was a sharp report, no louder than the sound of a light bulb popping, and Ogomo's smashed body was catapulted through the air.

Although I stopped to check, I knew he would be dead before he landed. I left him where he was, and climbed back into the Datsun. It was half past eleven. At nine o'clock in the morning, I would be on a plane heading back to London. I had a heavy heart. Yet again, a white man had come to Namibia and killed.

19

A rich blue-grey cloud of Bolivar corona smoke unfurled itself across the room, some of it rising to the stuccoed ceiling, some of it sinking to the Axminstered floor, some of it drifting sideways and turning into a mad eddy in front of the massive window. Somewhere out beyond the double-glazing, beyond the clacking of the wiper blades and the slashing of tyres through wet roads of London's Christmas-week traffic, was a man who called himself Patrick Cleary, who had to be found and found fast. Horace Whalley had gone on holiday to the Seychelles, and Ben Tsenong had gone into Tesco's in Oxford and vanished from the face of the earth. The mood in the room was not unlike the mood in a solicitor's office at the reading of a will, when the relatives, expecting to learn they have all been left vast fortunes, have just been told that the deceased died in debt.

The Director General of MI5 put the cigar back into his mouth and drew hard; the tip glowed bright red, and a good thirty-pence worth of Havana-flavoured exhaust went into his mouth and then out into the room in pursuit of the fast-vanishing first cloud. The officially dead chairman of the United Kingdom Atomic Energy Authority was busy doodling on a small card he held against the back of his diary. He was drawing short little men with big noses. He didn't like being officially dead and felt that the charade was being taken too far. He had been a prisoner in this building ever since his release from the Illushyn. No one outside, not even his wife, knew he was in England. But he had agreed to carry on like this until after 4 January, and he was reluctantly sticking to his word.

I was jet-lagged from my flight back the day before, and feeling the damp cold more than usual after my brief spell in the Namibian heat. The death of Ogomo certainly wasn't being used by the British press to sell their newspapers, not that it was likely he would have been plastered over the headlines. I didn't think the efforts of his life would have exalted him to a pole position in *The Times* obituaries, but I did think they might have been worth more than the only mention they did get in the British press, which was two lines on the overseas news page of the *Guardian* – Not that I was about to start writing letters to *The Times* about it. I had a feeling that if the authorities had looked hard enough, and found the car that hit him, and connected it to a German geologist that didn't exist, there might have been a few more lines; but knowing the type of man that had died, and the type of authorities they were, it was unlikely they would look hard enough to find the car and make the connection, and even if they did, they would probably assume it was the work of a right-wing German organization.

I had just finished relating to the two men everything that Ogomo had told me, and the not particularly pleasant method by which I had obtained his silence. Quoit made it plain, from the expression on his face, that he would have preferred the company of the chickens in the hold of the Illushyn to being in this room with me. He gave me the sort of expression that is normally reserved for a prospective house-purchaser's first sight of a damp patch on a bedroom wall. Fifeshire wasn't moved; deaths of enemies only upset him when they attracted publicity and he was called upon to explain them. He sucked in and blew out another massive cloud of smoke before he finally broke the silence.

'It is now crystal clear, from what you tell us, that we are dealing not with a bunch of ideologically motivated social misfits, nor a bunch of savages suffering from delusions of grandeur, but with the *crème de la crème:* top table of the Worshipful Company of International Terror-Weavers and Blood-Mongers. They're having a nuclear cocktail party on 4 January, and half the Western world is cordially invited. Isn't that about right, Flynn?'

'I think that sums it up very well, sir.'

'England, France, Spain, the United States and Canada. Are they going to blow up one nuclear power station in each country, or the whole damn lot? And how are they going to do it? What do you think, Isaac?'

Quoit eyed me nervously, looked at Fifeshire for a brief moment, then shot his eyes back to me again, as if he were afraid that if he took his eyes off me for too long, I might dash out of the room and reappear in a motor car. 'Mr Flynn,' he said, 'did this – er – Ogomo chap give any hint at all about how they might – er – blow up these power stations?' Quoit took his metal-framed glasses off and chewed for a moment on the end of one of the arms; then he took it out of his mouth. 'What I mean – er – is . . .' He squinted at Fifeshire, 'it is very important to establish this, Sir Charles—' he turned his head back towards me and squinted furiously, then put his glasses on for a moment to make sure I was still seated, and hadn't crept out and got behind the wheel of a motor car, then took his glasses off again. 'Did you get the impression that the purpose was merely to put the power stations out of action, for example, by knocking out the power cables, or – er – was the purpose to cause a leakage of radiation?'

'To cause a leakage of radiation, without doubt.'

Quoit bit furiously on the arm of his glasses again, then

once more removed them from his mouth. 'You don't think it might possibly be a bluff?'

'These people don't bluff,' said Fifeshire, 'not the team the Namibians have put together.'

'It's very difficult to know quite what they mean when they say "blow up" a nuclear power station. As you know, nuclear power stations are huge complexes, comprising a number of buildings and spread out over fairly large areas. They would need vast amounts of explosives to blow up entire power stations – hundreds of tons of high explosives. They could never smuggle that sort of quantity in. How could they? They could just go for the core, but unless they breached the containment building, that wouldn't do them a lot of good. And they would need a tremendous amount of explosives to do that.' He started to chew again on the plastic on the end of one arm of his glasses.

'What if they used an atomic device?' I asked.

Quoit was silent for a moment. He appeared to be having a problem. He looked up, turning his head from side to side in short, violent jerks. At first I thought he was having a seizure or a heart attack. 'Hrr,' he said, 'whrreer.' He stood up, holding his hand to his mouth, and took several paces around the room, with his head tilted first to one side and then the other. With the hand that was free, he pointed at his mouth with repeated stabbing movements. Fifeshire followed him around the room with his eyes, a thick frown on his forehead. Quoit bent himself almost double, shook his head wildly three or four times, then stood upright once more holding his spectacles out in front of his face. 'I'm sorry,' he said, 'I'm afraid I got my glasses stuck in between my teeth.'

I caught Fifeshire's eye. Fifeshire looked worried – not about atomic devices, but about Quoit.

'It would be possible to blow up power stations using nuclear explosives, certainly, and it would be very effective. If the objective of these people is to create widespread radiation fall-out, vapourizing the core by means of a nuclear explosive would be the best way. You see, the higher the explosion lifts the debris, the greater the distance downwind over which it would spread. Conventional explosives would lift the debris a few hundred feet at the most; a nuclear explosive that succeeded in vapourizing the core could make a plume fifty to sixty thousand feet high – and that would travel a very long way downwind.

'I think there are two ways these people could achieve their aims. The first would be to organize an internal sabotage of the power stations. One person in the control room of each power station, with the assistance of key accomplices, could achieve this quite simply. There would be no need for any explosives to be brought in. By creating malfunctions and taking the wrong corrective action, a lethal situation could be created in any reactor.'

'I thought the systems were meant to be foolproof?' said Fifeshire.

'They are foolproof provided fools are at the controls. Put a smart crook at the controls and the situation changes very rapidly. He can do a lot of damage, a very great deal.' He squinted at me through his glasses, looking a trifle unsure about whether he should be telling a confirmed mass-killer like myself information of this nature. He decided to go on, although the expression of doubt remained on his face. 'All nuclear reactors rely on a delicate balance of rods in their cores, and computers which are monitored by the controllers maintain this balance. If the rods are pushed too far in, the reaction stops completely; if they are pulled too far out, the heat builds up too much, and as the heat builds up, so does the pressure. There are escape valves for when the pressure gets too high, and emergency filtration systems for releasing coolant into the air, but if those escape valves are shut off, and the filtration systems jammed, the containment building's going to turn into a pressure cooker. The walls of the containment buildings are built strong enough to withstand jumbo jets crashing into them, and to withstand two thousand pounds per square inch of pressure from the inside; but in the event of the safety valves jamming when the reactor is out of control, there could be a build-up of one hundred times that amount within a couple of hours – and the containment isn't going to hold that. It will either start to crack, or it will just blow to smithereens. Whichever it does, it's going to release an almighty amount of fallout that would start travelling downwind, and cause serious contamination for a good hundred miles. The average nuclear reactor has several hundred times the radioactive content of, for instance, the Hiroshima bomb.'

'I thought,' said Fifeshire, 'that the British gas-cooled reactors use carbon dioxide as a coolant? Surely carbon dioxide, being lighter than air, would just rise straight into the atmosphere?'

'The carbon dioxide is lighter than air, but the radioactive materials that it picks up aren't, and they would start to drop out into the air as it rose. And don't forget, we don't just have gas-cooled reactors in Britain now – we have two PWR power stations, each with four pressurized-water reactors. They would send steam pouring out, and that all comes back down to earth.'

Fifeshire blew out another mouthful of smoke and watched it spread across the room, sinking here, rising there, spreading all the time.

'Wind eddies, swirls, revolves. If you're smoking your cigar outside, and I'm lying on the ground, with the wind blowing in the right direction, I'll get a good helping of your smoke. The principal isn't much different.

'There's a second major problem if the containment did blow to pieces: the blast would almost certainly sever the coolant pipes. The result would be that the core would become so hot that it would start to melt into a solid lump – and go on heating up.

'This is the worst nightmare of the nuclear energy industry – the Americans call it the China Syndrome, because some believe, if this happened, the core would start burning its way down through the centre of the earth, down towards China, China being the other side of the globe from the United States. We would call it here the Australia Syndrome, I suppose. Of course, it would not actually get to Australia, it would come to a halt in the first water substrata layer – not that that would stop the reaction. It would sit in the water for the best part of a couple of weeks before it burned itself out.'

'Sending up steam?' said Fifeshire.

'Yes, the steam would shoot straight up the funnel it had made, through the breached containment, and it would then spread out downwind.'

'Highly radioactive?'

'Highly.'

'And what about this substrata water: does man come into contact with it?'

'Good lord, yes, Sir Charles, elementary geography, you must have learned it at school: streams, rivers, lakes, rain, you name it.'

'And it would be polluted?'

'Couldn't touch it for centuries.'

'Didn't you fellows consider this angle when you built your bloody reactors?' asked Fifeshire, with more than a trace of anger in his voice.

'When you are dealing with something as potentially hazardous as nuclear fission, it is impossible to cover all the angles. We have to go, to quite a large extent, by what we call "risk relativities". By this, I mean, we have to say to ourselves, "How many people are going to be killed per thousand kilowatts of nuclear generated electricity, as opposed to other methods of generated energy? How many coal-mining accidents, for example? How many coal-miners would be killed mining the coal for coal-burning generators? How many drivers killed in road accidents delivering that coal? How many members of the public killed by the radiation and the carcinogens put in the atmosphere by the burning of the coal?"'

'The ecologists say, for instance, what about water mills? Good question: water mills, why not indeed?' Quoit took his glasses off and began chewing enthusiastically on the end of the arm. 'Did you know that the average water mill kills someone once every two hundred years. A proven statistic. To get the same electricity output from water mills as is currently produced by Britain's nuclear reactors, two hundred thousand water mills would have to be built. Based on proven statistics, that would kill, by drowning, one thousand people a year. There is no evidence to prove nuclear energy kills anyone at all.'

'No one, bar the occupants of a Russian graveyard five hundred square miles in area, whose existence your predecessor, Sir John Hill, refused to acknowledge; an estimated four hundred thousand deformed babies in America; an estimated ten thousand premature widows of uranium miners; not to mention about fifteen thousand further completely substantiated incidences of death and disease I could let you have, Sir Isaac, if you would like; but I don't want to put any ripples on your mill pond.'

Quoit looked distinctly uncomfortable, and Fifeshire kept out of it by concentrating on relighting his cigar. Quoit put his glasses back on. He wasn't going to rise to my bait.

'We have built in massive safety systems,' he said, 'against all operating accidents, and we have made nuclear power stations enormously difficult to sabotage, but it is impossible to guard against all eventualities. Whatever safeguards we come up with, if someone is determined to get through them, then sooner or later they will find a way. One just has to hope that no one is crazy enough to want to do this.'

'It's rather optimistic to hope that in this day and age, surely?' I said. Quoit glared at me.

'Isaac,' said Fifeshire, 'whatever you might think about the bunch of terrorists we are dealing with, however much we might all abhor their views and their methods, whatever they might be – zealots, fanatics – the one thing they most certainly are not is crazy.'

Quoit nodded.

'Correct me if I am wrong, Isaac,' he continued, 'but a disaster of the magnitude you have outlined, if I understand you correctly, could be brought about by perhaps one man with a few accomplices?'

'He would need several accomplices, some in quite senior positions, and he would need to be in a very senior position himself; but if that team was set up, and in place, none of them would have to do very much. Three Mile Island in the United States in 1979 showed the problems that can develop from one jammed valve. An operator misinterpreted the signals and thought the core was cooling down too much, when in fact it was starting to overheat. It was nearly goodnight to most of Pennsylvania. A team who knew what they were doing could easily put any reactor into an irreversible meltdown situation. I would think about six people would be needed.'

'We don't know how many reactors are targets,' said Fifeshire. 'We know there are five countries and at least one in each, and quite possibly more. For each one, they need six men in key positions: that makes quite a lot of people to rely on.'

'It does,' said Quoit. 'On the other hand, the average reactor has between four hundred and one thousand staff, so six out of that lot isn't a large percentage.

'However, in light of the connection with Mr Sleder, I am convinced it is the second option Operation Angel is going for: nuclear explosives. The most effective place to put a nuclear explosive would be actually inside the core itself. Only a very small device indeed need be used to set off a chain reaction that would completely vapourize the core – effectively turn the entire core into a massive atom bomb. The explosion itself would not be particularly large in comparison with other nuclear weapons, but the release of radioactivity would be on an unprecedented scale – many times larger than that any existing nuclear weapon might cause.'

'How would someone get this nuclear explosive into a core?' asked Fifeshire.

Quoit smiled. It was the first time I had seen him smile, and it wasn't a particularly heartening sight. It reminded me of the face of a python I had once watched, just after it had swallowed a rabbit. 'Disguised as a fuel element,' he said.

There was a long silence, then Quoit continued.

'Getting six men to infiltrate a power station might be a

problem; but getting in one small fuel element, a few feet long, a few inches in diameter, would be the easiest thing in the world. No one would bat an eyelid. Hundreds arrive every week.'

'Do all reactors use the same type of fuel?' asked Fife-shire.

'No, they don't, and the elements vary from reactor to reactor; but the manufacturing companies usually make the fuel for a variety of reactors.'

'And how is it put into the reactor?'

'Again it varies. On some types – some older reactors, and the pressurized-water reactors – they have to be shut down at intervals – three months, six months, a year, it depends. But on many types, the refuelling is continual, done by a machine. The reactor might have twenty-eight thousand elements in it, which stay in for about a year. About thirty-five a day are taken out and replaced. Just one accomplice in the fuel storage would be all that was needed to slip the sabotaged element in on the right day.'

'To how many reactors could this theory of yours apply?'

'If this sabotage is to take place on a specific day, dependent on wind direction, it is unlikely that reactors that have to be shut down for refuelling would be chosen, so that eliminates six, including Sizewell and Huntspill Head. We know that they are going to wait for a westerly wind, so power stations on the east coast can be eliminated, as a westerly would blow the radioactivity straight out to sea. That still leaves us with eleven power stations, that have between them twenty-eight reactors. And remember also, it is not just the sabotage of British reactors that could contaminate the south of England. There is Monts D'Arrée, in Brittany, Flamanville, in Normandy: both could contaminate the south-east of England if a southwesterly were blowing when they were hit. Similarly, there is the reactor at Bilbao which could contaminate the whole south of England.'

'What about contamination from American reactors reaching Britain?' I asked.

'It would be pretty diluted by the time it got here, but if there was enough of it, it certainly wouldn't be healthy to breathe it.'

'But healthier than jumping into mill ponds?'

He looked at me, and I could have sworn he was beaming lethal doses of radiation at me from his eyes. I turned to Fifeshire. 'Are you going to warn the other countries involved?'

'No,' he said, 'I am not. I'm not telling anyone, not anyone in this country nor anyone abroad, not the Prime Minister of this country, nor the President of the United States, nor anyone else. I think that our only chance lies in secrecy. You've established that those operating in this country don't know what Ahmed told you, and suspect it wasn't very much. The only other person who could have talked is stretched out on a mortician's slab in Windhoek.

'If I tell anyone in any other country, I might as well send a memo straight to Russia, that's how watertight their security services are. The same applies, quite frankly, to the PM here, and just about everyone else. I am not going to tell anyone at all until either I can tell them who to arrest and where to arrest them, or until I feel there is nothing more we can do. Right now, we, or rather you, Flynn, can do one hell of a lot. As they say in the RAF, right now, we have the height of them, and the sun behind us.'

I nodded. The chief of MI5 was being uncommonly lyrical. When he was lyrical, it meant he was enthusiastic, and when he was enthusiastic, it was usually bad news for me. I wasn't wrong.

Fifeshire turned to Quoit. 'If you are right about the fuel, Isaac, and what you have said certainly sounds plausible, then our friend Deke Sleder fits into this little circle very neatly, wouldn't you agree?'

'For sure. SledAtom – no, the other way around – Atom-Sled could certainly assemble such an element. But why has Sleder picked on Whalley? That doesn't make sense. He doesn't do the buying of fuel. That whole department belongs to British Nuclear Fuels – and they don't buy in fuel, they make the stuff themselves.'

'Does Whalley have any dealings with them?'

'Yes, he does. They come under his authority, but rather tenuously. He wouldn't often have any direct dealings with them – not unless there was a major problem.'

'Have there been any major problems?' asked Fifeshire.

'Not that I know of – certainly not until the time of my – enforced holiday.'

'Could that have been a reason,' said Fifeshire, 'for your kidnapping – to get you out the way?'

'I think someone ought to go and take a look at British Nuclear Fuels rather quickly,' said Quoit.

'I'll get straight on to it.' I said.

'Don't worry, Flynn, I'll deal with them,' said Fifeshire, 'I want you to take your magnifying glass and your spade along to AtomSled. We're going to need some fast digging. They're based in New York, although they've offices in the Sleder headquarters in Hamburg. I think New York is where you'd better start.'

I nodded, not particularly enthusiastically.

Fifeshire looked at his watch. 'The last flight to New York is a British Airways flight at 12.45 – if you hurry you should be able to make it. Did you have anything important lined up for Christmas Day?'

'I did particularly want to hear the Queen's speech.'

'I'm sure someone can record it for you.'

A certain young lady was not going to be too happy with me when I broke the news that I wasn't going to be joining her on Christmas Day after all.

'If you're going to go snooping around AtomSled, what better time than the Christmas holidays – everything slack and shut down for most of the time.'

'Of course, Sir Charles.' He was right, bugger him; he was always bloody right.

20

I had been in New York during Christmas week two years before, and it all looked familiar to me. It was a bitterly cold, overcast day and sleeting as I sat in the back of the cab in a tail-back on the Triboro Bridge.

The driver watched the jam through a haze of cigarette smoke. He drew on his cigarette in short puffs, inhaled very deeply, and then blew the smoke out quickly in front of him. Every time he blew the smoke out, he would shake his head three or four times and make a tutting sound. The plastic driver-identity card informed me his name was Enzo Roscantino, and the face that stared out from the cheap photo looked glum and faintly startled. It was a greasy, pug-shaped face, with high jowls, thick eyebrows and straight, thinning hair, covered in grease. For a bulky man, he spoke with a surprisingly gentle voice. 'Fucking Chreesmiss,' he said, 'whole of New York go fucking crazy at Chreesmiss. Why they don't stay at home – why they gotta go out block tha strits?'

I didn't know why they had to go out and block tha strits; I told him.

'Well, I don't a know either. You home for Chreesmiss?'

If I came here this time of year much more often, it was going to start feeling like home. 'No,' I said, 'I'm not home for Christmas.'

'You come to New York for Christmas? You crazy?'

'You got it in one.'

We were driving down Franklin D. Roosevelt Drive, passing around the edge of Harlem. Across the sidewalk, through a wire fence, I could see into a school playground. A teenage negro was standing there, all alone, watching a ball of paper burn. He looked as cheerful as I felt.

Enzo Roscantino dropped me at the Warwick. He studied the fairly generous tip I gave him carefully, his brow screwed in thought as he did his mental arithmetic; either his arithmetic was bad, or his idea of a generous tip and mine differed widely, but he just gave a curt nod and drove off. 'And a merry fucking Chreesmiss to you,' I said to the fast-disappearing, dented rear end of the Plymouth.

The front desk at the Warwick found me a room with a balcony that looked across onto an office block that was having a Christmas party on every floor. It was Wednesday afternoon; Christmas was on Friday. Provided I could get into AtomSled, I would have three clear days to go through Sleder's business to my heart's content. My heart didn't exactly leap with joy at the prospect. I flipped open my suitcase and began to unpack. It was nearly dark outside, and I was tired from my flight. I opened the French windows and stepped out onto the green astroturf on the balcony, leaned over the stone balustrade, and looked down at the traffic queuing up the Avenue of the Americas, and down West Fifty-Fifth Street, and listened to the blaring of the horns as taxi cabs and private cars hurled their mournful insults at each other.

It was bitterly cold, and a few flakes of snow drifted about. Across the street, on the same level as I was, I saw a light come on in an empty office, and a man and a blonde girl stepped in. He shut the door behind them and started kissing her. She resisted for some moments, but he persisted, then suddenly she seemed to fling her reservations to the wind, and started responding equally vigorously. Another affair was no doubt beginning. Another number, or perhaps two numbers, had started their short journey into the vast gullet of the American divorce courts. But that man, who was just disappearing below my eyeline with that blonde girl, right now, I envied him. Maybe she didn't look so hot close up. Perhaps she had a hooked nose and spots, and bad breath and dirty, scurfy hair, and stank of cheap perfume. Maybe she did, but I had a feeling that she didn't, and that he and she were having a good time over there, and I wasn't having a good time over here at all. There was nothing I was going to be able to do about that until I had found what I wanted and got my ass back on a plane to England and presented myself on Gelignite's doorstep; I hoped that maybe, just maybe, she might forgive me. But from what she'd said when I'd called her from London Airport, it didn't seem likely that she would.

I went to bed, and bad thoughts crashed around in my head all through the long night. I woke at eleven and thought it was four in the morning, and woke at a quarter to twelve and thought it was seven in the morning, and sat in bed until after midnight, too tired from my jet lag to get out of bed and do anything, and yet not tired enough to sleep.

I felt better after breakfast in the morning, and walked through bitter sleet to the New York headquarters of Gebruder Sleder, at Dag Hammarskjöld Plaza, where AtomSled was based. I crossed the road and walked up to the entrance of the copper and smoked-glass monolith that surged towards the sky, and in through the revolving door, which was the only entrance in sight. Glancing up and down inside the door, I could see it was fitted with a securi-counter, an electric security device which works on the simple principle of counting all the people that enter and leave the building throughout the day; if by the time the building is due to be locked up at night the counter has on record more people who have entered than have left, it signals an alarm to the security office. A simple and effective end to my plan A.

I looked up at the name boards; Gebruder Sleder and AtomSled occupied the sixty-fourth floor to the seventy-fourth – the top floor. The rest was a mixture of law firms, United Nations offices, and a plethora of anonymous-sounding corporate names.

I stepped into an elevator and noticed it only went up as far as the sixty-fourth floor – no doubt a security precaution on the part of the Sleder organization. I pushed the top button, the doors shut with a swoosh of air, and my stomach dropped to the ground like a balloon filled with water, whilst invisible hands tried to lift my head and neck up off my shoulders. A digital display before my eyes reeled off floor numbers faster than a bookie writing odds, then the water-filled balloon flew up from the floor and into the base of my neck, and a hefty foot trod on my head, and pushed it down into my shoulders. The digital read-out stopped, and the doors opened, and I wanted her, wanted all of her, wanted right now to own her, take her away to a warm, dark nest, to climb into it and never emerge.

She drew me like a magnet, out of the elevator, across the floor and up to the reception desk. I wanted someone to give her to me for Christmas. I stared into her eyes, then down at her body, most of which I could see clearly through the dress she wore, which appeared to have been made from a trawling net, then back into her eyes again. I concentrated hard on remembering that I had come up here on a recce, to take a brief look, not to carry away prizes.

'Is this Hazier, Cohen and Lipitman?' I said.

Her dark eyes stared right into the centre of mine, and her mouth opened a fraction. Whatever she was going to be doing for Christmas, she knew, wouldn't be half so much fun as spending it with me. 'They're the fifty-fourth floor – you've come to the sixty-fourth.'

'Stay here tomorrow,' I wanted to tell her, 'stay here tomorrow, and wait for me, and we'll spend Christmas here together on Deke.' But I hadn't come here to do that. 'Oh I'm sorry – I didn't read the sign right.' She was still staring at me, staring and smiling. I half-turned to go, swivelled my foot, turned my head, and then stopped. 'Are you doing anything tonight?'

'Not a lot.' She stared into my eyes and smiled a very evil smile.

'Would you like to come out and have some dinner?'

'No,' she said. 'I'd just like to come back to your place and screw all night long.'

I gave her a grin that was as evil as hers. 'I'm at the Warwick, room 2302.'

'What time will you be there?'

'Eight o'clock?'

'I'll try and wait that long, Max.'

A few minutes later the beam in the revolving door picked me up, registered me as having left the building, notified the computer, and awaited the next person. I walked on air up Thirty-Eighth Street. Life is a cunning creature; it keeps you down in the dumps for days on end, then, just when you've had enough of the whole thing, suddenly, for no reason at all, it pats you on the head, like a guilty owner who thinks he's scolded his dog too much, and gives you a biscuit. Right now, the girl on the sixty-fourth floor wasn't merely a biscuit: she was Oysters Rockefeller, a haunch of venison, a huge great chunk of raspberry cream pudding, a mountain of ripe camembert, a '69 Montrachet, a '62 Latour, a '67 Sauternes, a Remy Martin and a Romeo and Juliet corona. Two years ago, she had looked pretty damn good; now she was a stunner.

Unluckily for me, luckily for Gelignite, I came out of my thoughts at the very moment I happened to be walking past Tiffany's, the world's most famous jewellery corner store – and best avoided for breakfast . . . unless you happen to be into eating cut glass. Assailed by a potent mixture of guilt and seasonal cheer, I stepped off the New York sidewalk, through the doorway and onto the soft carpet. The shop was busy, but there was a general hush that needed only the clacking of a ball on a slowly spinning roulette wheel to set it off perfectly.

Walking among the glass cabinets, under a high ceiling, I had the feeling that it would make no difference whether I had one hundred pounds, one thousand pounds, one hundred thousand pounds, or even one million pounds. I, or anyone, could spend a whole day in here, writing out cheques non-stop for any sums, however large, and still not make even a tiny dent in the stock of just one department.

There were more rare animal skins on the backs of the women shoppers than you could ever see at a hundred museums, and there were so many cashmere and vicuña coats with velvet collars wrapped around the men, one might have thought someone was issuing them at the door-way as a standard uniform. The battery of lights everywhere wasn't necessary; there was more than enough light already provided by the reflections of the shining white, capped teeth of the clientele bouncing off the glittering gems and precious metals.

I bought Gelignite a silver bracelet. My American Express card did nicely, but could have done better, the expression on the courteous assistant's face told me. I left Tiffany's and took a cab to the City Hall, where I asked to take a look at the architectural plans of 101 Dag Hammar-skjöld Plaza.

Five minutes later, I was seated at a desk, trying to pre-tend I was an architect and struggling to make sure I got the ruddy things the right way up. The floor plans of seventy-four floors take a while to wade through, but it was long before I got to the end of them that I realized that if I was going to get into that building undetected, and have any chance of remaining in it undetected, then I was going to have to find some other means than via the ground floor.

From the City Hall, I took another cab, to 355 Park Avenue, the head office of a company called the Inter-continental Plastics Corporation. Intercontinental Plastics Corporation was owned, through a carefully maintained front, by MI5. The company made cabinets for computers, and had offices and factories around the world. Its annual profits paid for nearly half of MI5's running costs. I asked for, and was taken straight in to see, Ron Hagget, chief of US Operations for MI5.

Hagget granted my request without asking any ques-tions, and I was grateful to him for that; I never liked lying to my superiors.

'5.00 p.m. tomorrow,' he said, 'it'll be up there.'

'Thank you, sir.'

'How does it feel to be back?'

'Seems like it's getting to be a habit.'

'You're right, New York is a habit. It's as addictive as nicotine and ten times as bad for your health. Still – as they say over here – have a nice day, or what's left of it.'

'Thank you, sir. And a happy Christmas.'

'Thank you, Flynn. You too.'

'I'll do my best.'

'And Flynn—'

'Yes, sir?'

'I don't know why you're over here, and I don't intend to ask – as you know, I only run this outfit, I don't ask questions – but just do me one favour? Don't stir up any flack until after the New Year – I've promised my wife a holiday.'

I grinned at him, but then realized he wasn't smiling. 'It's not that kind of a trip,' I said.

'That's what I was told last time. I'm still clearing up the mess, and that was two years ago.'

He was referring to the wrecked car, demolished building and seven dead bodies I'd left behind last time, which he'd had to try and explain away to the authorities. The Americans don't like the British trampling all over their country, any more than we like them trampling over ours. It's all right to trample over Russia, or indeed any enemy country, but friendly countries are more sensitive, and none more so than the US of A.

Hagget was a frustrated man in his late fifties, with the ambition to get to the top, but not the brain or the political cunning. He was out of the limelight here, and had no real way of getting back into the limelight; he was nothing more than a Transatlantic courier for Fifeshire, maintaining the front, giving operatives assistance, and clearing up the messes they frequently left behind. And no one had left a bigger mess than I had. I wondered if anyone had ever bothered to explain to him what it had all been about. From the tone of his voice, and from the lack of an offer of a Christmas drink, I had a feeling they hadn't. It wasn't my place to tell, even if I had had the inclination, and anyhow, I didn't want to be late back to the hotel.

There was a knock on the door at a quarter past eight, and I went over to open it. Her Mystère de Rochas perfume plunged into the room ahead of her, through the keyhole and under the door. I turned the handle and pulled, and the perfume completely engulfed me. She stood there in a calf-length silver-fox coat, her neck loosely wrapped in a cashmere scarf, her hands in sensuous Cornelia James gloves and her legs in tall black boots. Her large brown eyes were opened wide, and her soft-red painted lips parted, and she leaned forward and kissed me on my lips for a long, long time; then she stood back and looked at me and grinned.

'Want to come in, or shall we stay out here?'

She strode into the room and sat down in an armchair, put her arms around her chest and hugged herself. 'Oooh, it's good to be in the warm. It's starting to snow.' She looked up at me and flashed her eyelids. 'Well, well, Max Flynn! Life is full of surprises.'

I poured her a glass of champagne and handed it to her.

'I see,' she smiled, 'you've really laid on the works!'

'Want to take your coat off and stay a while?'

'I'm not going anywhere – I just want to get warm. Cheers!' She took a sip of the Krug and took a pack of Marlboro out of her handbag. 'Smoke?'

'Thanks.' I took one and held out a light.

She inhaled deeply and grinned. 'Now, you're one guy I really didn't reckon I'd see again.'

'You figured I'd be dead by now?'

'No, I didn't figure that at all. I just didn't think I'd see you. I mean – there wasn't any reason to, was there? We didn't have anything going – you had a girl you were goggle-eyed over, and I was just your humble secretary.'

'I fancied you like crazy.'

'I knew you did – but you never asked me out.'

'Things were very difficult then.'

'Are they any easier now?'

'No – but I'm maybe a little wiser!'

'Cheers,' she said.

We chinked glasses. It was strange to be having this conversation. Her name was Martha. Two years ago, when I'd been in New York on my previous assignment, she had been allotted to me as my secretary. My cover then was Production Control Analyst for Intercontinental Plastics Corporation, and I had no way of telling then whether Martha was a genuine, innocent secretary, or whether she knew the true nature of both my business and Intercontinental's. On a number of occasions I had wanted to ask her out, but a steady bird and a busy schedule had prevented it from happening.

'I just saw Hagget,' I said, 'this evening.'

'How is he?'

'Sour as usual. Tell me, Martha – what the hell are you doing at AtomSled? How long have you been there?'

'Good agents don't talk,' she said.

'You want to bet?'

'Try me,' she grinned.

I did. She put up a spirited resistance, but at five o'clock in the morning she talked. Then I tried her again once more, for luck.

21

Hagget might have been sour, but he didn't let me down; at five thirty the small Bell helicopter was waiting at La Guardia airport, and I clambered in, clutching a soft hold-all. It was pitch dark, sleeting again, and a fierce wind was blowing across the concrete. The engine was already running, and the pilot nodded as I pulled the door shut and strapped myself in. The noise in the small cockpit was deafening.

'Y'okay?' he shouted.

I stuck my thumb up. He pointed to a set of headphones, and I put them on. It was like going into a different world as most of the roar and clatter was suddenly shut out. There was a burst of sharp, dipped speech from the pilot, a crackling hiss, then a reply from the tower. 'Any time you want, Charlie Zero Tango. Watch the wind.'

'I'll watch it. Y'awl have a good Christmas,' he said. He spoke with a heavy deep-South accent.

'We'll try.'

He reached forward with his right hand and pushed the throttle forward. The chopper shook violently, the body-work flapping so hard it sounded as though the whole machine was going to fall apart, then suddenly we lifted off the ground and hovered a few feet above it for some moments while the pilot fought against the buffeting wind to keep us stable. He opened the throttle full, dipped the nose slightly into the wind, and we started to climb upwards.

As the lights became smaller beneath us, we bounced uncomfortably about in the sky, and the pilot was fully occupied keeping the yawing, pitching machine in some semblance of level flight.

After about a minute and a half, he turned to me and pointed to my headphones. I lifted them off.

'Going to have a bumpy ride!'

I nodded in agreement.

'This is one hell of a night to go fooling around in helicopters.'

'I can think of things I'd prefer to be doing,' I shouted.

We were still climbing, and the wind was screaming outside. It was dark and eerie up here, and we were about level now with the tops of the tallest of the skyscrapers, heading in towards Manhattan at a faster rate than I, at this moment, relished. This was one hell of a way to spend Christmas Eve.

'You sure about what you want to do?' shouted the pilot.

'Yes,' I said, feeling very unsure.

'I don't know that I'm going to be able to set you down – this wind's worsening, and I don't know that roof at all.'

'Didn't you fly over it today?'

'Sure I did, half a dozen times; each time it looked worse than the time before. It's not fit to make a perch for a jackal. There's stuff all over the place – the roof of the elevators, ventilators, the air-conditioning motors are all up there. There's just one gap that's good enough, and if we get blown wide of it, you can bend over and kiss your ass goodbye.'

He was right. Landing on the roof of a building isn't easy. It's tough enough in broad daylight with a calm breeze. In the pitch dark, in a gale, on a roof that's not designed for helicopters landing, it wasn't going to be too clever. But then, Sleder hadn't exactly sent me an embossed invite to drop by on him; if he had, with his style for doing things, he would have had the roof levelled and landing lights installed.

'What the hell do you want to go fooling around up here for? Why don't you go in the front door?'

'I lost my key.'

'Oh, I just got it. Don't tell me. You're Santa Claus, right?'

'Right. That's what's in my sack—' I stopped talking suddenly, quite suddenly; anyone would have done. I gulped deeply. Only feet down below and to my right were the top windows of 101 Dag Hammarskjöld Plaza, looking more sinister and uninviting than I could ever have imagined.

'I ain't gonna be able to hang around for too long. I'm gonna set you down and then get my ass out of it. If I get caught by a gust, I'll be over the edge.'

'Okay.'

'Going in now.'

The chopper thumped down onto the black roof. I opened the door. 'Happy Christmas!'

'You too, Santa!'

I jumped down and the wind nearly blew me over backwards as I landed. The chopper lifted off without a moment's hesitation. In the pitch dark, and without its lights on, it had vanished into the sky within moments. The clattering of its engine and rotors faded, and suddenly Father Christmas was alone, very, very alone. The wind howled, tore at my clothes, trying to push me over to the edge.

I put down my hold-all, removed a powerful torch from it, and switched it on.

If this was the sort of thing Father Christmas had to do for a living, I decided he could keep it. The wind ripped through my clothing and through my flesh and through my bones, howling and whining against every object that protruded on the roof. I could dimly see the lights of the Empire

State Building through the thickening sleet, and I could see lights of other buildings over to my right. I was utterly alone; I had never felt so alone. I was on top of the world, in the heart of a city where most people had switched out the lights and gone off to have a good time. During the next few hours, millions of excited children would be climbing into bed and waiting for a bearded man in a red robe to come clambering down their chimneys – at any rate, those that knew what a chimney was. I didn't have a beard or a red robe, and I didn't have any presents to bring down Deke Sleder's chimney.

The beam of the torch found a small steel door, and I prayed that no one had tumbled Martha and prevented her from unlocking it. If I couldn't get in through that door, I would be a dead man by morning; no one could survive the chill factor created by the wind up here for a whole night – and since I'd dismissed my sleigh, there wasn't a wide selection of alternative routes back to the ground short of a mountaineering feat which would have qualified me to climb the north face of the Eiger with my hands tied behind my back.

I switched off my torch, pulled out my Beretta, and turned the handle. The door opened with no effort, and I relaxed, just a fraction, for the first time since I had kissed Martha goodbye that morning. I waited some moments before peering cautiously in and snapping the torch back on. I didn't expect a welcoming party, but I didn't want to take any chances. I shone the torch around. It was a concrete staircase, the fire escape to the roof, exactly as shown on the architect's plans. I pulled the door shut behind me, then, holding my torch in one hand and my gun in the other, I started descending. It was bloody creepy.

I came down onto a floor, went through a door and

found myself in a sumptuous apartment. It had evidently been furnished by an interior decorator to be all that the hospitality apartment of a successful corporation should be, with acres of thick broadloom, Italian porcelain lamps, bronze sculptures in the style of Giacometti, and a master bedroom that any exiled king would have been proud to have died in. It lacked a lived-in feeling, but fortunately it also lacked an occupant.

The larder had been stocked by someone who knew about good food. It was piled with tins of expensive delicacies, as was the freezer, and the booze cabinet had been stocked by someone who knew about good booze. At least I now had the consolation that my Christmas dinner might consist of something a little more exotic than the packets of sandwiches, chocolate bars and apples that lay at the bottom of my hold-all.

There was a large television set, the chairs looked inviting, and I decided it would be sensible to wait until daylight tomorrow to begin my search; the treasures of Sleder's office, on the floor below, would be my Christmas present to myself in the morning.

I helped myself to a large gin, a cold quinine, as tonic is called in the States, a generous portion of ice cubes from the electric dispenser attached to the fridge, and settled myself into an armchair that reclined as I sat in it. I lit a Marlboro, sat back, and decided that I didn't feel too bad . . . didn't feel too bad at all.

As I sat, I reflected on everything that I had learned in the last few weeks. Operation Angel was backed by the Soviet Union and fronted by Namibia. In France, Baader-Meinhoff, doubtlessly in conjunction with the French left wing, was involved. In Spain, ETA was involved. In the US it was Joel Ballard, a professional terrorist. He was in charge of Canada too, although doubtless there was an FLQ connection there. The Front Libération de Québec had been quiet for many years, and although many of their aims had been achieved, many had not. This was no doubt their chance of a return to the big time. In England, as usual, it was the Irish and, for a change, a Namibian with a grudge.

The deadline was eleven days away, and we had no idea which power stations were threatened. We couldn't take any of the people in because we had no evidence, and in any event it would have served little purpose, probably setting us back rather than advancing us. They were almost certainly all operating in individual units, or cells, as the IRA call them, which would be able to survive and continue their work, even without the leaders.

I wondered how much Fifeshire knew that he hadn't told me. Had he placed Martha in that job? She wasn't telling that. But she had told me pretty well all of what she had found out: about Harry Slan and American Fossilized, proving that Quoit was right in his theory – or at least, looked as though he was about to be proved right. The most important thing I had to find out in the next three days was whether Sleder was blackmailing Harry Slan and Horace Whalley, and perhaps others, merely because AtomSled needed orders, or whether Sir Isaac Quoit's hunch was correct.

What I wanted was very well hidden, and it took me until Sunday afternoon to find it; it was hidden in an ingeniously concealed spring-loaded drawer at the back of a filing cabinet in Sleder's own office. I had first to pull the front drawer right out, and then a second drawer popped up behind it. The front drawer had been the first place I had looked, and it was only when I returned to it and in a fit of frustration yanked too hard that I realized it would come out and that there was another drawer behind it.

The file in the drawer was marked, innocently but appropriately enough, *New Business*. It contained a buff folder, a sheath of papers, and a copy of Erica Jong's *Fear of Flying*. Inside the folder were several packs of Kodachrome X colour-negatives, and printed contact sheets. In some of the snaps I recognized my chum Horace Whalley; in the others were a total of eleven different men, none of whom could reasonably be described as good-looking, engaged in virtuoso performances with a bevvy of truly stunning young ladies. All had been captured, either for immortality or for some other purpose, in excellent colour, by a photographer who knew exactly what he was doing. I pressed a button on my ubiquitous Trout and Trumbull adapted Seiko digital quartz watch, and the face disappeared, exposing a tiny camera lens. The quality of my snaps would not be as these, but the fidelity of reproduction would be passable; Henri Cartier-Bresson might have turned in his grave, but it wasn't a one-man show at the National Gallery that I was after. I recorded the faces of each individual, then replaced the snaps in the buff folder. Next, I took the sheath of papers and went and sat down at Sleder's desk.

The papers were divided into five sections; one was headed *United States*, the second *Canada*, the third *Great Britain*, the fourth *France* and the fifth *Spain*.

Being not only patriotic, but also aware of who paid my rent, I turned my attentions first to the sheath marked *Great Britain*. The first page listed the names, locations and types of all the operating nuclear power stations in the British Isles. The second page listed the fuel types required for the advanced gas-cooled reactors, the magnox reactors, the pressurized-water reactors and for the one fast breeder reactor, and the third and fourth pages gave the exact technical specifications of the fuel required for each of the types.

The fifth and sixth pages gave the amount of fuel consumed daily, weekly and annually by each of the reactors, and whether they were required to shut down for refuelling or whether they were on a continual-feed system.

The pages that followed listed all the organizations that comprised Britain's nuclear energy industry, their addresses, telephone numbers and all key personnel of all sections.

In the bottom right-hand corner of the back of the last page was some tiny printing. It was so small as to be hardly legible to the naked eye and it took me some minutes of straining before I could decipher it. It said: *Printed in the USSR.* I thought about that for some moments. Sleder was without doubt a man who went to great lengths to get whatever he wanted. The information that was contained in here was readily available, surely, from a damned sight easier and more accessible source than the Soviet Union?

The other four bundles contained similar information about the nuclear energy industries of the other four countries, and all had the same tiny printing on the back of the last page.

The next sheath of papers interested me even more. The first page was a memorandum, undated, unsigned and not addressed to anyone specific. It stated simply: *All substitute fuel rods or bundles will be identifiable by the initial B in capital letter form following the third digit of their serial numbers. Under no circumstances whatsoever are any rods or bundles of B-marked fuel to be shipped anywhere without my personal authorization.*

There was a second memorandum. It stated: *Instruct Hamburg to allocate 72 bundles for British Nuclear Fuels Limited, 75 bundles for Electricité de France, 71 bundles for confirmation for Spain.* Under each word was a short string of numbers, and attached to the memorandum was a telex from AtomSled Hamburg which read: *101–5–5 /226–18–1 /40–28–2*. I picked up the copy of *Fear of Flying*, turned to page 101 and counted five lines down and then five words across. The word was *We*. The next two words were *are holding*. It was an old but very effective form of code – a book code. They would have a copy of the same novel in Hamburg. Unless anyone intercepting the message knew what the book was, it was virtually impossible to crack the code on such a short message as this. Sleder had evidently been reading his detective novels.

What I needed to know, and badly, was what was special about the B-marked fuel that they had to be marked at all, and what was so special about them that Sleder felt the need to communicate in code. I needed someone who knew about fuel bundles to take a very close look at one, and to do that, I needed to obtain one. I didn't have enough time to go hunting around Sleder's factories, and in any event I wasn't crazy about the idea of poking around a plant stuffed with radioactive nasties in case I ignored one *No Entry* sign too many and found myself in a *No Return* room. So I sat quietly at the grand master's desk and tried to figure out an easier way.

My train of thought was suddenly interrupted when my eyes told my brain that a shadow had all of a sudden fallen across the desk, and my brain figured out that since the chief source of light, the window, was behind the desk and my eyes could see nothing unusual in front of them, then the cause of the shadow must be behind me.

During the three-millionths of a second it took my brain to reach this not illogical conclusion, the nerve ends in my right temple informed my brain that a cold metal object had just been pressed against my right temple. The hammer, anvil and echo chamber within my ear holes on both sides of my head received a series of vibrations, which they passed on to my brain, and my brain decoded these vibrations into words from a human being, male, Caucasian, of strongly Germanic origins. 'Move and I'll shoot,' were the words.

A tidal wave of cold fear thundered through me and I felt that most of my innards had been flushed away. I froze for some moments, trying desperately to gather my wits, and to remember what to do in situations like this. I remembered. 'Didn't anyone tell you it's rude to enter a room without knocking?' I said. I wasn't absolutely sure, but I thought I could hear him thinking.

'I vill ask the questions.'

'Okay. History's my best subject.'

'Shut up. Who are you and vot are you doing here?'

'My name is Deke Sleder. I own the place.'

'Very funny. I happen to know vot Herr Sleder looks like. I have worked for him for ten years.' The gun pressed harder into my temple. 'Who are you?'

'The Ayatollah Khomeni – you probably don't recognize me without my beard.'

I felt the gun push harder.

'Vith a six-inch hole in your head, no one vill recognize you.'

'Herr Sleder wouldn't be pleased if you got blood all over his desk.' I was cursing myself madly for having been too damn complacent; I had left my gun in the bedroom.

'If it vas your blood, I am sure he vould not mind. Herr Sleder does not care for intruders.'

'I think I just heard someone call your name,' I said.

'In a moment, I shall get very angry with you. There is no one else in the building.'

He had fallen for it. Now I knew he was alone. That made

life a little easier – not much but a little, and every little helped in a situation like this. I wanted to see his face and his gun. The chair I was in could swivel freely. Whoever he was, he clearly wasn't going to pull the trigger or he would have done so by now. He was more interested in finding out who I was and what I was doing here.

I swivelled the chair round with all my force, ducked my head down, and as I came round, I grabbed his gun arm with my right hand, pulling him towards me with a violent jerk, at the same time bringing my right foot up into his crutch. He went over my left shoulder, skidded headfirst along the top of the desk, carrying most of the papers with him, and plunged off the end. Unfortunately, he was still clasping his gun, a .44 Smith and Wesson automatic, in his hand.

I heaved the massive desk up and pushed it down on top of him, and heard a winded groan as it crashed down. Either he was a lot tougher, or fitter, or both, than I had thought, for he immediately rolled clear, brought the muzzle of the gun up towards me, and fired a shot which flattened itself onto the wall. I sprang across the room and out the door, went through the fire door and up the concrete steps to the next floor. Just as I reached the top of the steps, I heard the fire door open and footsteps on the concrete. A bullet cracked up the stairwell.

I raced into the bedroom, grabbed my gun from its holster, and snapped the safety catch off. Then I dived down behind the bed, switched the gun to automatic fire, aimed at the door and waited. I heard his footsteps reach this floor, but then he continued on up; he obviously thought I had run up to the roof.

I went out into the corridor, and through the fire door. I heard the unlocked door to the roof bang open. I crept carefully up to the bottom of the stairwell. The door at the top was open and daylight was streaming in. He was up there, busy discovering that I wasn't. I hadn't expected him to be quite so careless – it obviously hadn't occurred to him that I might have a gun, and he displayed no caution at all when he decided that either I had jumped off the roof or I hadn't gone up there at all, and started to come back down. He stepped into the doorway, silhouetting himself against the sky. As he stared down the stairwell, I was the last thing he saw on this planet. He evidently didn't like what he saw. Whether it was me, or my Beretta 93R, I never did find out, because as he tried simultaneously to aim his gun at me and get back out onto the roof, I pulled the trigger, despatching three bullets up the stairs to greet him at a rate of twelve hundred feet per second. They didn't travel particularly quickly in terms of the speed of light, but they travelled quite fast enough to reach him long before he had the chance to pull his own trigger.

The three bullets hit him in the chest, putting an instant and irrevocable halt to that organ, essential for the pumping of blood around the body, about which so much good, bad and indifferent romantic literature has been written. The force of the impact carried him four feet backwards across the roof, and draped him in not the most elegant of poses across the raised portion of an air-conditioning extractor vent.

I cursed. I hadn't wanted to leave any mementoes of my visit behind. Dirty dishes can be washed, beds can be made, ashtrays can be emptied. Corpses are altogether more a problem. Fortunately it was dusk, and it would have been impossible for anyone to see what had happened – not that it was likely anyone would have seen even if it had been broad daylight. All the same, I pulled the man's body into the staircase. He was a large thug of a man in a cheap brown suit, with crew-cut hair. He looked like a low-grade body-guard, no doubt part of Sleder's private army of henchmen and thugs. There was a plastic ID card in his wallet. It stated that his name was Kurt Bruhnler, and he was an authorized security guard at 101 Dag Hammarskjöld Plaza. I searched through the rest of his wallet. There was no gun licence and his driving licence was German. Evidently Sleder imported his own thugs in preference to using the local brand. This particular one was going to require an import-reject sticker.

Hagget was yet again going to be an unhappy man, but I didn't want him to be an unhappy man for a few days yet – not that I cared about Hagget, but I needed time, and needed it badly; I didn't want anyone discovering this corpse just yet. A bunch of keys in Bruhnler's pocket gave me an idea. I went up onto the roof and found the key that fitted the hatch to the elevator motor room. I stepped in and looked at the maintenance certificate. It was dated 28 November. That would be the annual date. Provided nothing went wrong with the elevator in the meantime, it would be eleven months before anyone would go looking inside that hatch.

I pulled Bruhnler's body through and lowered him onto the roof of the elevator. Anyone riding up or down would be quite unaware of the joyless rider on the roof. Not that I intended to let him remain there for eleven months; I would ask the long-suffering Hagget to notify the authorities in a matter of weeks.

I didn't enjoy killing, but I enjoyed the thought of being killed even less. I wondered how long Bruhnler had been watching me, and it made me shiver. I wondered how he had come to be in the building, and whether he had been sent especially – but I decided that was unlikely. He had probably been given the job of keeping an eye on the building over the Christmas weekend and hadn't bothered on the first two days. On the Sunday afternoon, he had probably decided he had better check up, so that if anything was amiss, it wouldn't look as though he hadn't been doing his job when someone else discovered it on Monday morning. Although I shouldn't have done, I grinned at the thought of Bruhnler's strange tomb. Life has its ups and downs, and so, for Kurt Bruhnler, had death.

It was time to depart, and Bruhnler had at least kindly given me the opportunity to leave earlier than I had hoped. When Bruhnler had entered the building, the computer would have noted it. The fact that it was Max Flynn and not Bruhnler who departed was something that was unlikely to bother the computer greatly. All it was concerned with was balancing the numbers, and that my departure would do nicely.

It took me a couple of hours to tidy up and conceal, as best I could, the bullet hole in Sleder's office wall, and I was well pleased with my efforts. It was eight o'clock by the time I got back to the Warwick. I ordered some food up to my room, then sat down in the armchair, and continued the thoughts that Bruhnler had so rudely interrupted.

B-marked fuel rods and bundles – what the hell was special about them? It was looking more and more as though Quoit was right. I needed to get hold of one and quickly. I still didn't know which power stations they were for. Seventy-two bundles for England. I remembered that the daily average per reactor was about thirty-six bundles; that was two days' supply for one reactor – or one day's supply for two reactors. We could notify all the countries concerned, have them check all fuel bundles in every power station until they found the B-marked ones; but that wouldn't necessarily work. If the stations were already infiltrated, there was no way of being sure that whoever did the checking wasn't an accomplice and therefore wouldn't report anything. Those telexes were dated 23 December. It was unlikely that anything would have been shipped before Christmas, so the bundles were at the moment almost certainly still at AtomSled in Hamburg. They were probably to be sent between Christmas and the New Year, when most industries are running short of manpower and security tends to be lax. Sleder was evidently monitoring everything like a hawk. We had to stop the fuel leaving Hamburg until we could get surveillance organized on all AtomSled's factories and warehouses – the stuff could have been anywhere – and then we had to follow it to wherever it was shipped and stick with it. Sleder somehow, for a few days, had to be removed from the scene; just long enough to delay the start of the shipment until it could be identified. Getting a man like Sleder out of the way was not going to be easy.

I went to bed and dreamed dreams of mockery, and failure, and death, and woke in the middle of the night in a cold sweat – one of the great perks of my trade. Then I went back to sleep again, and this time the night was kinder to me.

22

I got up early and took a cab to La Guardia airport. I went to the Air Canada desk and bought a ticket for the eight o'clock shuttle to Toronto, then went to the bookstall and bought a copy of *Fear of Flying*. I had read it before and it didn't put me off air travel; it had about as much to do with flying as *Breakfast at Tiffany's* had to do with eating.

An hour and a half later the McDonnell-Douglas DC9 was sinking down slowly across Lake Ontario. Out to the right I could see bits of Toronto rising from the vast whiteness of snow: the CN Tower with its blinking lights, billed as the world's tallest free-standing structure, the black towers of the Toronto Dominion Centre, the silver-blue Commerce Court, a small concentrated clump of modern high-rise office blocks around these, and beyond them a massive urban sprawl stretching thirty miles down the lake and fifteen miles back from it.

Toronto has a special kind of cold in winter; there are plenty of places where the temperature in winter is lower, but nowhere I have ever been feels as cold as Toronto in winter. As I stepped down the gangway I could have told where I was, even if I had been blindfolded, by the icy blast that engulfed me.

I hired a Ford from Avis and drove out of Malden airport. The car had a tag on the ignition which warned that it ran on low-lead gasoline; it also had a catalytic converter to re-burn the exhaust gases, an economy metering device, a computer which worked out the consumption, several hundredweight of plasticized rubber glued to both ends of the car to absorb impacts, and a pint-sized engine that with the best will in the world, a steep hill and a following wind, was going to be hard pushed to propel this frugal, ecology-minded, four-wheeled battering ram up to anywhere near the eighty-five miles per hour mark on the speedometer, which, in the States, is the maximum speedometers on new cars are permitted to read. The Canadians will soon be stuck with it too.

I drove onto the massive Highway 401 West which had a battery of central lanes running in each direction, a similar battery of feeder lanes either side of the central lanes, and twin slip-lanes on either side of those. There was enough room on that road for the RAF to have landed a squadron of bombers abreast. I turned off onto Highway 400 and then onto Highway 7 North towards the village of Kleinburg, home of Canadian art.

I turned off before Kleinburg and headed across country towards a village called Terra Cotta. I kept the map sprawled out on the seat beside me, but the route I had worked out was simple to remember, and I didn't need to look at it. This road was packed with snow, and the over-light power steering gave me no sensation at all through the steering wheel as to what the front wheels might be up to. There is a knack to driving on hard snow, and since I managed to keep the car out of the ditches, on the road, and pointing vaguely forwards, I assumed I must have acquired that knack.

Some miles before Terra Cotta, I passed a gas station with a tumbled-down-looking café beside it. A large, rotting sign on the front of the café informed the world that its name was Rita's Rest-Up, and that it offered a wide range of gourmet delights from hamburgers to cheeseburgers. A couple of trucks and a beat-up old Chevvy indicated that trade for Rita, whilst not altogether booming, was not dead either.

Past Rita's Rest-Up was some wasteland, and then a crossroads with traffic lights. To the left was a furniture warehouse. I looked down to the right and saw the sign I wanted. It said *Antiques* in large white letters on a black background, and there was the mandatory, rotting, wooden cartwheel, bolted to the front wall of the building. I drove onto the patch of snow in front, which I presumed was the place referred to in a smaller sign which said *Patrons' Car Park*, and switched off the ignition. Before getting out of the car, I reached my hand inside the breast pocket of my jacket, unclipped the top of my holster, and switched the safety catch on my Beretta to the off position. Then I went into the shop.

It was dark, and piled high with the usual paraphernalia to be found in the type of shop that keeps itself one rung above the category of junk shop, not by the quality of its merchandize, but keeping its merchandize in some semblance of order and cleanliness. Anything that could be dusted had been dusted, and anything that could be polished had been polished, and anything that could be included had been included. There were bottles, jars, china with willow patterns, china with floral patterns, china with geometric patterns, Coronation mugs, a porcelain ashtray in the school of late twentieth-century Frank J. Woolworth, a chipped jardinière, a fading reproduction of a portrait of Lester Pearson, a former Prime Minister of Canada of whom Winston Churchill once asked, 'Who is that funny Canadian with the squeaky voice?'; a small paper-roll organ stood out from the rest of the artefacts as actually being quite old and quite pretty.

There was no one in the shop although a bell had pinged

as I walked in. After some moments a woman appeared and stood in the doorway, watching me idly. She was in her late thirties, but looked older. She was underweight and had no make-up on her face; she wore a cheap cotton dress with a thin, badly worn cardigan over it. Her skin was pale with thick wrinkles, and there were dark rings around her eyes. She might once have been very pretty, but now she was wracked with misery and more than a little trace of fear.

I turned the handle of the organ and a few tinny strands of 'Silent Night' twanged out. I looked over towards the woman. 'How much is this?'

'Isn't there a price ticket?' She had an English accent, North Country, probably Yorkshire.

'No,' I said.

'I don't know, I'm afraid – I can find out later for you.'

'Is the boss out?'

'No – he's asleep upstairs.'

'I can wait.'

'He won't be up until after midday.' She looked at a clock on the wall. It said ten fifty.

'Are you Mrs Sparrow?'

Her eyes widened and she jumped, as though she had put her finger into a live electric socket. Her face went even whiter and then flushed red. 'No,' she said.

She was.

'I am Mrs Barker.'

'How is Harvey?'

'I don't know any Harvey.'

'You've been married to him for fourteen years.'

'My husband's name is John,' she said coldly, trying to be matter-of-fact and not succeeding. She looked nervously at me.

I nodded and didn't say anything.

'Who are you?' she asked. 'And what do you want?'

'I want to buy a Victorian paper-roll organ.'

'If you come back in a couple of hours, my husband should be – er – back. He'll be able to tell you the price.'

'You just said he was asleep upstairs.'

'Did I? I made a mistake. He's out. It's just a store room upstairs.'

'Mind if I take a look? There might be some more interesting objects up there.'

'No, please. Why don't you go away and leave us? Leave us alone.'

I looked at her; there was suffering across every inch of her face.

'Who are you?' she asked again. 'Why have you come here? Didn't you people promise us a new life? New names, money to start a business, a new country? Wasn't that the deal? Hasn't he done enough for you? Didn't you promise that for the rest of his life he would be left alone?'

'Not me personally.'

'Well – your bloody government.'

'We're not entirely convinced he kept to his side of the bargain. You know what they say about a sailor having a girl in every port?'

She nodded, puzzled.

'Well, where I come from, they say that Harvey Sparrow has got a skeleton in every closet.'

Tears began to roll down her face. 'Would you like a cup of tea?' she asked.

'No, thanks,' I shook my head.

'I'm sick of him, sick to death of him and this life, this place, the constant deceit. I didn't want to go up and wake him, not because I didn't want to disturb him, but because I'd sooner lose a sale than look at his bloody face one more time than is absolutely necessary.' She started to weep, and sat down on the stool of a Spinning Jenny. 'Is it wrong to speak like that about one's husband?'

'Not if his name's Harvey Sparrow.'

'I want to go back to England.'

'You're free to do that. It's not you that's upset anybody – only him.'

'Maybe I will,' she said, 'maybe I just bloody will.'

I left her weeping and went up the stairs and found the bedroom. The former MI5 agent, who had earned for himself the not particularly flattering nickname of the Stoat, was still slumbering. He was on more hit lists than it was possible to count. Three different factions of the IRA wanted him dead, so did a dozen other terrorist organizations; the French, Italian, German and Dutch Secret Services would have given their back teeth for a pot-shot at him, and if they all failed, there was many a person inside MI5 who would have paid good money to have had his head in a cross-haired sight.

I crept into the room, my gun in one hand, and walked over to the bed. I ripped the bedclothes back, and rammed my gun into his naked stomach. 'Wakey wakey!'

He tried to sit up, but I pushed the gun further into his stomach. 'Sorry to remove your bedclothes, Harvey, I wanted to make sure you didn't have your tool wrapped around a trigger.'

'Flynn?'

'You got it in one.'

'What the hell do you want?'

'Got a little assignment for you.'

'Oh no. I finished with all that. Remember?'

'Yes, I remember. I remember how you near as dammit got me killed sending me into a goddam booby-trapped house, because you'd been out fucking a woman instead of doing your job – or was it perhaps that you wanted me to get blown up?'

'So, you're still alive. Don't get so uptight – and get out of my room. I got a deal from the British government whether you like it or not, and that deal sticks.'

'The government gave you a golden handshake because it believed that you had become a prime target for the Russians, not to mention half the rest of the world. That's why it let you retire at forty with a new identity and gave you enough money to set up your antique business. It didn't expect you to go promptly and make your peace with the Russians, and start to flog them secrets.'

'You're mad. This is rubbish.'

'Two months ago a KGB officer defected. His name was Anatole Mijkov. He told us all about you. Happier?'

Sparrow scowled. 'So you've come to tell me the picnic's over? You think this is a fucking picnic – here in this Godforsaken dump with a manic-depressive wife? Is that what you think?'

'You make your bed, you've got to sleep in it.'

'That's what I was trying to do.'

'Canada's obviously good for you, Sparrow, it's given you a sense of humour.' I lifted the gun from his stomach and tossed his bedclothes back over him. 'You've got a horrible body, Sparrow, I can't stand looking at it any longer.'

'Nobody invited you to in the first place.'

'I've got an assignment for you, Sparrow,'

'You can stuff it.'

'Then you're coming with me to Toronto.'

'What the hell for?'

'I'm taking you to the police and I'm going to ask them

to charge you, under the British Official Secrets Act, with selling classified information to the Soviet Union.'

'You're joking.'

'No, my friend, Canada hasn't given me a sense of humour. I am most definitely not joking.'

There was a silence, then Sparrow spoke. 'What's involved?'

'I knew you'd come round to our way of thinking.'

'I'm not agreeing – I want to know what's involved.'

'Nothing much. A little burglary and a long train ride. Get dressed. I'll explain everything in the car.'

'Car? Where are we going?'

'I'm taking you to the airport. You've got to make a flight to Seattle in exactly—' I looked at my watch – 'seventy-five minutes.' I pulled out of my pocket a thick brown envelope. 'Put this in your pocket before you forget it. It's plane tickets, train ticket and ten thousand dollars expenses.'

His eyes opened wide.

'And I want every cent accounted for. You aren't going on a freeloading holiday jaunt.'

'Really?' he said. 'You could have fooled me.'

I dropped Sparrow at the airport, then drove into Toronto and checked into the Four Seasons Hotel. It was twenty to one. I went to the cashier's desk and changed thirty dollars into quarters, then left the hotel and found a call box down the street. A few seconds before one o'clock, I dialled the number of a call box in Manhattan. It was answered before it even rang once.

'Hallo?' It was Martha's voice.

'How are you?'

'Fine, Max. And you?'

'I'm okay; I got what I wanted, or at least a lot of it.'

I decided not to tell her about Bruhnler. 'Anybody twig me?'

'Not as far as I know.'

'Good. When exactly is Sleder due back from Gstaad?' She had told me he had flown over there to spend Christmas.

'Tomorrow afternoon.'

'He's not going to Hamburg today?'

'Definitely not. He's going to a luncheon in Monaco and then flying out here tomorrow morning.'

'As soon as he's arrived in the office tomorrow, I want you to send a telex to AtomSled Hamburg – can you get to the telex machine?'

'Yes.'

'Okay. When you've sent the telex, I want you to jam the machine up.'

'How badly?'

'Enough to stop it receiving any replies for the rest of the day.'

It was unlikely there would be any reply the same day, since it would be late afternoon at the earliest in Hamburg before they received the telex, but I didn't want to take any chances. I took the pieces of paper on which I had written down numbers from the pages of *Fear of Flying* from my wallet, and read the numbers out over the phone. 'Good luck,' I said.

'You too, Max. Take care.'

'I'll call you Wednesday, 8.00 a.m.' I hung up, then dialled Fifeshire's number in London. I needed one boffin to be despatched smartly.

After I had spoken to Fifeshire, I went to the Toronto branch of Thomas Cook and had a good look at aircraft schedules and railway timetables, and then there wasn't a great deal more I could do until the following morning. Oscar Wilde once described the Niagara Falls as 'a vast, unnecessary amount of water, flowing the wrong way, and falling over an unnecessary amount of rocks. Sooner or later,' he said, 'every American groom takes every American bride to the Niagara Falls, and they must surely be the second biggest disappointment in American married life.'

His observations did not deter eight million tourists a year from making the pilgrimage down the Niagara peninsular – where, incidentally, the grapes for some of the world's most revolting wine are grown – to see for themselves, and I decided to do likewise. I stood in the teeming spray, as the water slid gently over the lip, before thundering down into the foaming abyss with a demonstration of power it would be hard to rival, and I decided his estimation of the cunning of the Marquis of Queensbury wasn't the only thing poor Oscar had been wrong about.

23

The train's horn blasted twice, and we flashed through a tiny station. *Short Richard's offspring divides nation with friendly underground railroad.* I looked at the clue for the hundredth time in the last twenty-four hours since I had boarded the train at Winnipeg. It was 6.45 p.m., Thursday, New Year's Eve, and Operation Angel was due to start in five days' time. The ground outside now was thick with snow, and the sky, which had been dark grey all day, was now black.

In a first-class compartment two carriages down, with drawn curtains and a locked door, Douglas Yeodal, the nuclear energy expert, ace lecturer and pacifier of the press, from Huntspill Head, was quietly dismantling and examining a nuclear fuel bundle with the letter B clearly stamped after the third digit of its serial number. The bundle had been obtained by Harvey Sparrow after a lengthy search, not a little bribery, and not a lot of burglary, from the storage depot of American Fossilized's Seattle plant.

I lifted my eyes from the baffling clue to fourteen across of the *New York Sunday Times* crossword and rested my gaze on Harvey Sparrow, who sat opposite me, finger working away at a bogey, with a generally indifferent expression on his face to his surroundings, his task, and probably to his life. He was under instructions that we did not know each other, had never met before, and were not to speak one word to each other, except for necessary courtesies, throughout the journey. To his credit, he had been professional enough not to have disobeyed my instructions, even though he must have discovered by now that at some point, in between his arriving at Winnipeg station and his ordering of a beer in the buffet car an hour after boarding the train, an unseen hand had removed his wallet from his breast pocket and replaced it with my own.

Between Sparrow and the window sat a man who constantly ran a hand across his face, as if checking his stubble. If he was worried about his appearance, he needn't have bothered; none of us looked too hot after a night of sleeping in our seats. There were beds in first class, but except for the one compartment I had been able to get for Yeodal, all the accommodation on the train with beds had been taken, and so we were slumming it.

The other person who didn't appear to be slumming it was Sleder. He wasn't in any of the open carriages, so if he was on the train, and I was damned sure he was, then he must have been behind one of the curtained windows of the first-class bedroom compartments. It hadn't taken me long to get put through to him on the telephone on Tuesday. The girl on the switchboard had answered on the first ring, and used the current jargon popular with the switchboard operators of all go-ahead New York corporations.

'Good morning, AtomSled, how can I help you?'

'By putting me through to Deke Sleder, please.'

'Just one moment. May I say who's calling, please?'

'My name is Max Flynn.'

'One moment, Mr Flynn, I'll see if he's in.'

Click.

'Mr Sleder's office,' said a new girl.

'I'd like to speak to Mr Sleder.'

'Oh I am sorry, Mr Sleder's in a meeting all day. Can anyone else help you?'

'No, this is very important. I'd like you to give him a message; I'll hold because I think he'll want to reply.'

'I'm afraid I can't do that, sir – he is not to be interrupted.'

'You'll have to interrupt him, this is an emergency. Will you please tell him that there is a problem with his B-grade fuel.'

She sounded dubious. 'Well, I'll try. Will you hold the line, please, Mr Flynn.'

Inside of thirty seconds, an American drawl with a heavy German accent came down the telephone. 'This is Sleder. Who are you? I don't know you, Mr Flynn.'

'If you want to find out, I'm going to be boarding the Rail Canada Vancouver to Montreal express, eastbound, in Winnipeg, at 6.00 p.m. tomorrow evening.'

'Is this a joke? You want me to travel across Canada? On a train?'

'I have a fuel element, manufactured by your firm. I am being met in Montreal by a senior representative of Atomic Energy of Canada Limited. I intend to give him your fuel bundle. Its serial number is 546B/98066/31. If you don't believe I have it, go and check North American Fossilized's store room.'

'So that makes you a thief.'

'Call it what you like, Sleder.'

'Do you want money?'

'I don't want money, Sleder. I want a fuel bundle that isn't faulty. I've promised to give one to the Canadians, and I'd hate to give them a dud one. Why don't you bring a nice one, in perfect order, and we can make a little swap?'

'I'm not sure that I understand you, Mr Flynn.'

'Well, you've got plenty of time to think about it. The

train leaves shortly after eighteen hundred hours, Winnipeg time. Maybe I'll see you on it.'

'One moment, I want to know—'

I didn't hear the rest of what he said, because I hung up.

To my right in the carriage was a man who had spent the whole of the last twenty-four hours – except for some times during the night when he tried to sleep – with his head buried in a succession of intellectual magazines, with the occasional incursion into James Gavel's *Tai Pan*; he was reading *Tai Pan* at the moment, and was making slow progress. In the last hour and a half he had read only nine pages.

To the left of Sparrow was a human gorilla. He was about thirty, with straight greasy hair brushed forward, and traces of sideburns running straight down both cheeks. He had several large and raw-looking spots on his face, a yellowy complexion, and a set of teeth that looked like the door sill of an abandoned car. He belched frequently and privately, and sniffed loudly and not so privately, occasionally wiping drips from his nose on his dirty tweed sleeve. He wasn't the sort of person it would be wise to sit next to if you had an open wound.

He spent the time either sleeping, with his mouth opening and shutting, or awake, playing solitaire on a small plastic travelling board he kept in his jacket pocket. When he slept, his head did not tilt forward but lay back against the cushion behind his head. Sometimes he did genuinely seem to be asleep, but most of the time I had the feeling he was watching the compartment through tiny gaps in his eyelids.

I pointed the tip of my ball-point pen back up towards the Gucci briefcase, and once more the digits on the tiny dial in the barrel began to rotate crazily. Whilst the pen was actually capable of writing, its primary function was not the business of writing at all. It was a Geiger counter that could detect radiation within a radius of several hundred yards. Right now, it detected a lot of radiation in the Gucci briefcase. It would have been stretching the laws of co-incidence too far to have considered that the content of that briefcase might be anything other than an AtomSled-manufactured fuel bundle.

For twenty-four hours, none of the three men. other than Harvey Sparrow, with whom I wasn't concerned, had lifted a finger towards their briefcases. In my phone call to Martha of yesterday, she had warned me that whilst Sleder was arranging to take a fuel bundle on the train, his main intention was to have me bumped off long before we got to Montreal.

The best way to thwart this not particularly pleasant plan, I had decided in the short while it took me to figure out, was to kill his hit man before his hit man killed me. But to do that, I had to find him first. As neither the hit man nor I had met each other before, we both had the initial problem of identification.

In case he thought of the bright idea of taking a look at his travelling companions' wallets, I had switched mine with Sparrow's. I had a feeling Sleder would use the hit man as his bag man, and all I had to do was fit the face to the bag to be in a definite position of one-upmanship. But the three did not make life easy for me; none of them would open his bloody briefcase. My arrangement with Sparrow was that one of us would be in the carriage at all times, and by facial signals he would indicate to me if I had missed the opening of a briefcase while I was out. In theory it was a simple proc-ess of elimination: the man who had the fuel bundle would not be opening his briefcase at all.

I decided to give it a break and go and see how Doug Yeodal was getting on. A lot hung on his findings, and I was pretty certain he was going to find something. If Sleder had nothing to hide, he wouldn't have got so bothered as he evidently had. I got up and walked down the aisle and through into the next coach, a first-class sleeper. I stopped outside a compartment where the blinds were drawn; it was in this compartment that I was sure I had seen a girl I recognized. I wondered whether to knock, and then decided against it. She had had as clear a look at me as I'd had at her. She had changed the colour of her hair, and now wore glasses; I hadn't changed at all. If it was the same girl, she would have recognized me without doubt, and if she was interested in seeing me again, she would have come and found me. She hadn't come. I turned and walked on down the corridor, into the next coach, and up to Doug Yeodal's compartment. The blinds were down, and I knew the door would be locked; I opened it with the key I had and went in.

'Hallo, Doug,' I said, and then I found I was talking to an empty compartment, and I turned very, very cold. There was nothing: no suitcases full of instruments and chemicals, no nuclear fuel bundle, and no Doug Yeodal. I checked the compartment number and the coach number. There was no mistake; he had gone, lock, stock and bundle.

The compartment was neat and tidy, there was no sign that there had been a struggle; and yet, the blinds were drawn and the door was locked. It didn't make any sense. There was no way Doug would have left of his own accord, no way at all. Something had happened. I didn't yet know what, but I didn't like it.

I walked up the rest of the train, and then back down, peering in every compartment that didn't have its blinds down, and I saw no sign of either Doug Yeodal or his suitcases. Unless what had been in that bundle had vapourized Yeodal, his baggage and itself, someone had come and taken him and his apparatus clean away.

I returned to my carriage. Harvey Sparrow wasn't in his seat and I wasn't very pleased; I assumed he'd gone either to the lavatory or to get a drink, which was bloody stupid of him; he knew his instructions were not to be out of the carriage if I was.

After an hour, Sparrow had still not reappeared, and I was not liking it one bit. I went to look for him, but the conjurer had been at work again. He'd gone. Two grown men had now vanished into thin air – and neither grown men nor anyone else vanish into thin air. An hour and a half ago, Sparrow had been sitting opposite me, picking his nose for all he was worth; now he wasn't on this train, or if he was, he was damn well hidden.

If Sleder was picking off my team one by one, he was doing an efficient job; there was only me to go. However, short of barricading myself in the guard's van for the rest of the journey, I wasn't quite sure what to do about it, and barricading myself away wouldn't get me very far, except, perhaps, to keep me alive, which ought to have been enough, but I didn't see it that way. I took the safety catch off my gun and returned to my seat.

The man opposite me continued to check his stubble and look out of the window. The reader on my right had somehow read one hundred and nine pages of *Tai Pan* in my absence, and the gorilla was busy moving solitaire pegs into new slots, and discarding taken ones into the plastic lid, with a rhythmic click, tap, click, tap, click, tap.

Suddenly I saw that the man who was reading *Tai Pan* wasn't reading it any more: his eyes were looking at me. He lifted his copy of the novel to reveal that he was holding an object which looked to me, at first glance, remarkably like a .44 calibre Luger; it required only the most cursory of second glances with my trained eye to establish beyond any reasonable doubt that it was indeed a .44 calibre Luger, with a device attached over the barrel that bore more than a passing resemblance to a silencer. I didn't require a third glance to see who the gun was pointed at. I looked over at the man with the stubble, and then at the gorilla; both of them had succeeded in producing Lugers out of thin air. Right now, I wished I could have done the same.

The gorilla stood up, followed by Stubble, and between them they blocked off the aisle in both directions. The intellectual indicated to me, with a remarkable economy of words, that I should stand up between the two. 'Up,' was all he said. It was enough. I stood up and stepped into the aisle. Then, sandwiched between the gorilla and Stubble, with a sharp object pushing into the small of my back, we shuffled in and out of step into the next coach, a first-class bedroom coach, and stopped outside a door with drawn curtains.

The gorilla slid open the door, and I was pushed in. The compartment was large – in fact two compartments turned into one. There was a man sitting in a lounging position, reading a document; he looked up as I and the three musketeers came in. I had never met this man before, but I had little difficulty in recognizing him from the newspaper photographs. It was Deke Sleder, and he didn't bother with any introductions.

'Perhaps you would care to tell me the meaning of this charade you have organized – but first, perhaps you would be kind enough to place your hands on your head, my acquaintances appear to have overlooked something.'

I didn't have much option, and Sleder reached across inside my jacket and pulled out my Beretta.

'How very observant of you, Sleder. That probably explains why you're a millionaire and they're just humble thugs.'

Sleder smiled, a short, dry smile. His blue eyes looked cold, cold as swimming pools in winter. 'We'll keep the jokes to a minimum, Mr Flynn. Now, please talk – you have the floor.'

'I don't talk to loaded guns,' I said, and sat down and stared at him. For some reason, it upset him quite a lot; he stood up and smashed me with the palm of his hand, and then sat down again. If he hadn't shown his colours before, he'd certainly done so now.

'Where are Douglas Yeodal and Harvey Sparrow?'

'Dead, Mr Flynn, as you will be in a few minutes too. Your technician man was removed from the train during the night – as was his luggage – through the window of his compartment. But do not worry – we are not litter louts – we arranged for everything to be collected. If you wish to see your friend Mr Sparrow, then it will give me great pleasure to show him to you. He did very kindly point out to us that he was Harvey Sparrow and not Max Flynn, but all the same, we felt it might not be wise to keep him alive.'

Sleder stood up, peeled back the carpeting from the floor, to reveal a hatch. He lifted up the hatch, and there was a very dead-looking Sparrow, his neck twisted horribly, lying in a large metal container attached to the underside of the compartment floor.

'Very ingenious,' I said.

'You may not know, or you may know but have forgotten, that my company has very extensive links with the railroad. I can get small favours done.'

'How very convenient,' I said, 'I have problems even getting a housekeeper.'

I was trying to figure out my next move and I wasn't getting very far.

'I am sorry to hear of your problems,' he said. 'In a few moments, you will be able to discuss them quietly with Mr Sparrow.'

'Tell me, Sleder, what the hell are you doing? What are you doing all this for? What's so damned special about your B-marked fuel?'

'That is my business and it is going to remain my business.'

'I've beaten you to it, Sleder.'

He pulled a sheet of folded paper from his inside pocket, and handed it to me. It was a telex; the one I had told Martha to send to AtomSled.

'The telex in that office does not connect with the telex network. It connects only with a second machine that is rather well concealed. This second machine prints out the message and holds it until a code is punched into the machine; only I know the code. You have held up nothing; the fuel shipments have been made already. You have achieved nothing except to waste a great deal of my time. I would like to know who you are, and what your purpose in doing all this has been?'

Three automatic Lugers pointed at me: one on my right, one diagonally opposite and to my right, the third diagonally opposite and to my left. My own gun was in Sleder's pocket. It wasn't hard to think of occasions, in life, when things had looked brighter. I was going to have to pull off something damn smart to get out of this one, and at this particular moment, no damn smart idea presented itself. The important thing was to keep talking, for as long as I kept talking, I was still alive, and as long as I was alive, I was in with a chance.

'It's been rumoured,' I said, 'that someone's trying to do a lot of damage to a lot of power stations. I'm trying to stop that happening. Does that answer your question?'

'About five per cent of it.'

'What's the big deal with the B-marked fuel?'

'I thought you already knew, Mr Flynn.'

'My guess is that it contains nuclear explosives.'

Sleder's eyes narrowed. 'I'm not interested in your guess-work, Mr Flynn.'

'But am I right?'

'I would not give you the satisfaction of telling you.'

'If you're going to kill me anyway, I don't see what harm it would do?'

'I'm sure you don't. That's why I am going to remain rich and alive, and you are about to become poor and dead.' He smiled, pleased at having turned my phrase. He nodded at Stubble, who reached up and brought down a small leather suitcase, also genuine Gucci, from the luggage rack, opened it up, and removed a syringe and a bottle. He eyed me the way a hungry man in a lousy restaurant would eye a shriv-elled lamb chop that had turned up on his plate when he'd ordered a sixteen-ounce T-Bone; he thrust the needle of the syringe through the top of the bottle, pressed the plunger all the way in, pulled it out again slowly, as it pulled the pale yellow fluid up with it.

Sleder looked at me with more than a trace of satis-faction on his face. 'Judging from the pin-pricks on Ogomo's arm, you know quite a lot about the use of this drug, Mr Flynn.'

I didn't reply. I was busy thinking, and I didn't want to lose my concentration and, as a result, my timing. The intel-lectual on my right was holding his gun over my arm. His eye was on the syringe. The gorilla by the door was also looking more at the syringe than at me. Sleder did not have a gun out and Dr Kildare alias Stubble, had his hands full.

I brought my right arm up sharply, smashing my knuckles into Intellectual's elbow, and the Luger flew across the compartment; I grabbed his arm with my left hand, pulled it down so hard over the arm of the seat that it snapped in two with a crack that sounded like a shot; he howled and half-stood up in his seat, which gave me enough leverage in my right arm to insert it under his shoulder and hurl him across into Stubble. I dived headlong for the gorilla in the corner, clamped my hand around his gun wrist, and rammed my left hand as hard as I could into his crutch, grabbing for his balls. For one glorious moment I had the Luger all to myself, then I felt an arm clamp on mine, there was a jarring thump and then everything went black.

When I came to, I couldn't move. I was lying lengthways across the seat, my hands and feet bound so tightly they were hurting, and I was conscious that the shirt sleeve of my left arm was rolled up. I opened my eyes and saw Sleder's face staring at me. His lips parted slightly, and at the same time I felt a tiny prick in my arm; I began, right away, to feel very good.

It's a drug, I told myself, Fight. You don't feel good, it's an illusion. I started to fight it. Fighting it felt good. I could see kindness in Sleder's face; it was full of kindness. Resist. Fight. Why? He's a nice man, they're all nice men; they're kind and they want to help me. Let them help. Answer their questions; if you answer them it will enable them to help you. There was a terrific, wonderful feeling from the centre of my body, which radiated outwards, basking every inch of me in happiness. I loved these people.

'What's your name?'

'Max Flynn. It's Maximilian, actually, Max for short.'

'How old are you, Max?'

'Thirty-two.'

'Who do you work for?'

Resist. Must resist. Drugged. Fight. But they're so nice. Everything is so nice. Trap. 'I work for Noddy.'

'Do you, Max? What do you do for Noddy?'

'I don't, I don't really work for Noddy. I lied.'

'We didn't think you did, Max.'

'I didn't mean to lie. Actually I—' Resist. Fight. Don't talk about work. Tell a story. Can't. Got to. Make it plausible. 'I'm a journalist.'

'Are you, Max?'

Sleder's face started jerking up and down. I closed my eyes and opened them. He was sticking his tongue out at me. I stuck mine out back, but he didn't laugh; in fact, he didn't move at all. I heard a little girl's voice. Sleder leaned forward, close to me, and then he disappeared from my line of vision. Something strange was going on, but I couldn't figure out quite what. That good feeling was going fast; I was coming back into reality and I wasn't sure that I wanted to – not until I saw her face staring at me. The final drops of the Pentothal drained from my bloodstream, and I found I was in a railway compartment with four dead men and a stunning red-head with a Smith and Wesson automatic in her hand.

She stood, frozen to the spot, her face sheet-white, and her gun-hand shaking.

'Thanks,' I said.

She shook her head, and looked nervously around. She looked like she was going to burst into tears. 'I've never killed anyone before,' she said.

'You should take it up professionally – you'd make a fortune.'

She looked at me, and some of the shock went from her face. She grinned. I had last seen her a shade over two years ago, as she had walked into the departure lounge at Kennedy Airport, and disappeared from my life. She hadn't been very pleased with me on that occasion, after I had caused her treasured Jensen to be riddled with bullet holes and badly bashed, but from the expression on her face, and her actions of the last couple of minutes, it appeared she wasn't still quite so upset about it.

'You look terrific, Sumpy.'

'You look like a chicken,' she said; 'I'll untruss you. Have you been reading your manual upside down?'

'What do you mean?'

'You got it all wrong: they should have been tied up and you should have had the gun.'

'It's funny you should mention it – I had a feeling something was wrong.'

She untied my hands and started working on the cord around my legs. Her name was Mary-Ellen Joffe, but I called her Sumpy on account of a passion she had for making love whilst soused from head to foot in Johnson's Baby Oil, her name being taken, in the nicest possible way, from the oil sump of a motor car. My legs came free, and I sat up. I sent Sumpy back to her compartment, and told her to order a stiff drink for each of us.

I set about trying to clean up the compartment. I rolled back the carpet and lifted up the hatch to where Sparrow lay. The accommodation hadn't been designed for five, but none of them were in any shape to do any complaining. I washed the bloodstains off the carpet and seats with the towels, and threw them out of the window. Then I went along to Sumpy's compartment.

She had drunk both the drinks, and two more were on

their way. A bit of colour had come back to her face. The steward delivered two double Scotches. I picked up one glass. 'To the human atom bomb!' I said.

She shook her head. 'Angel,' she said, 'your little guardian angel.'

24

Outside, beyond the black window, the dim glow of the snow-bound Canadian emptiness passed by. The train rattled noisily and shook gently. Cold air poured in through a dozen different places, and the heater was fighting a losing battle against it. I felt goose pimples on my shoulders, bare arms, and on that part of my chest which wasn't warmed by Sumpy's sleeping head.

Trying not to disturb her, I tilted my wrist and looked at my watch. It was a quarter past one in the morning; at a quarter to two, the train would stop at North Bay. In a few minutes, I had to start getting dressed.

'What's the time, Max?'

She was awake. I told her the time.

'I wish you were staying,' she said.

'So do I.'

'Why don't you go in the morning?'

'It is the morning. Every hour is important at the moment. I have to get to Slan. If any American power station blows and the Americans find out Britain knew about Operation Angel all along, there'll be more than just merry hell.'

'Why does Fifeshire play everything so close to his vest?'

'He doesn't trust anyone. He figures that the less people that know anything, the less chance of a leak. Whether he's right or wrong this time, we'll find out soon enough.'

'He never even gave me a hint it was going to be you on this train.'

'Obviously he was pleased with you,' I said, 'he wanted to

give you a really sensational treat. He even had me gift-wrapped.'

'I never had to shoot Santa Claus when I was a kid.'

'That's part of the fun of growing up.'

'Great,' she said, without a lot of enthusiasm. 'Who's going to win, Max, do you think? Fifeshire or Operation Angel?'

'I have no idea. If I can get a complete list of the American targets from Slan – and I'm sure I'm going to be able to – with Sleder dead, he'll talk, then we'll stop anything from happening in the States. Canada too, I hope. But England depends on finding those shipments, and we still don't have anyone to talk to. The two people who could help us have both vanished: one's gone on holiday with his wife, and disappeared; and the other one's just up-sticked and vanished. At the rate things are going, we're going to end up saving every other bloody country, and losing England – or at least a damn great chunk of it.'

'One of those "other bloody countries" happens to be mine,' said Sumpy. 'I am American, remember?'

'We all have our cross to bear.'

'Fifeshire's crazy – I don't think he should be keeping this quiet any more.'

'He should have armies out right now. We're talking about something that's going to happen in three days' time that could kill more people than both World Wars, and here we are, the only two people out in the field on the whole damn job, making love in a train.'

'Would you like to have five armies in here with us?' She kissed me again.

'Only if they looked like you.'

'And you'd tire the lot out, would you, Max? Instead of one helpless little girl?'

'If you're a helpless little girl, I sure as hell wouldn't want to meet the Bionic Woman.'

'Didn't I tell you that's who I am in my spare time?'

'No, you didn't. In fact you never did tell me who you really are at all. I had to go ask your mother.'

'I'm not allowed to tell you,' she grinned.

'When this is over, and if we're still alive, why don't we go somewhere quiet and peaceful, and have a few days together?'

'White sand? Palm trees? Rich blue ocean? Gentle breeze? Martinis on the rocks? You rubbing sun-tan lotion on my back and me rubbing it on yours? How romantic you English are! Together we save the world, and then we fly off into the sunset in a silver birdie!'

'Something like that.'

She laughed. 'I'm sure you have a nice girl in England, with a pale English-rose complexion, a Roedean accent and a merchant banker daddy, and she adores you, thinks you're pretty whizzo, and she goes bright red when you talk of doing rude things, and she wears pretty dresses and likes point-to-points, Ascot and Henley?'

'She doesn't go bright red when we talk of doing rude things.'

'Maybe I should read more up-to-date romantic novels.'

'What about it?'

'Uh oh.' She shook her head. 'We had a good time just now, and we had a good time two years ago in New York – we had a long good time then. Maybe in another two years we'll meet someplace else and have another good time. I'd like that, Max. But somehow, a quiet holiday – I don't know – I don't know I'm really into that.'

'We could arrange for a few Russians to keep crawling up around us and try and kill us – that sort of thing . . .'

She laughed again. 'Didn't you read the rule book? It says never to form emotional attachments.'

'Section 34, paragraph 12. What all good agents should remember.'

'Maybe that's our problem – both you and I, we're good agents, eh? Pretty damn good. I'm off to Montreal. Must make sure no one discovers Sleder's corpse who shouldn't discover it: so far as the world is concerned, Sleder is still alive. And you're off to Adamsville to persuade someone that he's dead. Think that could make for a steady relationship, Max?' She prodded me hard in the ribs. 'Up,' she said. 'You want to get to Adamsville, you'd better get dressed, or you're going to miss the last exit. And by the way, Max: Happy New Year!'

'I'll sing you "Auld Lang Syne" as I'm driving along.'

As usual, after a close encounter with Sumpy, I was covered from head to foot in baby oil. I washed it off my hands, and dried my body as best I could with a towel then pulled my clothes on. She was exactly as she'd always been.

On the dot of one forty-five, the train halted at North Bay Station. I didn't particularly want to be seen leaving here, not that there were going to be too many people around at this hour, on New Year's Day. I walked down the train until I was well past the station building, then jumped down, and, crouching, ran further away from the station.

There was a fence along the side of the track, with some street lighting the other side of it, and I soon found an easy gap to climb through. I jumped down, and landed straight in a four-foot snow drift. I fell forward and cursed, then picked myself and my bag up. There were creaking and rattling sounds from the train. I heard a couple of voices, then the slamming of a door and the train began to move off.

I looked around. I was in the middle of freezing bloody nowhere, with no map, no particularly warm coat, and the knowledge that Adamsville, Ohio, where I wanted to be by morning, was a good four-hundred-mile drive from here, through some of the worst possible conditions imaginable. I walked down the road and came to a row of houses, with snow-bound cars parked outside them. No good, someone might hear me, and I couldn't risk that. I walked on, and then found what I had been hoping for: a house at the top of a long gradient, with a car in the driveway facing out. It was a massive Oldsmobile 98 station-wagon.

I tried to get my flat skeleton key into the door lock, but the lock was frozen solid. I lit my cigarette lighter and put the key over the flame for several seconds; it then slid easily into the lock, and turned. There was a clunk that sounded, in the quiet of the falling snow, like a twenty-one-gun salute, as the electro-magnetic central locking device shot all four door-pins into the up position. I opened the door; it hadn't been oiled in years and creaked badly. I put the key in the ignition and fiddled it about for several seconds, until it turned, and the steering wheel lock disengaged. I did not attempt to start the car, but climbed out and cleared the snow off the wind-shield. Then I sat back in the car, removed the parking brake, put the gear shift into neutral, and we started to coast down the hill.

I had to use all my weight on the brake pedal, and my strength on the steering wheel, as, without the engine run-ning, the power assistance was not operative. When I was a sufficient distance from the house, I flattened the accelerator, turned my key hard over, and came as near to having a fatal heart attack as I hope I ever shall. The engine fired, first time, on all eight cylinders, all seven point nine litres of brute Yank V8, built in the heady days before oil shortages and pollution were of concern to the automobile world. It burst into life and the rev counter shot straight up to the three-thousand mark.

The noise of the engine shattered the still of the night, and must have shattered it for a good many miles around: the bloody car had no silencer. I snapped on the lights, shoved the shift into drive, and headed away as quickly as I could.

Down towards Lake Michigan, the weather was a bit better, and the roads were clear of snow. I arrived in Adamsville shortly after nine o'clock, and was directed to the American Fossilized plant which was several miles out of the town.

By nine forty-five Slan hadn't arrived. He was late, the receptionist informed me. He was usually in before she got there. She thought maybe he'd celebrated New Year's Eve a bit too hard and was sleeping it off. By ten o'clock, he still hadn't arrived. The girl gave me his home telephone number. I dialled it; the phone rang several times, and then it was answered by a hysterical woman who said, 'No, I can't speak now, not – now – you'll have to call back, Oh God, Oh God, Oh God,' and then hung up.

I decided I'd better go pay Harry Slan a visit at his home, and quickly. But I was too late. The entrance road to the smart middle-management-bracket housing estate was blocked by a patrol car. Behind it I could see a fire engine, an ambulance and two more patrol cars, and then the house. One side of the house looked an awful mess. A state trooper got out of the patrol car as I approached.

'I'm sorry, you can't come past here,' he said.

'I have to see Mr Slan – it's urgent.'

The trooper looked me slowly up and down. I was unshaven for two days, white, and shaking from no sleep and a long drive. 'You want to see Mr Slan, you're going to have to make an appointment with the Almighty.'

'What do you mean?'

'Are you a newspaper man?'

He seemed disappointed when I told him no, I wasn't a newspaper man. He had obviously been hoping to be quoted.

'Dead,' he said. 'They're scraping him off the garage wall. Must have been messing around with one of his nuke devices in the garage. People shouldn't ought to mess around with nuke devices in their garages.'

I didn't want to disillusion the Maigret of Ohio by informing him that if Harry Slan had been messing around with nuclear devices in his garage, nobody would be scraping Harry Slan off his garage wall: they would be scraping Adamsville, Ohio, off the map.

Someone had got to Harry Slan before I had. They'd made an awful mess of him, his garage and my plans. My list of helpful contacts was thinning out a damn sight too quickly for my liking. I didn't have the time to go and rummage in Slan's drawers, even if anyone had let me, which was doubtful, and I didn't have the time to start interviewing the five thousand people who worked at American Fossilized. Someone was going to have to break the good news to the CIA and break it quickly, and for that news to carry any weight, it was going to have to be broken by someone who appeared to have a lot more authority than an unshaven white-faced man in a stolen car with no silencer. I turned, and headed as fast as I could for Detroit and a plane for England, stopping en route for an overdue cup of coffee, mouthful of food, and a very long phone call to Fifeshire.

25

The newspaper vendor put a boiled sweet into his mouth and shuffled it around his toothless gums. He sorted out an itch on his cheek, checked for wax in his ears, and then put a hand up to see if it was raining.

The startling information of today, that appeared behind the mesh grill at the side of his news stand, printed to give the appearance of urgent handwriting was: *Volcanoes Kill Hundreds. Thousands Flee Two Eruptions.* I had not needed to pay money to this wrinkled purveyor of vegetable-rack liners and fly-swatters in order to slake my curiosity about his two eruptions. A customer, either of his, or of one of his eight thousand look-alikes had kindly left me a *Telegraph* in the back of the cab. The light changed to green, and with a menacing rattle of the diesel, we forged forward again down Knightsbridge.

One volcano was on an island called Coguana des Tyq in the South Atlantic Ocean, part of the same group of islands to which Tristan da Cunha, which had been devastated by a volcanic eruption twenty years before, belonged. The seismic readings and earthquakes resulting from the Coguana des Tyq activity made it the worst volcanic eruption of the twentieth century. A second volcano, Mount St Helens in Washington State, which had erupted previously in 1980, had now begun to erupt again, and the reason was being blamed on Coguana des Tyq. The prophets were having a field day, and dusty scrolls portending that two volcanoes simultaneously erupting signalled the end of the world were being pulled from a million doom-mongers' closets. For once, for many people, there was a damn sight more than a mere grain of truth in their prophesies. In a strange way, I found it comforting to remember that in a world full of sick people lusting for destruction, Mother Nature could rear her head in any way she liked, at any time she liked, and create acts of havoc that could make all human acts of destruction pale into insignificance.

The volcano in Fifeshire's mouth glowed a vivid red at the tip, and then the red faded away, leaving the tip a silvery grey colour; he opened his mouth and shot a plume of smoke out into the room.

The only other person in Fifeshire's office, apart from myself and Fifeshire, was Sir Isaac Quoit. It was eleven o'clock Saturday morning, 2 January. In two days' time, provided that England was still standing, Quoit would be permitted to come out of hiding. In spite of that, he didn't look particularly cheerful, and still continued to eye me with a mixture of fear and contempt. It was Fifeshire who spoke first.

'Seventy-two fuel bundles were shipped from Hamburg to Shoreham in Sussex on a small freighter, the *Jan Marie*, on 28 December, concealed in a consignment of kitchen equipment. The *Jan Marie* is at sea again at the moment, so the crew have not yet been questioned, but it is unlikely they would know much about what happened to their cargo once it went ashore. The consignment cleared UK customs on 30 December, and was in the forwarding agents' warehouse at Shoreham awaiting delivery to the customer – an East London discount retailing group. On the night of 31 December, the warehouse was broken into, and four crates were stolen. According to a check on the inventory list, these four crates contained spare elements for microwave oven units – a clever description, because, to someone unfamiliar, as most people are, with the inside of microwave ovens, they could easily be forgiven for thinking that's what the bundles were. Seventy-two bundles is two day's fresh fuel for one reactor, or one day's fresh fuel for two. Is that not right, Isaac?'

Quoit nodded.

'The rogue elements are probably concealed among these. If we can find these bundles, then our problems are over, wouldn't you agree?' He looked at Quoit.

'I would hope so.'

'At least, provided everyone else can find theirs too. I have here a report from Admiralty House. Naturally they know nothing of what is going on. This is a standard weekly intelligence report. The NATO fleet has observed that the Russians have been clearing all their shipping, both military and commercial, from the Atlantic Ocean, English Channel and North Sea. It's apparently causing some concern.'

'Submarines too?' I asked.

'No, only surface vessels.'

'Because they're worried about fall-out?'

'It must be. I can't think of any other reason – and the Admiralty can't think of any reason at all. If it was just military shipping, one might perhaps think there was a different reason, but civilian shipping as well – it all fits. Would you not agree, Isaac?'

'Ships are as vulnerable to fall-out as anything else. Most modern warships do have air-tight hatches and a system for washing down their decks automatically in the event of being subjected to fall-out, but no commercial shipping does to my knowledge.'

'Who have you informed of what we know, so far, sir?' I asked Fifeshire.

'Only the heads of the Atomic Energy authorities in the four countries. They are all instigating searches for B-marked fuel – I hope we're right about it.'

'So do I.'

'They have all promised to let me know the moment they find anything – or the moment anything happens,' he added ominously.

'What about this country?'

Fifeshire shook his head. 'If I tell the Home Secretary, he'll get in one almighty flap, and rush off and tell the PM. The PM will get in a bigger flap still, summon an emergency cabinet meeting and discuss the matter for three hours. Having done that, they will then telephone me, and ask me to come and discuss it with them. I will tell them what I am doing, that in my opinion it is the only thing to do, and they will agree and tell me to continue; so there is not a lot of point in telling them in the first place. I did put everyone formally on notice back in October. You were both present at the meeting. Now I am getting on with the job. There is nothing further to tell them that will be of any use either to them or to us.'

'If by Monday morning,' said Quoit, 'nothing has turned up, and there's a westerly blowing, what are you going to do?'

'Couldn't all the power stations be shut down?' I asked.

Quoit shook his head. 'In summer, perhaps, but not in winter. Nineteen per cent of the country's electricity comes from nuclear power. Take that away, and the conventional generating stations would not be able to cope. The whole country would be without electricity for days. Thousands of people, sick and old, would die.'

'Even more than that would die if the country were contaminated by fall-out.'

'I don't think shutting down the stations would make any difference,' said Quoit. 'If these people have got this far, I'm certain they would have a contingency plan against the stations being shut down. If they cannot be stopped, then the only way you are going to protect the people of this country is to evacuate them.'

'Evacuate the entire country?' said Fifeshire. 'Excellent idea, I'm sure, Isaac. How do you propose getting fifty-five million people off this island by Monday morning? And where exactly would you put them if we did so?'

Quoit looked at him and said nothing.

'It's not going to be much use shoving them into empty hotels on the Costa Brava,' he went on, 'if the ruddy Spaniards are going to have their reactors blown up too.' He paused for some moments. 'And if we did evacuate, how long before everyone could come back? It wouldn't be a few days would it? It would be a year for the lucky ones, ten years for some less lucky, and several centuries for the less luckier still.'

'I agree with you, it's a major problem.' said Quoit. 'We've always been aware of it. We have plans for minor accidents – and major accidents – but not for a sabotage of this nature. This comes under the category of war – nuclear war, if you like, if they're going to use nuclear explosives. That's a different ball-game entirely. You've either got to get the people into fall-out shelters, or out of the downwind path. Until you know which are the target power stations, almost any area in the country could be in jeopardy, and by the time the reactors blow, it will be too late for evacuation.'

'Evacuation is impossible,' said Fifeshire, 'completely impossible. It's been discussed many times.'

'So what will you do?'

'You cannot see radioactive fall-out, you cannot smell it,

you cannot feel it; unless you have a Geiger counter, you wouldn't know it was present, neither in massive doses, nor in tiny doses. Correct?'

Quoit nodded.

'So how would the public know if they were subjected to a massive dose?'

'How would they know? It depends how the reactor is blown up, and how close they are. If a nuclear device is used, the people up to about fifty miles downwind would be dropping dead like flies, that's how they'd know.'

'Literally dropping dead? Maybe the ones very close to the power station would die immediately or very quickly, but further downwind – say fifty to one hundred miles – surely not? If a power station blows up fifty miles from London and the wind blows the stuff over London, the Londoners aren't all going to drop dead on the spot are they?'

'No. A few would die fairly quickly – within a couple of weeks probably – the rest, during the next five to fifteen years. And of course there would be a horrendous incidence of deformed children born.'

'Would everyone in London be affected?'

'No – probably about fifty per cent.'

'No one would be able to prove anything would they? Not conclusively? A high incidence of deformed children, and of cancer five years later. That's a long time; people forget. What could the people do anyway?'

Quoit stared at Fifeshire. A look of horror was on his face. 'Do you mean, Charles, that you are suggesting nothing would be done to protect the public should these power stations be blown up?'

'Yes, I am. There isn't anything we could do, and if we tried to do anything at all, let the cat out of the bag about what had happened, it would cause blind nationwide panic.

We would have to put the country onto full nuclear alert and stop all movement throughout the country. No one would be any the better off for knowing.'

There was a silence in the room while Fifeshire's words sank in.

'What about protecting the services?' said Quoit.

'Yes, of course we would do that. We would mount Operation Midwicket – which is what we call the soft nuclear alert, as opposed to Operation Longstop, which is the full-scale nuclear alert. In Midwicket, certain key ministers and military personnel and civil servants quietly move into nuclear shelters – without their families. The whole operation is carried out as if it were an exercise only, to avoid panic, and these people would never know it was anything more than an exercise. The Atomic Energy Authority, if questioned about its detonated reactors, would categorically deny any leak of radiation whatsoever.'

'Well, I think it's disgraceful,' said Quoit.

'Let's hope we can find our elements,' said Fifeshire, 'and maybe it won't come to that.'

'They would need a truck,' said Quoit suddenly. 'They would have rented it. They must have had one to transport the bundles from Shoreham! Surely there can't be many people who have rented trucks at this time of year? What if you called all the truck-hire people and asked them for descriptions of all the people who had hired trucks during the last week?'

As a nuclear energy expert, Quoit might have been brilliant. As a fledgling detective, he wasn't quite so hot.

'Assuming that we did that, Sir Isaac – and I am sure you are right that not many people hire vans at this time of year, even so I am sure you would find it runs into several thousands; it would take us months to get around to everyone. It is Saturday today, and half of the van hire firms in England are probably shut. Even if we got a description – say of Whalley or of Tsenong – what would that tell us that we don't already know?'

Quoit thought for some moments. Fifeshire put his hand to his mouth to hide a smirk.

'Perhaps you're right,' said Sherlock Holmes. 'It wouldn't tell us much.'

'I think our only chance,' I said, 'is to search the fuel stores of every power station. As we cannot tell or trust anyone, I'll do it myself. I've got the rest of today and the whole of tomorrow. I'll make an order of priority and work through the power stations one by one.'

'An order of priority?' queried Quoit.

'Yes. I'll assume first that London is the target. I'll go to all the stations that, if blown up in a westerly wind, could contaminate London. If those don't pan out, I'll move northward.'

'You'll never get round them all in time.'

'Yes, I will – I'll use a helicopter. It can't take that long to check the fuel stores, surely? I'll inform them I'm doing a spot inventory check; they're used to spot checks. Unless you can think of something better?'

Quoit couldn't.

At half past three on the following afternoon, the first of the B-marked fuel bundles turned up in the stacking line at the fuel store at Trawsfynydd in Wales; behind it sat another thirty-five. Either Ogomo had lied about the wind, or London was not the target – a westerly from here would have blown the stuff over Liverpool and Manchester.

At a quarter to two in the morning, with my eyeballs hanging out on their stalks from tiredness, I found the second thirty-six, stacked and ready to go in the morning into the reactor at Calder Hall. If this one had blown, it would have taken out Newcastle.

For the second time in twelve hours, I instructed an army CO to place a nuclear power station under arrest. I instructed warrants to be issued for the arrest of Whalley, Tsenong and Patrick Cleary, whoever he was. Then I telephoned London and left a message for Fifeshire. Then the jet lag, and the three nights without any real sleep finally caught up with me, and feeling not a little pleased with myself, I leaned my head forward onto the desk in front of me, and was about to fall into a deep sleep, when the phone rang. It was Fifeshire, and he was not a happy man.

26

A van drove swiftly through the thick fog that shrouded Shropshire. It was a real pea-souper, and the van was going swifter than a van should in these conditions. But its driver was well trained, damned well trained, at driving in conditions such as these; he almost preferred conditions such as these to plain clear daylight. All the usual dashboard instruments were to one side; the centre of the dash was occupied by a large radar screen. The screen told the driver that the road ahead was clear. Next to the driver sat another man, with an identical screen in front of him; like the driver, he too was glued to the screen.

The exterior of the van was painted a rather dreary brown colour, and was in need of a good polish; emblazoned along each side, and along the rear doors, were the words *Harris the Bakers.*

The interior of the van, sealed off from the driver and his mate, was altogether a different matter. It had six seats, in two rows of three, facing each other, all covered in Connolly hide, and there was an elegant mahogany table in the centre. There were no windows in the back, but at the touch of a button the occupants could see any direction outside that they wished, on the large television monitor attached to the top of the table. To the left of the monitor was a radio-telephone that could connect directly into the telephone system of almost any country in the world.

The air inside the back could be set to any temperature the occupants desired, and, if necessary, the outside air could be shut off completely and they could switch to the van's own ten-hour supply. The equipment also included a refrigerator, well stocked with food and milk, and an equally well stocked cabinet of soft drinks, including a large quantity of Malvern water.

Behind the seats was a padded space which had been especially designed to accommodate a quantity of small dogs, and it was currently occupied by several puzzled corgis. The six seats also were occupied by six no less puzzled adults. They were the Queen, Prince Philip, the Queen Mother, the Prince and Princess of Wales with their baby in a carry-cot, and Prince Andrew. Two similar vans, a short way behind, one marked *Latin's Poultry* and the other marked *Brights for Fish*, contained other members of the Royal Family, and an assortment of ladies-in-waiting and secretaries.

The bread van turned into what looked like the driveway to an old manor house, and indeed once had been, and headed up the twisting mile-long drive. The van drove past outbuildings which had once housed farm machinery, but now barracked special members of the Coldstream Guards, and pulled up outside what looked like a timbered Elizabethan manor.

The interior of the house was not exactly classic Elizabethan. There was a dome of reinforced concrete, a battery of TV monitors, and a massive descending stairwell. A silver-haired man in his late fifties, wearing the battle-dress uniform of a Brigadier, led the Royal group into the building and down the stairwell. On the first level down, they walked through a rounded doorway which had a massive, two-foot-thick steel door with a rotating plate in the centre, and a large dial, not unlike the door to a bank vault. The door was open, and secured back.

The party went down to the second level and through a second, identical doorway, then down to the third level and through yet another identical doorway. They came into a very large and brightly lit operations room of open-plan design. There were over one hundred desks in the room; each desk had two telephones and one computer terminal.

The Queen then parted company with the rest of her family who were taken on down into their living quarters, and she was led through the back of the operations room, down a short corridor, and into a room hung completely with maps and charts. In the centre of the room was a huge rosewood table, of elongated oval shape, around which sat the Prime Minister, the Cabinet, and a battery of advisors.

In an office further down the same corridor, Fifeshire sat, shrouding himself in cigar smoke and firing his words through the cloud. I wondered if, perhaps, he was trying to simulate giving orders in battle conditions.

'Did you have a good journey?'

'No,' I said, 'flying in choppers through thick fog is not my scene.'

'Nor mine. Damned foolish. Did you notice the wind getting up?'

I nodded. 'Westerly.'

A massive cloud of Havana smoke appeared in front of my eyes, and his voice boomed through it. 'You're wondering what the devil is going on, so I'll tell you everything first, and then you can ask questions.'

As the smoke lifted, I half-expected that he might have disappeared, but he was still there.

'The Americans, the Canadians, the French, and the Spaniards: they all found AtomSled's fuel bundles, in position in various reactors, ready for loading into the cores. Now for the bad news: at the Chinon reactor in France, at eleven o'clock last night, four men carrying explosive charges were arrested. A Spanish reactor at Lemoniz went critical at one o'clock this morning: there were no B-marked fuel bundles at Lemoniz. According to their latest report, the reactor is now completely out of control.' Fifeshire took the cigar away from his mouth for some moments, and I could see his face was very white. 'Do you know what this means?'

I nodded. I knew what it meant. I said something I don't normally say when in the presence of a superior. I said, 'Oh shit.'

'I don't think I could have put it better myself,' said Fifeshire.

'We've been duped. Hook, line and sinker.'

He nodded. 'That's what it looks like, I'm afraid. Total red herring, the fuel business; and it's worked a treat. God knows how many stations are going to blow up today. And where the hell do we begin?'

I sunk my head into my hands. 'How the hell have we been so stupid?'

'I don't think you or I have been in the slightest bit stupid. We are gatherers of intelligence, not scientists. We can't be expected to understand every aspect of modern science – but we are expected to use good advisors. Sir Isaac is this country's number one expert in nuclear energy; we used his advice.'

'Maybe we should have left him on the bloody plane. Where is he now?'

'In with the brass. He's trying to explain how you split an atom.'

'This is one hell of a time for a science lesson. Maybe he should have explained it to them before the country ever built its first sodding power station. Can we get him out?'

'Do you need him?'

'I have a hunch,' I said. 'If I'm right, then I'm going to need him and a helicopter fast.'

'What's your hunch?'

'A power station that's got a black university student doing a work-study course at a nuclear power station that's East of London. That's what we've got to find. I think they're going to do one power station only. I don't think they have the manpower to do more. We need to speak to the heads of personnel at Hinkley Point, Inswork Point, Bugle and Huntspill Head.'

Fifeshire again disappeared behind a screen of smoke. When he emerged, he was holding the telephone in his hand. He barked down it. Within ten minutes the phone rang back. Ben Tsenong was at Huntspill Head. So was Horace Whalley.

As the helicopter hurtled down across Wales, the fog thinned, then vanished behind us. We clattered over the Bristol Channel and looked down on water that was thick with white horses. The wind was whipping up – a strong Westerly. The weather conditions for Operation Angel were absolutely perfect.

Heading up the Channel, down below, was a powerful cabin cruiser. It seemed to be making for a small port on the Somerset coast. I thought it was an odd time of year for a luxury cabin cruiser to be out, but then it went from my mind as Huntspill Head nuclear power station appeared in view, hunched menacingly on the shore. It looked for-midable and oppressive. Its four round domes and square vacuum chambers, in pale grey concrete, rose from the ground looking like the tomb of a Martian emperor. I won-dered what was going on in there, whether it had already begun, if we were too late to do anything about it and were going down to certain death – and that didn't worry me. What did worry me was a girl in London, a pissed-off girl whose boyfriend had stood her up for Christmas and New Year's Eve, who had hung up on him when he'd called to apologize and tried to tell her that she had to get her ass out of London. I wasn't going to let that crazy gorgeous girl get her lungs full of plutonium, and her thyroids full of iodine and her stomach full of gamma rays. I thought of a fanatic young black student, and a weak civil servant, and an anonymous zealot who dreamed of a free Ireland. I checked the magazine of my Beretta, took the safety catch off, switched to automatic fire, nodded to Quoit to follow me, and leapt to the ground before the skids of the chopper had even settled.

A figure came hurrying across to greet us. It was the man I had met only a few months ago, when I had come to see a nervous lecturer, Doug Yeodall, who was now dead, assure the world's press that a nuclear power station could never blow up. Ron Tenney held out his hand. 'Hi there, did you have a good flight?' he said with his soft voice that had a hint of an Irish brogue.

I nodded back and gave his hand a firm shake, which were all the pleasantries I had time for. 'Tsenong and Whalley,' I said, 'where are they?'

'Why, what's up?'

'Do you know where they are?'

'Sure I do. They're at the number three reactor face.'

'At the reactor face?'

'Carrying out support point inspections.'

'Is there a problem with your support points?'

'No, not that I know of.'

'Whalley's meant to be on holiday in the Seychelles. What's so special about your support points that he left his wife, without taking the time to tell her, and flew straight back to England to come and have a look at them?'

'I don't understand what you mean?'

We walked inside, past the security desk. I stopped and turned to him. 'I'll tell you what I mean. They're about to blow your fucking power station up, that's what I mean.'

Tenney led, I sprinted behind him, and Quoit did his best to keep up. We ran through several doors, past a massive tank of water, past stacks of barrels, radiation warning signs, vending machines, men in overalls, and then came up to a door with a large sign: *Danger. Authorized personnel only. Protective clothing must be worn beyond this point.*

Tenney opened a cupboard door, and pulled out a handful of clothing. 'Got to put these on – none of us would last thirty seconds without them.' It took several minutes for us to get dressed: first, black knee-high boots, then a white one-piece suit, complete with hood, visor and breathing apparatus. We stepped into these, and zipped them up; even the gloves were part of the suit.

'Same material as they use for astronauts' suits, for when they go out of their spacecraft – that's what they were developed for originally, the moon landing,' said Quoit, shouting through his visor at me.

'I think the moon's a lot more hospitable place than where we're going now,' shouted Tenney.

'I wouldn't disagree with you,' said Quoit.

I was busy trying to get my gloved trigger finger in through the trigger guard. Tenney eyed the gun with a frown. 'Don't forget to wash that when you come back out – it'll be contaminated.'

'I think it already is,' said Quoit distastefully.

Tenney strapped large watches onto our wrists. 'We have one hour's supply of oxygen. The buzzer will go in fifty-five minutes and if you hear it, just get the hell out. But we shouldn't be in there anywhere near that long. Okay?' I nodded through the visor and gripped the Beretta tightly. We walked through the door and Tenney shut it firmly behind us. We were in a small room with a massively thick porthole window. I looked through the porthole, expecting to see Dante's Inferno, or worse. Instead, I saw a vast cavern, dome-shaped ceiling all around, and a massive blue steel structure, looking like a giant windowless space capsule, in the middle. This was the pressure vessel, inside which was the core. A mass of thick pipes ran from the side of it into a much smaller capsule, and from that into a tall, thin cylinder, about twenty-five feet high. The core itself was about thirty feet high, and sat on four massive hydraulically sprung struts.

A short way to the right was a massive steel robot arm with a giant pincer hand. The controls for this arm were underneath the porthole. It was used to carry out dismantling work on the core for refuelling, maintenance and for inspection purposes; this had to be done by remote control – no suit would protect a human being from an open core.

At the top of one of the metal struts was a figure in a white suit; even from here one could see clearly what he was doing: he was taping something to the strut. We went through a steel door and into the decontamination room which contained an enormous and powerful shower, followed by an air-drying chamber. We went through another steel door, closing that behind us, and into the pressurization chamber. We went through into another chamber, and finally came to the door into the reactor face. Tenney led the way in, and Quoit followed. I hung back some way behind him. Something was bothering me, bothering me a lot more than Whalley and Tsenong, and I wasn't sure what it was.

I went through, and if the place hadn't looked like the Inferno, it certainly felt like it. There was a heat stronger than I had ever felt before – intense, claustrophobic; I felt as though I had entered a microwave oven. I looked around for some solid object; just to my right was an enormous valve fixed to the floor. Quoit pointed at the figure up on the support strut; I could see from where I was standing that whatever he was taping to the strut, he had already taped the same to one other strut, and to several of the pipes at the point of connection to the core.

The figure turned his head and looked at us for a moment, before turning back to his work. I saw his face clearly through his visor; it was Whalley.

Quoit started to run over to the core. I hung back. I couldn't see Tsenong, and I was looking around for him. Quoit reached the base of the strut and was about to start climbing up to Whalley, when two black holes appeared in the back of his suit. He shook violently twice, threw his arms out, and fell over sideways, I flattened myself behind the valve, my eyes doing the best they could, despite the restrictions of the visor, to scan the full three hundred and sixty degrees around me. I saw a flash of white behind a cluster of monitoring gauges, and I fired a burst of three bullets. A figure in white stood up, clutching his arm, and through his visor I could see clearly the face of Ben Tsenong. He had one arm clamped over the other, and he started to run for the door. I swivelled my gun round at him and was about to pull the trigger again when a bullet smacked off the handle of the valve right beside me, ripping a chunk out of the enamel paint; it was then that I knew what had been bothering me.

The voice of the man that Horace Whalley had met in the field, the voice that I had heard before and couldn't place – it was here that I had heard it before, when I had come down on the day of the press conference and Ron Tenney had shown me around. Ron Tenney with that soft voice, that hint of an Irish brogue: Ron Tenney was Patrick Cleary. He had come around and was right behind me and I fired off three bullets without even aiming, just to scare; another bullet smacked the floor beside me. I saw the bastard, saw him grin, I was sure, as he stepped behind an air-vent housing. I sprawled myself flat on my stomach. There was a flash of white, and I fired another burst, then cursed myself; the white had vanished long before I pulled the trigger. I waited. I caught a glimpse of something out of the corner of my eye, something moving. It was the pincer hand of the robot and it was moving over towards me, and it was moving damn quickly. I had fifteen rounds in the gun, nine had gone. I had to get the bastard fast.

There was a flash of white. I sprang onto my knees, fired another burst and sprinted madly forward, if the lumbering motion that is all one is able to perform in these suits could be called sprinting. I reached the other side of the housing. Cleary would be wondering where the hell I was. He might know how to pull a trigger, but he sure hadn't been taught much about gun-fighting.

I sat, knowing he was over the far side, and the pincers still moved steadily and swiftly towards me. I hoped it would bring Cleary out in curiosity; it did. He stood up behind the housing, I sprang my arms up and fired a burst of three bullets straight through his neck.

I leapt up, ran around the back of the housing and grabbed his gun, a Walther automatic. I gripped the gun firmly in both hands and aimed at Whalley. A crashing blow hit me in the side of my shoulder, flinging me over onto the ground. I got to my knees and the shadow of the robot arm, pincer jaw wide open and coming down at my head was right over me. I rolled out of the way, making a grab for the gun and getting it, but the arm followed; I ran back several steps, but the arm ran back; any move I made, it could make too, and almost as quickly. It made a dive at me, and I side-stepped just as the jaws clamped shut.

I sprinted for the door; half-way there, the jaws knocked me to the ground. I rolled over, got up again, the jaws smashed me down again, then came back down towards my face. I don't know where the effort came from, but somehow I managed to fling myself sideways. I grabbed the door-handle, turned, pulled, and fell through the doorway. The arm smashed into the doorway, the pincers closed over the door, then pulled back. The door must have weighed the best part of five hundred pounds, and the pincer pulled it straight back, ripping it from its hinges, and lifting it up in the air.

I ran through the chambers, not stopping at the shower room, but carrying straight through: Tsenong was there, by the porthole, but semi-slumped, one hand on the robot controls, one hand holding an automatic. He was looking very ill, whether from loss of blood or from radiation poi-soning through the massive rip in his suit along his arm, I did not know. Through his glass visor I could see his eyes; they were burning with hate, and I remembered what I had read in the psychologist's report. He deliberately and slowly brought his gun up towards me. I pulled the Walther's trigger twice. He jerked back sharply against the wall. The hatred in his eyes seemed to vanish, and was replaced with an expres-sion of surprise; his eyes stayed open and he did not move.

I grabbed the controls of the robot. They were simple. I swung the arm over towards where Whalley was still fever-ishly working. He didn't notice anything. I brought the pincer right up behind him, then grabbed him just below the shoulders, pinning his arms to his side. I plucked him up and carried him through the air over towards where the door had been. His legs were kicking frantically. I put the pressure on a little harder, just to make sure he couldn't escape, then left him, about four feet in the air, and ran back through the chambers to him.

His face was a picture of terror. 'Where is the detonator?' I yelled.

'Individual, on each charge,' he screamed. 'Two minutes, they're all going off in two minutes, you'll never stop them, never be able to stop them in time. Get me down, get me down!'

'You'd better stop them.'

'I can't, I can't, I just finished the last one, I can't stop anything. Please put me down, put me down quickly.' He was screaming hysterically.

'It's your firework party, you get the front row seat!'

'No, help, please, I'll tell you anything you want!'

'Which other power stations?'

'None, this only!'

'How can you stop those charges?'

'I can't, really can't, we must get out, we're all going to go up, oh please, oh please!'

I turned and left the bleating creature, and ran back to the controls. If he was telling the truth, then the only chance was if he did the defusing while I carried him to the charges. No other way would give us enough time. I started the arm moving and swung him back over to the last charge he had attached. His legs were kicking like a rabbit's. Long before he reached it, the charge blew. Then the one on the other strut also blew. The struts disappeared and the whole core tilted crazily to one side, held from falling only by the battery of piping. Whalley's legs were bicycling crazily. I hoped he was enjoying his seat in the Royal box. Then, in rapid succession, three charges attached to the pipes blew, the core, in a cloud of steam, crashed upside down to the ground, and part of its steel casing fell away.

The room began to get brighter and brighter, a strange, creamy-white light, that just kept on brightening, even though steam poured everywhere from a hundred directions, the light just kept getting brighter. I rushed out into the corridor, looking desperately for someone to tell. I had the choice of about five hundred different people. All hell had broken loose, and a klaxon started, wailing and stopping, wailing and stopping. I stood in the middle of it all, feeling like a prize lemon, wondering if I ought to go and take a shower.

27

The day Huntspill Head blew its top was a day the locals would remember for a long time to come. The town was five miles from the power station, but the Shockwave rippled through like an earthquake. People fell over in the streets and in their houses. According to official records, four hundred and twelve claims were received for new window panes, as buildings contorted slightly and glass dropped out. The tremor lasted no more than ten seconds, and then it was over. It happened three hours and ten minutes after I had left.

Almost everyone in the town looked westwards, towards the nuclear power station which they had fought so hard to stop being built, convinced that finally their fears had come true. They saw first a small plume of smoke rise; it rose for several seconds and then curved over westwards; then the containment building of reactor number three ceased to exist. It turned into a brown, grey and blue cloud, billowing out for several minutes in all directions, and then the billowing stopped and nothing more came out of the blackened crater in the ground.

The cloud rose, and spread out, until it was vaguely the shape of a fat cigar; it was four miles wide and fifteen miles long, and expanding quite quickly. It moved swiftly, blown by the fifteen-mile-an-hour wind westwards, straight down the Bristol Channel and out towards the Atlantic Ocean.

Only four people died as a result of the explosion and the subsequent lethal cloud; shipping in the Channel and out in the Atlantic was warned of the cloud's size and direction, and was able to steer clear – all shipping, that was, except for an expensive cabin cruiser which had broken down in the mouth of the Channel. The cabin cruiser had sailed only a few hours before from a tiny marina near Huntspill, and was bound for Kinsale. On board the cabin cruiser were the skipper and three technicians from Huntspill Head; one was an electrical inspector, one a computer programmer and one a hydraulics engineer. There were three empty seats on the boat: these should have been filled by Patrick Cleary, Horace Whalley and Ben Tsenong. The centre of the cloud travelled straight across the boat, and although the four men went below, the polished teak decking offered them little protection. By the time the cloud had passed by, neither the men nor the boat were very nice to look at. Within half an hour, the last of the four men had died.

I had flown from Huntspill Head straight back to Strategic Headquarters in Shropshire; the reactor was still intact, and the southwesterly was blowing strongly.

'It's out of control,' said Fifeshire. 'The technical expression for it is a "power excursion accident" – except it's not an accident.' Surprisingly, he did not look as grim as he might have done; something was up, but I didn't know what, and I didn't think that anything, right now, could be anything but bad. I thought about Gelignite again. I had tried three times to get her on the phone to tell her to head north and keep going north as far as she could go. I nodded at Fifeshire.

'The way I understand it,' he continued, 'is that two of the four struts on which the pressure vessel containing the core sits, have been blown away; the coolant pipes have also all been fractured. The core has fallen upside down, breaking its outer pressure vessel, and therefore losing all of its coolant.

'Being upside down has caused the control rods to fall out. They are situated at the top of the core, and normally in an emergency, if all other precautions and systems fail, would drop straight down into the core, under the force of gravity, and the reaction would stop. Being upside down has of course stopped this, and in fact, the reverse had happened: the rods having fallen out completely means that the temperature of the core is rising at a fantastic rate – no one ever figured that the control rods might be removed altogether.

'The net result is that the containment of reactor number three is filling with steam, and the core is expanding this steam fast. All the escape valves and filtration systems have been jammed by Whalley, Tsenong and their chums, so the pressure is building up, and any moment there is going to be an almighty bang. Apparently, a very big bang is preferable to a small one. The boffins believe that if the bang is sufficiently big, it will blow the core to pieces rather than let it continue to heat and have a situation that Isaac Quoit described as – what was it . . . an Australia . . . no, a China Syndrome. If the core is blown to pieces, there will be a short emission of radioactivity, making a cloud that will be large, but which will be a once-only cloud. If the core stays intact, there will be stuff pouring out of the ground for days.'

'Is there anything anyone can do to make sure it does blow to pieces?'

'Yes. By just leaving everything as it is and not attempting to open any valves, or anything. They are ninety-nine per cent sure that the bang will be big enough.' Fifeshire smiled broadly, and pulled a cigar from the box. 'Mind you, if you think we've got a few problems, you want to thank your lucky stars you're not in America: they've got five re-actors down the West Coast doing exactly the same as this.'

'What about the Canadians?'

'They've caught them. The French, as you know, they caught last night, and the Spaniards have somehow man-aged to shut down.'

'So it's just us and the Americans in the soup?'

Fifeshire's smile turned to a large grin. I decided he was definitely cracking up. He started shaking a piece of paper at me. 'Volcanoes!' he said. 'Volcanoes!'

I wondered if there was anybody here who could certify him.

'Coguana des Tyq, Mount St Helens,' he said. 'Look at this weather report!' He thrust the sheet of paper at me. I read it. It was an emergency weather report, put out to all shipping at half past twelve. It stated that the wind would be starting to veer and that easterly gales were imminent.

'What do you mean, "Coguana des Tyq"?' I said.

'Haven't you read your newspapers?'

'I've had quite a busy schedule lately, in case you hadn't noticed, sir.'

'Volcanoes – two erupting at the same time.'

'I was aware,' I said.

'Well, it often happens, apparently, when there's a volcanic eruption, that the world's weather pattern gets disrupted. This is precisely what has happened – only with two, it's even worse. There's some vortex or something they've created, I don't quite understand it all, but the point is that it's causing our winds to veer to the east. All the stuff from Huntspill is going to go straight out into the middle of the Atlantic, and then probably get blown north up into the Arctic. It'll have dispersed almost completely by the time it gets up there.'

'All the same, I wouldn't want to be a penguin right now. What about America?'

'Same thing. The idea was obviously to blow up the west coast stations, so the fall-out would blow eastwards over the whole of America. Now it's going to blow over Siberia.'

'Oh dear,' I said, 'the Russians won't be pleased!'

'No.' he smiled, 'I don't expect they will.'

I sat back and lit a cigarette. There was a long silence.

'You look glum, Flynn,' he said.

'I don't like to fail.'

'You didn't fail.'

'What do you mean? Of course I did. The reactor is going to blow up. So, okay, all the stuff's going to be blown out to sea; fifteen million Englishmen aren't going to be decimated; but that's no thanks to me, to any of us – it's all a bloody fluke. Next time, it could be very different.'

'There isn't a "this time" and a "next time" in our business,' said Fifeshire, 'there's no official beginning and end. Ours is an ongoing process. We're forever walking down a dark tunnel, snatching at patches of light. We win some and we lose some; but often we don't know whether we have really won, any more than we know whether we have really lost.'

I looked at him. His talk of dark and light had reminded me of something. 'Are you any good at crosswords, sir?'

'Try me.'

'"Short Richard's offspring divides nation with friendly underground railroad." Three words. Five letters, five letters, and four.'

'Where's the crossword from?'

'The *New York Sunday Times*.'

He thought for about three seconds. 'It's from the civil

war days, the division between the northern and southern States; Mason Dixon Line.'

'Of course, staring me in the face,' I said.

'Any other clues you're stuck with?'

'No, but there's one puzzle we haven't yet solved: Sir Isaac Quoit.'

Fifeshire nodded. 'You know what I think? I think the whole damned business with him was a red herring. Like the fuel; it was to distract us from what was really going on.'

'I'm sure you're right, sir. But what the hell do we do with his body?'

'Smuggle it into Russia, Flynn. Unless you can think of a better idea?'

I sat in silence for a long time, trying to think of a better idea.